# Andalon Arises

## Dreamers of Andalon - Book 2

T. B. Phillips

Deckplate Publishing LLC

---

*Andalon Arises*
Dreamers of Andalon, Book Two

Published by Deckplate Publishing LLC


Cover design by Lynnette Bonner of Indie Cover Design
Front cover art by Jenny Kuehner Bechtold
Map artwork by Cary Beshel
Book interior design by Stewart Design, https://StewartDesign.studio



ISBN 978-1-73318-051-1

*To my wife, Jaana*
*You are truly my best friend. I appreciate you and your support throughout my endeavor to bring this story to the world!*

*To my mother, Jennie*
*Sorry for making you blush as you read certain pages of Book One. Not sorry that it will happen again in Book Two*

*To my friend and artist, Jenny*
*You did it again! Thank you for bringing my ships to life!*

*To my friends Beth, Maria, and Cary,*
*Thank you for believing in Andalon!*

Fjörk
Ataraxia
Ashen Tundra
Diaph
Eston
Estowen's Landing
Logan
Norton
Caldera of Cinder
Steppes of Cinder
ANDALON
Middleton
Forbidden Wastes
Weston
Eskerra
Soston
Ashen Waste
Islands of Deception
N
W
E
S

Southern Continent
S
Cargia
Metzi
Tlaloc
Nazcla
KEY
- Hacienda
- Puebla Aztecá
- City
CwB

N
Winter Oracle
Oslot
Autumn Oracle
Bergin
Summer Oracle
Spring Oracle
ASTIA

# Part I
# The Gathering

*Emotions of water but born of land,*
*Lord of beast and friend of man.*

– *The Oracle of Astian, 50th year of order*

# Prologue

The boy ran as fast as he could, ignoring the sting of both insects and humidity as he fled. His pulse drummed a rhythm that clashed with the sounds of feet pounding the dense jungle floor. Sweat beaded against dark skin as he raced headlong into the darkness, fearing his pursuers and refusing to look behind. Nothing incited terror like the witches of the rainforest.

He stumbled twice, losing ground, but quickly recovering his feet both times. Knowledge that he was the swiftest runner in his village fueled hope as he led the chase, small and nimble enough to duck below branches. He gracefully jumped over debris and felt his margin closing, ignoring the ache in his chest and daring not to slow as he fled. He refused to succumb or accept that he was overtaken.

Movement on both sides shook the foliage and Parumba braced for whatever leaped out. Instinct spurred the youth and he gracefully jumped into the air, grabbing a vine and swinging into a tree. He barely cleared the ground as two large shapes converged beneath his legs. Higher he climbed while the cats paced, biting and clawing the air. The chief's son paused to catch his breath while watching the animals.

His heart sank at the sight of the jaguars. They circled, perhaps planning to hold him for their masters. The human forms of the beasts were far more dangerous than these and Parumba fought panic, desperate to flee before they arrived. He scanned the jungle for signs of their approach and searched his mind for a path of escape.

One of the animals stood with forepaws on the trunk and terror gripped the youth as the cat began to climb. Thinking fast Parumba closed his eyes and felt for the second beast still on the ground. He could feel the jaguar's mind but bonding the beast would be futile. It was already claimed. He searched instead for a thread and found a tenuous strand of thought. It extended into the jungle. He severed it cleanly and immediately lashed the beast with one of his own, taking over the cat's sentience.

The world changed as Parumba abruptly looked up at himself in the tree. His vision widened and things at a distance blurred. The other cat was climbing swiftly, almost to his position. As the jaguar he leaped as high as he could, catching the animal's leg in his strong jaws and dragging it down. Pain shot through his body as the beast thudded down on top of him. He screamed a roar while the other whelped.

The confused beast stared back as it regained footing. Parumba lunged with a second attack and bit, trying to sink his massive teeth into her skull. Claws ripped out flesh and both hissed and scratched until one of his nails found soft tissue. His opponent moaned a bloodcurdling howl as an eye ruptured, abruptly breaking connection with her master and fleeing into the jungle. He gave chase as the animal, but the boy hopped down from his perch to flee in the opposite direction.

A third cat pounced from the underbrush and tackled the boy, claws sinking in his back and pinning him to the soft jungle floor. Soon, three humanoid creatures loomed above. Although dressed alike, he could tell that two were female and one was male. They draped their muscular bodies in animal skins and hid faces behind hooded masks the resembled the beasts they mastered.

"Ahgnut, retrieve the cats while we bind the boy." An emotionless female voice commanded, sending the man racing into the jungle. To Parumba she said, "Someone has been showing off his magic to the other children in the village." Shaking her head, she added, "Thankfully one of them told your father. I guess he fears us more than he loves you."

"Lies!" the boy groaned. Anger filled Parumba and he extended his mind, attempting to sever the connection between the beast atop him and one of the shamans. He reached out with force but felt a hard kick in the ribs when he touched the link. All around him the jungle floor came to life and vines wriggled like snakes, wrapping his arms and legs until he could no longer struggle. The boy finally accepted defeat and lay still beneath the heavy weight of the animal.

The second woman, naked except for the furs of a jaguar, bent over his restrained body. She held out two tiny caterpillars with long green horns atop their heads and slid them gently into Parumba's ear canals. He cried out as the larvae burrowed deeper into his head until they could no longer. He felt their tiny horns bite into his skin, locking them in place. The world around him muffled as he listened to his own screams.

By then Ahgnut had returned with the other jaguars. Parumba sensed the one-eyed beast and tried again to connect. He held her briefly, but his concentration broke when the caterpillars screeched and hissed in his ears. The intensity of the pain prevented his magic. Desperate, he tried to unwrap the vines that bound him, but the larvae screeched a second time. The sound did not stop until he succumbed. The humanoid creatures hauled him atop one of the jaguars and tied him securely. He could only weep as they dragged him off to their cave.

He passed out several times on the journey to their den, occasionally waking and finding himself deeper in the jungle. Each time he roused Parumba would strain against bonds or try to regain his bearings. Eventually he stopped struggling and accepted that he was a prisoner. His youthful mind raced with thoughts regarding his fate. The last of these drifted toward his father, the man who handed him over to save his village. *I hate you, Father.*

When they finally reached their destination, the boy lifted his head enough that he could see a dark entrance to a small cave. They dragged him inside by his feet, allowing his head to bounce against wet stone. One of the women found a crevice in the wall and a secret door swung open, revealing smooth walls that had been polished to a sheen. Inside smelled fresh and clean, unlike the musty air of the cavern.

As the door shut behind them, Parumba realized that the ceiling glowed with a strange light. He stared, marveling, until he began to see dark spots in his eyes. They hoisted the boy and slammed him down on a finely polished slab. As the spots in front of his eyes faded, he realized that he was in a large chamber with hundreds of tables, each holding with a man, woman, child, or infant. Each had been stripped naked to accommodate strange tubing running from every opening in their bodies.

He tried to struggle when they ripped away his clothing, reaching out with his mind and causing the larvae in his ears to scream once more. Determined, he fought through the pain and untangled some of the vines that bound him. He froze when a strong hand grasped his shoulder. Something cold and sharp entered the skin of his neck and a metallic taste filled his mouth. He quickly grew dizzy, losing contact with his extremities one by one. He eventually lay paralyzed on the table, staring up at the strange lighting.

The sorcerers waited for his body to still then slid the tubes into his mouth, nose, and sensitive parts. He eventually felt the edges of his vision darken and tears streamed down both cheeks onto the slab, his last thoughts focused on his father and revenge. When sleep took over, he became another specimen in the den of the Jaguars.

# Chapter One

Eusari Thorinson watched her crew load milled lumber aboard her ship. *She Wolf* had held up well on the voyage to Estowen's Landing, and the heavy supplies she ferried had not strained recent repairs. It had only been a few months since dragging the hull across a reef and then aground. That had been during the infamous raid on Pirate's Cove, the attack that deposed Lord Stefan Nevra.

At the time she had believed her ship lost, and it would have been, had it not been for her friend Sippen Yurik. But he completed the repairs in record time, restoring seaworthiness and upgrading her weapons. *She Wolf* had not been the only casualty in the attack, and much more lumber was necessary to restore the fleet. The little engineer had constructed three drydocks in The Cove and he and his team cranked out new vessels every three weeks.

A massive black wolf lay at her feet. Gelert growled low, alerting that someone approached from behind. She turned and greeted her uncle. "You shouldn't sneak up on people, Shon."

"Aye. That's true, dearie. For what it matters, I wasn't trying to." He walked a wide berth around the animal, clearly cautious from a previous meeting. "You're lost in your thoughts," he observed, "what troubles you?"

"I was thinking about our world and how much it's changed in such a short time." She ran her hands along the hilt of one of her many hidden knives, toying with it nervously. She finally rested her palm along a newly made pistol resting in a holster on her hip. There was a time when all she took into battle were blades. *That's also new,* she thought. *Even the way we fight has changed.*

Shon Wimbley nodded and touched his own pistol as if in agreement. "Will you be making another run?"

"Probably not. We've enough ships now to run the supplies. I need to be home for the elections." *Home.* She marveled at the phrase, once so foreign to her. A word nearly as strange as "family" had been before she had met Braen Braston. "You're sure that you won't return?"

"No, dearie." He strained his eyes up at the town, once abandoned and now a haven for his outlaw army. "We've much work if we're to help your Northman with his war. I need to recruit and train soldiers on these." He pointed at the rifle slung on his shoulder. "I'll keep the mill running and make sure The Cove is replenished. You'll need more ships for the coming wars."

Eusari allowed a smile for her uncle. "Did you ever think you'd be on this side of the law?" The once constable answered honestly. "If it weren't for their Falconers then I think that I wouldn't have made the switch." A troubled look crossed his face. "I just can't abide by their tactics."

His words returned her thoughts to a room littered with slabs. Atop the smooth tables slept men and women of all ages, some were mere children. She shivered at her inability to save them from the Rookery in Diaph. "I can't believe we're merely a farm to them."

"Aye, and I won't rest until we've found a way to free all of Andalon."

Eusari's eyes rarely met another's, but she looked deep into her uncle's. Not long ago she trusted only two living men. Now, she had more friends and family than she had ever hoped for. "Uncle Shon. I... I'm sorry that I doubted you, before."

"Nah. Don't worry about it, dearie. I walked into your life without warning. Trust takes time." He knelt before Gelert. The wolf looked away, not meeting his eyes. "I see that some will take longer."

"He remembers your deceit."

"No, dearie. He probably senses some lingering doubt through your connection." He watched her face. "It's okay. You've grown much in the past few months and someday we'll be family in more than name."

Strangely, Eusari didn't feel anger at his candid words. She stared at the deck and asked in a weak voice, "What was she like, my mother?"

Shon's voice broke slightly. "My sister was the most giving woman I'd ever met. She was beautiful with eyes as green as yours and hair just as raven."

"Did she love my father?"

"Of course, she did."

"I mean, what was their relationship like? I... I can't remember."

Shon closed his eyes, remembering a time long before. He let a smile take over when he spoke about his friend and mentor. "Your mother loved Franque. She defied our own father to marry him without even a dowry. At the time he was a mere deputy, but he rose quickly to serve as constable of Brentway." A tear formed in the corner of his eye as he spoke. "I loved him as much as she did, only differently. Something about him drew men to follow, kind of like your Northman."

"I'm glad that he died before he could find her like... like that." Eusari felt a lump form in her throat as she thought of what Skander Braston had done to them both.

"Aye. It would have broken Franque. He loved her so much."

Eusari caught herself in the midst of vulnerability and quickly changed the subject. "Any luck finding more emotants?"

Shon shook his head with a hint of disappointment. "Nay, dearie. I've dispersed instigators to every town in the Empire. They're teaching about the real work of the Falconers and their relationship to the crown."

"And none have turned up?"

He shook his head again. "Not a one."

"They'll come." She abruptly turned back toward the harbor entrance. "We're shoving off soon, so you need to disembark." Eusari paused then added, "Shon, take care of the children."

"I will."

"They're more than air emotes. Remember that they're children."

Shon looked at the five teenagers on the pier, laughing without a care despite the desperate state of the world. "Their connection to the others will reach this far, you think?"

She nodded. "Samani seems to think that it will. He said that a youth in Weston contacted him all the way in Diaph. That's roughly the same distance to The Cove."

Shon hugged his niece and then turned to leave.

"Uncle Shon!"

With a glance over his shoulder his eyes met hers once more. "Yes, dearie?"

Speaking intimately was still difficult for Eusari. "Take care of yourself, too. Don't try and take on the Empire by yourself. Promise me that you'll wait for Braen." He tipped a quick salute and walked across the brow. She watched as he slapped two of the youths on the shoulders and walked with them, laughing with comradery into the hidden village of Estowen's Landing.

Before long her first mate reported. "Captain, *She Wolf* is loaded down and ready to set sail. But I warn you, our draft is low in the water. We'll be slower than normal, even with Caroline blowing on the sails."

Eusari nodded. Marita had stayed behind at The Cove and the crew carried a younger and less experienced emotant on this voyage. She had not been with them during the attack on Pirate's Cove and Eusari wanted to shield Caroline from the dangerous missions. "How low's the draft?"

"We're displacing five extra feet from the load."

The captain, clad in her traditional black leathers, frowned. "That's a lot. We'll be considerably slower."

"Aye. We need to be leaving before the tide runs out or we risk running aground in the channel."

"Then make ready the sails and shove off immediately, Pete." She smiled as her friend ambled off on his wooden peg leg. She remembered the first time they had met. Peter Longshanks had been a gunner on her original crew before she had lost her best friend and first mate, Sa'Mond. She had wanted to die after losing him, but Braen had pulled her out of despair and helped her win over her crew, still skeptical over following a woman pirate. Peter had fought alongside of her during the mutiny and remained by her side whispering wisdom all along the way.

Within an hour they cleared the channel and drifted with the wind toward the south. Pirate's Cove lay a week away if the wind cooperated, but she expected that time to double with the added weight. Without an escort vessel *She Wolf* would be a sitting duck, exposed to both the elements and hostilities. Thankfully, the winter storms had ended for the season, and spring weather was more favorable for a southern voyage.

"Sail Ho!" A voice called down from the rigging, "Too far for identification!"

Eusari felt the hair on her neck bristle. This far north the ship would hail from Fjorik or one of the Imperial cities. Either way the sighting spelled trouble. Her thoughts turned to Caroline, instincts warning her to try and outrun the ship. However, *She Wolf* was too slow and overburdened to outpace a ship that may carry Imperial Falconers. "Hold steady on this bearing."

Devil Jacque, the quartermaster, raised a spyglass to the horizon. "Captain, she's Imperial, but appears to be without extra wind. Don't suspect any birdmen." He lowered the glass and pointed the eyepiece toward Caroline, suggesting they use the girl. "What are your orders?"

Eusari paused while the men stared. Normally she would have given an order, but this decision was tougher than most. She and Braen weren't ready to reveal their use of emotancy, especially to the Esterling navy and the Falconers. If she outran them with this low of a draft, then she would give away a potentially effective tool in the fight to come. When she finally spoke, her voice carried determination, "Mr. Longshanks."

"Aye Captain?"

"Prepare to strike colors when the ship is in range to see. Allow them to come alongside and board for inspection of goods." She watched as Pete and the rest of the crew paled. Striking colors was a cowardly act at sea, and they had all sworn to The Cove that they would rather die in battle than be hanged by the Empire for piracy.

"Jacque." She had given the order, but her quartermaster only stared at the deck, angrily grinding his teeth with dancing cheeks. "Jacque!" She yelled his name a second time, and he lifted his eyes to meet hers.

"Yes, My Captain?" He spoke through gritted teeth, a rumble of dissention in his tone.

"Place a couple of sharpshooters in the crow's nest. Then go and prepare all three raiding teams. Place them in the longboats, out of sight and undercover until the enemy boards."

A look of confusion crossed the quartermaster's face, but then realization replaced his grimace with an understanding grin. "Aye Captain! Right away, Mum!"

"Pete, get Caroline below decks and safely hidden away. Lock her in my stateroom if you have to. Just make sure she isn't topside when they board." *I want to shield her from witnessing the bloodshed,* she thought.

"Aye!" Both men raced away and called the ship to order. They were careful not to appear like they had ordered battle stations.

The other vessel pulled alongside *She Wolf* in less than an hour. The galleon had thirty guns and could maintain a crew of nearly two hundred. Eusari commanded only thirty aboard the sleek two-masted sloop. Even if she had a bigger crew, she was limited to eighteen guns.

They soon learned that the larger ship was *Desperation,* a vessel captained by Bartholomew Cartwright. The ship of the line grappled alongside and Eusari awaited his arrival on the lee deck, wanting to avoid both wind and spray. Within minutes the enemy crew had sent seventy men aboard with swords drawn.

"This is the famed *She Wolf?*" The captain roared with laughter at the tiny woman dressed in black leathers, gloved arms crossed across her chest. "And you must be the famed phantom wolf, the she-devil and Lady Captain." He casually strode forward and reached out his hand, stroking the fur of her cloak. As he reached to scratch the ears of the hood a low growl could be heard from behind a crate. He instantly stepped back and drew both of his swords. "What in the unholy hells is a wolf doing aboard a ship?"

"Easy Gelert," when Eusari spoke the words seemed to purr out of her throat, "let's not kill him until he's had a chance to surrender."

"Surrender?" Bartholomew and his men roared hysterically at her words, but she and her sailors stood fast on the deck.

Without flinching she responded, "You and your men will lay down your swords."

The crew that hadn't boarded manned the rails to watch the show. They shared the merriment and laughed along with their captain. He asked, "Just like that?"

"Actually," Eusari purred, "you will also give over your vessel, Captain Cartwright." She raised her gloved hand into the air and dropped a black silk handkerchief to the deck.

As soon as it left her hand two claps of thunder could be heard from atop the crow's nest. With all eyes on the wolf, no one noticed her sharpshooters. Bartholomew sprang a red hole in the top of his head. Nearby another man fell with him in unison. On cue, three tarps flew back from the longboats and rifles ripped into the topside crew aboard *Desperation.*

Eusari's men on deck drew their pistols and fired into the invaders, causing them to panic. With swords drawn her crew cut down man after man while those in the longboats finished off those on the other vessel. The battle ended in minutes, with *Desperation* losing more than one hundred men. Several of the survivors surrendered very quickly after realizing the awesome firepower of her weapons.

*She Wolf* did not lose a single sailor. She ordered the captives locked away below decks on the Galleon, intending to press many of the soldiers into service. Now, with a ship of the line at her disposal, she tied off her own and towed it back home to The Cove. With the help of Caroline, the winds favored the larger sails and she made the trip in a week.

# Chapter Two

Robert Esterling awoke with a start, heart racing and beating out rhythm with his anxiety. Drenched with sweat, he stared at the ceiling and willed his body to relax. He drew a breath into his tight and aching chest, feeling the passages of his lungs constrict. *Of course,* he thought, *my breathing always suffers in the spring.* He pulled himself up in his bed and practiced his breathing exercises.

Next to him a woman stirred. She rolled over and touched a hand to his chest. "Are you okay?"

"I will be. It's always worse at night."

"I love you, but I told you not to spend so much time outdoors today. This always happens when the wind blows pollen."

"I love you more than I can put in words, Sarai." Robert gazed upon his bride. Her radiant smile seemed to glow on its own, seemingly brighter than the moonlight spilling through the window. Her skin had fully healed, and her scars enhanced her natural beauty, especially when she smiled. Her hair had grown back where it could, once thickly flowing blonde rendered patchy where she had burned.

She pulled herself up beside him and kissed his cheek before nestling against his shoulder. "Have you done your thing yet?"

"No, not yet. I keep hoping that someday I won't have to. I need to outgrow this and not rely on magic." He breathed a few more times in through his nose and slowly out of his mouth before finally giving up. The air in front of him began to swirl slowly, building a current. He drew this into his lungs and felt the branches of his airways open, muscles relaxing. After exhaling he felt a remarkable change and his pattern resumed.

"You're stubborn."

"As stubborn as a Horslei? You shouldn't throw rocks when your own house is glass, My Love." He beamed at her reaction.

Her nose wrinkled in disgust. "Glass house?" She playfully smacked his shoulder. "My dear prince, I deserve a palace of gold. Don't ever forget."

A thought bothered Robert and he quickly turned somber. "I wish that you could see my palace in Eston. The roses will be in full bloom by now. Spring was always my mother's favorite time of the year. That's one of the promises my father made when he built up the city to span the river. He vowed that Loganshire would be protected from the northern aggressors and Crestal Esterling would have roses."

"I wish I could have met him." Nuzzling in she added, "We'll get there soon enough."

"We have to get out of Eskera and retake Weston first. The blockade is strangling the city and more troops are amassing in Soston. It won't be long before they march on us, Max is sure of it."

"He should know." Sarai wrinkled her nose at mention of Robert's mentor and friend, Maximus Reeves. "He's a war-monger."

Ignoring her disgust, he continued, "My brother placed ten thousand soldiers in Soston, so far. I've seen them, myself, through the eyes of Arne."

"You can fly that far and hold the connection?" Her eyes marveled at how strong he had grown with his powers in such a short time. The bond with his eagle further amazed her.

He nodded. "We've been taking daily flights, pushing farther from Eskera each day. We reached Soston yesterday and I'm going back today." He stopped talking. He did not want to alarm his love by describing what he had seen.

She recognized his sudden change and sat up, silk sheet sliding from her chest and exposing her breasts to the night. Heedless of the cold she pressed, "What aren't you telling me?"

Robert searched her eyes for quarter, but saw no way out of answering. "There are more ships arriving sometime today."

A shiver down her spine made her suddenly aware of the chill, and Sarai lifted the covers to her neck. "He means business. Robert, we need to flee Eskera and take our chances in Weston."

"I need to hold out a little longer. Max and General Lourdes believe that more soldiers will defect to our side, and I want them to find me."

"How many have joined you so far?"

The Esterling prince allowed a quiet humility to pass through him. "Only about five hundred."

"Then you have your answer. Robert, I love you, but we need to flee. Help isn't coming. Not by sea, at least." She snuggled back into his shoulder and closed her eyes. "Now go back to sleep."

He stared at the ceiling for several minutes, even after the rhythm of slumber returned to her breathing. *She's right. If more were coming, then they'd have already arrived.* The entire campaign against his usurper brother felt hopeless. He finally closed his eyes tight and willed himself to sleep, lulled to slumber by the warmth of Sarai at his side and the sweet scent of her hair.

Sleep brings dreams. For Robert Esterling these were as tiring as the awakened world. His consciousness drifted upward toward the heavens until he connected with Arne and drifted on the breeze. Flying south he focused sharp eyes on the Misting River delta as it flowed out to sea.

A line of twenty ships sat at anchor, forming a semi-circle around the mouth of the river. These were clearly war galleons instead of transports, with rows of guns staring down any ship that dared to enter or leave the harbor. Escape was not an option. Robert commanded the city of Eskera, but his brother controlled the ocean.

He turned east along the coast and drifted with the wind toward the city in the far distance. The sun was rising over Soston, making it a beautiful sight from the air. Tall pines and broad palms grew out of pure white sand against teal blue water. More ships lined the harbor, this time troop transports and heavy barques with three masts each. The city was well protected with natural sandbars channeling traffic into a single opening protected by two forts. Large guns loomed on short but wide parapets, ready to strafe any invader.

Beneath the pines Robert counted thousands of tents, each emblazoned with his family crest. Only, something had changed. He drifted as close as he dared and focused sharp eyes on the image. The flower was gone and only an eagle remained. Looking closer he could tell that the soldiers among the tents wore black armbands, each emblazoned with his mother's rose.

Out of nowhere several hawks filled the air to meet him, scattering the flock of seagulls accompanying his flight. With a screech he flew higher into the sky. Eventually they turned away and circled, unable to follow at the higher altitude. Having seen enough, he turned westward to inspect the route the army would follow when they invaded Eskera.

The narrow road wound through tall pines and marshes. *That's good,* the prince thought, *the swamps and deep cover will slow them.* Robert had many talents, and the foremost advantage over his brother was his military mind for battle. He had trained to lead armies since birth, schooled in tactics by his mentor and recently revealed biological father General Maximus Reeves. Max had been trained by the greatest tactician in the history of the Esterling Dynasty, Major General Merrimac Lourdes. Robert considered himself lucky to have both men fighting beside him during the early days of his civil war.

Of course, Marcus collected his own military minds. Although he had shunned training, choosing instead the pastime of bedding damsels, he was raised by his own mentor and true father, Captain General Matteas Brohn. That man was ruthless and cunning with a history of bold and sometimes dubious tactics. Brohn always struck without giving quarter and without regard to humanity.

Robert had recently survived an assassination attempt while in Weston, no doubt the calling card of Matteas. He shivered when he thought about the failed attempt. It had been the first day he had channeled his powers and used air as a weapon against the men. He killed them, and, by doing so, drew his first blood as a warrior.

His life had changed on that single day and thinking about it forced his mind to drift. He had experienced intense dreams for several weeks before that morning and had awakened with a strange feeling of prophesy. In his sleep he travelled more than a thousand miles in the air to witness an assault on the town of Diaph. He watched as several people manifested strange powers during the raid, working together to save captive children and steal weapons.

But that wasn't the only disturbing scene he witnessed. The small force had entered a Rookery, a place of such secrecy that that not even the royal family was allowed admittance by the Falconers. There, through the eyes of another man as gifted as he, Robert saw the disturbing images of people laid out on stone slabs. Tubes ran from every orifice. *I wish they could have saved the people,* he thought. But they were ill-equipped to remove the tubing, and somehow knew that doing so could kill them all. *What was the meaning of that place,* he thought?

*"It was a farm."*

Robert felt himself teeter in the air, losing control of his altitude and falling several dozens of feet before righting himself. Abruptly, a face entered his vision. He saw a smiling little girl of about thirteen summers with a face full of freckles. *"Who... Who are you?"*

*"I'm Marita."*

*"How... How are you communicating with me?"* But inside Robert knew the answer. He had stumbled upon the same thought-sharing with the man in the Rookery, bound by air and at the mercy of the looming Falconer.

*"Just like that."*

*"Like how?"*

The girl laughed. *"Just like you talked to Samani in the Rookery. He told us about that, said you have the same powers as us. He's the one who told me to find you. We've been trying for weeks."*

*"I found him first!"* Another face appeared before him, this time of a round-faced boy of about nine summers.

*"Yes, Sebastian, but I figured out how to talk to him, so I win the prize."*

Robert was amazed by the childhood innocence of his visitors, listening intently as they argued in his mind. *Like me?* Robert's thoughts turned to Taros, the Pescari boy who had wielded fire and burned down the gates of Weston. It was his inability to control emotion that had burned Sarai.

*"Oh no! She was so pretty! I hope that he didn't kill her. Is she...? Is she ok?"* The girl named Marita looked genuinely concerned and shocked. *"He's lucky you didn't kill him."*

*"How did you know about her?"*

*"You just showed me, when you thought about her."*

*"She's fine."*

The boy interrupted. *"She looks different now. Uglier."*

*"Sebastian! How dare you! That was an awful thing to say. Can't you tell that he loves her no matter what she looks like? You need to go. Wake up!"*

Robert worried that the girl could read his thoughts so easily. *"I must admit that it's a little scary with you reading my mind."*

The girl answered honestly. *"I'm sorry, communicating like this is hard to control if you aren't fully in our dream world."*

*"Dream world?"* The conversation did not make any sense to the prince.

*"Oh yes! It's wonderful!"* The girl's lips turned up at the corners as she giggled. *"Let go of your bird and let me take you there."*

Robert considered her offer, curious to know more about the strange children, but politely declined. *"No, I will not. Maybe another time."*

*"That's okay! We're still working on the trees and mountains, anyway. But when you come, you can help us with the rivers and lakes."* Her smiling face dropped, and she took on a serious expression. *"Before I forget, I was supposed to pass you a message."*

*"A message? From whom?"*

*"From Samani, silly. He said to come to Pirate's Cove and join us. We have a lot of work to do and need your help."*

*"What kind of work?"*

*"The rebellion! Braen and Eusari are leading a rebellion!"*

Robert's heart fell from his stomach, plummeting three hundred feet in the sky. Careful to control his thoughts he answered, *"I'll think about it."*

*"Don't think too long. There's an army about to march on you."* For a moment she again looked serious as she tried to remember something important. *"Oh yeah! And Samani wants to know your name."*

*Robert.* He tried to send his name, but the word was lost in his mind. Somehow, the connection had been lost and the prince sat upright in bed, drenched in sweat and again wheezing.

Anger gripped him as he thought about his mother and her killer. Marcus had blamed him for that conspiracy and poisoned the people against him. Robert had never met the outlaw, the man quickly becoming a legend. *They call him the Kraken, the King of the Deep.* Tales of his exploits had already reached Eskera and the child had unwittingly confirmed that Braen Braston, the scourge of his family, was mounting a rebellion and recruiting an army with magical powers. *I'll never lend aid to a pirate.*

# Chapter Three

Market day filled Logan city. The favorite holiday brought people to celebrate spring and prepare for planting season. Their buckboards lined the streets as farmers loaded seed and supplies. Sounds of merriment competed with merchants shouting their wares, and puppet shows acted out brazen political satires. Whether shopping or pausing for entertainment, the festival goers felt the warm sun as they laughed and rekindled friendships.

One young girl watched a troupe of actors perform the crowds' newest favorite, *The Kraken King.* Men, women, and children booed as the evil pirate Braen Braston lopped off the Queen Regent's puppet head. It rolled off the stage onto the ground and pig's blood spewed from an apparatus in the neck of the doll. The girl watched the audience blanche at the brazen display of violence. Kali smirked at their naivety, her entire life having been exposed to senseless and excessive pain and bloodshed. She had seen it all in her fourteen summers, starting with the loss of her mother when she was only five.

She searched the crowd for a new mark until her favorite scene caught her eye. The puppeteer held up two large squids, designed to represent the legendary Kraken of the ocean depths. She loved the myths about the beast and would often sit at the docks listening to the sailors tell the tales. Every child in Andalon knew that if you sailed too far east, the beasts would tear your ship into splinters. She stared intently as the puppet pirate king rose up and took control of the strings of the beasts, directing them to rip apart the parapets of the fortress, tossing defenders into the water.

She had seen the show several times and knew the ending awaiting the miniature Pirate's Cove. In life, Braston brought total destruction to the city he had intended to keep as his own. By now nothing could tear the crowd away from the enthralling carnage on the magnificent little stage.

A wealthy merchant and his wife stood nearby, eyes wide and huddled together in fear of Braston's magical and massive tidal wave. The thought of dark arts repulsed the woman, and she burrowed into her husband's shoulder. He wrapped his arms around his love, his fat belly raising his tunic above his belt. This created a perfect scenario for the redheaded thief, and Kali acted quickly.

Moving in close and careful not to jostle the pair, the girl slashed two strings and dropped the heavy purse into her waiting satchel. Neither man nor wife noticed the lightest sound of coins jingling. At the same time, deft little fingers worked the clasp on the women's heavy golden bracelet. It slid easily into the thief's pocket. Feeling emboldened, she took an extra second to lift a loaf of rye bread. She drew it from the woman's shopping bag and stowed it with the coins.

Kali felt eyes watching and adrenaline surged, causing her back to stiffen. Constables and their deputies scoured the city on market days, many wearing plain clothing to hide in the crowd. She searched the surrounding people, wondering who had seen her crime. She had two witnesses. One was a young girl clutching a princess doll in a regal dress. The toy clashed with the child. Although she looked clean and well looked after, her own clothing was tattered and badly worn. *She's only a poor farmer's daughter,* Kali assumed and dismissed the threat.

Her eyes focused on the other witness, a boy leaning against a fruit stand. He was tall and lean with coal black hair. His steely eyes bore through her soul with obvious hatred. She recognized him as a member of the Wolfpack, a local gang who claimed and worked the lower sector. He would pose a problem.

She casually approached another target, trying not to tip the boy that she had noticed him spying. *You're welcome to watch,* she thought, *maybe you'll learn a trick or two.* The street gangs in Logan were nothing more than loosely organized groups of miscreants and orphans. Usually, they committed only petty larceny but worked their turf with permission of the Thieves' Guild. Known for hefty fencing fees, the guild accepted items from all sources and those included Kali.

The only consequence for working someone else's street would come if the boy caught up with her. She doubted that he would, but secretly hoped that he would try. She smiled at the prospect of a fight, and several surprises awaited anyone challenging her right to work the street.

Kali spied another boy moving the opposite direction through the crowd, no doubt running to gather reinforcements. Applause rang out from the audience, signaling the conclusion of the performance. People would be tossing coins to the players, and several would realize their missing purses and shout for the nearest constable. She wanted to pick one more pocket before fleeing and would have to work quickly.

Her new mark was a drunken soldier enjoying the festivities and winter mead. He ambled toward three whores standing on the doorstep of their brothel. He hefted a heavy bag of coins and jingled them, no doubt judging which quality of girl he could afford. *No, stupid girl,* Kali tried to warn herself, *don't be greedy.* She knew that she should pass him over and leave safely, but his lechery fueled her desire to punish him. *Men like him prey on women like mama,* her mind insisted, *and he's just like the man who killed her.* That thought was enough to risk capture.

She moved in close, pleased that the women had not noticed their potential client. He had returned the purse to his belt, tucking it in rather than tying. *That makes it tougher to grab,* she thought, *but I like a challenge.* The plunder would require more creativity, but Kali would take the coins.

He was nearly in range of the whores and Kali worked fast. One final glance toward her watcher revealed him and others moving in with determined looks. Thinking quickly, Kali loosened several buttons on her blouse, revealing much of her freckled chest. After running her hands through her wild red hair, she swept in with a flourish, wrapping her arms around the waist of the sodden soldier. "Hey there, handsome!" She shot a theatrical glance over her shoulder and indicated the three girls on the corner. "If you're looking for a good time you can get me for half their price."

The drunk pushed her away with force, too embarrassed that she had touched him to notice his now missing purse. Pointing at the three street women he said, "I want a professional, not a child."

She feigned hurt at his words and discreetly slipped the prize into her satchel. "Are you sure? There are some men who'd prefer a child." She batted her eyes with a fake look of pout. "They charge gold, but I'd do it for a copper"

The man chuckled, "If you'd do it for a copper then you've got diseases."

By now the legitimate prostitutes had noticed the exchange and one of them, a busty blonde in her late twenties, pushed Kali away from the soldier and spoke with gutter speech, "This is ow cornah! Move away from ow customah!"

Taking advantage of the intervention, she shouted an apology and ran. She only had a short time before the soldier would realize that he could no longer afford any of the girls. Worse, the Wolfpack was already in hot pursuit. She sped down market street with haste, ears listening for whistles from constables. Hopefully they wouldn't have time to waste on a common thief.

Kali ducked around a butcher shop and into an alleyway. Footsteps echoed the pursuers closing in. Normally she would have run into a crowd, jostling her small frame through and using people to block the would-be assailants. She had been chased hundreds of times through these streets, sometimes by a constable but most often by a failed mark who felt their purses lift. Safety always came with crowds for a street urchin, especially one as old and wise as she. But she had a different strategy in mind.

In all of her fourteen years, she had never led a chase into an indefensible position. The streets of Logan were narrow, and this alley even more cramped. Kali wheeled around with a wide smile stretched across her freckled face. Four boys, all larger and a few years older than she, skidded to a stop and stared her down. The oldest, a dirty teen of about seventeen summers, pushed coal black hair out of his eyes and spat out a stream of gutter speech, "Yah made ah blasted mistake. This turf be the Wolfpack's."

The girl continued smiling as she watched the boys form a semi-circle, trapping her against the dense ivy climbing the brick wall of an ironworks. She knew that she shouldn't have been working streets owned by a gang, but she had already lifted a week's worth of rations before the boys had noticed her. That, and what was about to come next, made her morning excursion worthwhile. "These streets belong to a different pack now. You'd best stay out of my way."

The boys laughed in unison. One of the younger boys looked to the oldest and asked earnestly, "Can we rough her up, Matt?"

"No." The wiser and more experienced leader shook his head with an evil grin. "You don't be roughin' up girls as pretty as she. You teach 'em a lesson they won't soon fuhget, and you do it with their skirts ovah thah head."

A growl turned the boys' attention and filled them with fear. Six snarling dogs emerged from hiding places behind crates. Kali knelt down beside the biggest, hugging and kissing the top of its head. She whispered into the animal's ear loud enough for the boys to hear. "The big one has an evil heart. You should harm only him and let the others go."

Matt's companions stepped away from him with caution, most likely weighing their lives over loyalty. With eyes locked on the dogs they backed toward the alleyway entrance. He remained frozen in place, afraid to move. The animals snarled as they circled, trapping him as he had done to Kali. Defiantly he found his voice, betrayed by cracking fear. "I... I'm sorry. I wouldn't really rape yah! I... I just wanted to scare yah off ah turf."

"Like I said. There's a different pack in town, and we roam all of Logan." Kali snapped her fingers and the dogs returned to her side. She narrowed her eyes and added, "Stay out of our way." At her final command the dogs sat in unison.

Matt trembled at how well the dogs obeyed their master, but what happened next horrified him beyond reasonable terror. An army of roaches and spiders emerged from the rubbish and crates, tiny feet clattering as they advanced. He whimpered as they halted six inches away, leaving a narrow trail leading away.

"If you see me again, don't look at me," Kali warned. All at once the army of insects moved an inch closer and then stopped. Matt jumped and urine ran down the inside of his breeches. With a smile she added, "In fact, don't even see me." The boy nodded between sobs and ran from the alley.

She turned to face the wall and willed the ivy to animate, twisting and braiding into a strong ladder. She made her way onto the rooftop, the ladder unwinding after each step. From this vantage she gazed out at the city, pleased with her morning and excited about her newly won turf.

Movement overhead caught her attention and she paused. Fifteen hawks circled overhead, scanning the streets. *What are they looking for,* she wondered, remembering the ramblings of the old man, *or who?* She crouched low and moved across the rooftops, making her way with stealth and avoiding the crowded streets.

After a few minutes Kali arrived at her hideout. Standing atop an abandoned warehouse, she tripped the latch to a narrow vent and slipped inside. She had long ago barred the main door, making the roof the only entrance. Only weeks before she had added noisemakers inside, hoping they would alert her of intruders.

Once inside she surveyed the comfort in her tiny apartment that had formerly been a foreman's office. She lifted some rugs in the corner to reveal a small chest. She never had the key, but locks had never been a problem for Kali. She took out her pick and popped it open, revealing a small fortune of coins of all color and shape. To this she added her newly acquired spoils, including the bracelet.

Exhausted and cold from her ordeal in the streets, she curled up under several blankets and tightly closed her eyes. She soon drifted off to a dreamless sleep. Hours later bells rang violently, arousing her from her slumber. Her eyes shot open with alarm as she realized that danger approached.

She held her breath and listened to sounds of movement outside the building. Looking down from the barred window, she had to squint to see through the grime covered glass. Several hooded figures had gathered. They shook the large doors below, trying to gain access. Her heart raced as she recognized the Falconers, remembering the birds that had circled above. In her carelessness she had led them to her safe place, and now she must leave.

The specters focused on the heavy wooden doors, dust swirling and forming a dust devil. *Shit.* She broke her thoughts away from their ministrations and threw her belongings into her satchel. Along with the gold she grabbed some dried meat and a few overly ripened fruits. She had one chance for escape. She already had a destination in mind but had hoped for more time to plan her travels. It was now or never.

Kali moved a box away from the wall revealing a loose plank in the wall. She pressed on the board and made an opening, then tossed her satchel inside the space. She squeezed into the narrow gap, pausing only to return the crate to hide signs of her escape. Once inside she slid a bar into place, sealing the exit. The sound from inside the wall was deafening as the doors of the warehouse imploded. A powerful gust of wind shook the entire structure and the skeletal frame strained under some outside force.

Abruptly the roof lifted off and flew into the night sky, stars brightly shining down from above. Beneath her, sounds of heavy feet rushed inside. She closed her eyes tightly and silently made her way through the crawlspace in the wall. *If I can just make it to the tree,* she thought. But as she neared the opening, she spotted several large raptors perched high in the branches, eyes darting everywhere in the night and presumably searching for her whereabouts.

She knew the truth about the Falconers from the old man in the city square. She had first met him a month earlier when he had begun preaching about the awakenings. At first, she had dismissed his ramblings as some crazy new religious zealot. There were always plenty of those in the city. But his words hit home when she first experienced hew own powers. She knew right away that she was also an emotant.

Kali had spent much of her time with the old man. She listened to his warnings about the Falconers, the agents of an alien culture beyond the sea. He had no doubt seen her watching and listening, but never approached until the previous week. She had been kneeling, talking into the ears of stray dogs when he spoke directly to her. "I've seen those alley scavengers many times, but I've never known them to allow a human close enough to touch."

"They like me," she had responded with indifference. Like the animals, she rarely allowed strangers close enough to engage in conversation. She secretly hoped that he could sense her power.

"That they do." He had turned to leave, and she had been amazed that he didn't intend to press for her secrets.

"Is there a safe place?" Kali's words had the intended effect and the old timer paused with a slight smile on his lips.

"I'm sorry? Is there a safe place for whom?"

"Is there a safe place for emotants? A school, maybe? Somewhere they could run to when the Falconers come to reap the ones they've missed." Her eyes met his, still smiling like a proud grandfather entertained by a child's antics. "Somewhere to learn how to control it?"

"Yes. And it isn't far. If one were to journey up the Logan River into the Forest of Diaph, an emotant could find others like her."

"Or him." She winked at him, slyly. "I was only asking for a friend."

He had nodded, a glimmer of humor in his eye. "Of course, you were."

The next day she had convinced herself that she would seek him and press for more information. But when she arrived three Falconers had already bound him with their magic. She watched as a local magistrate and constable read out a death sentence for the old man before the beast-like administrators dangled his neck from the highest branches of a tree. They apparently no longer cared to hide their powers from the public, not with agents like the old man exposing them to the world.

A nearby shriek returned her attention to the warehouse. She had to get the birds out of the tree. Seeing that their talons were tightly wound around the branches she focused on the trunk. It began to move slowly to the side as if it were gently moving in the squall. *Thank the gods that they can't fly in this windstorm.* Finally, she released the great oak and it whipped upright like a sapling. The birds were flung across the street, crashing into the brick of a silo. One by one seven raptors fell to the ground, crippled or dead from the impact.

The Falconers howled screams of raging pain somewhere inside the building and she heard pounding feet rushing to her secret room. They tried to batter down the door. She scurried out of the opening and leapt onto the waiting branches of the tree, quickly swinging down and sprinting to a narrow gap in the ground. She slid into the sewer just as a wisp of wind, similar to the ropes from which her old friend had dangled, narrowly missed catching her arm. And thus, she escaped into the night. The Falconers could not follow her into the crack to the cistern, and their airborne eyes could not see through the streets into the maze of tunnels beneath Logan.

After she finally felt safe enough to stop running, she drew a piece of paper from her satchel. Before he had been arrested, the old man had tied a string around the neck of one of the alley strays. She had known it was he who left the message because she had seen him petting the dog shortly before the Falconers had arrived. Of course, the animal had sought her out later and delivered the simple note with two words scribbled in a shaky hand. *Estowen's Landing.*

# Chapter Four

Fatwana Nakala pulled the shroud over a motionless body. This oracle had been a young man in his early twenties, his life stripped away before he had fully lived. He had shown much promise as an oracle but failed to transcend deep into Ka'ash'mael before his heart gave out. The initiates had recorded very little up until his passing, but enough clues corroborated what she already believed. Unfortunately, she had no one to whom she could confide her belief and tucked the latest transcription into her robe.

She touched the stone altar beside the corpse. Fatwana's own sister had died in the same fashion and this shrouded husk brought back painful memories. *How many more must die*, she thought, *giving up their young lives for the Council?* Her sister had died after revealing the awakening of a powerful emotant, one who even the Chancellor feared.

Ashima's final prophesy had thrown the Council into an uproar as they argued over the interpretation. For years the Astian Council had focused attention on the prophecies regarding one man, the destroyer foretold many centuries before. The awakening of all four powers seemingly confirmed their fears. The Kraken King would be the doom of the Astian way of life, and he would lead an army of emotants.

"Rest easy, Kalani, your death was not in vain." She spoke the words for the priests standing around her, waiting to anoint the body. In her mind she screamed opposition. *Of course, your death was in vain. All of you have sacrificed young lives for nothing.*

She paused when her eye caught a glimpse of a dark object that had rolled onto the floor. The covens revered the oracle beads as relics and the source of omniscience. But Fatwana knew the truth thanks to the work of her brother, Samani, who had been hiding in Andalon. She defiantly left the black bead where it lay, a discarded symbol of her faith in the Council, and left the priests to their ministrations over the body.

A figure stood outside when she opened the door to the oracle room. "Fatwana. Another dispatch has arrived from the Council."

"Thank you, Adelina." As the lead sister turned toward her cell, she noticed that the young woman lingered, eyes locked on the white room as the door closed. "Is there something else, sister?"

The girl lowered her eyes submissively and shyly shifting her weight before answering, "One of the initiates told me that Kalani gave the ultimate sacrifice."

"Yes. I only just left him. Why don't you walk me to my cell?"

"Thank you."

"You look troubled, sister. Tell me your concern."

"Kalani and I..." Adelina blushed and Fatwana could tell that the youth had shared intimacy. "We were friends."

"You mean that you were lovers?"

The girl blushed a deeper shade. "Yes, lead sister. I'm sorry."

"There is nothing to apologize for, sister Adelina. You have not broken any rules." All four oracles urged celibacy, but sexual interactions were not forbidden within the covens. "The dangers of forming a relationship are great, though, as I believe you are experiencing. Do you need a day or two for mourning?"

"I... Yes, please. And may I see him? To say goodbye?"

Fatwana shook her head. "I am sorry. Once the priests have taken over, we are strictly forbidden to have contact with the soulless husk."

"He had something of mine, a favor that he kept in his pocket."

Alarmed, the lead sister stopped abruptly. "Now that is against the rules, sister. We may not keep property."

"I know, lead sister, and I'm sorry."

"What kind of favor are we talking about? A trinket? A note?" Fatwana resumed walking and Adelina followed.

"A ring, lead sister." Tears welled up in the girl's eyes and she stopped, burying her face in shame.

Fatwana approached and placed a hand on her shoulder. "This is indeed a violation. Jewelry is strictly forbidden, as I am sure that you're aware."

"I'm sorry, lead sister. I truly am."

"You're to be confined to your cell while I decide your punishment." She wanted to act with leniency and compassion, but her foremost task as the lead sister was to enforce the codes of the coven. "But I will tell the others that it is for mourning and I want you to treat it as such. Do you understand?"

The girl nodded. "Yes, sister."

"Good. Now go and leave me in peace. I have work to do in my own cell."

The girl scurried away and Fatwana opened the door. She flipped a switch on the wall. The overhead lights were dim and illuminated a simple apartment free of adornment or decoration. In the corner rested a small bed for sleeping and a chair for sitting or reading. In the opposite corner sat a single writing desk. Atop the desk rested one of only two computers allowed in the coven.

She sat down and accessed the network. The connection was painstakingly slow as usual. The Winter Oracle was situated high in the mountains north of Astia, and the transmission lines were buried long ago. She had once read that people of the world had long ago communicated via objects that floated in the sky, but that was before the Great Eruption first ionized the atmosphere. It was also before the Final War when all of the great nations destroyed each other out of greed and survival.

Her connection to the network was confirmed and she quickly found the dispatch from the Council. The statement was vague in details but clear in direction. *The Council demands the immediate return of all oracle representatives. Arrive with haste.* Fatwana frowned, thinking about the disastrous outcome from the last time they had summoned her. She had been put on display and forced to announce the emotants, as if she were responsible for their awakenings. Fatwana sighed. She had no choice but to obey the summons.

Adeline left the lead sister in a hurry, embarrassed that she had admitted to breaking sacred laws of the coven. Tears flowed and her sobs were inconsolable as she sprinted down the passageway. Luckily the halls were deserted during mealtime, so no one saw her unsightly state. She began to hyperventilate and paused to catch her wind.

One hand rested on the wall as she bent over, shaking as she focused on each breath. But she tasted more salt from her tears than felt air enter her lungs. Finally, after what felt like an eternity, she began to breathe with control and regularity. Footsteps sounded around the corner and they were coming closer. Panic took her breath a second time.

Embarrassed by her condition, she ducked into the nearest door, shutting it quietly behind her. She leaned against the cold metal, listening to the sounds on the other side. After a moment the footsteps passed by and she felt that it was safe to move. She looked around and instantly realized where she was.

She gasped. *This is the room in which he died*, she thought. For the second time in several minutes, Adeline had broken another rule of the Coven. She had desecrated the oracle chamber with her unclean presence. She fell to her knees and wept silently, hands over her mouth and thinking about the horrific consequences that awaited her.

Even the body of Kalani was missing. Only a few minutes had passed since Fatwana had exited the room, but everything had changed. When Adeline had previously peeked inside, she had clearly seen the priests standing over her lover's husk. But the altar stood empty. *How could they have moved his body so quickly?*

Fatwana's cell was not far away down the passage and she had not heard them leave. *Where did they go?*

Curious, she stood and walked the room running her hand along the stone slab, still warm where his body had lain. Bending over she placed her cheek in the spot upon which his head had rested. With her right hand she gently caressed the surface where his chest would have breathed his last. Fatwana was correct that they had formed a relationship, but it was not a mistake as she had suggested. Their love was as true as any lovers from legend and she must seek him in the afterlife.

She knew what she must do. As soon as her mourning period and punishment ended, she would request to move up in rotation. She was not due again for another month, but she would volunteer for extra assignments. She wanted to endure the Ka'ash'mael and hoped that it would bring death. She yearned to transcend her soul and leave her husk behind.

Muffled screams beyond the wall caught her attention. She snapped back to reality and stood, leaving the altar behind. *The stone is thick, how can I hear through it?* She felt along until she found a slight depression atop one of the edges and pressed. A hidden door slid open and the hideous screaming overcame her ears.

Softly she tiptoed down a corridor, careful not to reveal her presence. She knew that she should turn and run but fear and curiosity pushed her onward, down the dark hallway toward a glowing sliver of red. She arrived at a door, slightly ajar, and discovered that the light came from within. Silently she crept forward until she could see inside.

Six coven priests stood around a polished altar very similar to the slab in the white oracle room. Except this entire room was carved out of a deep onyx. The ceiling, the walls, and even their robes were darker than the night. Sinister lights glowed red, casting a strange shadow on each of the faces within. Adelina gasped when she recognized her lover's naked form atop the slab and fear locked her feet in place.

Mesmerized she watched as one of the priests fell to the ground in agony, spilling a bowl of oracle beads. The others kept at their work, ignoring both their comrade and the round white balls rolling across the slab. Adeline stared as dozens bounced on the floor, one even rolling near her hiding place at the door. *Why are they white?*

She strained her eyes to see her lover spread out on the table. The priests stood over his body, chanting and waving their hands over his skin. Another fell to the ground writhing in pain like the first. His body shook and convulsed. *Why don't the others help them?* After the third fell to the floor the fourth placed his hands atop Kalani's forehead. With his eyes closed, his muscles spasmed in rhythm with the convulsions of the others. *It's as if he is drawing power from them!* And then Kalani sat up from the table.

The three men on the floor rose up and helped Adeline's lover into a standing position. Then, one of them brought a robe and dropped it over his head. Another placed a feathered collar around his shoulders and then she understood. She had seen one of the Falconers during her vision of Fatwana's brother several months before. She could no longer contain her fear and let out a single gut-wrenching scream.

Everyone in the room looked at the door but no one moved toward her. Kalani stared blankly, apparently not recognizing his love. One of the priests placed a black bead into the Falconers mouth and his pupils instantly dilated. Fear sent Adeline racing from the room and down the corridor, hoping to get free but not knowing where she could hide. When she entered the oracle room she slipped on a forgotten black bead on the floor and fell. Her head struck the stone altar.

The corners of her vision swam as everything around her pulsed. She rolled over and tried to stand but wisps of air wrapped tightly around her hands and feet. She lost her balance a second time and toppled forward, splitting the skin above her left eye on the stone. Through a crimson smear she made out the Falconer looming above. With a weak voice she begged, "Kalani! Stop! It's me!"

"Kalani?" Her lover appeared confused.

"Yes! You are Kalani! I know that you are in there!" She slipped in her own blood, smearing it against the white and ruining the purity of the sacred place. "Come back to me, Kalani!" Sobs caught in her throat and she coughed. Tears and mucus streamed down her face.

"Yes. I recognize that name," the Falconer said, "I am Kalani." One of the priests whispered into his ear and another wisp of air noosed around Adelina's neck.

Gasping, she clawed at the invisible rope, feeling, but unable to grab ahold of the strands. She felt as if she clawed at water, trying to grab a reflection. Tiny speckles of light and darkness danced in her vision. Her eyes bulged as she fought to breathe. There would be no afterlife for Adelina as darkness won out over the light.

# Chapter Five

The spring sun warmed Pirate's Cove while birds sang songs of life and restoration. Three months had passed since the tidal wave cleansed corruption and greed, ushering in a new era of change. All around the city people worked to rebuild their livelihood as well as the buildings around them. But their work was not drudgery. Their tenacity and willingness to strengthen and recover after the setback represented the resilient spirit of freedom.

Freedom rings with complexity and the word meant so much more than independence to the townspeople. They enjoyed choices unavailable to the rest of the world and each person had settled for different reasons. Some arrived with comfortable means and looked to increase their wealth, while others arrived with nothing and aimed to create their own legacy. Whether choosing a quiet life in the town or a daring and bold one on the sea, the decision had belonged to them. But none of them had expected their lives to change so quickly with the arrival of Braen Braston.

The sun had risen over a solitary figure pushing a broom in the streets. He looked out of place with his tall and muscular frame bent over the simple tool. A passerby would correctly guess that the Northman had been born to wield an axe or push a plow into the hard and frozen ground of his former kingdom of Fjorik. But his choice every morning was to help another family rebuild from the disaster that he had brought in the name of liberation.

At first the people feared him and that was understandable. He represented change that challenged their comfortable patterns of convenience. But each day they emerged one by one to work beside him and their sentiment shifted. He met each citizen with a warm smile and tender sincerity. Calm and caring, his patient nature comforted and offered a future without kings and harsh taxes.

But Braen Braston was a man of controversy. Word had spread of his past and especially of his birthright, both of which were secrets he had worked for years to hide. As the oldest son to the late Krist Braston, he should have inherited the northern kingdom and its wealth of resources. Instead, his younger brother had usurped his claim and blamed him for the murder of their beloved father and ruler. But that was only the first regicide of which he was wrongly accused.

More recently, the mainland civil war had dragged him into dark politics. Artema Horn, the former ruler of The Cove, betrayed Braen with intent to sell him to his brother. During that fateful night and failed exchange, the Queen Regent's own Captain of the Guard had seized an opportunity to assassinate her in favor of her son, Marcus. So far, the rumors had fueled a slanted perspective regarding the real nature of Braston.

On this day, the bearded captain had chosen to clean a storefront overlooking the once magnificent harbor. He paused to gaze upon the naturally defensible position, with gun turrets protecting the single entrance made narrow by treacherous reefs. These battlements had been ripped apart during his attack, the hardware tossed into the water by legendary creatures. Their intervention had earned him the whispered title of Kraken King. Now recovered, rebuilt, and restored, The Cove again enjoyed protection.

Below his vantage point he observed the progress made on the new wharf and pier. The tidal wave had splintered the old, but his engineer had quickly rallied the rebuilding effort. Six strong vessels tied off with newly stained wood shining in the rising sun. Beyond the ships, three new drydocks stood proudly and shipwrights added to the fleet. His eyes focused on the third dock, covered with tarps to hide the project within. The new ship was to be a surprise even for the Kraken King.

*Thoughtful Sippen,* he thought with a smile. This day marked the christening of the vessel and he could barely contain his excitement. Braen hated surprises. When he tried to sneak a peek under the tarp, his own crew had escorted him back to the palace, teasing and laughing at his impatience. Everyone understood though, he had sacrificed his famed *Ice Prince* onto the rocks below. Only his securely packed wine stores had survived the wreck. He planned to use one of those special bottles during the launch of his flagship.

The door behind him opened and Braen turned to greet the shop owner. The man wiped his hands on his apron but made no attempt to reach out a hand in greeting. Instead he crossed his arms across his chest with defiant indifference. Braen nodded his understanding and spoke apologetically, "I was just finishing up and will be out of your way."

At first the man said nothing, staring at the large man with a questioning and cold calculation. Finally, he spoke, "We were fine, you know. We didn't need you to save us from Nevra."

This was a common sentiment among the townspeople, who cared not who ruled The Cove. Leaders were only figureheads to whom they owed their taxes. Braen again nodded. "I'm not here to convince you otherwise, Sir." He gestured at the window of the storefront, now free of mud and debris. "I'm just here to clean up my mess."

The shopkeeper laughed despite his attempt to remain apathetic. "You're a piss poor nobleman, do you realize that?"

"I get that a lot." Artema Horn had often told him the same and he had always answered with, "No, that ship has sailed. I have no titles."

"I hear people throwing around the title of 'Kraken King' behind your back. Isn't that what you are, now? Are you our new king, Braston?"

"Not a king and barely a Braston." His conversations with the townspeople usually went this way and were always awkward. He did his best to speak candidly, and again seized the opportunity to explain his vision. "The Cove doesn't need a king. I'm proposing a new type of governing body with elected officials. Three leaders with clearly distinct and separated powers. They will represent your interests, and serve terms agreed upon by you."

The shopkeeper chuckled. "And you're running for one of these positions?"

"I am. But only to get things started before I move along. I hope that you vote with your heart."

"My heart?" The man's face darkened. "My heart says to kick you off my doorstep. My wife and I are old and can't make any more children." His eyes misted as he talked. "You nearly took our child from us. Charleigh was outside playing when you hit the town with your magic. She was lost for hours."

"But you found her alive?"

"We found her. She was barely breathing and buried in the mud over the ridge. Buried with the soldiers that your people killed." Tears completely filled the man's eyes. "She still has nightmares, Braston. She dreams that she's drowning every night and it's your fault."

Braen didn't argue or try to defend his actions. The shop owner's words begged for listening, and that was a skill the large man had perfected in the past months. When the man had finished, Braen simply stated, "I am deeply sorry that my brashness has affected your family."

"Well." The man scoffed. "That proves you're not a nobleman."

"Why is that, Sir?" Braen noticed that the man had uncrossed his arms and appeared more relaxed.

"Noblemen never apologize for what they take."

"Thank you for your time and your story. I'll get out of your hair." Braen turned to leave.

"Braston." Something in the shopkeeper's voice had changed. It softened.

"Yes?" The captain turned to see an outstretched hand and reached out his own to grasp it.

"The name's Ralphe Station." With their forearms clasped in the northern custom the businessman added, "Good luck with your endeavor. It's monumental."

Braen nodded, then picked up his broom and walked up the hill to the palace. *We'll change this world. One person at a time, if necessary, but we will change it.*

Hours later Braston had washed up and dressed in his finest. The christening would be a formal event, symbolic of rebuilding efforts. As he buttoned his coat, he murmured his complaint to Samani Kernigan. "Does this uniform have to be so stiff in the collar? How in the name of Cinder am I supposed to fight in this thing?"

"You don't." Samani laughed at the Northman's lack of refinement. "Rulers let others do their fighting." The man from Astia had made himself comfortable in a soft chair and helped himself to a bottle of wine.

"I'm not a legitimate ruler, yet."

"You will be."

"I don't know." Braen paused to form the words that had been troubling him. "Adamas Creech has been campaigning hard against us. He appears to have the merchant and tavern guilds in his pocket."

Kernigan let out a long sigh before drinking from his glass. "I told you to let me handle the elections. Don't stress yourself over the details."

"What you're planning feels wrong, Sam. I want the people to own this decision." A previous conversation troubled him. "Besides, I promised Eusari that she would be elected by the will of the people. That we wouldn't interfere with the process."

"Speaking of Eusari, *She Wolf* arrived an hour ago. That's the reason I called on you."

"I thought you made yourself comfortable for my wine." Braen felt excitement fill his heart. He had not seen his lover in several weeks and yearned to wrap her in his arms.

"Well, that was the reason I came in person. I wanted to see if you had any more bottles of the 754 red."

The bearded captain paused in buttoning his jacket and raised an eyebrow. "If I did, then you can bet that they're hidden from the likes of your bottomless gullet." He looked at his friend questioningly in the mirror. "Who told you I had that vintage?"

"Amash bragged to me that he once cracked open a case with you and Sippen." He sighed again. "Alas, we were not friends, then, and you still doubted my loyalties."

Braen chuckled and straightened up his jacket. "How do you know that I don't?"

"Because you still have questions for which I, alone, have answers." Samani rose from the chair and made for the door, pausing only long enough to pick up the bottle of wine. "Let's go. Sippen told me not to allow you to lag behind. He said that you'll talk to everyone in town between the palace and the docks if I don't escort you."

"I swear, sometimes he's more of a nursemaid than a confidant." But Braen knew that his little friend was right and allowed Samani to lead him to the docks. Along the way his thoughts turned back to Eusari.

There was a time when Braen agonized with yearning for a different woman. He had dreamt nightly of Hester, his childhood friend and once betrothed. His brother, Skander, had forced her into marriage as a statement to an exiled Braen. She was an unwitting pawn in a trap to lure the legitimate ruler out of hiding and into death.

Eusari Thorinson had completely replaced thoughts of Hester over the past months. She was a beautiful and delightfully complex woman, although deeply troubled. At first, she had confused Braen for Skander and focused her revenge on the wrong Braston. Artema Horn had used her to deliver the prince, beaten and drugged, to the usurper from Fjorik. But she had realized her mistake at the last moment and they escaped. Since that night in Estowen's Landing the pair had become friends and eventually lovers.

Their walk took the two men past the storefront Braen had cleaned earlier that morning. The sight of a little girl playing on the porch made the captain pause. Little Charleigh had bright round eyes that matched her chestnut hair. When she recognized the bearded man, her eyes filled with shock and Braston's heart sank as he imagined her drowning in the mud. *She fears me.* He felt his feet freeze on the street, unable to move another step. *What am I doing,* he thought, *Am I going to try and apologize to her? Why am I stopping?*

The door to the shop opened and Ralphe Station emerged with his wife. The bald shopkeeper wore a reassuring smile that contrasted the woman's apprehension. Braen felt his feet take over as they led him toward the shop. Samani let out an irritated sigh which was ignored.

"Captain Braston, I want you to meet my wife, Sofie, and our daughter, Charleigh."

Braen nodded a greeting to Sofie who eyed him nervously. "Pleased to meet you, Ma'am." The child stared up with confusion on her face. He knelt before her with a tender smile. "Hello, Charleigh."

She looked up at her parents questioningly and they both nodded that it was okay to speak with the stranger. When she answered it was with confidence, "Hello."

"Do you know who I am, Charleigh?"

"Yes. You are the man who made the wave come." He had been wrong in his earlier assumption. The child was not afraid.

"I'm sorry that you were hurt when that happened. I understand that you were trapped and afraid."

She nodded, looking down at her doll. "I was, but then the woman found me."

"What woman was that, Charleigh?"

"The lady with black gloves."

"Captain Eusari?"

She shrugged. "I guess. Her doggy found me, and she dug me out. I never got to thank her."

Braen addressed the girl's parents. "We are on our way to the christening of the new ship and Eusari will be there. Why don't you come along as my guests so that Charleigh can meet her?"

Ralphe let out a chuckle. "Guests of the Kraken King, himself. You don't get an invitation like that every day." After a nod from his wife he added, "We'll be there."

Braen turned to Samani who anxiously glanced at the sun. It had risen to midday and they were holding up the ceremony. Kernigan waited until they were out of earshot when he whispered, "Next time we're taking a carriage, Braston."

# Chapter Six

Fatwana watched from the doorway as the initiates loaded her single bag. She eyed the car with lonesome dread, afraid to leave her coven. She never liked traveling, especially for the kind of business that the council demanded. Worse, whenever she journeyed on the government's purse, it made her feel ostentatious. *Such waste,* she thought, embarrassed that the rest of the coven would see her step into such a luxurious coach.

It was sleek and shiny, one of the new models that could run on electricity. That technology had been lost to the people of Astia for so long, much of their power grid still affected by the instability in the atmosphere. She marveled to see such an advancement so far from the capital and wondered briefly if it was new to the Oslot constabulary. Shrugging she guessed that she would know soon enough.

Rain drizzled down, soaking the ground and dampening her mood. It added to her disdain for travel. Thankfully the trip would not take long. After boarding the train in Oslot, the ride would only take a few hours to the capital city of Bergin. She drew a deep breath and then stepped out into the rain.

Subba held a parasol and somehow managed to keep her partially dry as one of the initiates opened the door. He then rushed around to the other side, sliding in next to the driver. "I hope that you're not too soaked, lead sister."

"I'm fine, thank you for asking." Fatwana liked the oracle with whom she had chosen to travel, although it should have been Adelina's duty. She had disappeared and no one had seen her since

Fatwana ordered confinement. It wasn't often that anyone left the coven, although some occasionally did. The grief over Kalani must have been too much for the girl to bear.

But her replacement was trustworthy and would be a pleasant companion if boredom struck. Thinking of the girl brought a thought to her mind "Subba, has there been any word from Adelina?"

"No, sister. Nothing."

"And no one saw her leave?"

"No one. Kareshi brought food to her cell after dinner, but she wasn't there."

The wind picked up and a downburst of cold rain pummeled the windshield. She shivered at the thought of the girl wandering alone down the mountain. "Strange that she didn't swap out her robes for heavy wool."

"Yes, sister. Several of us searched outside but found no sign of her. Though it's possible that she made it down, I fear..."

Fatwana turned and looked at the man, always sweet and kind to his peers. "You fear what?"

His eyes pointed to the floor and his expression dimmed. "I fear that she is still inside the coven and that we will find her, eventually."

Fatwana nodded. "Sometimes grief makes us act foolishly."

"Surely she wouldn't." Confusion covered his face. "Not if it meant losing her chance to join him in transcendence."

Fatwana's voice turned motherly. "Why did you join the Oracle, Subba?"

"Because I yearn to transcend. When I was young and first heard the priests talk about afterlife, I set my life on that journey. After they tested me and I learned that my soul showed promise, I left immediately for a coven."

"Does it worry you that there is no afterlife for the family you left behind?"

"Of course. That's why I said my goodbyes before leaving." His eyes betrayed distant homesickness.

"Then you won't miss them after you transcend?"

"Well, yes. I suppose that I will." He seemed thoughtful, speaking from his heart.

*Most oracles would have lied,* she observed. Honesty was another trait that she liked about the man and wondered about herself. *How would you have answered?* After clearing her throat, she gave him truth of her own. "I lost my sister, Ashima, recently.

"Yes, lead sister. I remember."

"But before that I lost my brother." Her kind smile dropped when she spoke of Samani.

"Did he transcend, as well?"

"No. He chose to leave the Oracle." Fatwana paused to let the words sink in. Subba looked astonished. "But I have learned that he finally found a new home."

"Another oracle?"

"No. He joined the Humanitarian Freedom Society. You see, sometimes people will give up everything they have for something they suddenly believe they need."

All color left the man's face. "What would someone choose over transcending?"

Fatwana fell silent, staring at the raindrops on the window. She felt his staring eyes, large with disbelief and waiting. Unable to speak honestly, she chose to watch scenery.

After a while the terrain flattened. Forest turned into cultivated farmland and soon rows of tiny buildings dotted the landscape. One large building stood in the center of smaller houses and each of the communes were identical, save the numbers painted on the side of the central building. Normally Fatwana would have observed a flourish of activity in the compounds, but the rain had driven the workers inside.

Subba finally broke the silence. "Compounds thirty-two and thirty-three are without power."

Fatwana looked out the passenger window and saw that he spoke true. "I have heard that's happening more frequently as the cities draw more."

"It seems strange, since the electricity is farmed here."

She looked up at the tall windmills spinning in the storm. "It's collected here, but the distribution center is in Oslot. The cities get priority and so they randomly roll blackouts in the rural areas."

Subba nodded. "I wish there was a way we could harness more energy by means other than wind and water, perhaps from the sun?"

She shook her head. "I read that there was a time that was possible in ancient times. Unfortunately, that technology and many others were lost during the dark age. Some say that the ancients could fly across the sky and even to the moon, but I doubt that was true." The look on the oracle's face reflected amazement. "Subba, do you know what the oracle beads are?"

"Yes, lead sister. Every initiate knows. They are the essence of foresight and seeing. They allow us to know and anticipate the world's problems while watching over the Andalonians. To prevent the birth of the Destroyer who will kill us all and tear down our cities."

"And who can use the beads?"

Subba looked troubled, as if she tested him. "Only the worthy."

"And who are the worthy?"

"Astian people with a soul capable of transcending planes."

"To where, Subba."

"To the Collective Soul, lead sister." He pointed toward compound fifty as they drove by. "Just as the people of Astia work as a collective, so do the oracles lucky enough to transcend."

Fatwana nodded and smiled with motherly praise. At this Subba lit up and beamed, assuming he had passed her exam. *Haven't you ever wondered where they come from, Subba?* But she couldn't ask that question, not with a government driver at the wheel. She watched the young man with his idealistic dream of transcending. *He's too brainwashed like the others,* she thought, *just like I have been.* But that was the way with the Oracles. *We're promised a heavenly paradise for our ultimate sacrifice.* Although lately, she doubted that martyrdom was worth the price.

They rode in silence the rest of the way and her mind mulled a conversation with Samani from their youth. His voice resonated in her head, deepening the lines in her face. "The people in Andalon are human like us, Fatwana!"

"No, Sam. They're monsters with powers to destroy instead of build." Her younger self had argued. "That is why our ancestors keep them across the water."

"But how did they get the powers in the first place?"

"I don't want to get into that."

"Because you don't want to admit that our ancestors made them when they first experimented with foresight."

"That's preposterous. You can't 'make' someone."

"So, you admit that they *are* someone and I win the argument. They are people, simple as that."

"You twisted my words!" Her younger self had often been frustrated with his ability to turn debates to his favor. Her little brother was a master manipulator.

But then Ashima had spoken up and the older siblings quieted to hear their baby sister, intelligent and wise for her years, "I read that our ancestors did create them. That's why the practice of life science is forbidden by anyone working outside of the government and without permits."

"How?"

"Something to do with traits. Like the color of eyes or hair. Sometimes a redheaded mother will have a baby with raven hair. The same thing with foresight. If you are born with the ability to see, even a little bit, and mate with another with that same trait, then their child could be strong." The other siblings laughed at the thought of people making babies in the name of science.

"That sounds like a fun experiment I'd like to participate in." The teenage Samani was thinking about the sexual act, of course.

Fatwana still had her doubts, "Why did they move them across the water, then?"

Samani answered, "That's what I've been trying to say. The experiment backfired, and, in addition to foresight, they created other abilities. People emerged with powers over living things and even the wind and water, as well."

"Then why didn't they just kill them?"

Ashima spoke, again. "Because you can't just kill someone out of fear."

"Well then they should have sterilized them and let them die out." Her attention returned to the present as they approached the outskirts of Oslot. She and her sister had never figured out the answer to that question, never speaking further of why the Andalonian people were kept alive. It was enough for them that they were controlled by measures taken by the council and closely monitored by the oracles.

She thought about the black bead she had left on the oracle room floor the day before. *We need them alive to farm the essence of the bead. But you figured that out, didn't you, Samani? That's why you left and joined The Society. You wanted to prove that you were right.*

The city of Oslot starkly contrasted both the Winter Oracle and the communes they passed on the drive. Tall buildings flanked the road and everywhere people scurried to their assignments. *Seems we arrived at shift change,* she observed. The driver had to stop and wait as a mass of people crossed the road from the apartments, hurrying to the factories and bakeries.

Fatwana watched them closely as they passed, engaged in friendly conversation and occasionally smiling. Before he left, Samani had told her that the Astian people were not free. That they were slaves without collars working for the collective. At the time she had argued back that the collective ensured equality, providing for all so that none lived in poverty. *But how is wealth measured? I own nothing but these robes and the hope of transcending. Would owning more make me happy?*

These people possessed little more than she. Their clothing was simple, made from materials farmed in the communes. Their homes were just as sparse, with furniture enough for necessity, but nothing more. Her thoughts wandered to the ring that Adaline had given to Kalani. A simple token, but one that had most likely been hidden and passed through her family for generations. She wondered what the priests had done with the bauble when they disposed of the husk.

The crowd finally parted, and they again moved through the city, leaving behind the third ward and the industrial quarter. As they drove, they briefly passed the second ward where the educated classes lived. If one was lucky enough, they were chosen from the schools to receive higher education and assigned this ward. Ashima could have easily been promoted, but she happily took assignment to the same oracle as her siblings and shared their eagerness to transcend.

Despite their earlier delay, they reached the depot in time to catch their train. Subba retrieved the bags and the driver handed him their passports. The pair made their way in silence, ignoring the staring eyes of the people waiting to board. They walked quickly then showed their documents to the travel master who directed them to their car. Once aboard, they learned that they would share a private cabin.

Fatwana collapsed on a sleeper seat while Subba stowed their bags. "I'm hungry. Will you go to the dinner car and retrieve our rations?"

"Of course, lead sister." He bowed and departed, closing the door behind him.

Soon after, she heard a tap on the door and panic twisted her gut. She jumped to her feet and smoothed her robes before a young woman dressed in simple clothing entered. Fatwana closed the door behind her then turned with eyebrow raised, waiting for her to speak. "Well?"

"When you arrive in Bergin you will tell your partner that you feel ill. Instead of going directly to your car and driver you will say that you need to use the facilities and separate from him. Let him watch you go inside the building. Go straight through and out the rear entrance where you will again meet with me."

"That's it?"

The girl nodded and then quickly opened the door and scurried out. Fatwana watched as she left, anxiety building as she willed her heart to slow its pounding. *So that's how the Society makes contact,* she thought. She had wondered how long they would take after receiving her message. It had been a risk, but one that she was ready to take.

# Chapter Seven

Hester hated the winter. Truthfully, she hated the winter less than she hated her husband, but the season always forced her to spend extra time with him. On this day she had avoided Skander by mulling over the inventory reports. Food stores were greatly depleted from the strong bite of the season, but Fjorik had survived. Of course, he wouldn't care about that report. He never did.

He was only interested in updates from the armory and those regarding troop strength or ship building. All he had talked about the entire winter was his plan to raid Esterling holdings and townships. She wished the channel would thaw so that she could be rid of the animal, even if only for a short time. That would be soon, she hoped.

Something on the table caught her eye. Among the dispatches lay a single message, neatly folded, and placed aside. *Why would he have folded it?* Hester plucked it from its perch. The words instantly disrupted her morning as she gasped with shock and disbelief. She read them many times before understanding. Rising with fury, she searched out her husband.

Hester checked the usual places but turned up nothing. Even the staff were no help, offering ideas like the practice field or the armory. She had already checked both obvious places. She eventually found him in the unlikeliest spot in the castle, the former chambers of his late father, Krist Braston.

Skander feared the room in which he had murdered his father. He avoided it, not out of remorse but from superstition. He had once been so deep in his cups that he claimed Krist Braston paced the halls of the palace, unable to join the heavenly feast. But she occasionally found her husband here, staring out the window or pacing the floor like a lunatic. She cautiously opened the door to peer inside.

On the bed she spied Bronhilde, a buxom chamber maid. The girl lay upon her stomach and was entirely disrobed. Hester's husband loomed over the girl in the same state of undress. In his hand was a crimson knife, dripping from his perversion. The girl moaned her pleasure as Skander carved fair skin. Several healed scars revealed that this was not the first time. Mortified, Hester gasped. The eyes of the lovers searched the doorway for the source of the sound.

The queen quickly regained her composure, fighting hard to slow her racing heart. With eyes locked on the blade Hester managed words, "When you finish, I need to speak with you, husband." She shut the door and leaned against the other side, pulse pumping fear that fogged her mind. Sounds of laughter from inside set her feet moving, anger replacing shock.

She hurried to her own chambers and rushed inside, collapsing on the bed and shuddering. With trembling hand she raised the folded dispatch and read. *A bounty of five hundred thousand talents has been offered for the capture or killing of outlaw Braen Braston. He is wanted for regicide in two kingdoms and for the destruction of Diaph and Pirate's Cove. He is guilty of rape and mutilation in Atarax, as well as inciting violence throughout the Eston Empire.*

Her thoughts returned to Skander and his scarlet blade, dripping with Bronhilde's passionate release. "No," she whispered into the room, "not Braen. He isn't the monster." A kick at the door sent it flying open with brute force, and she sat up straight on the bed. "Get out, you beast."

"Get out? You summoned me, or did you forget." He leaned in, reflecting her eyes in his. "What was so important that you interrupted me during my private time?"

She thrust the dispatch into his hand, "Explain this."

"So?" He let out a laugh that landed cruelly on her ears, "My brother's a wanted outlaw and that bounty will keep him in hiding."

"How much of that was him and how much was you?"

The chitter in his laughter turned maniacal as he responded, "You don't want to know the answer." He leaned in close, foul breath in her face. "But I will show you, anyway."

His fist connected hard against her cheek and the entire room went black.

Hours later Hester awoke in agony, face down on the bed and stripped completely naked. Everything hurt, but especially the skin on her arms and legs. Her entire backside was afire with pain unlike any she had ever experienced. She closed her eyes and prayed for death. But Skander would not have been that sloppy. He wanted her alive.

She finally mustered enough courage to try and stand. Trying hard not to roll onto her back she gingerly positioned her left foot on the ground. It held her weight. With a shove she pressed up, right foot contacting the floor. She shifted slightly off balance and crashed onto the boards with a splattering thud, crying out as skin ripped between her shoulders.

The nightstand was close but seemed to loom just out of reach. Time was quickly wasting, and Hester yearned for the elixir inside. She pulled her legs to her belly, forcing her body to roll onto her knees. Bloody hands grabbed hold of the sheet nearby as she pulled herself upright, close enough that she could reach the open drawer.

She felt inside with searching fingertips and found only emptiness. It wasn't there. Panic took over, pumping adrenaline and giving her enough strength to rise to her feet. She desperately searched the room, scanning with terrified eyes that shone like sapphires against the crimson smeared upon her face. They rested on the far wall.

Skander had found the bottle and must have hurled it across the room in his fit of rage, staining the stone with the impact. The contents had seeped into the rug below. She tried to run forward but stumbled and fell. She crawled, ignoring the pain, and hoping to find a puddle. All dignity had fled, and she would lap it up like a dog. Hester cried sobs of grief when she could not find any usable amount.

Then she noticed a spot on the rug that had absorbed quite a bit. Desperate, she gathered it to her face. Placing the corner in her mouth she sucked hard, trying to drink, but tasting only dirt. She pulled apart the fibers and pressed harder, slurping what little she could, and came away with a bloody tongue. With trembling fingers she plucked a shard of glass and tossed it aside.

She climbed to her feet using the wall for balance. Ignoring the scarlet handprints, she focused on a new goal and staggered one step at a time to the three-way mirror. *How bad, this time,* she wondered. It was not long before the reflection answered with a cruel image.

Skander's handiwork sharply contrasted her previously flawless skin. Every part of her front was savaged by his anger. He had left her badly battered with more than bruises. Her eyes, adorned with eyeshadow earlier that morning, swelled with yellow and purple. Welts had already risen on her arms and legs, remnants of a cruel belt and the wild swings from a madman. Her once perfect breasts had been marred by his foul and hideous mouth. What had once been milky white were ravaged by his teeth as claret marks evidenced his derangement.

She slowly rotated; eyes locked on her reflection as it revealed the damages on her back. Skander was careful not to reach the layers beneath the surface as he flayed. Every portion of her skin bled from his artwork. He carved designs that would certainly scar, no doubt a claim upon his property. She would forever wear the image of the Braston family crest.

# Chapter Eight

A spring storm raged over the city of Weston. Rain drenched the streets with heavy droplets that pounded instead of pattered on rooftops. Large chunks of ice shattered pottery left outside, and the winds howled and broke tree limbs while swirling the dark clouds overhead. But the most dangerous storm raged in the hovels and townhomes of the people. They had split in two over the arrival of the Pescari, and protests from both factions were a daily occurrence.

Cassus Eachann stared from his window and watched the ravaging weather. "I'll give you the contract to develop the new sewer, but the roads have been awarded to another."

Liam Creegle bowed his thanks. "Thank you, Your Lordship. Will that be with the standard ten percent for you?"

"I find that inappropriate for a contract of this magnitude." He considered, "No, we should agree on fifteen." He turned from the window and ignored the disappointment on the leech's face. "And don't forget that you must include a sizable contribution to the Humanitarian Faction. I am thinking an additional five percent would be appropriate. You know, to aid the cause of the poor and desolate in the city."

Creegle appeared ready to crack at the unreasonable bribes but nodded. "That's agreeable, Lord Eachann."

*Good,* thought Cassus, *he's not a complete moron.* The contract would last years and increase both of their coffers. Turning down his terms would be financial suicide. "Then it's agreed. Percy will draw up the contracts and you'll begin construction within the week.

I want my constituency to know that they have my whole-hearted devotion and I will provide their every need."

Liam Creegle bowed and scraped as he backed from the room, escorted by Percy Roan. Roan resembled the stereotypical clerk, bookish and mild tempered. His fingers on his writing hand were perpetually stained with ink, and, when he spoke, his voice barely broke a whisper. Despite his benign appearance, the man was nearly as ruthless as Eachann. His contract writing and genius negotiation skills had made them both sizable fortunes enviable by even the Esterlings.

It wasn't long before Percy returned to the room. He chose a soft chair and reclined, crossing one leg over the other. "That went easier than I expected."

Cassus agreed. "He's desperate to get on board with us early in our takeover."

"As have many others."

"What other deals are near closing?"

"I think Lehman will bite on the labor recruiting options for the mining initiative."

Cassus let a grin take over his formerly stoic face. "That was a genius move, by the way."

"Thank you."

"I'm serious, to think that the savages are taking over the labor force for the mines? This is audacious. Our legitimate company pays them wages, showing the humanitarians that we care enough to provide jobs. That legitimizes them as citizens."

"You mean voters," Percy asked.

"What did I say?"

"You called them citizens."

"As long as they appear and think that they are, then yes, they are both citizens and voters. We will tax their wages and charge them also through our subsidized companies for transportation to the mines, housing in our tenements, and for the food they buy in our markets." He smiled. "Are the brutes still running them out of the shopping districts in the rest of Weston?"

Percy nodded. "They get harassed any time they leave their district, unless they're traveling in our 'protected' caravans."

"Hmm. Let's plan a crackdown for a few weeks or a month on the brutes," Eachann decided. "Tell them that we'll continue to pay them, and any who are arrested or injured by the city guard will be compensated accordingly."

"I'll make the arrangements. What do you want to do about the boy?"

The governor was momentarily confused. "What boy?"

"Their chieftain. The boy named Taros."

"You've found him?"

"No. We don't believe he's in the city."

"If he's not in the city then what about this vigilante they call the agent of Felicima?"

"You think that's him?" Roan appeared dubious. "It has to be. If it isn't, then another Pescari has power over fire. Three more bodies have shown up in different parts of the city. Each as charred as the rest."

"Are we sure that it isn't a copycat? Someone pretending to be the boy to keep the legend alive?"

"There's no evidence that an accelerant was used on the fire.

"I see." Percy pondered the information. "Yes, and that's troubling. The Pescari are unstable and prone to violence. We may need to consider taking their weapons in order to prevent future riots."

"That's my sentiment as well. Start putting together the logistics of that."

"It will take a lot of planning. That act alone could create a riot. Let's see if they'll offer them up voluntarily first. Is there anything else, Cassus?"

"Yes. How are the gaming enterprises performing?"

"We've awarded permits to three, so far. But the owners are asking when they can introduce prostitution."

"Westonese or Pescari?"

"Westonese."

"No. That would lose the moderate or undecided voters. Block the sale of Westonese, but any true citizen who wants to buy a Pescari woman may do so without penalty. But no brothels! Just tell them not to bring the girls out of the district or they'll be arrested and fined."

Percy understood the order. "I'll get word out through the discreet channels."

A loud crack of thunder caused both men to jump. Cassus moved to the window and peered out. "Lovely, that started a fire."

"Shall I dispatch the fire brigade?"

"In this weather? Not a chance. Wait until a few more of their hovels have burned, and then charge in to save the day. In fact, also set a few fires in the Westonese middle class neighborhoods." Observing shock on his assistant's face he explained, "So that I have a legitimate disaster to point back on when I raise police and fire taxes in the fall."

A knock at the door silenced both men. It opened and a messenger handed Percy a pile of dispatches. He flipped through them, pausing briefly, and raised an eyebrow. After a while he carried them over to Eachann's desk and tossed them down. "The top one's interesting."

"Oh?"

"It seems that Marcus Esterling put an exceptionally large bounty on the exiled Braston. Says that he's committed atrocities throughout the continent."

Cassus read it over. "The sick bastard's been busy. Do you think it's true? The part about him taking over The Cove?"

Percy shrugged. "If it is, then where's Nevra? He's invested a significantly large amount in our endeavors."

Cassus considered the possibility. "Find out if he lives, and if not, draft something that turns his shares over to a fictitious party. Then use this 'crisis' that Marcus Esterling is whining about to depress the market. We'll buy his shares for coppers and return golden talents when it blows over in a month."

Another tap at the door announced the arrival of their next appointment. The door opened and an older, slightly hunched man entered. The steward's hair was thinning, and his baldness gave him a horseshoe appearance on top. The strands that remained were neatly combed over the other side.

"Your Excellency, may I introduce Lady Genevieve Flowers? She wishes to discuss pressing matters regarding the humanitarian efforts of the city." He bowed after speaking and an older woman of obvious wealth and comfort entered the chamber.

"Thank you, Phillip." The steward quickly closed the doors and exited.

"Lady Genevieve!" Cassus rose from his desk, eager to welcome his lobbyist.

Percy also rose. He bowed politely out of respect for the important visitor, then stepped aside and chose a different chair. The gesture excluded him from the company but allowed him details of the discussion. He picked up a quill as if he would record the meeting.

"Lord Eachann." She held out a single hand adorned with a white glove.

Her nasally and ostentatious voice burned both men's ears, but the governor did not let it show. "Please call me Cassus." He bowed graciously and took her hand, kissing the top of her glove as if she were a queen. "I was so excited to see your name on the schedule today. It has been too long since our last meeting." He helped her to a chair and sat across from her attentively. "To what do I owe this honor?"

She blushed at his flattery. Cassus was considered eligible to the Westonese nobility, having been widowed only a year before. "Lord Eachann... I mean, Cassus." Her cheeks went rosier at the mention of his given name. "I wanted to personally thank you for intervening on behalf of the Pescari against that filthy traitor, Robert Esterling."

"Oh that? It was my honor to stand up for the refugees against his immaturity and rash war mongering." He whispered. "Quite honestly, I would do it again."

She leaned in and scanned the room for invisible eavesdroppers. "Isn't it terrible that he kidnapped the sweet Sarai Horslei?"

He donned a sad expression that better conveyed false concern. In a low voice, he mournfully agreed. "Most terrible, Lady Genevieve. She was a friend and a colleague in our humanitarian efforts to aid the underprivileged." His face grew grim and somber. "Alas, I fear that if she were returned to us, it would be too late."

Concern and shock crossed her face and she reached out both gloved hands to grab his forearm. "Whatever do you mean, Cassus?"

"The boy is cunning and has a tongue turned silvered by his breeding and frivolous wealth. He is no doubt working on her as we speak and..." He shook his head. "No. I dare not say."

"Say! Say!"

The anxious expression and eagerness in her voice forced Percy to stifle a snicker. He covered his mouth and tried not to laugh. But Eachann's performance was legendary and held her on the edge of fainting. Cassus slowly and quietly let the woman out of her misery. "I fear that she has been turned. That she will sympathize with him and the war hawks. I fear that she'll desire wealth and power as a queen instead of our noble endeavor of aiding the Pescari."

Genevieve turned chalk white and fanned herself for air. "That would be scandalous!"

"Worse. It would be a humanitarian disaster of epic proportions." Fake tears formed on cue. "She may even help him to completely reverse the progress that we've made, so far!"

Tears formed in her own eyes and high-pitched squeals that may have been sobs poured from her chest. Eachann offered his handkerchief and she snatched it from the air. She blew her nose, emitting the shrillest and annoying sound either man had ever heard. Percy had to cough to cover up his laughter and Cassus hid his face in his hands. Luckily, she mistook his muffled laughter for sobs of his own.

"Oh, Cassus! Let me help you to find her. Maybe you can form a special cadre of city guard to sneak into Eskera and rescue her!"

He raised up his face, eyes red, then spoke in the most serious of tones. "That kind of operation is too expensive, My Dear. Where could I find that kind of money?"

Both men stared as she pulled off her jewelry. She pressed her earrings, necklace, and rings into Cassus' palm then said, "I will send more. Also, I will talk to the women of the better houses and convince them to do the same. Just..." She let out the shrill sound and sobbed a few more times before adding, "Just find her, Cassus!" She stood and ran from the room, gown flowing like a banshee as she squealed and sobbed. She frightened the entire palace staff as she ran through the halls.

Eachann watched her leave then turned to his partner. "Well, Percy, it seems we have found another source of revenue to fund another cause."

The clerk's eyes were red with laughter as he replied, "I'll draft up the donation forms and create a new account."

# Chapter Nine

Sippen Yurik stood on the pier, anxiously shifting his weight from foot to foot. Braen and Samani were late. He had wanted this event to be special for his lifelong friend, and the excitement of the reveal was almost too much for him. When they had crashed *Ice Prince* against the rocks, he had sworn that he would build for Braen the greatest ship ever designed. Today he would unveil the most magnificent marvel of Andalonian technology.

The entire city had turned out for the ceremony, eager to see the vessel that had been kept secret for so long. They lined the wharf and even sat atop houses and shops. Everyone jockeyed for the best view of it sliding out from dry dock. All dignitaries were on the pier. Eusari and her wolf stood with Peter Longshanks while Amash Horslei and Alec Pogue hung back from the rest, their conversation low enough that the others wouldn't overhear. Even Captain Adamas Creech attended, despite competing against the others for a seat on the triumvirate council.

Gunnery Sergeant Krill stood nearby, adorned with eyepatch and wooden leg. "Relax, Matey," he told the engineer, "He's a comin' down the road."

Sippen pushed his spectacles up on his nose and spied Braen walking with Samani and a local family from The Cove. "Huh... Who is wuh... with him?" Sippen hated his stutter. He never minded being shorter or smaller than everyone else, only his speech bothered him. It was worse when he was anxious, and this day tested his limits.

Eusari strained her eyes against the midday glare. "That little girl looks familiar."

As the procession wound its way through the multitude, Sippen smiled at the awe in which the crowd held his friend. Many moved away from him in fear, while most pressed close to either touch or be recognized by the Kraken King.

"He sure knows how to make an entrance." The voice came from Amash. The son of the late Abraham Horslei, former governor of Weston.

"That he does, Matey." Krill's smile was a ludicrous sight, filling his wide face and making his one eye appear overly large.

"Wait." Eusari's finally recognized the little girl and her family. "That's the girl Gelert and I dug up." The wolf whined at the mention of his name.

By the time Braen and the family pressed through the crowd, he beamed joyfully. Moving first to Eusari, he wrapped her in a tight embrace.

The woman captain hissed, "Propriety, you idiot! The entire Cove is watching!"

"Sorry!" He whispered, then wrapped up Sippen and Amash in the same embrace. For Creech and Pogue, he offered a dignified handshake that the approving crowd cheered.

After the crowd quieted, Amash stepped forward to speak the words Sippen had written down. The little man mouthed along as Horslei spoke, "People of The Cove! Today is a day for celebration! You are witness to the future of Andalon. You are witness to the birth of power wielded by the people instead of monarchs. Three months ago, you were liberated from a man who enslaved both women and children for his personal profit, gain, and fame. Today, you are witness to a future that promises the will of the majority over the wealthy few!

The crowd stood mesmerized at his words and Sippen stood behind the others, nodding his approval of Amash's prowess as a speaker. With his stutter he never would have dared such a speech in public. He braced himself for the introduction of Braen. This was the part they had rehearsed several times.

"I stand here to introduce the man who liberated you. He was born a prince but gave up that life of privilege to live as you do, self-reliant and not beholden to the wealthy. He spent two years living amongst you as a man instead of a king, serving The Cove. After Lord Nevra seized power from your beloved Artema Horn, he sacrificed even his own ship, his sole possession in the world, to stand against tyranny."

Eusari and Adamas both turned to Sippen with raised eyebrows, but the little man stared straight ahead, still smiling. Even Braen shot the little man a look of caution.

Amash had the people in a frenzy. "I introduce to you the son of Krist and friend of Artema. He is Lord of the Kraken and master over sea and inlet. He is the future of The Cove, Braen Braston!"

The people roared their applause. Braen, red with embarrassment, shot Sippen a look that meant they would talk about this later. The little man smiled and shrugged while his big friend faced the crowd. They hushed immediately, hungry to hear him speak. "Brothers and sisters of The Cove, I salute you. I am honored by the introduction from Amash Horslei, the man who freed loyalists from the palace dungeon and fought on the day of liberation." Having said these words, he turned and again wrapped Amash in a brotherly embrace. The crowd cheered even louder than before.

After the people again quieted, the bearded captain stepped toward the family who had followed him onto the docks. Braen gestured toward the child and spoke briefly in the ear of the father, who nodded agreement. He knelt and said something to the little girl, who offered her hand for him to take. He guided her toward his friends. Gelert stood and nuzzled the child, causing her to laugh loudly and hug him back. The crowd was perfectly silent at the display, shocked at how tender the terrifying animal had responded.

Braen turned back to the crowd and explained, "Many citizens were affected by my decision to assault the walls using forces of nature. Innocents were harmed, and for that I am eternally sorry. But, now that our mourning period is over, we should celebrate their sacrifice. Our future is one with better lives free from oppressive rule."

Many in the crowd applauded, although less than Sippen had hoped. Braen still had a long way to go in earning the trust of the populace. He watched as his friend gestured toward the child. "Today Eusari Thorinson is reunited with one of the hundreds of citizens she personally rescued. Her compassion and instincts are truly for the people, as evidenced by the gratitude of this family touched by her quick thinking on that day."

He paused as the applause washed over them all, watching as the family walked toward Eusari. They also embraced her, thanking her for finding and digging out their beloved child. The captain of *She Wolf* blushed, wiping a tear and smiling back at the mother. The multitude of people, moved by the display, cheered wildly. Braen had forced her to bathe in the praise, knowing full well that she had spent her life in shadows. She would certainly have words with him later.

Sippen stepped forward and whispered into his friend's ear, letting him know that the time had come. This was his day, after all, but he was giving away all the recognition and appreciation. Yurik moved into position next to the dock, signaling his shipwrights. On his signal they removed the tarp. The midday sun reflected off the ship with a radiance that seemingly made it glow. The crowd drew in a collective gasp, as did the dignitaries on the pier. Braston stood with mouth agape at the magnificent sight, noticing at once his Kraken banner flying high atop the mast.

The source of the brilliant reflection turned out to be a complex array of copper sheeting. They lined the entirety of the hull, providing armor for battle and protecting from the elements and ocean pests. The ship appeared sleek and fast, clearly representing the future of The Cove's tenacity. She was outfitted with the most modern of weaponry, all guns rifled for extended range. Sippen's new technology was also easier and faster to load for rapid firing.

While the crew of boatbuilders readied for launch Braen whispered to Sippen. "What is her name?"

"*Malfeasance.*" Sippen responded proudly without the hint of stutter, placing a bottle of 754 in his friend's hand.

Braen turned to the assembled crowd. "I give to you and your generations to come, *Malfeasance!* May she demonstrate to the world the strength of The Cove!" He smashed the bottle against the hull and the crew pulled a series of levers, launching the vessel into the water with a splash. The warship immediately righted itself and the crew quickly tied off its new berth.

The crowd frenzied at the sight of the new flagship. After their cheering had died down and many of the people had dispersed, Braen turned to Sippen and swept him up in a bear hug. "That's the most amazing sight I have ever seen. Is she as fast as *Ice Prince?*"

"Fuh... faster, I hope."

"I can't wait to take her through sea trials and shake her down."

"Shuh... She's yours, Braen."

"No, She's all of ours." Braston turned and saw that the family lingered on the pier.

The woman spoke. "Thank you for letting Charleigh be a part of this. We hope that she'll finally have closure."

Braen nodded and watched at the child, still hugging the wolf, and introducing it to her doll. "Well, at the very least she has new friends who will go to great lengths to protect her."

The shopkeeper agreed. "It seems that's true for all people of The Cove. You still have a lot of opposition, just so you are aware, but I'll help spread the word as much as I can before the elections." All eyes turned instantly toward Adamas Creech. He stood on the pier marveling at the craftsmanship of *Malfeasance.*

The parents finally pulled Charleigh away from Gelert and departed. After they had gone Braen turned to Eusari. "Sorry about that, but you needed recognition to help your position in the polls."

She shot him her signature glare but answered, "I'm getting used to it."

"What is that new ship in the harbor, alongside *She Wolf?*"

She smiled broadly, excited that he had noticed. "That's a gift. I brought *Desperation* to The Cove."

"We have enough of that as it is." They shared a laugh and then he turned serious. "You had trouble, then?"

"Nothing we couldn't handle. But I did capture a hundred men, many of whom may take up our colors after they meet the Kraken King."

Braen nodded. "I'll speak with them one by one in their cells." He turned to his engineer. "Sippen, you'll have to strip the vessel of its name and repaint it. Remove any clue of her origin. Otherwise the Esterling Armada will recognize her and set bounties. Hopefully, they'll think her lost at sea."

Amash interrupted, "Braen. Before you have him do that, Alec and I have a matter to discuss with you."

"Regarding Captain Dominique and Mattie?" The look on Alec Pogue's face told him that it was. Several months before, his wife and daughters had been kidnapped and sold by the former Pirate King, Stefan Nevra. That man sat in a cell, but his conspirator, Dominique, had not returned to the Cove.

"Yes." The captain of the guard spoke, "We've word that he's in Eskera. If I'm to find Mattie and the girls, then I need to question him before he moves on."

"That's a problem. I've heard that the entire harbor is under blockade."

"Nonetheless we want to risk it.

Braen looked toward Amash who nodded his agreement. "I don't know. It's too risky and I can't give you one of the new ships. If you get caught, they'd learn our secrets."

Horslei pointed at the galleon tied off beside *She Wolf.* "You won't have to, Braen. It seems that the gods have provided for us in our time of need and *Desperation.* Let us take her as she is. If Eusari has captured a hundred men, then we also have a hundred uniforms. I think I know how to get through the blockade."

Braen warily watched Captain Creech as he spoke with Sippen's shipwrights. His back was turned and had not heard the plan. He looked thoughtful for a moment then added, "Eusari, you won't like this, but I want them to take Marita along for this mission."

She darkened. "Braen, you know how I feel about using the children."

"I know. But she recently contacted another air emote in Eskera. It seems he was the same boy that contacted Samani from Weston."

Her face softened and Braen let out a breath as she spoke. "Okay, but only if she wants to. She isn't a soldier that you get to order around like your private army. Remember, she's still a child."

"I promise."

"Good. Now I'm going to go wash off the sea and have a decent meal. Meet me later?" Her eyes sparkled when she spoke the last part and Braen's heart leaped at the thought of embracing her in private.

"I'm looking forward to it." He smiled as he watched her saunter off then addressed his friend from Weston.

"Amash, I have one more thing for you to do in Eskera. Prince Esterling is holed up there as well. After you get what you need from Dominique, I would like for you to contact him as an ambassador of The Cove. Let him know that we seek alliance. His brother is behind the slander of my name and I want Robert to know the truth. Tell him about what happened in Estowen's Landing and the part that Artema Horn played."

Both men nodded, said their 'goodbyes,' and made their way from the pier. After they had left Braen turned to Sippen with a warm and brotherly smile. "You're truly remarkable, Sippen Yurik."

"Ah... I'm just a man, Braen."

"A brilliant man with a heart of gold. Thank you for everything you've done throughout the years."

Sippen said nothing in return. He didn't have to. He would always follow the rightful ruler of Fjorik and his best friend, no matter the circumstance. Nothing would sway his allegiance and loyalty from the son of Krist Braston, the Lord Kraken.

# Chapter Ten

Marcus screamed into the face of Lord Chancellor Campton Shol, "I am the rightful ruler of the Esterling Dynasty!"

Matteas Brohn stood in the corner, sipping a glass of wine. "Saying it louder doesn't make it true, Boy."

The king shot his captain of the guard a stare that would chill any other man. "You're only here because you've been loyal. Don't tempt me to find your replacement."

The Captain General took another sip and set down the glass. He crossed the room in three steps and grabbed the boy by the tunic, lifted him from his seat, and then shoved him against the wall. With a snarl he growled into the boy's face, "I'm here because I screwed your mother nine months before you crawled out. If you had any sense, you'd know that the council rules and the king profits." He dug his fingers into Marcus' cheeks and forced him to look at the chancellor. "And that man has the backing of both the council and The Falconers. You'd do best to find your place."

Chancellor Shol watched the exchange with amusement but carried on as if it were a minor interruption. "As I was saying, I sent a dispatch on your behalf to the governors and the Kingdom of Fjorik. We believe that Skander Braston is planning to resume raids after the thaw. We're hoping to convince him that we've forgiven his aggression against Atarax and blamed it on his brother. Hopefully, that will pacify his lust for revenge. We're also planning to negotiate a new treaty that keeps him off our shores."

"I have the biggest navy in the world..."

Brohn had resumed sipping from his glass, but paused to correct the king, "Continent. You have no idea what Astia has."

Marcus shot him a wary glance, anger building toward his father and mentor. "No one else knows about them, so I have the biggest on this side of the ocean."

"Whatever floats your boats, Boy."

Campton continued, "The Astian Council is unconvinced that Andalon is stable. We need peace with The Cove and Fjorik so that The Falconers can resume their work."

Matteas raised a brow. "Then why exaggerate Braston's crimes? Why not recognize him in The Cove and call it a day?"

"Because we need him removed." He pointed at Marcus. "He is going after his brother and, later, you, My Liege. You made a good decision to blame him for the death of your mother, but we can't reach him."

Realization finally crossed the king's face. "You are hoping one of the pirates will cash in on the bounty and take care of him for us?"

Shol agreed. "Exactly. It's our best option."

"What about my own brother? He's a problem and holds Eskera."

Brohn answered. "We have the harbor securely blockaded. Our armada and overwhelming troop strength will march soon from Soston."

"What are we waiting for? Why haven't we attacked?"

"We're waiting for the grass to green up enough for the horses, then we'll march."

Marcus had calmed down considerably, but Shol could see that anxiety still had a grip. "What is it that bothers you, My Liege?"

"Is Robert really like a Falconer? Did he really kill ten?"

"Nonsense." Shol shook his head. "Those are rumors spread by his followers, just as Braston's call him the Kraken King."

"Then how did he defeat our forces? We had bigger numbers."

"Betrayal, sire. Merrimac Lourdes surprised The Falconers and turned his army on ours. We won't let it happen again."

"Matteas, how many have defected to his side?" The concern on the boy's face had grown.

Shol interrupted, "None besides Lourdes. Your troops are loyal." His answer earned a raised eyebrow from Brohn. Since the boy still wasn't convinced, he continued, "sire, rest assured that you rule the Empire. You're a strong leader and the people adore you. But the council behaves like spoiled children and you need to trust their pacification to me." The boy remained silent, biting his lip out of frustration. "Nonetheless, the ball is about the begin and I recommend that you get ready." His eyes followed the boy from the room and then turned to Brohn.

The Captain General asked, "Why did you lie to him?"

"Which time?"

"About his brother for one." The soldier sipped his wine then added, "And second, you and I both know that he's not in charge of shit. He needs to know that troops are defecting and marching to Eskera. Our army has lost a quarter of its force and daily musters continue to fall lighter each day."

"I've planned a special treat for the defectors," he replied. "But those troops will return to our side after we crush Robert in Eskera. We'll make an example out of his death as soon as we've taken the city."

"When it comes time for that, I hope that you do. But your featherheads failed last time, so let's wait and see how it turns out." Matteas tilted back his wine glass and then followed his son.

A stone panel moved and then swung away. An imposing figure wearing robes and a feathered collar stepped out of the passage. Shol glanced up briefly and then back to the door. "He's right. Ten of your finest failed."

"They were not prepared for his power, but we will not be surprised again."

"That's happened several times now." He listed them off with his fingers, "Don't forget about the forest and streets of Diaph."

The specter nodded. “We now know what we are up against. We prepare daily and know the limit of his power. The boy could only split five times.”

“But what about the pirates? What can Braston do? What about the woman in black who defeated you?”

Kestrel removed his hood and revealed his bald head. His skin was stitched together in several places and part of the skull had caved in from impact. He was a hideous sight and Shol shuddered at the number of priests that it took to resurrect him. Two of them nearly died in the process. “We will find her.”

“How many of the others have you retrieved and restored?”

“Many but not all. The boy in Eskera ordered those burned before the priests could reach them.”

Campton felt anger welling up inside. For eight centuries The Falconers had maintained order on the continent. He couldn’t let it fall apart under his leadership. “I think we need to call upon your southern friends.”

Kestral nodded his agreement. “I think that is wise. They have other skills that may prove useful.”

Campton nodded his agreement then added, “The boy wants technology.”

“Will you give it to him?”

“Of course not. The Council would never agree. Giving them cannons to fight Pescari was risky enough. No, they’ve already been helped along too far. If we can’t contain this, then my father may order a cleansing and start anew.”

“That hasn’t happened for nearly nine hundred years.”

“No,” Shol agreed, “not in the north, it hasn’t.” He put a hand on the shoulder of what was left of his childhood friend, searching for the soul that once resided in these blank and emotionless eyes. “I won’t fail, Kestrel. We need to destroy Braston and the other awakened emotants. We shall bring them out of the shadows.”

Kestrel nodded agreement then asked, “What of your brother? Where did he flee?”

"I wish I knew, but when we find him my father's orders are clear."

The Falconer bowed and replaced his hood, leaving the way he had entered. Campton focused his attention on a large wall map of Andalon, trying to figure out his next move. *There are so many, and more awaken each day.* He reached out a finger and touched a piece of land to the south, "Yes, Kestrel, the skills of your friends will be very useful."

# Chapter Eleven

Felicima dropped low beneath the walls of the city, lightly coloring the sky red as she prepared to sleep. Even as she faded the glow on the horizon raged as the Steppes of Cinder burned. The angry caldera in which she rested erupted more frequently, no doubt the result of her nightly tantrums. She grew indignant at the recent injustices toward her children and her nightly rest grew more interrupted. Each morning brought more soot and ash with the westerly winds.

Teot emerged from his hovel and started the long walk to the meeting lodge. He frowned at the many Westonese merchants who had set up shop. The governor had promised the district would remain exclusively Pescari, but these newcomers ran the seediest businesses. Although the brothels and had been kept at bay, several gambling and drinking halls had moved deeper into the sector. He paused outside one such establishment, listening to the sounds of his many kinsmen wasting their hard-earned wages inside.

Coin was sparse for his people and the concept of money new, introduced by the Andalonian benefactors. General labor was easily found in the city of Weston, especially with the rebuilding of the western gate and wall. More recently Teot's kinsmen earned their coin by working the coal mines east of the city. The hard work demanded much of a man's energy, but allowed them to stay largely out of the eye of Felicima while they worked below ground.

His concentration broke when a woman laughed inside a gambling den. Teot frowned. *Women should not be celebrating in public.* He walked to the door and strained to see past the brute barring the door.

"Paying customers only." The doorman held his hand out for Teot's coin. The Westonese man carried himself with the same bearing as the city soldiers, most likely earning extra wages while providing security for the games within.

"I only want to look."

"That costs money too. Pay up or move along."

Teot shrugged and went along his way, but his frustration had grown. He didn't see much past the guard but had glimpsed enough debauchery to fuel disgust. By the time he reached the meeting lodge, the others were seated around the sacred flame and sage smoldered in bowls.

The elders sat in a circle around the pit and Daska poured water atop the rocks that glowed red with heat. Steam rose into the air around the men, all stripped to the waist and sweating beads down their backs and chests. Teot removed his jerkin and took the empty seat next to the old man. All eyes fell upon him.

"The shappan is still missing." Daska spoke the words without emotion, stating a fact but asking the question that all in the lodge were asking.

"He is well," Teot answered.

"Well of body or of mind? There is much distinction between the two."

The missing chieftain's uncle let the words wash over him. Unlike like cooling sweat from the steam the accusations fueled his anger. "He is still shappan, to speak otherwise would offend Felicima."

"Do not condescend by preaching knowledge of Felicima to an elder!" Daska's words erupted with the ferocity of the caldera and Teot fell silent. "You are son of Dromond, one of the greatest shappan the Pescari have ever known. One would think you would have learned humility."

"My apologies, Elder Daska."

The older man nodded acceptance and asked, "Where is Taros?"

"There is a stone mill along the river. He meditates within, awaiting a sign from Felicima."

Another man added to the exchange, "While he awaits her message, he is missing the many signs in the city."

Teot wanted to protect Taros but could not ignore the truth behind the words of the council. "You speak true, Pleot. Tonight, I heard a woman's voice in the gambling tavern."

The man spat on the rocks. The spittle sizzled and quickly evaporated. "The young Pescari are acting like Andalonians, tempted by wealth and quickly losing touch with our ways."

Daska bowed his head in a long pause, considering his words. All eyes fell upon him, waiting with anticipation for the elder to speak. When he finally did, his voice was low and quiet. "The youth are indeed acting sinfully, but the disease of greed has spread to Pescari of all ages. I have heard stories of blasphemy and debauchery from the mining camps, where our young women entertain our men like whores."

The elders gasped and Daska continued, "But that is not the worst of our problems. We are quickly becoming reliant upon Cassus Eachann and the Weston council. He provides the work and coin as well as the means of spending it. He sent soldiers to protect us from acts of hatred by the Westonese, but, in reality, they trap us like cattle. They force us to eat the grass that we trample into dirt and our own filth."

Pleot interrupted, "Our people are lost. Felicima will unleash her fury upon us if she cannot see our shappan."

Daska nodded and threw more water down, making the steam fill the room. The heat of it raged as hot as the men's emotions. "You speak true, Pleot. His people are losing their way. And now the Westonese are asking for our weapons?"

Pleot nodded and held up his hands. "Soldiers have been moving door to door asking for us to give up both bow and blade. They say that we don't need them since there's nothing to hunt in the city."

"That's true," another elder answered, "we buy what we want with Westonese gold. There's no need to hunt any longer, and the wars are over now that our people are united under the shappan."

Daska wrinkled his face at the boy's name. "Start taking our weapons to the mines. Hide them away so that we'll have them if and when we need them."

Daska spoke wisely but Teot did not condone the air of command in his voice. "Are you speaking as shappan now, Elder?"

"Someone needs to as long as your nephew hides."

"Challenge him to Shapalote before you make decisions for him."

Another of the elders, a grey headed and shriveled ancient named Romond broke his silence. All heads turned and even Daska was surprised. "There is an alternative to Shapalote, if we decide to remove the shappan."

Teot shifted his weight uneasily. Taros was his nephew, the son of his late sister, Lynette. Although familial ties should be put aside for the good of the greater Pescari need, brazen talk of removing him was an insult. Out of respect for council and the ways of his people he bit his own tongue and allowed Romond to continue.

"No man or woman among the Pescari can challenge the shappan while he wields the power of our goddess. But if he has abandoned us, then he has conceded his authority under Shapalote and the elder council can choose another to lead. If he returns after we have chosen another, or before but with a damaged mind, then we can lawfully claim the right of Paramalote."

The lodge went entirely silent except for the sizzle of water dancing on hot rocks. Teot felt his heart drop at the mention of assassination but knew that the elders were not plotting. They were merely considering options if Taros did not return. With a trembling voice he addressed them, "I will find my nephew and speak to his heart so that he returns to his duties and his people." Daska and the others nodded their approval. "If he will not, then I will be the one to claim the right of Paramalote. He is of my blood and I will be the one shunned by spilling it on the ground."

Daska raised his hand in acquiescence. "Fine. The right will be yours." He paused to pour water on the rocks and watched the steam rise. "Of course, once we discover who is the new the agent of Felicima you may lose that right to another."

Teot spit on the rocks, then rose from the circle. He retrieved his jerkin before leaving the lodge and walked into the night. The cool air bit into his hot skin and would have taken away his breath except that he was too troubled to feel. Sounds of sinful Pescari echoed down the street, no longer fearing their goddess or hiding their celebration. He paused in front of the same tavern as before, pulling his shirt over his head.

Teot watched as a Pescari woman exited the tavern holding the arm of a Westonese man. They laughed and kissed openly in the night air, publicly displaying their impropriety for all to witness. *Has she no shame, this woman?* Rage burned inside of Teot as he followed them, keeping to the shadows of the city.

The woman led the man around the corner to a tenement that housed several families. He peeked through the window to see which apartment they entered and then followed. Although they were trying to be quiet, they were quite noisy in their drunkenness, making it easy to track them. He paused at the door and waited. Once he was confident that they had gone into a bedroom he tried the door. It opened easily, allowing him to trespass.

The apartment was small, and he stood in a tiny kitchen with a small hearth. *What am I doing? Their sin is not my concern.* But sounds of their passion soon reached his ears. A knife lay forgotten near a chopping block and he absently reached for it, gripping it tighter as the woman moaned louder.

He scanned the tiny apartment. Two rooms were separated from the main area by curtains. Despite this family's eager adoption of Westonese culture, they, like many others, couldn't bring themselves to sleep behind closed doors. He peeked inside the first. A pallet of straw lay in the corner and two small bodies slept peacefully in a single blanket. Teot thanked Felicima that the lovers had not awakened the children. He made a quick prayer that she keeps them asleep no matter what happened next. As he moved toward the second room something caught his eye in the kitchen.

A wooden bin sat near the hearth and several pieces of black coal rested within. His eyes shot to the bedroom where sounds of lovemaking intensified. *How does a single mother afford coal?* He looked down at the floor and saw black marks on the wood. Closer inspection revealed that they were not scuffs. They were stains where a Pescari man's work boots had trodden, leaving behind evidence of the mine in which he worked. Realization fueled his anger and boiled it into rage.

He dashed to the second curtain and pulled it aside. The Westonese man and the Pescari woman lay spent on a small pile of blankets. They panted from exhaustion with eyes closed, wrapped in an embrace. A single flame danced atop a candle on the windowsill, casting shadows as the couple drifted into a drunken sleep. Sinful sweat beaded on their naked skin.

A glint of reflected light caught his eye. On the floor next to the woman, a single golden coin lay where it had been carefully placed. Teot stared at the Westonese god. *To how much sin must these coins contribute?* His hand tightened around the hilt of the knife as he knelt beside the couple.

His hand drove the point deep into the chest of the sleeping woman, piercing her heart. Her eyes shot open in alarm, but his hand clamped down on her mouth, stifling her cry. Her nails dug deep into his forearm and warm blood dripped down to his hand. He brought his face closer to hers and stared at the monster reflected in her glassy orbs. His burned the color of fire.

Ferocious heat boiled inside Teot. He felt at his wounds and recoiled. He had not expected the icy chill of his skin. Suddenly, the candle snuffed and instantly pitched the room into blackness. He pulled the knife from the woman's breast and plunged it again, this time into the eye socket of the sleeping man. The blow killed him instantly.

Unquenched, the heat within Teot grew. He was as angry as before and the sacrifice did little to quell the burning. He stepped back and stretched out his trembling hand. With a satisfying release he directed the cleansing flames of Felicima. The stained and filthy body of the whore blackened beside her customer. He was careful not to mar the second body, leaving him whole. When her husband returned from the mines, he would know that her sinfulness had drawn the agent of the Felicima.

# Chapter Twelve

Barely a breeze blew across the Southern Ocean and the waves crested low and far apart. The sun shone while clouds drifted lazily, high above the water without any threat to sailors. It was a perfect day for sailing, but Amash Horslei hugged the rail of the ship. Every now and then he would empty the contents of his stomach over the side, retching until his insides hurt from effort. It had been this way for two days.

Alec Pogue had laughed at his friend on the first day but felt sorry for the man on the second. "You okay, pal?"

"Probably not." Amash clasped his hand over his mouth and turned over the rail, sending what little water he had consumed in the past few minutes over the side.

"We should be arriving at the blockade before too long. Do you have the stomach for going over the plan again? Or would you rather me handle things?"

Pogue had spent the greater part of a decade locked on land as The Cove's captain of the guard. But, previously, had been a sailor by every meaning of the word. He cut his teeth on hemp lines as a baby, common for a child growing up in Eskera, and was born to a long line of seafarers. He could handle command of the ship on his own but made every effort to include his landlubber friend. Unlike Pogue, Horslei was the son of a horse breeder, born in Weston and more at home in a saddle than on deck.

"You can handle just fine without me, if you don't mind."

Pogue laughed loudly. "Well then, I think we'll just blow through the line and race for the harbor. I grew up here and know the best heading and approach. If we're chased by the Imperial Navy, I think the harbor will accept our struck colors. There's a civil war going on, so defections are common." A serious expression crossed his face. "Of course, we can count on being arrested as soon as they figure out that we're from The Cove. Eskera has no love for pirates."

Amash nodded his agreement then went back to his previous task of lightening his stomach over the side.

Alec slapped him on the back. "No worries, Mate. I'll handle everything while you work on the important task."

Horslei responded with a raised fist with a single finger pointed toward the heavens. He tried to speak, but quickly clasped his hands over his mouth.

As he walked away, Pogue's thoughts returned to Mattie and the girls. *Eliza's nearly seventeen summers.* He fought back a sob at the thought of Nevra's men stealing her away and the raping she must have endured mere days before her sixteenth birthday. *And Alexa. How could she have survived such a fate?* That sweet girl was barely past fourteen and Mattie had done a good job grooming her to be a scholar. She was mentally stronger than she was physical. *Gods, I hope she didn't break.*

Alec blamed himself for their fate. Mattie had begged him many times to give up his position in The Cove and take his family to a small town in Loganshire, where he could work as a constable. The thought had allured him, but he served Artema Horn at the time, and he was a man who always got his way. Of course, now The Cove knew the truth. The former pirate king was a master manipulator whose every move served personal ambitions. *Why hadn't I just listened to Mattie?*

Worse, he blamed himself for not trying to find her sooner. He pulled a piece of neatly folded parchment from his pocket. He carefully opened it and stared at the message, now stained with months of tears as he reread every word. Of course, by now, he knew them by heart. *You are married to your career and I refuse to be second behind that mistress. Don't try to find us. Mattie.* It had been so believable that she had left on her own instead of kidnapped. *I should have tried to find her then.*

When he had learned the truth, he lost his senses and tried to murder Lord Nevra. The man's words echoed in his mind. *Did you see in my ledger where I had sold a thoroughbred? I called her that because she was tough to break in. I had to let Turat help, but he mostly enjoyed your little girls. So did Captain Dominique during his voyage, from what I understand.* Rage again bubbled up, but despair quickly replaced the anger. His only hope was to find Dominique and learn where on the southern continent they had been sold.

"Sail on the horizon!" The call came from the topside watch and sent men running to their stations.

Amash, surging with adrenaline, pulled himself from the rail. He asked the captain, "Fight or flight, Mate? Which will it be?"

Alec quickly folded and stowed the letter then studied the pair of galleons on the horizon. They had not yet turned but would soon. "Break out the uniforms, boys. Let's be ready for either."

*Desperation* tied her sails and allowed the two galleons to come along side. Imperial sailors worked quickly and tossed over lines and laid out planks for the boarding. Several soldiers milled the deck, and everything appeared routine. Captain Moran waited aboard his flagship, *Terra Flora,* for them to finish. Maritime interdiction was tedious work, with most of a crew's time spent waiting for something to do.

He did not expect trouble from this ship of the line. *Desperation* was well-known throughout the Empire and he looked forward to seeing his old friend Captain Cartwright. He tried to remember the last time he had seen Bartholomew. They had been good friends at the academy and served together as midshipmen aboard *Diligence.* It would be nice to catch up while his men conducted their duties.

The sailors finished tying off and Moran crossed the rails with ten of his soldiers. He strode toward Cartwright, eying his crisply ironed and meticulous uniform. *He always wore it smartly,* he thought, smoothing his own as he approached. His friend stood on the forecastle, looking over the bowsprit toward the city of Eskera. Moran called out, "Bartholomew, old chap! How many years has it been?"

The man who turned to greet him was most certainly not Cartwright. Bartholomew was round faced and jolly. This man was chiseled and hard, his body muscled and athletic. His raven hair was neat, whereas Bart's was blonde and unkept. The stranger before him wore a tight beard angled to a point below his chin. Cartwright had always been shaven. Moran froze.

He asked, "Who are you?"

The stranger casually strode forward, reaching an outstretched hand. "Captain Alec Pogue at your service. I'm happy to make your acquaintance. Captain ...?"

"Moran." He eyed the crew with growing suspicions. "Where is Captain Cartwright? This is *Desperation,* is it not?"

"Ah. Bart was relieved of command only a few weeks ago." He leaned in to whisper so that the crew would not overhear. "It seems that he had a slight problem with a scandal."

"A scandal?"

"Oh yes. One involving the wife of Admiral Stapleton, I fear."

"But she..."

"Yes. Contracted a disease quite foul, from what I was told. When Stapleton found out the gossip, he had poor Bart brought in and keel hulled."

"Oh my! How did he take it?"

"Ol' Barty? I hear that his head exploded over the entire affair. He's been a mess ever since."

Captain Moran took in the information and considered. *He was always quite lascivious.* He looked up as two of his soldiers approached.

"It's all in order, Captain. No contraband, only normal rations."

"Well then, Captain Pogue. It seems that all I need to see are your dispatches and we can send you on your way."

"Absolutely. I have them right here." The stalwart captain patted his pockets for the paperwork. "I say. It appears I'm mistaken." He searched his jacket and made a show of feigned forgetfulness, probably hoping Moran wouldn't press. "I did have them. Perhaps I left them in my stateroom?"

"No problem. My men will retrieve them." Moran signaled for two crewmen to return below decks, then movement caught his eye.

Pogue's hand slid down just slightly, but undeniably, to his sword belt. With a flash both men drew and all men on deck did the same. A sailor standing on the forecastle gave an order and a thunderous boom rocked the ship. *Desperation* fired a full broadside into both ships, ripping their gun positions to shreds. Sailors threw off the planks and drew knives, quickly sawing the lines to set the ship free.

Moran called for assistance but the reserve soldiers aboard *Terra Flora* could not lend aid. The blast had knocked every man from their feet and their ears rang from the concussion. *Desperation* fired a second volley and the deck violently shook. While Moran staggered Pogue advanced.

Never had the captain of *Terra Flora* witnessed such mastery at the art of swords. Pogue wielded two with more grace than the greatest instructor at the Academy had swung one. He parried each blow Moran attempted and returned an immediate counter with his off hand. Steel sang aboard *Desperation.*

The sails unfurled overhead, and the ship swayed. He lost his footing. Thankfully, Moran's misstep did not cost him his life. Pogue paused briefly to yell to someone aft, "Marita! Give us wind, dearie! Make it blow!"

Confused, Moran turned to see a young woman raise her hands in the air. The sails abruptly filled with wind and the ship lurched ahead with breakneck speed. Everyone on deck stumbled except for the girl. *By Cinder's grace! She's a Falconer!* Moran raised his eyes just in time to watch Pogue's sword hovering overhead.

"Mercy!" He pleaded. "I surrender!" He laid his weapon at the feet of the pirate and braced himself. The towering man crossed his blades and placed them against his throat.

"Sorry, Mate. We can't afford to take prisoners after what you just saw. Well, perhaps your crewmen, but not an Academy man like you." He felt the swords slice his neck and the world went black.

Alec Pogue severed the neck of the Imperial captain and watched him bleed out on the deck.

"Why'd you kill him, Alec?" Amash looked less green than before, but the bouncing of at these speeds was beginning to work on his stomach.

"He saw what Marita did. We can't let the Imperial Navy know that we have an emotant on board, can we?"

"No. I suppose not."

"Do me a favor and drag him to the rail next time you puke? Just kick him over the side when you have a chance." Alec turned his attention to Marita. She was humming quietly, pleased with the speeds she provided. At times the mast creaked under the strain of the sustained winds. "You okay, dearie?" She shot him a smiling thumbs up from behind her freckles. *Weird kid*, he thought. "Just dial it down a bit. Don't rip off our mast."

"Sorry Captain Pogue!"

"Thank you." The ship slowed just a bit and he relaxed.

Amash had already dispatched the body and pulled Alec aside. "You aren't worried about the effect that will have on her?"

"What do you mean?"

"She just watched you nearly lob a man's head off."

"Amash, we've known each other a long time. Other than that time with Nevra, have you ever known me to act rashly or in a harmful way toward children?"

"Not at all, Alec."

"Then trust me that it was the right decision. Besides, the child emotants that Braen recruited have already experienced violence. One beheading won't stick in her mind. For Cinder's sake, she was in Atarax and witnessed the brutality by Skander Braston."

Alec turned toward the city and watched the harbor growing larger in the distance. A glance aft reassured him that no one followed, and he called again to Marita to slow the wind. In no time at all *Desperation* arrived at the port of Eskera with stricken colors. He was correct in assuming two things: that the harbor guns would not fire upon the vessel and that they would be arrested for piracy immediately upon arrival. They went willingly.

# Chapter Thirteen

Taros stared at the waterwheel as it turned. It had a cracked seam that slapped the water with an audible splash every time it made a full revolution. When it did, light water droplets sprayed his face, but the boy didn't mind. He found the mist refreshing and relaxing, even though he always felt perpetually cold.

He had wintered away from his people and had chosen this spot for several reasons. First, it provided a vantage that overlooked the Steppes of Cinder and the nighttime glow of the Caldera. He worried about the state of his childhood home. The fires had spread at an increasingly alarming rate, nearly devouring the plains in only a few months. The flames were close to breeching the forbidden waste and would eventually reach the Misting River.

Secondly, the millhouse provided seclusion and a profound lack of visitors. Other than an occasional visit from Teot, he wished to speak to no one else. He viewed conversation as a distraction from his quest for answers. He had become a spiritual hermit, questioning his relationship with Felicima. He pondered the truth of her existence and the reason for his powers.

Finally, the mill sat on a small island surrounded by a creek that fed the river. The water seemed to serve as a buffer for his ability to draw in heat, and he never lit a flame in the fireplace. He had isolated himself entirely from flame. After he had nearly killed Sarai, he wanted to stay far away from anyone else he could accidently harm.

He sat like this, staring at the waterwheel and meditating on Felicima, when he heard a polite cough. He turned his head and saw the granddaughter to Elder Daska. She held a basket on her head and seemed anxious for conversation. Despite that she had obviously walked far to find him, he tried to send her away. "I do not wish visitors. You should leave, Flaya."

She set the basket on the ground and bowed respectfully. "My apologies, Shappan." She glanced mournfully back toward the city from whence she had walked. "I've come such a long way, please allow me to rest a while before I make the second journey."

He shrugged and turned back to the waterwheel. Uninvited, she brought the basket and placed it in front of him. Then she settled down directly beside him.

"Can you not rest somewhere else?"

"Since I am here, you may as well eat the food that I brought." She began to draw out carefully wrapped bundles that he recognized immediately as traditional Pescari fare.

Taros grunted his dissatisfaction but caught a whiff of something wonderful when he did. His stomach growled, betraying his hunger. He asked, "Is that smoked rabbit?"

Flaya laughed at the sound of his belly. "It is. I smoked it all morning so that I may bring it to you when the flavor was best." She glanced back toward Weston. "I would hate to waste the timing by carrying it all the way back."

Taros felt his mouth salivating at the thought of perfectly smoked game. "Perhaps I was hasty, and you should share a meal before you leave?"

"Perhaps." She drew out an animal skin and spread it out on the ground, laying out items one by one for the boy chieftain.

Taros watched closely as she drew out a small knife and carved the rabbit. He wondered, *why haven't I paid attention to her before?* But he knew the answer and pushed the thought aside. In all his life he had never considered her or any other Pescari woman attractive. But watching her now, he couldn't remember why not.

One thing that she had in common with the others was her stern face and determined jaw. Pescari women rarely smiled, but when she had laughed, he caught a brief glimpse of vulnerability. In that brief moment he thought of Sarai, the pretty blonde woman in Weston. She had a tender face full of abundant smiles. He had been so smitten with her that he was blinded to anyone else.

Flaya had beautiful brown eyes, now that he took the time to notice them. Her cheeks were tan and arched high across her face. Her lips just the right shade of rose and puckered like one beginning to open. He couldn't help but notice that she had not adopted the Westonese style of dress like many Pescari girls in the city. He felt his manhood respond to the way her body curved gracefully beneath her loosely fitting buckskins.

She blushed shyly when she caught him staring. "Shappan, I am not the rabbit."

He quickly realized what he was doing and apologized, "I am sorry, Flaya. I have not spoken or looked upon anyone in a long while."

Without answering she picked up a slice of game and popped it into his mouth with her fingers. The meat was decadent and melted immediately. It was even better than his mother used to make. He smiled and the girl laughed.

She locked her eyes with his momentarily, but then started to wrap the meat. "I am rested. Perhaps I should begin my walk."

Taros felt panic well up inside and his mind scrambled for something to say. "Wait!" The word came out too forcefully and he saw her recoil a little in shock. "I mean... You don't have to go yet. Please stay."

She smiled deviously and unrolled the meat. It took him a moment, but he finally understood her joke. It felt good to laugh for the first time in months. They sat like that, eating the meal and making small talk for quite a while. Before long Felicima dropped fully from the sky and disappeared into her fiery home.

Taros felt himself relax as they lay, looking up at the stars. With a full belly and Flaya's company he felt free. He realized suddenly that he had not allowed himself to enjoy life since the day his village had burned. As shappan he bore too much responsibility to waste time staring at the heavens.

Tender fingers gently touched his hand. He felt his intertwine with hers as his heart leapt in his chest. This feeling was new. He welcomed her touch and wished they could lay like this forever. Until this night, the only other girl who had ever touched him had been Sarai. But he had misread her gestures. What she had intended as friendship he had mistaken for intimacy.

There was no mistaking that Flaya held his hand with a lover's intent. After a while she rolled onto her side and nuzzled her head into his chest. He held his arm out to the side, afraid to move but yearning to touch her skin. He finally took a chance and cradled her, touching her delicate skin with his fingertips. She responded by nuzzling closer.

Her breath was rhythmic, setting a slow tempo that countered his racing pulse. He turned his head to gaze upon her and saw two dark pools staring back. She smiled and pulled him closer, touching his lips with hers. Their mouths lightly danced, teasing and tasting. After a while she pulled back with gentle tug. They both laughed into the night and embraced again. His second kiss was as magnificent as his first.

Taros had never suspected that two people could share so much through physical contact until she swung her leg over and sat astride his hips. She rocked slowly back and forth, pressing into his manhood. At first, he was shocked by her sudden movement, but the gentle pressure of her body intensified his arousal. They locked eyes. Flaya raised her arms and pulled her buckskin dress over her head, exposing soft breasts that were starkly white against her tanned skin. And then she truly taught him passion.

Flaya rose before Felicima, gathered up her clothing, and slipped out into the dark. She left Taros sleeping soundly, exhausted and spent by their lovemaking. She would visit him the next evening and every night thereafter until she fully held his trust. She enjoyed his touch immensely and looked forward to more.

The walk back to Weston was easy. The Andalonians built roads everywhere they wished to go, making traveling in the dark faster and without obstacles. She made good time and was soon standing before the gates. She stood beneath the looming structure pounded, waiting for them to open.

A soldier answered her knock. "Go away. The city is closed until sunrise."

"I live within the walls and am returning home. Please let me in." Now that she had stopped moving, she felt the cold air on her skin and wished she had worn a fur.

"What district?"

"The Pescari." She shivered against the chill and hoped to Felicima they would let her in.

One of the guards looked out from little door that exposed only his eyes and she could hear him whisper to his counterpart. "She's a Pescari woman and she's alone."

"Probably one of the whores returning from the mining camps. Go ahead and let her in."

The sounds of bolts sliding were music to her ears as the gate slowly crept open. Once inside one of the men blocked her path. "Thank you." She put her head down and tried to move around him.

"Where are you going, dearie?" He leaned in lecherously, tasting her skin with his eyes.

The other man had closed the gate behind her. "Let her go, Dabbon. She's obviously had a late night."

"What's another customer, then? It's been a long night for me, as well. She's pretty enough that I'd pay double. Name your price, dearie."

It took her a while to figure out what the men were saying in their language, but she soon understood. "I am not a whore. I do not charge."

"So, you give it for free then? I like that price even better." He grabbed her and pushed her into the guard shack, catching her before she could set her feet. Her face hit hard against the wall and within seconds he was pressed against her and inside. She struggled to move, trapped like a rabbit in a snare. Her hand reached down to the satchel on her belt. The knife she had used to cut the meat lay within if she could just get her arm beneath his breastplate.

Luckily, he finished quickly. He threw a copper coin on the ground and rebuttoned his trousers. The other guard appeared uncomfortable but said nothing. "That's how you treat a whore," Dabbon said. "Take 'em quick and don't worry if they ..." Flaya's knife cut both his sentence and life short as blood gushed from his neck. The eyes of the second guard grew large and she shoved the blade deep into the left, pressing it as far as the handle would allow. She triumphantly felt the blade sink into his skull.

"You there! Stop!" A shout of alarm came from above as another watchman witnessed the murders.

Flaya ran as fast and far as she could, leaving behind the gate and two dead soldiers. Boots on stone pounded in the distance and whistles broke the silence of the night. She fully became the rabbit then, fleeing the pursuing dogs. She darted into an alley and crouched, panting as torches bobbed by. Her worst fear became reality when two burning lights came her way. She searched in panic for a way out.

They came closer, bring the sounds of angry voices. "She killed them both. Sliced Dabbon's throat from behind like a coward and then rammed her knife deep into Sett's eye! When I find her, I'm going to gut her open and drag her back to the barracks by her hair."

She silently prayed to her goddess for deliverance. They were nearing her hiding spot when she opened her eyes and spied a newcomer. The shadowy figure approached the men from behind with a large Pescari blade in his hand. He was cloaked and the night was dark so she could not see his face, but she knew that he was the agent of Felicima.

His drove his sword through the first man and parried a blow from the second. The soldier whirled so quickly that she thought her savior would surely fall to his blade. Only the blessings of the sleeping goddess saved the mysterious stranger. At the last second, he stepped to the side and blocked the blow.

She watched as he reached out with his free hand and grabbed the man by the throat. They stood like that eye to eye, with the soldier staring up at the newcomer. But Flaya could tell that he was not choking the man. He was doing something far worse. The man began to sweat as his body heated from within. Smoke billowed out of his ears and his mouth and nose until flames erupted from his skull. The hooded stranger released his grip and dropped the guardsmen in the dirt, smoldering and steaming within his armor.

Realization leapt in her heart. "Taros?"

The man shook his head in response. *No, not Taros.*

Teot threw back his hood. With his finger to his mouth he urged quiet, motioning for her to follow. She ran to him, taking his hand, He led her from the alley and back to the Pescari district. He stayed with her until they reached Daska's home. Finally feeling safe she asked of him, "You are the agent of Felicima?" He nodded. "I prayed and you answered. Thank you, Teot."

He leaned close and whispered back, "Tell no one what you have seen." And then he was off into the night.

Flaya slipped quietly into her grandfather's lodge. She was careful not to disturb him, but found the aged man sitting on the floor awaiting her arrival. "You're home late. I assume that it went as we had hoped."

"Yes, Grandfather. May we speak later? I am exhausted and want to rest."

"No. We will talk, now. Were you successful? Did the boy lay with you?"

"Yes."

"Good." He reached out a cup of white liquid. "Drink this so that the child will take in your womb."

"No, Grandfather. Not this time, I..."

"Drink it!" The man shouted so loudly that she cowered. "If we are to gain control of the shappan then you must ensure that you bear his child."

"But tonight I..."

He firmly placed the cup in her hand and brought it up to her mouth, forcing it between her lips. "I said to drink."

Most of the contents found its way down her throat, but some drooled out from the corners of her mouth as he poured, ignoring her wide and terrified eyes. *Felicima save me. Save us all if it is the wrong one,* she prayed.

# Chapter Fourteen

"Well, I want to meet the girl!" Sarai Horslei interrupted, tired of listening to the men dominate the conversation.

Robert nodded. "You will, I promise." His advisors had gathered in his war room and discussed the arrival of the stolen galleon. To Major General Lourdes he asked, "You're telling me that they just sailed the ship into the harbor with a white flag? Then a little girl disembarked with a message for me?"

"Yes, Your Highness. She is named Marita." The name sent shock down the boy's spine. He remembered the smiling freckles from his dream.

"She sailed here from Pirate's Cove?"

"Yes."

"And she has freckles?"

"Again, yes, Your Highness."

Sarai watched her love with concern in her eyes. "What is it, Robert?"

"It seems that part of my vision was real and Braen Braston has sent an envoy to parlay." He laughed dismissively. "He probably wants to give terms for my surrender. Does he realize that he's meeting with the wrong brother?"

Maximus Reeves interjected, "Robert, at least meet with his diplomat. Hear what he has to say. We've been cut off from the rest of the world and it would be nice to get some news for once."

"You want me to meet with a dead man?" Robert chuckled and shook his head. To General Lourdes he ordered, "Read that part, again, for Sarai."

"It is my esteemed honor to introduce my friend and ambassador, Amash Horslei. Originally of the city of Weston and..."

Sarai furrowed her scarred brow in disgust. "Is that a joke for me?"

"I doubt it." Max shook his head. "There's no way he would know you're here."

"Unless he heard the rumor out of Weston that I was kidnapped by Robert."

"Details like that move slow, Sarai. I think we should meet with the girl first. Then, if you're both satisfied, we can drag this 'ambassador' out in chains and let you decide." Max held up one finger and addressed his king. "But I urge you to remain open minded, sire. We need more allies and access to a navy would help end the blockade."

"At least they were kind enough to donate a galleon to our meager armada." Robert tried to act casual, but inside his anxiety grew. The girl from his vision terrified him. *How can I be afraid of a little girl?*

A few minutes later Max opened the door and led the auburn-haired girl into the war room. She was tiny, freckle faced and about thirteen summers. She smiled with an innocence that the rest of the people in the room had lost. When her eyes settled on Robert, they rounded with disbelief. After a moment her strange smile widened.

"It's you! The boy who flies in dreams!"

Robert blushed, he never thought of his nighttime adventures in such a fashion. "You know me?"

"Of course, I do! Sebastian and I talked to you! I didn't know you were the prince!"

The look of shock on her face was genuine and confused Robert. "You really didn't know that you'd be meeting with me?"

"No! This is wonderful!" She beamed brightly and walked closer. The guards reacted but Robert waved them off and let her through. She approached and touched his face. "It is you! Samani will be so happy! He told us to find you and I did! Twice!"

"Marita," Sarai asked softly, "you've seen King Robert before? You've met him?"

"Yes! Sebastian and I dream-walked for months and found him, just like Samani told us!"

"Who is Samani, Marita?" Robert could sense that something was off with the child, but she was certainly the girl he had met in his dream.

"You know him. You met in Diaph." She was a pitiful sight, standing before Robert and the others and rambling. She acted so young and so obviously touched in the head.

"What did I see of him, Marita?"

"He said that he was wrapped up in air and you visited him. You asked him to save a woman before someone burned her." Her eyes fell on Sarai as if seeing her for the first time and grew wide-eyed. "You're her, aren't you?" Her smile fell and a mournful look took its place. "You're much more beautiful now."

Sarai shot a look of surprise at Robert, but he looked away. "Marita, if you weren't here to see King Esterling, then why did you come?"

"Alec is looking for his wife and Amash is helping him. Since they were coming here, Braen asked them to deliver a message."

"Amash? What is he like, Marita?"

"Yes. He's big and really smart. I like him, but he doesn't sail very well. He threw up the entire voyage. He made me laugh."

Sarai turned to Robert, "I need to see him to know for sure, but it could be him."

Maximus Reeves nodded and whispered to a guard. The soldier departed and returned a few minutes later with a tall man with broad shoulders and hair as blonde as Sarai's. Chains bound his feet and hands, so he shuffled into the room. Despite the shackles, he bore his head with dignity and held it high with confidence. When his blue eyes settled on the exiled prince, he addressed him with a Westonese accent. "Greetings, Your Highness. I bring tidings and a message of solidarity from The Cove."

Next to Robert, Sarai gasped. Her nails sunk into his arm and he watched his love expectantly. Tears formed in her blue eyes and she nodded her head violently up and down. He looked back at the man who bore a striking resemblance to her father, Abraham Horslei.

Amash could barely move in the shackles as the guard led him into the room. Two generals and several soldiers stood between him and the prince, each eyeing him with distrust. He could tell that they were ready to pounce if he tried something aggressive toward their ruler. *They are loyal to the boy; that's good. It's a sign that he has some leadership in him.* He had rehearsed his greeting and spoke it directly, hoping to get straight to business. Time was of the essence.

After he had spoken, the girl beside the prince reacted in a way that caught his attention. *Did I say something wrong?* He narrowed his eyes and looked closer. She would have been a beautiful young woman had she not endured some sort of accident. Most of her face was hideously scarred and a good portion of her hair had been permanently burned off. Her eyes glowed like fierce sapphires through her scars.

All at once he knew her. Although it had been several years and she had grown into a woman, he recognized his sister. "Sarai? Is it you?" The voice of the dignitary gone; the words uttered on a soft whisper. *What happened to her?* Despite the scars, she was the most beautiful sight he had seen in years. She leaped from her chair and ran toward him, wrapping her arms around his waist and crying into his chest. He wished he could put his around her, but they were locked in irons. "I don't understand. How are you here?"

She pulled back and wiped her face on her sleeve, smiling up at her brother. "It's a long story and I think we have much more to talk about first."

The self-proclaimed king cleared his throat and addressed one of the soldiers. "I think we can dispense with the chains. I'm not in any danger and Lord Horslei should be treated with respect." To Amash he added, "I apologize for your treatment, it's just that we believed you dead."

"I understand completely, Your Highness. I would have taken the same precautions." After his hands were free, he embraced his sister and felt his own eyes misting.

After they were all seated, one of the generals asked, "How well do you know this Braen Braston?"

"Very well. I've been his friend for nearly two years in The Cove."

"Why did he kill my mother?" A glint of anger in the prince's eyes betrayed his intent.

"He didn't. That was done by Matteas Brohn at your brother's request." He recounted the story of the failed exchange exactly as Braen had told it to him.

The other of the two generals nodded his head. "That sounds like Brohn. He must have seen an opportunity to place Marcus in power. He always had ambition in him. And that part about Artema Horn's role makes sense. That crafty son of a bitch would do anything for a pile of coins. I never did trust him."

The prince turned to his general. "Max, this changes things."

"Indeed. We have options that we didn't before." The general addressed the other, "What do you think, Lourdes?"

"How big is Braston's fleet?"

"That's a slight problem. Most of the ships in The Cove were destroyed when he took it over. But he's rebuilding quickly and has some technological advantages that you'll need to know about. He has unbelievable fire power."

"Then my recommendation is that we work together on this. But getting a message back through the blockade will be difficult if not impossible. He's not much help if we can't tell him what we need."

Marita giggled and everyone turned to the little girl. Amash nodded and she smiled back with her odd thumbs up.

"Did I miss a joke, or something?" The general frowned at the exchange.

"No General. It's just that she has a unique way to message The Cove."

Robert's eyes grew wide with realization. "You have a network? How many more Dreamers do you have?"

It was Amash's turn to be confused. "How did you know about the Dreamers?"

Marita answered, "Because he's the boy from Weston."

"You? You have emotancy?" Horslei felt his head swim. "You have control over air?"

Robert shyly looked toward the others as if afraid to answer. Finally, Sarai spoke up, "Amash, he killed ten Falconers in the battle of Eskera."

Horslei considered his sister's words. "That's twice more than we have. But I really suggest that you speak with Braen."

# Chapter Fifteen

Anxiety gripped Fatwana as the train slowed. Her pulse pounded in her ears while her chest fluttered. She adjusted her seat, propping upright to counteract the jittery sensation coursing her veins. She was desperate to flee and escape the next hour, suddenly regretting her decisions.

Subba napped soundly across from her, but she impatiently lifted the shade and allowed light to flood the compartment. The capital city of Bergin sprawled outside the window, ten times larger than Oslot and with hundreds of thousands more people crammed into its wards. The thought of stepping off the train sent a shudder through her spine, but she had committed down this path. Her brother's message had forced her to act.

Subba stirred. "Have we arrived?"

"Yes. But it is late and the ride to the Council Building will take another hour. We'll most likely be put up for the night in lodging and meet with them in the morning."

The sound of the brakes announced that they would disembark soon. Subba stood and stretched before pulling their bags from stowage. "This is my first time in the Capital, lead sister. Will there be time for sight-seeing?"

"I doubt it, but I may be wrong. It all depends on how the meeting goes. If the council puts us on standby, then we may be here several days." Fatwana opened the door and Subba carried the bags. The shuffling line of people was crammed into the narrow corridor and Fatwana felt another attack of panic. She stretched to see what was holding up their departure.

A uniformed policeman stood in the doorway, scanning faces as they disembarked and comparing them to a photograph in his hand. One by one he checked the passengers, dutifully searching for a particular face. Her stomach lurched as she thought of the girl. *If they catch her will she implicate me? Do they know what I've done?* She began to tremble and no longer had to lie to Subba about feeling ill. She suddenly worried that she may vomit before leaving the train.

When they approached the officer, she stared down at his belt. She had seen guns before, but the sight of them always made her nervous. Her mind raced. *What would he do to me if I run?* She swallowed and stood tall, trying to walk with the same confidence she portrayed in the Oracle.

He barely glanced at her face and looking past her into the crowd. He focused again on the photograph and waved her on. "Keep moving," he said.

As she stepped off the train, Fatwana was relieved and thankful for the cooling breeze. She moved away from the crowd and waited for Subba. He hurried over with their load, overburdened and nearly dropping bags. "I wonder who they're searching for." He was slightly out of breath as he scanned the depot for their car. He pointed, "There it is."

"Subba, I don't feel well. I think that traveling has unnerved me, and I need to use the restroom."

He nodded. "I understand, lead sister. I'll load the bags and meet you at the car."

The facilities were exactly how the girl had described, with doors both in front and back. She stepped in, pausing at a sink to check her reflection in the mirror. Her face was ashen, with bags under her eyes from lack of sleep. She took a moment to wash her face before exiting through the rear, it did nothing to calm her nerves.

She halfway expected the girl not to show. With heavy police presence she would surely be recognized as an activist. But Fatwana found her waiting as promised, resting on a bench with an open book. She casually stood as Fatwana approached.

The stranger whispered, “Took you long enough. We need to go.”

“I don’t think you understand. I’m not going with you. I was only going to give you this.” She pulled a small storage disk from her sleeve and thrust it toward the girl’s hand.

“Put that away! Do you want to be seen on camera?”

“I’m sorry, I don’t know how to do this.”

“Just keep walking and pretend we aren’t together.”

“But I have a car waiting and need to get back.” A tremendous blast roared from behind. Fatwana whirled around just as the train exploded a second time. She gasped when the barrel of a gun jabbed her ribs.

“Start moving and do exactly as I say. Now, go!”

Chancellor Jakata rested in his chambers. Soft orchestral music played quietly, and the lights were low. He relaxed in an overstuffed recliner enjoying the ambiance and letting the music calm his mood. The day had been very demanding, and the Council had called an emergency session. To top it off, violence erupted in the capital.

He swirled the wine in the glass and watched the trails run down the edge. After a moment he put his nose inside the goblet and breathed in the bouquet. It was pleasing, rich and oaky with a hint of flowers. He let out a sigh and took a sip. With closed eyes he chewed the wine, forcing the flavor across his taste buds. This was not his favorite but proved a decent vintage. His beloved 754 was becoming more difficult to obtain.

His assistant sat in another chair, waiting patiently. In his lap was an open folder, full of matters that required the chancellor’s attention. “Sir, if we could discuss the train bombing.”

Jakata opened his eyes and glared. “Gaurin, I’d rather that we don’t at the moment.”

The man persisted, drawing out a photograph. He glanced briefly, then held it out with earnest. “Fatwana Nakala is missing and was seen walking away from the explosion.”

"Coincidence."

"I think not." He pointed at a girl in the photo. "We've been watching the girl next to her for few weeks. She's a low-level member of the Society."

Jakata sat up and frowned at the picture. "Was Fatwana abducted?"

"Possibly. Or she's decided to follow in her brother's footsteps."

"Why would you think that?"

"There is a discrepancy in her recent reports and transcriptions. One of the Da'ash'mael events was omitted from her records. The priests reported three for the day, but she only provided transcriptions for two."

Jakata downed his wine, speeding its work against his irritation. "We've never had reason to doubt her loyalty before. Maybe she simply forgot. Or she sent it and the connection was bad. You know how difficult it is to connect with the Oracle that far north."

Gaurin nodded agreement. "Nonetheless, she's missing."

"How many people died in the attack?"

"The preliminary estimate is twenty-two. They were small bombs placed in a specific car."

"Specific car? How specific?"

"The priests from the northern oracle were transporting six new Falconers, each on route to Andalon. Thankfully they had already exited the car and only four of them were killed. They are working on bringing them back as we speak."

Jakata shook his head in disbelief. "How did the Society know they'd be in that specific car?"

"We're looking into that."

"Make it a priority. Also, raid Fatwana's cell and make a full sweep of her computer. I doubt she'd defect, but there could be something we're missing."

# Chapter Sixteen

The vastness of Lake Norton dwarfed Kali as she stared across the waves, unable to find land in any direction. Growing up in the streets of Logan, she had never paid attention to the body of water, regarding it only as a border between her world and the money that filled wealthy purses. She had never imagined that she would purchase passage across, much less marvel at, the expansive waterway. But in all of her dreams, the lake was never this large.

Overhead the weather had cooperated for several days and the waves remained gentle beneath her feet. During the trip she had listened to many a sailor's story about fierce storms and overturned vessels, but mostly they liked to joke about the weak stomached landlubbers who dared to sail during high winds. She considered herself lucky that she had made it this far without showing the crew her breakfast.

One of those crewmen was only a few years older than she and had quickly befriended her during the voyage. Johan approached with excitement filling his face. "Cap'n says that we're almost across and should be nearing Eston soon."

Kali shrugged casually, trying to mask her own excitement. "Why is that a big deal?"

"You've never seen the Span, have you?" The boy's eyes sparkled with enthusiasm as he spoke. Without waiting for her response, he continued, "It's two huge bridges that cross the Logan River! At the very top they're connected by another bridge with the biggest market you'll ever see! It's right smack dab in the middle. The biggest in the world!"

"I've seen big markets. Logan has an entire market sector." His resulting laughter embarrassed the girl and she felt her temper rise. She turned her attention back to the horizon of water.

"I'm sorry," he said after realizing he had insulted her naivety.

"I've never been out of Logan," she admitted.

"Then you really need to see Eston. It will take us an entire day to cross it by river."

"You're lying."

"Seriously," he insisted, "It's the largest city in Andalon." He thought for a moment then added, "Largest in the world, even!"

Kali shrugged to hide her curiosity. *Surely, he's lying.* A question suddenly entered her mind, "Where are you from?"

By his reaction she surmised that no one had ever asked him that question. After a time, he responded. "Middleton. It's on the east coast of Andalon."

"What's it like?"

"It's big. Not as big as Eston, but bigger than Logan."

"How much bigger?"

He scrunched up his face as the calculated. "At least five or six times. Maybe seven."

She nodded. No wonder he had laughed at her response. "Does it have a Span like Eston?"

"No. The bay is too large. It's several hundred miles long from the entrance, and its hundreds of fingers weave between jutting peninsulas with gun batteries. No armada would dare attack it by sea; there's no reason for a Span."

"Why'd you leave?"

Johan's eyes dropped to the deck, suddenly glistening with homesickness. The moisture reflected the afternoon sun. "My paw died a year ago, so I had to find work."

"Where's your maw?"

The boy replied, "I never had one."

"Oh." She looked away casually pretending that she hadn't noticed his tears. "I never had a paw, so I get that."

"Why are you going to Diaph?"

"My business." She spoke the words with a sharp finality, suddenly wanting to end the conversation.

"I am hoping to get to Estowen's Landing, myself."

Her attention snapped to the boy. "Why did you say that?"

With trembling hand, he pulled out a folded parchment and smoothed it flat. "I was told that would be where I can find others like me."

"Like you, how?"

Johan shrugged dismissively and didn't answer.

Her gaze narrowed as she stared, looking for a sign that he knew her true destination. *How can he know where I'm going?*

After a while he softly answered. "I have a special thing that I can do."

Her heart raced with excitement, but she asked with feigned indifference in her voice, "How special?" *There's no way that he's like me,* she thought, silently hoping they were the same.

"Watch." He reached his hand into the water and waited. Soon an entire school of trout swam to the surface and the largest, easily twenty pounds, rested against his hand. Johan slowly pet the fish as it kept careful pace with the boat.

"How do you do that?"

"I don't know. It only started about a month ago."

An idea crept into her mind as she thought about the stray animals in the alleys of Logan. "What if I help you get to Estowen's Landing?"

A smile curled on the boy's face, showing his eagerness for a companion. "Deal." He reached out his hand she gave it a firm shake.

Kali strained her eyes against the horizon and focused on the massive structure in the distance. She pointed. No longer able to hide her excitement her voice cracked as she asked, "Is that the Span?"

Johan shook his head with a knowing smile. "No, Kali. That's only the first bridge. It'll be several more hours before we reach the center."

Her eyes darted, marveling at the banks downriver and beyond the bridge. She curiously wondered why the stone walls reached so deep into the city, "Where's the harbor?"

"Underneath the Span." He responded, "It's the safest place in the city."

She shivered as their tiny vessel approached the looming gun mounts, impenetrable from invasion either by land or sea. A long wharf sat on the starboard riverbank where soldiers inspected cargo. Johan and the crew worked the rigs and slackened sails as the coxswain guided the rudder. As they changed course, Kali stared up at the massive stone archway blocking out the sun. *It's like a cave,* she marveled. Tiny droplets of water dripped from the ceiling, forming tiny stalactites, and raining down on the awestruck girl.

Johan followed her gaze upward. "Wicking water created that. Isn't it beautiful?"

She responded, "But not as beautiful as the vines." Hundreds of thousands of feet of green ivy trailed the stone maze of grout and granite, creating a carpet among the dripping columns.

"Wait until you see the palace. The city is full of rose trellises. That's why they call it the 'Rose Palace' and why the Esterlings favor that flower on their crest." After he had spoken, he hopped onto the deck to tie off lines.

Kali finally turned her attention away from the cavernous underside of the bridge. She turned to ask Johan another question but froze, silent with eyes wide and mouth agape. Five feathered specters in flowing robes trailed down the winding staircase and passed through the gatehouse above. Each bore their raptor on their arm and stared directly at Kali. *Surely these are not the same Falconers from Logan,* she thought. *How could they have beaten me here?*

Johan frowned. "What's wrong, Kali?" She lifted her hand and pointed over his shoulder, causing him to turn. "Oh, them? Sometimes they come down and watch the guards search the boats. It's okay."

She stammered, "What are they looking for?"

"I don't know. I've never seen them do anything but watch the boats."

One of the hooded men paused to converse quietly with a soldier. When the guardsman pointed toward the boat, Kali pleaded, "Johan, we need to leave."

"We can't. They won't let us pass under the city if we don't submit."

"But you don't understand, I..." A screech cut off her words as the falcons fanned wings and rose into the air.

The great birds flew directly at Johan, causing him to crouch and cover his face. They clawed and tore at his flesh as he cried out, screaming for mercy. When none came, his cries turned to rage. Suddenly, the river beneath the wharf exploded, ripping boards to splinters and knocking the Falconers off balance. One fell into the river and was instantly surrounded by the water, now alive and clutching the man with flowing fingers. Despite how hard he tried to swim, he was pulled below the surface by an impossible current.

The boy grabbed the neck of one of the birds and wrung with all his might. Kali blanched as his face contorted with anger, and she found herself unable to turn away. He squeezed and did not let go until the bird fell, lifeless, onto the pier. He then faced the four men scrambling to their feet. Another wave of water tossed the boat into the air and Kali lost her footing. She fell hard to the deck just as the cresting surge washed the Falconers against the boards. The remaining birds dove and ripped flesh from the boy's face.

One of the Falconers regained his footing and wisps of air coalesced around Johan's hands and feet. He yanked hard and the boy fell hard against the pier. Suddenly, a gust of wind sent him sliding hard against the archway.

Kali looked on with anger replacing her earlier fear. "No!" She cried out, drawing the Falconers' attention.

A single strand of air caught her by the neck. Breathless, she felt a tug and slammed against the wall alongside her friend. As her head hit stone the grip released, and Kali gasped for life. *We're both going to die,* she thought. The girl lay like that, hopelessly staring at the stalactite ceiling above. She wished that she had never discovered her powers or the truth about the Falconers.

But then an idea brought hope. "Johan," she whispered, "wick the water back from the stone." The boy's eyes were wide with fear, and she could tell that he could barely breathe. But something in his gaze flickered and she knew he understood. "Now, Johan!"

The dark grey of the archway slowly lightened as if the sun had baked it on a hot afternoon. Shards of grouting turned to powder, above, falling harmlessly into the river. One by one the tiny stalactites stopped dripping, but the four monsters never noticed. They busied themselves with the task of forming a sled of air upon which to carry their captives.

Kali's vision swam from the impact, but her hands were free. She managed to touch a single vine, grasping it in her palm. Her other hand felt for Johan until she eventually contacted the bare skin of his ankle. She would have to hurry. His lips were turning blue.

The water within the boy surged against the power she held within. The sensation burned as she concentrated on the vine. As a child, she would watch the plants in the summer, thirsty and parched from want of rain. When it finally fell, those shriveled husks would drink enough to fill both stalk and leaf until they again danced in the wind. Just as roots passed water to their stems, Kali drew the water the boy had collected and fed the climbing ivy. The sudden growth filled the cracks and crevices above. They had come alive, and Kali convinced them to wriggle deeper into the stone.

Beside her Johan groaned. One of the Falconers had knelt down and pulled out two green caterpillars. She watched with horror as these crawled into her friend's ears. Abruptly the flow of water stopped, and the boy's screams echoed under the massive structure of stone. Without the flow of water, she could no longer make the vines grow.

The nearby birds screeched again, and four sets of Falconer eyes snapped toward Kali. Wisps of air coalesced around her hands, pulling them away from the vines and trapping her tightly in place.

She stared back defiantly as one of them spoke. "We did not expect to find two emotants traveling together. Where were you traveling, girl?" The air around her skin burned worse than the water she had drawn from Johan. The specter repeated the question, but she gritted her teeth against the pain and refused to answer.

The hooded man drew out two more of the caterpillars. He confidently strode toward Kali and asked, "How did you find each other?" When she ignored the question, he held out the larvae. "Answer me, child."

The bonds constricted the more she resisted, and Kali gasped. Air twisted around her chest and neck. Her breathing slowed. *I don't want to die here,* she thought, *not without finding others like me.*

Despite the strength of the wisps she wriggled her fingers and felt at her bonds. At first, she felt nothing, just missed again and again as she clawed. *Relax,* she cautioned herself, *focus on where they should be.* More calmly she tried again, this time feeling a buzzing sensation. All at once the feeling grew, intensifying as invisible heat burned her fingertips.

She closed her eyes and pressed her back against the thick vines climbing the pillar. The slightest tickle of a leaf found her neck and she grinned up at the menace looming before her. In a whisper she answered, "Kiss my freckled ass, you feathered freak."

The connection between air and leaf complete, Kali transferred it from her bonds into the ivy around her. The leaves seemed to know which part they wanted, soaking in the nutrients as the discarded portion dissipated like vapor into the air. She focused on the vines directly above the Falconers, forcing them deeper into the crevices and rapidly expanding them in girth. With her mind, she squeezed them behind each stone.

The hooded monsters turned their eyes upward as debris shook free and rained down. They laughed in unison, making an eerie display. Sounding more like a demon than a man, the lead Falconer spoke. "Valiant try, child, but your ignorance keeps you in our charge. The vines are gripping the stone tighter than before and will only make the structure stronger from the pressure."

"Maybe," she answered, "until I do this." She knew each strand intimately, having traced them from root to frond. She found the branch that she needed and reversed the process, robbing it of the sugary sweet substance that acted as blood for the plant. Without lifeforce it shriveled and dried, shrinking like one discarded along the forest floor. The ceiling didn't even shake as the stones fell, crashing down upon her foes.

Abruptly, her bonds released their grip and Kali quickly dragged Johan away. Falling stones crushed the pier behind them just as they reached freedom. Water splashed high into the air and the nearby soldiers dove into the river to avoid the flying splinters and debris. Her friend scrambled to his feet and raced alongside her up the riverbank. Neither stopped until both felt confident of their freedom.

Kali wheeled around in anger, her face red and seeking revenge. The pressure in her head throbbed as she controlled the remaining vines, but she held on a little longer. She felt like a dam was breaking on the inside.

"What are you doing, Kali? We need to get away!"

"Not yet. Not until the soldiers are far enough down river to get away."

"Away from what? What are you talking about?"

"Away from this." Kali released the vines which abruptly released the stored air and water. In an instant they resembled shriveled plants of summer desperate for an evening storm. The ramparts and batteries atop the bridge were too heavy for the weakened foundation. Both teens watched with awe as the structure rained down on the river Logan, crushing boats and burying the Falconers.

"Look at the river, Kali." Johan pointed at the bank along which they had run. "You rerouted the flow and it's flooding the fields."

Exhausted, she watched as the water slowly filled the low areas, creating a wide marsh. "Is that bad?"

"Only for the Imperial Navy," he responded. "No ship will be able to sail in water that shallow!"

"I don't care," she replied, eying the encroaching river as it pushed their path further south and into the Diaph Forest. "As long as those birdmen don't follow us to Estowen's Landing."

Marcus Esterling was perpetually bored. Usually his parties brought him some reprieve, but the extravagance and expense of this ball did little to bring him joy. Beautiful women in expensive gowns twirled while men brayed and boasted about wealth and hunts. In the corner of the ball room puppeteers entertained those too drunk to dance, but not so much that they would collapse. He turned his head from the display with disgust and felt ill. *I'm a mere puppet,* he thought, *no different from them except for my lack of strings.*

Matteas Brohn stood over the wine cart, sorting through the bottles and frowning until he found one worthy of his palate. Marcus once looked up to the man who was really his father, but now found the sight of him disgusting. A patsy to a master race of people a continent away, Brohn groveled at their feet like a dog given a bone. A dog who kept the rightful king on a leash. *What does that make me then? Am I the bone on which the dog gnaws?*

The orchestra played a tune that the crowd found delightful, with a fast tempo and high acoustics that danced above their heads. A low cello bellowed out notes that pumped their hearts with excitement. Everyone was joyous except Marcus. He choked on the melody, and the rhythm nauseated his gut, pushing up bile that tickled the back of his throat. Suddenly in need of air, he rose from his throne. Attendants scrambled to fawn over their king, but he waved them off.

He pushed through the crowd toward a side door. There he found a room that was empty except for a bookshelf, an overstuffed chair, and a window. The chair faced a roaring fire and the window overlooked the harbor. Seeking the breeze he chose the window. Marcus stared out at the numerous warships loaded with stores and munitions bound for The Cove. Their mission was to bring death to Braen Braston, or so he was told. *I didn't order their preparations,* he mused, *I don't order shit in my own kingdom.*

The massive harbor was a beautiful sight from this vantage. Protected by the high walls of the city, his enemies would never reach the bulk of his fleet. The river flowed slowly eastward, toward Diaph and eventually out to sea where attack was impossible from down river. The steep walls killed the wind for all vessels but those carrying Falconers. On both banks an intricate ferry system dragged the rest upstream since oars were hindered by the narrow channel.

Nearby bells tolled in earnest, suddenly alerting him to the west. A column of grey smoke rose into the air. *It can't be a fire,* he thought, *it isn't dark enough.* Judging the distance, he estimated that trouble loomed on the western battery. *Odd, there's no threat from that direction.* The door opened and Matteas Brohn entered the room. Without taking his eyes from the harbor Marcus asked, "What is it? An attack?"

"We're not sure. But you need to move to a secure location."

"Why not move Lord Shol? He's the real leader."

"True, but we need everyone in the ballroom to believe that you're worth more than you are."

*There it is,* he thought with a grin, *actual honesty from Daddy.* Pressing for more, he asked, "Would you rather play this role?"

"Hell no, Boy. I'm in a good position where I stand."

"As long as I'm alive, you mean."

"Pretty much. Now hurry your ass and let's go."

But the boy king held his ground, staring out the window. "Does that seem strange to you?"

"What? The smoke?" The general shifted his weight impatiently.

"No. Look at the pier. The ships are leaning."

"Every ship lists."

"No. That's not what I mean." He strained his eyes. The water level seemed to be dropping rapidly. Both men stood in silence, staring with amazement as the ships sunk one by one into the mud. In mere minutes the mightiest fleet in Andalon was grounded, their heavy bellies pressing deep into the muck.

Matteas gave the boy a strong shove then ordered, "Go!"

# Chapter Seventeen

Braen Braston made his way slowly down the steps to the prison cells. The air below the surface smelled musty and itched the back of his throat as he breathed, but he didn't mind. Something about the cold stone and soft humidity reminded him of his home in Fjorik. He had spent much of his boyhood playing in the cellars of the palace, and he smiled at the thought of the many hours spent counting and examining the dusty bottles in his father's wine collection.

Unfortunately, this visit below surface would create memories of a darker and less enjoyable experience. Stefan Nevra had wintered in confinement, and the new council was no closer to deciding his fate. Although Braen led the temporary league in drafting a constitution and funding city operations from the treasury, a trial of this magnitude must wait for the officially elected triumvirate to decide the man's fate. Thankfully, elections were scheduled for later that very day.

So far only five candidates ran for leadership spots. Braen, Eusari and Amash were among the favorites, and Samani all but assured them that they would win. Adamas Creech vied for a spot, but the ruthless captain often proved unpredictable and was known to employ cunning tactics. The fifth entry was a wild card that no one had expected.

Everyone had been surprised to learn that Nevra still held a small contingency of backers. Some of the merchants felt that he had been wrongly removed from his throne. As a result, he received enough nominations to find his way onto the ballot. Like him or not, Braen and the others had to recognize the legitimacy of his campaign.

The problem that troubled Braston remained the charges leveled against him by Alec Pogue. Stefan originally hailed from the southern continent, and as such, retained contacts in several kingdoms outside of the Eston Empire. These had proven very profitable for the man, and his wealth rivaled that of the Esterlings. According to Pogue, one of his business ventures involved the capture and delivery of slaves to wealthy plantation owners.

The problem lay in proving that he had been behind the crime. He had confessed in front of Alec and Amash but recanted his confession as soon as he had been confined. Events in his ledger coincided with dates of various disappearances but did not directly implicate his involvement. Hopefully the two men would catch up with Captain Dominique in Eskera and bring him in for testimony.

The jailer met him at the gate. "I'll need you to leave your weapons here, Lord Braston."

"Not a lord, barely a Braston." He removed his belt and handed over his cutlass and axe. He had been leaving his broadsword in his apartments more and more these days, opting instead for one of Sippen's pistols.

"The prisoner asked for better accommodations, so we dragged a mattress in from one of the other cells. Now he's asking for books."

Braen nodded. "I think we can provide reading material. I don't see any harm in that."

The soldier escorted him down the long walkway between cells. Few of them were occupied since crime had tapered off during the cleanup of the city. According to Amash, that was due to the increase in jobs. Apparently when people have proper employment, their level of honesty increases, and petty crime drops off.

The jailer turned the key in the lock and pushed the door open. "I'll be nearby, just holler if you need me, sir."

Braen nodded and entered the tiny room. The straw mattress lay in the corner and upon it sat the ugliest man he had ever known. His face resembled a rat, and pox scars covered dark skin which hung loose on his bony frame. A greasy smile curved on his lips as his visitor entered. "You finally decided to have that little talk with me, Braston? You know, if we had met when I first summoned you, we may have made a different arrangement, you and I."

"I'm not here to make business deals, Lord Nevra."

"Stefan. I'm always urging you to use my given name and yet you refuse. What is it that you don't like about me, Braen?"

"I don't even know where to begin on that topic." Braston forced himself to look into a pair of beady eyes. "I'm not here for small talk. I'm here to collect your final campaign statement so that the council can read it aloud before the elections."

"How nice of you to retrieve it yourself. A common page could have done that. No, Braen, I think you have other questions." He handed over a sheet of paper with black scribblings. Not trusted with a quill or sharp objects, the man had written it with a piece of coal. Braen tried hard not to smear the writing.

"I actually do have other business."

"Ask away, my friend."

"Not your friend." Braen wanted to lean against the wall but refrained. The entire room reeked with the man's repugnance. "You know the southern lords better than anyone in The Cove. How amiable would they be to an alliance?"

Nevra's brow rose up questioningly. "Against the Empire?"

"Against anyone and no one in particular."

"They don't run things on the southern continent like Andalon does. Their system of politics is different. Each lord is independent and has no affiliation with any other. The only allegiance in the south is with their wealth. Besides, most of the people on the continent live in small villages deep in the jungle. The lords don't have large populations of citizens like the north and there's no standing army. They are essentially warlords with hired mercenaries. Any help they could offer would be inconsequential."

Braen nodded. The information matched what Amash had told him. "What do you know about the people down there? Do the Falconers oversee them, as well?"

Stefan let out a cackle that showed his brown teeth. "You really know nothing about anything, do you, Braston? Stop beating around the bush. You want to know if powers exist that can be useful in your fight."

"Fights. And yes, that's exactly what I want to know."

"I can't give you the answers you seek, but suffice to say they have something far worse than Falconers overseeing their people."

"Then I must be going. Thank you for the statement and your time, Lord Nevra." He turned to leave, pounding on the door three times to signal the guard.

"If you seek an alliance with the south, Braston, you'll need to tarnish your conscience a bit. The only currency we southerners understand is dealing the capital of flesh and bone." The door was shutting behind Braen, but he heard Nevra call out from behind, "And I don't think you have the stomach for darker dealings."

After Braen had left, Stefan released his grip on the object hidden in his hand. The shiv felt good to hold during the conversation, all the while imagining himself stabbing it into the arrogant fool's neck. If only Braston had known just how closely he stood to death. There was no water nearby for him to draw from, and without his swords he was just a mortal man. But there would be time for that fun later.

He toyed with his weapon, flipping it over in his hands. The first time he had reached his hand into the slit in the mattress, he was shocked to find the piece of metal. Apparently, some prisoner had taken the time to sharpen a spoon into a blade. Although not razor sharp, the tool was usable and would be effective in time of need. The more he held it the more he ached to put it to use.

Talking about his former home had stirred a feeling of nostalgia. He usually suppressed these thoughts, having left the continent to seek fortunes elsewhere for good reason. Growing up he had hated the jungle and the perils within. Perhaps his surroundings and abundant supply of time contributed to his memories, but he allowed his mind to wander back to his former home.

Despite his current status he was not always a lord. He was born into a small village near one of the larger plantations. One summer when he was young, a plague spread among his people, killing a vast majority. Luckily, he and his mother survived, although he still bore the scars from the horrible illness. After they had recovered, she took him away to find work on the plantation.

Plantation life was difficult but offered better comforts than the village. His mother was pretty, and so she worked in the kitchen of the manor. Young Stefan was the same age as the manor lord's son, and so he was allowed to play with him and be his companion. That was where he learned to read. Every lesson that Charro received was passed along to Stefan. They were the best of friends until Charro's father learned that they were also lovers.

The enraged manor lord took his anger out on Stefan's mother, beating and bashing until no bone was left unbroken. The cruel man forced Stefan to watch while soldiers held his eyelids open. No matter how badly he wanted to look away, he could not. Stefan would carry the image of that event for the rest of his life.

A squeaking sound caught his attention. Gently he rose from the mattress and crawled over to the rat gnawing on a piece of discarded bread. At first the creature merely sniffed, but eventually committed to eating the offering. In a flash Stefan scooped the animal into his hands and held it tightly. Beady eyes stared up as the rodent struggled to get loose. "What's wrong, little rat? Don't you want to be my friend? I'm lonely in here and you can come visit me. Would you like to talk to me?"

Pain shot through his hand and blood trickled down. The animal had latched on to the meat beside his thumb and Nevra squeezed. The animal squealed from the pressure. "You little shit!" He stood up and ran to his mattress. "I'll teach you a lesson, you worm." He held the rat in one clenched hand and grabbed his shiv with the other. "You're nothing and I'm better than you!" He lifted it above the animal and said with a sneer, "You're my slave and I can do with you what I want."

He pressed the tip of the sharpened spoon hard against the animal's chest, ignoring the squeaks and squirms as it tried to get free. He giggled with glee as the device ripped skin, slowly piercing the heart. After a brief struggle, it fell limp. Nevra, suddenly aware of his deed, dropped the lifeless animal onto his bed and gasped.

Tears flowed down his cheeks as he realized the damage his anger had caused. He poked at the rodent and begged it to wake up, "I'm so sorry. I didn't mean to. Please wake up!"

His voice fell soft until his begging turned into a chant. His words were nearly inaudible as he spoke to the animal's lifeforce, willing its tiny soul to return. He sensed activity in the brain, just a flicker but enough to touch. He added his own to what he found. *Careful, he thought, not too much. Just enough to restart the organs.* He became one with the animal then and felt the torn chambers of the heart mend. His own muscles began to quiver as he felt the animal respond.

Of course, the animal that awoke had changed. The same beady eyes looked upon Stefan, only they no longer feared him. They obeyed. Stefan bent over and kissed its tiny pink nose.

Samani Kernigan took Nevra's campaign statement from Braen and read it three times. "I have to read this out loud?"

"To be fair, you do." Braston obviously felt the same hesitation but was a man of honor.

"You do realize I'm ready to rig this election, right? You, Amash, and Eusari will win if you say the word, but I need to know soon." Samani had worked diligently through the months to ensure the outcome, and everything was in place.

"You know how I feel. I promised Eusari that we'd win legitimately and without interference. We have to trust in the people and keep the campaign fair. Every statement is read verbatim, without changing a word. Got that?"

With a sigh, Samani acquiesced, "Fine. I'll read it."

They made their way to the docks where the entire town had gathered. The new ships stood in the harbor with colors raised like magnificent sentries standing to protect The Cove. There were enough to call them a fleet now, with more coming every month under Sippen's team of engineers. The light reflected off their armored hulls and seemingly glowed.

Some of the older ships moored, as well. They had trickled in one by one as word of the new government spread, and every captain had returned except Dominique. Some were curious about Braston, but most were eager to put their letters of marque to use and resume pillaging.

Every candidate, except Horslei and Nevra, stood on the pier ready to address the crowd. After each statement, the people would fan out to three polling places based on their district of residence. Soldiers stationed at every site would screen the residents and ensure each voted only once. They would also escort the ballots to the palace for counting.

Samani stepped forward to address the crowd. "People of The Cove, you know me. I served in Artema Horn's Inner Sanctum during his entire reign and advised previous kings before him." Some cheers came from the crowd at Artema's name, but some shouts of "traitor" and "criminal" heckled, as well. Samani was unsure if those were meant for him or for Artema. "The council has been hard at work drafting our new constitution to both protect you and establish your ownership over the government. It was ratified last night, and copies are available at the polling stations." This time only cheers met his ears and he paused to allow the applause to die down.

"You will choose your own representatives to the new council based on your place of residence. You will also choose from these nominees to lead the council as a triumvirate, a three headed leadership equal in power and ending the age of kings!" This time the crowd roared, hungry for the power that they believed they would hold in participatory government. "The candidates will randomly draw stones painted with a number signifying their order of speech. I will draw for the absent candidates and read their statements."

Sippen Yurik held the bucket high above his head and walked before each contender. Adamas Creech drew number one, Eusari drew number three, and Braen chose number five. *Good,* Samani thought, *let his words be the last and the most remembered.*

Creech wasted no time and stepped forward to start the show. "The Cove has always invited foreigners from both continents to enjoy the spoils of a granted marque." He spoke with an eloquence that matched his flamboyant attire. "To invite foreigners is one thing, to allow them to invade our beloved soil and force a new form of government upon us is oppression. After I am elected, I will work to restore the Pirate's Guild to the true hands of the people. Yes. I will wrench it from the hands of a smiling tyrant from the north and place it in yours."

A cheer erupted from a large section of the assembly. Samani frowned, not expecting his words to resonate with such a large number. He leaned over to Eusari and whispered into her ear, "No matter what he says about you, remain calm and don't let them see your anger." She nodded and continued smiling at the crowd.

"And then we have his wench, the whore who shares his bed as well as fuels his revolution." Creech pointed a perfectly manicured finger at Eusari.

Samani felt his heart lurch as he watched her stiffen. *Oh shit,* he thought. Her hand slowly worked its way into her leather jerkin where she kept her assortment of blades. *Don't do it, dearie,* he silently pleaded.

"What has she done for us except destroy most of our defenses with her sharpshooters and fancy weaponry? Why doesn't every captain of the guild share such awesome firepower if this isn't a tyranny?" More of the crowd clapped and many of the sailors on the wharf began chanting for access to the guns. "A vote for me is one against tyrants and for the rightfully deserving people of our Cove." He finished his speech with a flourished bow. "Thank you!"

Samani let the deafening applause die down and stepped forward. A quick glance let him know that Eusari still held her hand close to her knives. *At least she's still smiling.* But he knew her well enough to recognize the anger behind her clenched teeth. He drew out the first of the two prepared remarks.

"Amash Horslei provided the following, and the words spoken are his own." He cleared his throat more for effect than necessity, even if it felt dry after Creech's insults to Eusari. "My brothers and sisters of The Cove. Today marks an auspicious occasion for our beloved guild; one that will establish precedence for social contract theory with our representatives and provide an opportunity for recourse should they fail in their duties in popular sovereignty."

*Damn it, Amash!* Samani could tell instantly that, although the man was brilliant and well educated, he had missed his audience. The crowd stood dumbfounded, whispering for their neighbors to translate. Kernigan thought fast and ad-libbed. "It's a good day when you can hold your government accountable and take action to remove them if they fail to act on your behalf!" His quick thinking worked, and the crowd erupted in applause and chants of "Vote them out!"

Samani stepped back and glanced at Braen who shot a disapproving stare. His pulse quickened when Eusari stepped forward, awfully close to Creech and with her hand in her leathers. "Yes. My esteemed opponent speaks true. I share a bed with Braen Braston, but I am not his puppet nor his prize." The women in the audience screamed their approval, drowning out the cat calls of the men. "My words and my mind, just as my body, are mine. No man will ever convince me otherwise. I am empowered and strong because, as a dear friend once taught me, I choose it for myself."

She drew something out of her jerkin and Samani held his breath. She was in striking distance of Adamas and a single knife could end the day with bloodshed. Instead of steel she drew out a folded piece of paper which she carefully opened and continued her speech. Samani let out the air in his chest with an audible sigh. She turned and gave him a knowing wink as she talked.

"But today is not about me or any man on this stage. Today is about selecting leadership into an age of prosperity. Vote for me and you choose to balance strength with compassion. Ignore the words spoken today out of hatred and negativity and select the leaders who will provide you with protection against the wars that rage around us. Thank you."

Samani could not believe his ears. He had never heard her speak with such passion or with as many words, for that matter. *She was brilliant!* He resisted the urge to join the wild applause from the crowd and waited until every clap had ceased to sound. And then he swallowed hard to prepare his next statement.

"And now I read the statement from Lord Stefan Nevra, unable to attend due to pre-trial confinement." He closed his eyes to steady himself before continuing. "Again, these words are not my own." He swallowed hard and shook his head in disbelief at the words on the paper.

"People of The Cove. Braen Braston is a murderer and a foreign invader. He has forced you to accept a form of government that usurps my legitimate rule as your king. I was chosen by Artema Horn who faked his death so that he could enjoy uninterrupted retirement. I apologize that I chose to spread the lies to you, as he suggested. Had I told you the truth, I would still be your benevolent king."

The crowd murmured and Samani could see many heads bobbing and pointing at Braen. "Captain Braston wants to put me on trial for crimes that he cannot prove, but neither he nor any candidate before you can wield the scepter of justice over my head, because I am the law and your rightful king. Raise me from my prison and restore me with the power of your revolution. Kill Braston. Kill Horslei. Kill Kernigan. Kill Creech. Kill the she-bitch. Kill them all."

Samani stepped back and crumpled up the paper, tossing it into the water in front of him. All eyes stared at him expectantly. Creech broke the silence by leaning close to Eusari. "And you thought 'my' speech was full of mudslinging? He's way more eloquent with his insults." She nodded agreement through her still clenched smile.

Only Braen remained unaffected and stepped before the silent crowd. "Yes, I'm an invader, but he and Adamas are wrong to call me foreign. I love The Cove, and the destruction and lost lives that I brought with me are on my conscience every night. Artema Horn was my mentor and friend, but he profited from a deal he made with Marcus Esterling and turned his back on all of us. His 'retirement,' as he called it, is actually an abandonment of every citizen of The Cove."

He stood tall on the pier, facing the crowd with the regal stature of a king. As he spoke Samani could not help but marvel how different everything would be if this born leader had stayed in Fjorik. *But the prophesy foresaw that he wouldn't.*

Braen continued, "And to think that he left Nevra in charge? A man accused of stealing your wives and daughters and selling them to slavers? I cannot tell you how he will be judged, but I can promise that a vote for me is for justice and fairness." His voice boomed over the silent crowd, no one speaking out of fear of missing a single word from the Kraken.

"The concerns regarding my war against my brother and the claims that it is personal are valid. I will not conceal my motive, but I will not press any of you into a war against your will. If elected, I will ask the council to promote me to the rank of admiral with war powers to sail a volunteer armada against Fjorik and Marcus Esterling. There are spoils to be gained in such a war and I will outfit every crew that participates with the new weaponry. Our allies on the mainland are amassing an army that will assist with raids from the ground, helping to ensure our success. The time to strike with revolution is now, and a vote for me is a vote for a different world." When Braen finished speaking he turned to Samani and whispered. "Do it. Win this by any means necessary."

# Part II
# Choice and Consequence

*Pain and suffering early known,*
*Raised a king without a crown.*

*– The Oracle of Astian, 702nd year of order*

# Chapter Eighteen

The streets of Eskera were always busy no matter the time of day. People bustled from place to place despite the late hour; the market full of vendors peddling all sorts of wares. Lively tunes radiated from buildings as musicians entertained. Renowned for music, a budding prodigy would travel far to learn from the masters of the arts. Visitors loved the energy that surrounded the city, but Alec Pogue paid no heed. He was a man on a mission.

He made his way through these streets every evening since arriving in the city, determined to find his quarry in a brothel or tavern. When they had arrived in port, there was no mistaking Dominique's ship *Aggressor* tied off to the pier. He spent the first few days watching and listening for signs of the slave trader, but quickly learned that the ship, like all other warships in the harbor, had been seized by King Robert and pressed into service. Alec had to look for Dominique deeper in the city, searching the pubs and restaurants near the entertainment district.

Eskera enjoyed more than modest wealth, not because of its resources, but because all trade up and down the Misting River paid usage taxes in her ports. Even with the blockade, the people within the walls acted as if no war loomed in the East or drew nearer each day. The district was full of all types, from sharply dressed merchants and escorted women in flowing gowns to prostitutes and peddlers of questionable wares.

Alec stood outside a theater, scanning the crowds partying in the streets. *This city could be razed next week but no one's worried,* he thought. *It's been so long without conflict that they believe war is only fought by soldiers in the field.* He felt the eyes of residents on balconies above the shops but felt confident that he blended in.

A whore ambled up, deep in her cups and stumbling from too much revelry. "Ow bout uh tumble in the alley, yuh lawdship?" She slurred her words as she pawed at him.

"Not interested." He gently pushed her away, mindful of his purse. The woman shrugged and quickly found a buyer to take her into the shadows. Alec shook his head, trying to keep it clear, but thoughts of Mattie and the girls bubbled up to the surface. Alexa would be of age soon, and Liza was already a woman. He hoped it wasn't too late, that they hadn't succumbed to their fates and chosen the same profession as this drunkard. Of course, if he were to believe Lord Nevra, they had already been forced into it against their will.

He nearly killed the man on that day and silently wished he had. But his old friend Amash had dueled away his rage, insisting that the monster stand trial for his crimes according to the code of the guild. But the blatant confession haunted Alec. Nevra's poxed face had contorted when he hissed out his claim that he and his men had taken advantage of all three. With pleasure he told Pogue that Dominique and his son had sold them as whores on the southern continent.

Hope still clung to his heart that they were unharmed; that their minds weren't broken from the abuse. *Gods please grant them the strength to heal.* Mattie was a fine mother, and, as long as they remained together, he knew they would be fine. Or at least he hoped.

A flashy uniform caught his eye across the street, scarlet in color and nautical, contrasting sharply with the white of the king's army. He focused on Adolphus Dominique, the son of the slave trader, emerging from a gambling den with two pretty girls on his arms. His heart leaped in his chest. *They're the right ages.* But as he stepped closer, he could tell that these were not his girls.

Following the lad was easy in the crowd, with so many people for concealment. A proper short sword hung at the boy's side, meaning that he was either classically trained like his father or a fool. It was safer to assume that he was well trained and experienced. Alec touched the dual cutlasses at his own sides. Only one man had ever bested him with blades, and that had been his protégé Amash. Of course, he had been recovering from a wound in his side at the time, but Horslei had shown considerable talent with the two bladed technique. It was a pity that the era of swordsmanship waned with the advent of Braston's new weapons. Any man can pull a trigger, but only a master swung steel and lived.

The boy and the two girls walked through the first ward. This was the home to the wealthiest of Eskerans, especially the noble families who controlled the old shipping rights. But new wealth slowly joined the old and freshly built houses dotted the streets. Manor homes popped up on lots sold off by the families who had slowly lost their grip on the city's high society. Adolphus steered the young ladies into one of these.

Grinning with victory, Pogue hurried back to the palace to retrieve Horslei. Out of breath he approached his old friend. "I found the bastard."

"Great! When do you want to do it?"

"Tonight. Right now." Pogue was already buckling his leather chest plate with high protective collar. It would protect him from glancing blows.

Amash watched him with concern. "You expect a fight?"

He nodded. "Both the kid and the father are skilled with the sword. This may turn bad quickly, and I don't want to risk dying before I find Mattie and the girls."

Amash grabbed his sword belt from the table and buckled it to hang in the same fashion as Pogue's. He paused midway through fitting his own armor and froze, eyes fixated on the open door. "Shit, Alec." He nodded toward the little girl in the doorway.

Marita smiled her trademark grin at the duo. "Oh goodie! You found him!"

Alec turned slowly to meet her voice and nodded. "Don't let anyone know that we have. Also, if you're questioned, fib and say that we've been here all night."

"But that would be a lie, Captain Pogue." She spoke with sharp condemnation that sent panic through both men. Alec drew a deep breath and imagined the girl giving them up to authorities because she thought pirates followed a code. Amash started to speak, but Marita cut him off with a giggle. "Just kidding! But your faces were funny. But I won't be lying because I'm going with you. If they're that good of swordsmen, then you'll need my help to bind them."

"Absolutely not," Amash shook his head, adding emphasis when he added, "No."

"Wait." Alec put up his hand, not to the girl but to his friend. "She's right. We can't go in there overburdened with ropes or chains to tie both men. Plus, Adolphus will be in bed with two women." He walked over to Marita who still grinned. Kneeling, he gently placed his hand on her shoulder and locked eyes. "dearie, what we do tonight is dark business."

"I know, like what you had to do to the captain on the ship."

"Yes, exactly like that. It's the kind of thing that could get us in trouble, but we do it because we have to. If you go with us, you must lie through your teeth, or we'll all hang from our necks at King Robert's order. It's the code! Do you understand?" She nodded vigorously, thrusting her thumb upward to match her ludicrous grin. "Good. Then go put on dark clothing, preferably britches like Eusari wears."

Her eyes grew wide at the mention of her mentor. "I can be like her tonight?"

"Exactly like her, dearie. Now hurry!"

The girl scurried off and Amash took a step toward his friend. "What the hell was that?"

"She's coming because we need her."

"No. This is like when you tried to kill Nevra. You need to calm down and use your brain not your heart, Alec!"

"She won't be in danger."

"It isn't about the danger! Kids are like sponges. They see everything adults do, and it affects the development of their conscience.

She's watching and learning, Alec. She already saw you slit Captain Moran's throat. Don't make her a part of this, especially after what she witnessed in Atarax."

Pogue looked thoughtful for a moment but shook his head. "We need her tonight. After this, I promise I'll be more careful."

An hour later the trio had scaled the wall around the manor and crouched behind a bush. Amash reiterated his concerns, "I don't like this. We don't know how many, if any, guards are inside. We also don't know what rooms they're in."

"True, but we have Marita." Alec pointed at two windows lit from within. "dearie, will you gently blow those tree branches against those windows? Don't break them, just jostle them enough to get someone's attention."

"Are you daft?" Amash bristled. "The point is not to draw any attention at all!"

She nodded and did as she was told. The window furthest from the main hall showed movement, and a bare-chested teenager looked out into the courtyard. "Do it again, make it look like a storm is brewing." The branch hit the window hard and the boy quickly threw it open to batten down the shutters. "It's him. I'm sure."

"Nice thinking."

"I sometimes have good ideas, that's how I became a captain, remember?" Still in a crouch he made his way to the window adjacent to their target's. He pulled out a thin blade and tripped the lock. Once they were all inside, he whispered, "This is certainly the master suite, but Matthieu isn't home." They could tell that the room was used, but not currently occupied. "Amash, look around and see if you can find any ledgers or ship's logs. If Esterling took his ship, then Dominique would have brought them here."

The big man nodded and went to work. Alec smiled down at the grinning Marita and asked, "Are you ready?" She responded with another silly thumbs up. He eased open the door and peered out.

"No guards. Give me a twenty second head start and follow me to the next room." She nodded.

He slid into the hallway and tried the doorknob, turning it with satisfaction. As he pressed it open, he found three figures lying in the bed. Thankfully, the girls had fallen asleep intertwined with each other, so his target was alone on the near side. He crept quietly and drew a knife, placing it to the boy's neck and placing a hand over his mouth. Adolphus awakened with a start, eyes shooting open and wide. As he did, Marita took over by gagging and binding him. His eyes betrayed panic.

In a whisper Alec ordered, "We'll let your legs work so that you can get up and walk into the next room." He nodded toward the girls in the bed. "Wake them and you all die. Nod if you understand." The boy nodded vigorously. "Good, now go."

Together they slipped into the room where Amash appeared defeated. "Nothing. It must be in an office."

"I doubt it." He pushed the boy into a chair. "Strap him in good and release his gag. Boy, if you scream it will be your last. We just want information." The teen nodded his understanding.

"We'll start with easy questions. Where are your father's ledgers?"

Adolphus coughed as the gag released. "Back on the ship."

"Bullshit." Alec stepped forward with his knife, digging the tip into the boy's tender thigh. Pogue ignored the trickle of blood and pressed. "They are in this room, tell me where." The boy's eyes shot to a painting on the wall. "Good boy." To his friend he ordered, "Check it out."

Amash moved the canvas to reveal a hiding spot. He held up three ledgers triumphantly. "Got it!"

Pogue removed the knife, leaning in and speaking deliberately, "And now for question number two. Where did you slave trading bastards take my wife and daughters?"

Eyes finally focusing on his captor, Adolphus smiled in recognition. "Oh, Captain Pogue. You should have asked for a smaller dowry and Daddy wouldn't have taught you a lesson."

Alec's fist instinctively flew, connecting with the boy's nose. Blood splattered the wall and gushed down his mouth before dripping onto his chest. "Where did you take them."

"You broke my nose!"

"Yes, I did, and your cock is the next thing I injure." He shoved the blade against the boy's naked crotch. "Tell me now or those girls in the next room are the last you ever touch with this worm."

Fear suddenly broke the boy. Tears ran down his cheeks and urine sprayed down his leg and onto the floor. "Southern continent."

"I know that. Tell me where."

The boy's eyes pleaded for mercy as he answered, "We sold them to Charro Valencia."

"Good, where's his villa?"

"On the northern shore of Cargia."

Alec pressed, "What else do you want to tell me?"

Tears continued to flow as the boy whimpered. "Nothing, Captain Pogue. There isn't anything else. We delivered them to his villa and came to Eskera after we received Horn's dispatch. You know the order to stay away from The Cove for a few weeks? By then Prince Robert had taken the city and seized *Aggression.* I swear to you that's all!"

Alec pressed the tip into the tender parts of the boy and leaned in wickedly. "Did you enjoy using this on them, you little maggot?"

"Who?"

"My daughters and my wife, you little shit!"

Adolphus shook his head violently. "I didn't! We didn't! I swear we just sold them for coin and to teach you a lesson!"

Alec sheathed his blade and drew both cutlasses, crossing sharp edges against the boy's neckline and holding them like a giant pair of glistening scissors. "Tell me the truth!"

"I swear, sir! That's everything! I cared for Liza! I wouldn't have defiled her like that!"

Amash called tenderly to his friend, "Alec." He gently pulled back on his arms, taking the swords and placing them on the bed. With hands on Pogue's shoulders, he turned him around to lock eyes. "Alec. That's it. We know where they are and have the ledgers to confirm his story."

"But I need him to admit that he raped them. I need a reason to kill him."

"No, Brother, you don't. If he's a rapist, then we'll get the girls' testimonies and let the king or Braen deal with him."

Pogue started to answer, but something in his friend's face caught his attention.

Amash abruptly shouted, "Marita! No!"

Alec wheeled around and saw that the little girl had picked up his blades. She held them crossed along the boy's neck, just as he had, before. She stood over the whimpering teen with her toothy smile glowing in the night. "Sorry, Mate," she said through her smile, "we can't afford to take prisoners after what you just saw." With one fluid motion she drew the blades outward, slicing a red "x" where his throat had been. Blood spurt from both sides, spraying her grinning face as he died. Then, she turned slowly to the two men and gave a crimson covered thumbs up. Even her once white teeth were covered in blood.

Alec took the blades. "Marita, why did you do this?" But he knew the answer. She had spoken the same words he had said to Captain Moran.

The girl looked confused, inclining her head and dropping her smile. "Aren't you proud of me, Captain Pogue?"

Alec did not know how to respond.

# Chapter Nineteen

Mattie hurried across the courtyard to the manor house. The plantation was large, but thankfully the servants' quarters were closer than those of the field hands. She preferred to call them servants and field hands over their proper title of slave. Since she and the girls arrived, Mrs. Pogue had learned to readjust to many differences on the southern continent, including their abrupt change in status.

She had expected the worse when they departed The Cove, but Captain Dominique had ensured that they traveled fairly well. The journey was uneventful despite being locked in a stateroom for an entire week. At least he had provided protection and kept her and the girls free from his men's pawing eyes and hands. She actually felt bad for his son, Adolphus. She could tell that the boy genuinely cared for Liza, and it pained him that he wasn't allowed visits.

All in all, the trip went fairly quickly, and they weren't sold at market. Rather, Matthieu had prearranged a private transaction on one of the larger plantations. They were loaded in a cart and driven directly to a manor perched on a coastal cliff. The view was spectacular and overlooked the ocean.

When they had first arrived, she stared across those blue green waters, praying that her beloved Alec would arrive with swift rescue. She had prayed that he would see through the letter her captors had forced her to pen. Surely, he would have assumed she was under duress and immediately search. But months had gone by without his arrival, and, until he did, Cargia made a beautiful prison cell.

But each day the passing months of captivity worked to convince her that he would never find them. *Surely, he wouldn't believe that I'd leave him,* she often thought, *he knows that I love him, doesn't he?* But then she would remember their last conversation. She regretted hounding him to leave The Cove for a life on a farm. *Well, I got my farm, after all. Albeit as a slave to a sugar plantation.*

The first time she had seen the property owner she had been worried about hers and the girl's roles in the manor home. But he had proven to be a fair and gentle man, and, thankfully, one obviously disinterested in female company. Charro Valencia was flamboyant and dressed as colorfully as the parrots flying around his villa. His head was cleanly shaven and his dark skin without blemish. When he smiled, his brilliant white teeth unnerved the others in the room. The man was perfection and standing in his presence felt like you were standing the home of a god.

She hurried to the kitchen where the steward, Mrs. Pritchet, lorded over the other women of the house. "Where have you been, Mattie. Do you want the lash?"

Mattie didn't think Valencia allowed her to whip slaves, but she shook her head and kept her eyes lowered when answering, "I hung the laundry as you instructed, Mum."

The older woman's eyes narrowed. "So, it's my fault?"

"No, Mum, but my chores are finished, and I thought I'd clean and organize the kitchen before preparing the midday meal."

"What's wrong with the way my kitchen is now?"

Mattie could tell that she hit a nerve but pressed. "The storeroom is a mess and Nannette thought she saw a rodent yesterday. We can never find anything we need because there's no method to the storage. And these cutting boards need to be sanded and refinished or the lord will get sick one day." After a pause she added, "and it'll be on you."

Pritchet snarled, revealing several rotted and missing teeth. Instead of menacing it gave her a comical appearance that invoked more humor than fear. Mattie couldn't help herself and chuckled. She quickly brought up her hand to cover a smile.

Pritchett raised a plump finger and waved it in Mattie's face, "The lord will hear of this, for sure. Defiance from a slave is always punished." She moved in closer, the java beans strong on her breath, and said, "I hope he lets me beat it out you personally."

Mattie stood taller, looming over the disgusting woman by an entire head and added, "Oh, yes, and your floors are disgusting. I've seen kennels that I'd rather wade in when cooking."

A loud crash interrupted their exchange, and both women looked to the servant stairs. A copper chamber pot tumbled down with a series of bangs, spilling its contents and spraying it on the walls and landing below. A few moments later a young teenage girl poked her head around with a look of horrified guilt. Her arms were full of pots and apparently one had slipped from her stack. "I'm sorry, Mum."

Mattie's heart sank for Alexa, but it was clearly an accident. Knowing her sweet daughter, she would clean it immediately. She started to speak encouraging words when the kitchen steward flew into a fury. Aghast, she watched Mrs. Pritchet grab a wooden spoon and run at her youngest daughter.

The horrible woman grabbed Alexa's raven hair and swung her into the wall, rubbing her face in the feces. Then she threw the girl down on the ground, looming with the spoon raised high. She brought it down with force, striking the cowering child across her hands. Again and again the utensil pounded flesh until it broke with an audible snap. Finding herself without a weapon, the steward reached her fist into the air. Mattie caught it.

One advantage of being the wife of the Captain of the Cove's City Guard is extensive training in self-defense. She reacted in an instant, twisting the woman's hand into an awkward angle until the portly woman knelt before her on the ground. Mattie stood above Mrs. Pritchet with the offending hand securely locked into place. With a hiss she addressed the woman, "This is the first and last time that you or anybody else touches a member of my family. Slave or not, we're not property that you can trash about."

She wrenched the hand further, convincing the woman that her arm would dislocate. She added additional pressure on the thumb to emphasize her resolve and Pritchet whined mournfully, clutching her right shoulder with her left hand. "If anyone threatens or touches us other than the lord, I assure you that you'll lose the rest of your teeth while you sleep. Is that understood?" The woman nodded furiously. "Good, now clean up this mess for Alexa while we clean out the chamber pots."

Charro Valencia stared at the woman kneeling before him. He noticed, as he had on the day Dominique had delivered her and her daughters, that she was astonishingly beautiful. He also observed that she held herself with a bearing of a lord's wife instead of a scullery slave. Although she humbly knelt before him, her eyes revealed her true feelings regarding her crime. They were cold and dark without remorse.

He sighed, "I know that you are new to my continent, but do you realize how many laws you broke this morning?"

"Not as many as if I had broken her thumb, My Lord."

Despite himself, he laughed at her obstinance. "She says that you attacked her unprovoked, is that true."

"No, My Lord. That woman is horrible. She beat a chambermaid over an accident, and I intervened before she did further harm."

"A chambermaid who happens to be your own daughter, I believe. Is that true, as well."

The woman stared directly into his eyes, not with anger, but with confidence and bearing. "Yes, My Lord, but I would have done the same regardless of the child's origin. No one will harm a child in my presence."

"Fair enough, but I cannot have slaves attacking my paid staff. By law I'll have to pay for her injuries and suffering. I must give compensation for her sustaining them in a work environment." He watched the woman closely and added, "You realize that those costs will be added to your indentureship?"

She nodded, eyes never leaving his. "Yes, My Lord."

"That woman is vital to my household. She maintains order over my kitchen and staff and procures all food supplies and stores." He returned to a chair behind his desk and added, "I need her. She keeps this manor house running."

"That woman is robbing you blind, spending your money on inflated prices and splitting the profits with her cronies in town. The kitchen is unsanitary, and the pantry disorganized. You'd do better to hire a new kitchen steward."

*This one is so bold,* he thought, *I like her.* Changing the subject, he asked, "What's your name?"

"Mattie Pogue."

"Why did you choose to come to the southern continent, Mattie? Did your husband die, and you hoped for opportunity for you and your daughters? Because you're going about it the wrong way if that was the reason." He genuinely liked the woman. He had seen slave attacks before, but never one so calculated. She had used appropriate force, and the situation was one he would have probably interfered with himself.

"We were kidnapped from The Cove and brought here against our will by Captain Dominique."

"I see. Well, that claim is made by many a slave, although it is usually a ploy to end their indentureship early." He had heard enough. The woman was obviously intelligent and found a new way to play an old con. He started to rise, but her words stopped him.

"My husband is the Captain of the Guard for Artema Horn. He is Alec Pogue, proven by battles on the sea, and taker of many of Cargia's vessels before he retired from a life at sea."

Charro sat back into his chair, amused by her commitment to her lie. "And he serves him currently?"

"Yes. Up until the day we were stolen."

"Can you prove this?"

Her eyes grew wide with hope and she reached shaking hands into a pocket sewn into her dress. "Yes, My Lord. I've carried this with me since the day of my capture. Artema Horn gave it to my husband just the night before, and I found it while ironing his uniform." Tears filled her eyes and she trembled. "At the time I thought nothing of it."

"And now?"

"It's the only memento of him I possess." She wiped away her tears and held it toward him. "Besides my girls, it's all that I have in this world."

Normally Valencia would not have allowed the conversation to go on this long, but the woman intrigued him. He read the words on the letter. He was surprised to see that the signature truly resembled that of Horn. They had exchanged many business transactions in the past, and the mark was easily recognizable. The letter was brief and merely thanked a Captain Pogue for his many years of service. "This looks in order, but I'm sorry. It proves nothing. You may've stolen it from another woman, or found it lying about."

"It's true, I swear on the gods."

"Regardless, Artema Horn is no longer in charge of The Cove. There have been recent... How do you say? Developments."

Her eyebrows raised with concern. "Like what?"

*She is certainly dedicated to this story,* he thought. "Horn retired and we've received conflicting reports on who is actually in charge. My sources say that Lord Stefan Nevra presides." He watched carefully for her response and was shocked when she did.

The woman hissed at the name. Her body recoiled and she stood, forgetting her humility. "No. That cannot be so. I pray to the gods that it isn't!"

"And why is that?"

"His men were our initial captors." She shivered, "I'll never forget that disgusting Turat and how hard he tried to get alone with my girls. "Nevra's ill in the head, My Lord. He is much of the reason I've begged my husband to take us away to Logan."

Charro felt his heart turn over in his chest. "If you've met Stefan, describe him."

"Walnut brown skin covered with scars from some childhood pox. The scars are pronounced and mar him from head to toe."

"Common knowledge, do better."

"His eyes squint and he rarely looks anyone in the eye, choosing instead to bury his rat-like face in his ledgers." She paused. "When he scribbles in them, he bites his lower lip and mutters to himself."

Charro Valencia fell silent at the accurate description of his former lover. When he finally spoke, it was low and quiet. "Mrs. Pogue?"

"Yes, My Lord?"

"The consequences for your insolence are steep. You are charged an additional fifty talents to cover her losses." The woman tried to speak, but he threw up his hand. "Silence!" Her mouth clamped shut and he continued. "I'll also look into your claims about Mrs. Pritchet's embezzlement. If they're false, you'll be confined ten days for slander and fined an additional fifty talents for further damages." He watched as she regained her composure, defiantly confident in her statements. "If you speak true, then you're promoted to the rank of Kitchen Stewart in her stead." He smiled at her shocked expression. "You are dismissed, Mrs. Pogue."

# Chapter Twenty

A break in the spring storms brought out Westonese people eager to spend their coin while catching up on latest gossip. Percy Roan watched the display in the market from his balcony, pleased that sales taxes would flow and balance out the slower previous month. He wondered silently if the poorer sections of the city fared as well as his own. Soon sounds of argument drew his attention to a particular clothing shop.

The owner stood on the threshold shouting at two Pescari women. They were young, perhaps in their teens, and clad in Andalonian attire instead of buckskins. One of them held her sack of coin high in the face of the merchant and screamed back, "Why is our gold no good? We are citizens and earned our coin!"

"Earned it on your backs, most likely," the shop owner's wife shouted over the shoulder of her husband, "You foreigners are nothing more than thieves and rabble!"

The second Pescari woman chimed in response to the accusation, "We earn it working in the mines!" She stepped forward and spit into the face of the Westonese woman. "We cook for our men and feed them for coin to spend where we please!"

Percy clicked his tongue aloud and shook his head. *Shouldn't have done that, dearie.*

As he predicted, the shop owner screamed for the city guards. They had already heard the shouting and were moving toward the commotion. Having witnessed the assault, they quickly grabbed the women and shoved them to the ground, shackling their wrists before leading them away. The crowd murmured displeasure at the interruption of their morning but quickly resumed their business. Soon this would be one more reason to gossip and the story would get juicier as the day wore on.

During the scuffle, the purse fell forgotten onto the street. Percy watched closely as the shop owner carefully hid the treasure with his trouser leg. After everyone had resumed their own business, the merchant bent and retrieved the coins. He slipped the bulging sack into his pocket and returned inside. Percy made a mental note to have a conversation with the man and ensure that he received his cut at the end of the week.

*If only the heathens would remain in their district,* he thought about the women, *then we wouldn't have these problems.* Of course, he and Cassus Eachann shared no intention of stopping them from roaming into the richer sectors. Events like these demonstrated the need for added security and higher taxes. *Besides, we've improved their lives monumentally! They'd still be living off the land if we hadn't accepted them into our culture!*

The women would be lashed and returned to their district within the day, although, there would be trouble with the Pescari from this. More would have to be arrested before they learned their lesson. He would need to speak with Lord Eachann about a proactive solution to prevent riots. He had a meeting with Cassus in an hour and would discuss it then.

They planned to meet with new donors and discuss improvements to the harbor. With the Esterling brat in control of Eskera in the south, Weston had an opportunity to improve its position. It would become a key stop along the Misting River. Percy Roan rose from his chair and left the remains of his breakfast for the kitchen staff to retrieve.

Concerned Pescari men filled the meeting lodge, murmuring their frustrations and trying hard to keep their tempers low. Daska and Teot sat at the front of the congregation, and the other elders gathered behind the two men. Daska tapped a drum five times, and the grumblings fell silent. By the fifth beat no one spoke, and all eyes were on the two men. He reached out the talking stick and handed it to Teot.

The uncle of the shappan stood and addressed the gathered. "Felicima led us to this city for a reason but has yet to reveal her purpose. In the meantime, our culture is crumbling. The inhabitants of this city worship the gold in their pockets and are enticing us with its power. This god of wealth makes Felicima angry and she will punish us."

Daska retrieved the ceremonial stick from Teot and added, "Women are whoring with Westonese men for gold, and our backs are breaking while we dig to further the wealth of our Andalonian masters. We have become their slaves and they control us with their golden god."

One of the men raised his hand, and the elder passed the stick through the crowd. Once he held it, he spoke chilling words, "My sisters were arrested in the market this morning. I told them not to leave our district, but they insisted that the quality of clothing was far better near the homes of the wealthy. The guards took turns flogging their backs with leather whips while their bare chests were exposed to the crowd. This was all under the eye of Felicima."

He passed the talking stick through the crowd, and another man added his own story. "They are seducing our youth with lies about our culture. They force them to attend school and endure hours upon hours of teachings that persuade them to turn from our goddess. Last evening my son told me that she is not alive, and that she is nothing more than a fireball in the sky that warms our world. He said that there are no gods, only mankind."

This brought the council to break protocol, and they shouted with anger until Daska again beat the drum. They quickly quieted and Teot retrieved the stick. Before he could speak, a single voice shouted from the back. "Where is the shappan? Why has he forsaken us?"

Teot cast his eyes upon the man, rebuking him with a single look. “My nephew is gone, and I can no longer support him as shappan.” Ignoring the gasps of both the warriors and the elders, he continued. “Felicima has passed her power to another, more worthy of our people; a shappan with maturity and experience as both a warrior and a leader.”

Shouts of defiance rang out in the lodge and Daska beat the drum. “Who shall we follow, Teot? You? Prove your worth!”

With both hands, Teot pointed at several dark braziers. In a flash they sprung to life, crackling and snapping as sparks licked the air. The men gasped and dropped to the floor in reverence. Even Daska had not expected the display and he too fell to his knees. “If Taros returns, I will demand that he step down. If he refuses, I will challenge his right to rule through Shapalote.”

The doors to the lodge burst open and the night wind chilled the room, threatening to snuff the flickering torches. Their fire danced against the interruption but held their glow. A Pescari youth in buckskins approached and addressed the elders. “Soldiers are in our district! They’re demanding that we turn over our weapons and are going door to door taking them away!”

Fire reflected in Teot’s golden eyes as he strode from the room. He found the activity in the streets exactly as the boy had described. Soldiers exited homes with bundles of bows and blades that they discarded into the backs of wagons. Many of the Pescari complied out of fear, while the bravest who resisted were quickly outnumbered.

Rage filled the warrior as he stared down two approaching soldiers. With an outstretched hand, one of them ordered, “Place your blade on the ground.” When Teot refused, the man pressed, “Do it now, and there won’t be trouble.” He placed his hand on the wooden handle of the club at his side.

“Your trouble is only beginning in the eyes of Felicima,” Teot responded loudly so that all present would hear, “and she is not pleased with either of our people.” With a wave of his hand, the club at the man’s side burst into flame. All at once, every soldier in the street screamed out in pain as their own cudgels did the same, some while in use.

The men behind Teot stared in awe until Daska yelled, "Attack them and drive them off!" At his command the warriors sprinted toward the wagons, intending to gather up weapons and turn them on the soldiers. "In the name of Felicima, kill them!"

But the soldiers recovered quickly and drew swords while the waggoneers spurred horses. With precision they formed a thin line to protect the retreating caravan. Teot and his men clashed with the remaining soldiers, driving them back. As they neared the gate marking the boundary of the district, Teot reared back. He channeled his inner heat and anger. Then he froze in his tracks.

On the other side of the gate stood several ranks of mobilized soldiers, not the city guards his men had pushed back, but lines of well-armed imperial soldiers. *Tonight did not happen by chance,* he thought, *they planned for us to rise up!* Instantly the sky above filled with arrows, so many that he could not burn them all as they rained down. All around him men screamed in agony as the soldiers fired upon both friend and foe. He caught the second wave more easily but was unable to stop the heavy iron portcullis from dropping into place behind the fleeing guardsmen.

The fierce battle was over almost as soon as it had begun, ending with the district completely locked down. Within an hour the entire city guard had mobilized and encircled the Pescari. If anyone had wondered why the new governor had given them this particular ward, they no longer questioned. The high walls encircling the neighborhood included two gates which were easily closed and locked at the first sign of trouble. Steel portcullises were impervious to fire, and the rioting people were trapped inside an open tomb of stone.

Cassus Eachann watched from his vantage high atop the city walls and addressed the six Falconers standing beside him. "Issue every soldier the steel weapons that we made with the coal and iron the Pescari mined for us. He can't destroy those. We'll also cut their water for a few days and teach them a lesson. Keep a watch and let me know if any more than the one exhibit emotancy." As an afterthought he added, "Is the girl with the boy?"

The tallest of the specters nodded. "Yes. She walks to him every evening and returns to the city each morning before first light."

"Good. Don't let the girl into the city tomorrow. Have the guards turn her around with a rumor at the gates or something. She'll run straight to him and he'll be forced where we please."

"We already have the trap set and he'll have no defense this time."

"Good." Eachann nodded approvingly. "Contact Lord Campton Shol with your report straight away." He turned and faced the specter then added, "Let him know that it was my plan that worked."

"Don't overstep your authority with us, Governor." The order had its intended effect and Cassus immediately regretted his tone. "But rest easy, that I'll let him know that you've trapped the entire population of abominations. He'll no doubt reward you handsomely for your contribution to the Empire."

"He damn well better, since I just went against every voter in my constituency."

"Worry not. I'm sure that he'll secure your future in this city. For now, continue to work for the greater good of your continent."

"The continent?" Eachann scoffed. "I don't give two shits about Andalon."

"Neither do we, Governor."

The politician continued to stare down at the trapped Pescari as he mentally calculated the cost of repairs to the district. The funds, of course, would funnel through his city contracts and into his own pocket. With or without the refugees, Cassus Eachann was the wealthiest man in Weston.

# Chapter Twenty-One

Hester pulled at the hooded cloak. She made certain to completely hide her face. This part of Fjorik was unsavory and darkness emboldened dangerous shadows. She would not have come at night, except to maintain secrecy, but so far only eyes had followed her through the streets. With relief she arrived at the tiny cottage near the end of the docks.

She raised an unsteady fist to the wooden planks and knocked, ignoring the nerves that wrenched her belly into knots. The cuts on her back burned as she pounded on the door and she flinched from the pain with every strike. *Why aren't they healing more quickly,* she wondered, *what else did he do to me?* Her unanswered knock fueled anxiety and her impatient eyes scanned the shadows.

Panic raised her hand a second time, and she rapped louder and more violently until a face peeked from a single fogged windowpane. Hester pulled back her hood and the person ducked out of sight. A few heartbeats later the door slowly opened. She pushed past the young woman and searched her memory for her name. "Is she here, Gretchen?" She looked around the shabby interior and peered into the single bedroom in the back.

"No, My Lady." The tawny haired girl shook her head with eyes glued to the floor, refusing to look at Hester. "She's due back soon, though."

"Then I'll wait." Two chairs sat around a small table next to the stove. She longingly eyed them, wishing that she could sit and cursing the pain that sitting would cause. The woman and the girl stood like that for several awkward minutes until Hester finally cleared her throat. "Go boil some water, girl. I'd like some tea."

"We don't have tea, My Lady." The girl's eyes never left the floor as she spoke, hiding behind her locks of hair as if she could disappear behind them.

"Herbs, then. I'm in pain and need something to numb my skin."

Gretchen shook her head to the contrary, hair flying about as she did. Her voice was meek and tiny when she responded, "I can't give you anything for pain, My Lady."

"Don't be silly, of course you can." Hester eyed her with curiosity. "You conjured something before."

"I don't have anything to give you that won't affect the baby in your womb."

Hester stared back in shock. She opened her mouth to chastise the girl, but fear held her tongue. *What if she's right,* she wondered. But then she remembered the broken vial and the elixir soaked into the rug of her chambers. *Surely, it's too soon to know,* she reasoned.

Just then, the door to the cottage blew inward, startling the queen and breaking her gaze from the odd child. A figure entered and locked the door before setting a basket of herbs and vials on the tiny table. The woman removed her coat and hung it delicately on a hook. With a sigh she collapsed onto one of the empty chairs. No one spoke, they only stared, the older women at each other and Gretchen at the ground. Finally, the witch pointed at the chair across from her.

Hester responded, "I can't sit, Delilah. I'm in too much pain."

"What did he do to you?"

"He carved me up like one of his whores. I never thought he'd do it to me, but he finally did."

"Why would you be different, Hester? He's a dangerous monster."

"He only marks his property, and, until now, he saw me as something else. My family's wealth finances his luxuries and I've kept this kingdom running since he took it over. I've been too valuable."

Delilah nodded along as she listened. "But no longer? What changed?"

"He's raiding again. Broke the peace with the Esterlings and plans to use their own steel against them."

"That makes no sense. The Falconers would destroy his ships."

"There's something different about him, Delilah. He's changed and become something darker and more dangerous."

The older woman absorbed the words, listening intently and nodding. "I saw him take much of the fleet when he left last week. Where did he go?"

"I think to Diaph. Braen raided it in the fall and left it vulnerable. Skander's angry with Marcus Esterling for breaking a deal and stealing his gold. He wants to pour salt on a wound that he was too weak to have inflicted himself."

"My coven sister is there, in Diaph. I'll need to get word to her to flee." Delilah turned to the girl standing in the middle of the room. "Gretchen, boil some herbs to dull her pain."

The girl shook her head and refused to move. "She can't have them. She's with child."

"Is this true?" The older woman's eyes shot back at Hester with alarm. "What about the elixir I gave you?"

"He knocked me out and had his way with me. Somehow he found the bottle and smashed it against the wall."

"When was this?"

"Two weeks ago."

Delilah stood, suddenly appearing less tired than before. "Why didn't you come to me then?"

"I couldn't walk. I've been in bed with my chambermaid tending my wounds. I sent her to fetch you, but she said you were away."

The woman's eyes shot again to the girl. "Gretchen, did a woman come from the palace?" Hair flew as the girl shook her head. No one came. "Hester, it's too late to stop conception."

Hester's eyes glazed as tears formed. "Then give me something to kill it."

"It won't work." The girl's voice silenced both women. "The child is a powerful emotant of winter. The drug won't kill him."

Hester turned to Delilah. "What's she talking about?"

The old woman's eyes had grown distant and filled with worry. "Take off your clothes so that I can mend your wounds, child. I'll explain as I do."

Hester complied and gingerly peeled off the layers of cloth. Yellow pus oozed from the red and raised edges of the cuts, and the smell filled the room as soon as her clothing dropped to the floor. Delilah followed the lines with her eyes.

"You said that your maid tended your wounds? More likely she caused them to fester at his command." She turned to the girl "Gretchen, I need supplies from my special trunk. This is beyond herbs and natural medicine."

"Which antibiotic do you want?"

"Grab the penicillin and erythromycin ointment. If we don't act fast, she won't survive the voyage."

"Voyage?" Confusion spread across Hester's face. "I'm not going anywhere."

"Yes, you are, dearie. We have to get you to Braen and make him believe this child is his."

"But I've not lain with him in two years. How would that be possible?"

"You'll need to change that, and soon. Lay face down on the bed so that I can apply the ointment. I'll explain everything, but I warn you that the world is not as you believe, Hester. Andalon is only a tiny part of it and there are powers and weapons far greater than swords."

# Chapter Twenty-Two

The night wind carried twenty warships up the Logan River. The vessels made a magnificent sight, low in the water and sleek while loaded with marauders hell bent on plunder. They made good time and their steady pace ensured arrival just after midnight, when the moon would be highest. Eventually the current won the battle against the sails, and the crew oared the rest of the way. Other than the sound of gentle splashing, the night remained silent.

The crisp air compelled topside men to raise their collars as they rowed, but one man ignored the chill as he focused on the prize ahead. The captain of the lead vessel stared straight ahead, nervously fidgeting with his knife and a piece of whale bone, a practice called scrimshaw that many sailors adopted to pass the time. Unlike beautiful carvings and etchings that one would expect from an artist, a closer look as his artwork would have revealed indiscriminate scratches in the ivory bone. He scarcely looked down, except to ensure he did not cut himself by mistake.

"Artur!" Skander Braston called over his shoulder to a bald warrior wielding a two-handed axe.

The First Mate stepped forward. "Yes, Your Highness?"

"Prepare the men. This raid is not like any other they've joined. Diaph is well fortified and there may even be Falconers present."

The man blanched with mouth agape, revealing several missing teeth. With a trembling voice he asked, "Falconers, sire?"

"Yes. My dear brother completed half the work for us by removing the harbor defenses. From dispatches I've seen, the southern wall may even be down completely. But the rest of the guns are intact, and they may turn them on their own city if they get desperate. I want you to handle those."

Artur nodded his understanding, face still troubled by the thought of specters waiting with dark magic. "But the Falconers, sire?"

"I have a plan for them, just worry about the guns." The city walls loomed ahead. To his right a signal flame lit atop a watchtower. *Good. They know we're coming.* After a moment, a second light answered from atop the walls. Soon bells tolled throughout Diaph. "Get them ready. Make preparations for a cannonade to soften our landing." After a pause he added, "And I want the Berserkers out front when we land."

Artur relayed the order to a signalman who lit two torches. The man went into a dance of flame with a series of movements that conveyed both messages. Within seconds, horns of acknowledgement sounded from the other boats. "All ships are ready, sire." Ahead, the city came to life with torches of their own that lit the night sky.

Once his fleet had reached cannon range, Skander gave the order to lift oars. The heavy gunner ships drifted with the current, ambling until their broadsides faced the city. They anchored positions so that the water flowed around the ships. Once in place, the small boats halted as well.

The northern king smiled as he commanded, "Start the bombardment." The signalman resumed his fire dance and soon the big vessels lobbed heavy shot into the harbor and eastern armaments.

Skander stood on the forecastle of *Ice Slayer.* He nodded to Artur who knelt to light a circle of torches around his captain and king. He wanted each crewman on every vessel to witness the power he was about to wield. Above him the clear skies darkened, and storm clouds built into a magnificent storm. The tempest drifted slowly toward Diaph as it grew. Every sailor gasped when the river changed course.

The draft of the Fjorik ships slowly lowered as the current beneath them lessened to a trickle. Ahead, the river seemed to flow into the harbor, flooding the city. Skander focused so intently on directing the path of the water that he nearly lost his grip on the storm above. Lightning flashed and he roared against thunder as he reestablished control. Finally confident that he could maintain both the weather and the river, he allowed his ships to settle into the mud. With a growl he ordered Artur, "Send the Berserkers."

The signalman danced and fifty marauders aboard two ships chanted and swayed. A strong gust on its way to feed the storm carried their crazed song into the night. Faster they chanted until their voices became animalistic and inaudible, a grotesque cacophony of grunts and growls. Skander never turned from the city, but knew that the fighters built their fury by biting their shields and slicing their own skin. Each was locked in an herbal frenzy. With a scream, one of the men had leaped from the deck and onto the soft mud. A heartbeat later the others flooded over the side of their longboats and the Berserkers charged Diaph.

"Now." He growled to Artur who relayed the command. The rest of the soldiers disembarked with more discipline than the first wave, carefully forming a shield wall. Skander, finally confident that he could hold both the storm and the river, joined his force of sixteen hundred soldiers and sounded the charge, "Fjorik! Attack!"

As he and his men ran, his head began to thump. His ears rang but he ignored the pain caused by holding the water in place. He almost lost it when his father's voice boomed in his mind, resonating with the sound of thunder above. *Your brother did not lose a man when he raided this city, yet you will send my most elite fighters to their doom.* Skander tried to ignore the words from the spirit, but he could not. The bound warrior, forbidden from entering the heavenly feast, continued to mock him. *You know nothing about tactics, only killing. This raid will fail, and you will ignite the war that will end our family line.* The king gritted his teeth and pressed forward.

And then a moment of doubt took over. *What if father is right? What if I'm leading us into a war we cannot win?* He missed a step and stumbled, slightly losing his hold on the flowing body of water just ahead. Some of it streamed down the riverbed toward his advance, but he quickly recovered both his footing and his link.

*Of course I'm correct, Skander. I tried to teach my sons to be generals and kings as well as fighters, but you never listened. You were so convinced that you were smarter that you ignored the advice of experience. Now you're doomed to die a failure.* Skander roared his defiance into the night.

By the time they reached the harbor, the Berserkers had cleared the front line. Many bled or were pierced by arrows, but they fought on with exuberance, pressing the remaining defenders where the former wall had stood. Skander smiled as he spied the small cannons the city had gathered for protection. Their big guns were destroyed by Braen and these had no range on his attack. Moreover, the flooding water backed them toward higher ground.

Once Fjorik troops were in place, he released his hold on the river and allowed it to flow naturally. The pressure in his head eased instantly and the voice of his father fell silent, helping him to scan the battlefield with clarity. Movement among the enemy forces caught his attention. Three men in feathered hoods paced casually behind the defenders. Almost immediately, a strong gust of wind blew toward the Berserkers, forming a cyclone that drew strength from the storm above. The tornado swirled as it ripped at the elite force before spitting them out. In the blink of an eye, his front line was gone.

Skander seethed as he reached into the storm. He could feel the pulse of it and found the particles in the clouds. His rage shook these until the storm intensified, charging the sky and igniting it with white flashes of lightning. And then he knew what power he truly held. He poured hatred for his brother and father into the storm just as the first volley of grapeshot ripped through his men. Unfazed, he connected fully with the storm, carving the cloud with his mind and swirling the ice within. His electric scrimshaw glowed against the clouds.

Everyone on both sides of the fight paused to stare. Even the Falconers marveled at the intricate swirls and unmistakable sigil of House Braston. The sabre cat came to life and ripped a wolf to pieces above the city while portions of the enemy ranks broke. Skander cackled as men threw down weapons, fleeing toward the northern gate. Their exit left the Falconers alone, trying to rally to hold the rest in line. And then the baby cried.

*No,* Skander thought. *Not now.* He hated the wail of the infant. Ever since he had raided Atarax he carried the infant inside, unable to extinguish the agonizing cries. Usually they came at nighttime, keeping him awake and unable to rest. *But why now?* He watched as more of his men fell and he realized that the night would not be won without considerable loss.

The northern king screamed into the night, his voice drowning out the wailing for just a brief second. In that moment he flooded hatred for Hester into the swirling clouds above, remembering the rage he had felt when he discovered her elixir in the nightstand. *No wonder she has never whelped a child. In two years, my seed should have taken hold and ensured an heir, but the witch had blocked conception with her potions.*

He poured all of his pain into the storm and watched as it burst into a white ball of lightning. The Falconers exploded on the ground and men flew in all directions around them. He bellowed his command and sent his warriors toward victory with a single word, "Charge!" They pressed, overwhelmed the defenders, and gave no quarter to prisoners. The city was his.

After the killing came the pillaging. The storm above had dissipated rapidly, but the tempest on the ground raged for hours until daybreak. Skander watched his men load the spoils onto the ships with disinterest, his mind already focused on his next move. He enjoyed the moment of clear headedness, free from the voices and wails. He heard a throat clear behind him. "What is it, Artur?"

"Sire, we found something... unusual."

Skander raised an eyebrow. "Weapons?"

"No, Your Highness. The armory had already been looted before we arrived. They had little in the way of weapons."

"Then what is it that gave you a need to interrupt my thoughts?" *Especially when they are finally only my own.*

"You need to come and see for yourself. We think it's the roost of the Falconers."

Suddenly curious, he allowed his friend to lead him to a stone building, simple and free of adornment. The wooden doors had been battered by his men and lay discarded on the ground. Once inside, he noticed a strange overhead glow in the ceiling. He climbed onto a table and touched the light, recoiling from the heat within. "How do they work?"

"We don't know."

"Is this what you brought me to see?"

"No, My Lord. In here, please."

They passed through several doorways until they reached a room full of hundreds of stone slabs. People of all ages lay atop each one, stripped of clothing and with strange tubes running in and out of their bodies. He paused next to one, a man of no more than twenty summers with long blonde hair and beard. He followed the tubing to a small glass bottle with black fluid dripping into a pool within. He examined the sleeping form and watched the eyes flicker as if in a dream. Shrugging, he ripped the tubes from the man. Nothing happened.

Skander noticed that Artur examined the form of a woman on the next table. "Have all of the fun that you want, just make sure you kill them when you're finished." A gasp from the man on the table snapped his attention, just in time for the body to sit up with eyes open and mouth sucking breath. "What in the hells?"

The man raised his hands and a blast of air shot toward Skander, sending him flying across the room and into the wall. Artur moved in with his ax but stopped when his king yelled, "Wait!"

The man stared at Skander with confusion in his eyes. "Where am I?"

"Diaph. What do you last remember?"

"I was playing in the field when Mommy called me in." Tears filled his eyes, childlike and scared. "I was making the leaves blow around. Then a falcon landed beside me and the man came."

Skander rushed over, placing a hand on his shoulder and feigning compassion. "What is your name?"

"Brion."

*His mind is of a child,* the northern king mused. With kindness in his voice he asked, "Brion, how long have you been here?"

The child in a man's body looked around, taking in the other sleeping forms. In a trembling voice he answered, "I don't know."

"How old are you, Brion?"

"Ten summers at harvest, sir."

A wide grin covered Skander's face when he turned to Artur. "Wake them and treat them well. Find them clothing and get them aboard the ships immediately." When his friend nodded understanding he added, "Treat them like honored guests and ensure the others do as well." He paused, then said, "Before we leave, I want the entire city burned to the ground. Leave nothing standing, do you understand?"

Artur responded, "Yes, sire. But what does it mean?"

"It means that we just won this war."

# Chapter Twenty-Three

Fatwana stared at the girl sitting across from her. The terrorist gave nothing away with her expression and said little since the train station. The antique weapon in the girl's hand added to her sinister appearance and Fatwana hoped that it was too old to function. She had never seen one in person, since the possession of anything designed to kill a human had been outlawed more than a thousand years before. Only the police squads and the private army of the Council carried weapons.

"You can put that away now." She spoke with a coolness that cloaked her nerves. "I'm not stupid enough to run away."

"You're not my prisoner, Fatwana." The girl flashed a smile, but her lips quickly settled into a worried fret.

"Then why did you point that at me?"

"We didn't have time to argue."

"Argue? About what?" Fatwana asked casually.

"About coming back with me to headquarters."

"This isn't going as I had planned." Fatwana looked around the interior of the van.

"Exactly. This meeting is on our terms."

With eyes darting back to the gun, Fatwana asked, "Can you please put that away? It's making me nervous."

The girls shrugged and holstered the weapon inside her jacket. "Since we're almost there, I suppose I should introduce myself." She outstretched her hand, "I'm Cassidy." Fatwana took it in greeting, fighting against the panic within.

Soon the vehicle slowed and eventually came to a stop. Fatwana heard doors slam and then the rear of the vehicle opened, revealing two men in coveralls. They were from the metalworks sector, judging by the dark green they wore. From their surroundings she intuitively knew that she was not in an actual factory. The warehouse was empty except for some crates stacked orderly against the far wall. As they walked by, she saw that these were stamped Pots or Pans. "Where exactly is headquarters?"

"That isn't for me to say. If the Dragon wants you to know then he will tell you."

"The Dragon?"

"The Dragon is our deliverance from the Council." Fatwana detected reverence in the way the girl spoke of her leader. "He's been away many years and only recently returned to lead our cause."

"Away to where?"

"Why, Andalon, of course!" Cassidy almost seemed to laugh when she spoke. "He's returned to destroy the system that keeps the people of both Astia and Andalon enslaved."

"So, the Society truly are revolutionaries?" She clutched the storage device tightly in her hand. *What am I doing involved in a revolution? I only wanted to stop the farming of the Andalonians.*

"Not exactly," the girl answered while an elevator opened on the wall. The women entered first followed by the men. "But the Dragon will explain."

Cassidy slid a panel aside and inserted a key. With a turn the car descended, going the opposite direction from the options on the display. When they reached the bottom, the doors opened to reveal a large cave bustling with activity.

Cassidy led her onward. It grew obvious that the lead sister's first impression was wrong. *This is one of the lost cities,* she marveled, *buried under centuries of warfare and volcanic ash.* Hundreds of people hurried about their tasks. Fatwana first noticed their clothing, brightly colored crimson. Their dress contrasted sharply with the bland coveralls worn by the people walking the streets above.

She asked, "Everyone here is part of the Society?"

"Yes. You called us revolutionaries but we're more than that. We are truly a society with laws and government. We even have our own army. We crave freedom for ourselves and the Andalonians. We hope to live peacefully beside them after we remake the world without the Council."

"How do you know that's even possible? They're chaotic and their powers stem from unstable emotions."

"While you hide away in your oracle trying to see things from above, we're busy placing agents on the ground across all continents. We've been grooming them for centuries, and we're ready to rise together."

"Is that how my brother reached Andalon? Is that what he does there?"

"I don't know your brother. But I assume that he's either making contacts to aid our war against the Council or he's supporting those who do. We have hundreds of agents spread out among every city."

"Tell me more about the Dragon."

"You'll meet him soon enough." Cassidy's response held a finality that abruptly ended the conversation.

Sounds of industry clanged and hissed around them as they walked. Fatwana scanned the factories, taking notice of the large fans lifting dark smoke to the surface. Here and there men loaded crates into trucks, and the lead sister tried to peer into one as they passed. They were all tightly closed or covered with tarps. Her curiosity finally won out and she asked, "What are you producing down here that you have to hide it from The Council?"

Cassidy retorted, "That's for the Dragon to share if he chooses."

The women walked in silence the rest of the way and finally approached a stone building of gothic architecture. The cobblestone street leading to the entrance curved around a circular fountain, revealing a sight unlike any Fatwana had ever seen.

She could not believe her eyes. Although the structure was heavily damaged and the dome had been buried beneath layers of dirt and ash, the Society had excavated the entire entrance. The high archway was accented by six tall pillars on each side. Carved religious statues adorned the massive building, depicting figures whose names were long lost to civilization. The massive wooden doors were mostly preserved and hung on their hinges, useless except as adornment.

The inside of the structure was far more beautiful. No light shone through the stained glass windows, but the paintings held as much color as the day the artist lay brush to stone. Above the golden altar, one painting prominently stood above the others. Several women adorned in robes knelt before the corpse of a man. He was stripped to the waist and nailed to crossed wooden stakes with arms outstretched to his sides. Fatwana could almost hear the women wail and pray to the winged spirits adorning the other artwork.

"This is the den of the Dragon, Fatwana." She led the sister down a long walkway between rows of wooden benches.

At the foot of the altar sat a regal man with a welcoming smile and jovial eyes set under a head of fiery red hair. He looked to be in his early forties, close to her own age, and she could not help but find him beautiful. Prying her eyes and regaining her composure, she asked, "So, you're the Dragon?"

"I've been called that name, among others." His green eyes twinkled at a private joke as he spoke. He waved his hands at the magnificent house of worship. "Welcome to my home."

"It's marvelous. Fifteenth century Europe?"

He nodded. "Yes. And eighteenth and twentieth centuries as well. Our ancestors enjoyed destroying masterpieces in their pursuit of redefining their identity. But they missed this one."

"Like they haven't found you?"

"This is only one of our bases of operation. We've lain low and avoided drawing their attention until now. We felt that it was best to remain as ghosts until the prophecy was fulfilled."

"Are you The Destroyer?"

The Dragon's laughter came honest and from deep inside. "In a way we all are, Fatwana."

"Why are you so focused on destroying the power of the Council? The people of Astia are content."

His demeanor changed at her question, growing suddenly serious. "The people of Astia are sheep, blindly giving their lives for their rich and spoiled masters." The fire in his eyes seared Fatwana's nerves as he spoke. "The Council has enslaved all mankind. They lock their subjects in wards and communes, unable to consume what they produce for the state while the elite and leaders eat the fat."

"And you'd rather feed the fat to the people? How do you know they won't devour each other?"

"For a time in our history most of mankind lived free of tyranny," he responded, "and we can do so again."

"Some but not all, and even those living under democracy couldn't preserve it. After a while they gave up self-rule in favor of global government."

"No, Fatwana, they did not. Nothing was given freely. It was stolen by each generation under the guise of social reform." He pointed a finger toward the ceiling. "The people up there are the result of generational apathy. They are no more than children living without purpose."

She protested, "Their purpose is to feed the collective."

"Exactly. The purpose that fed our ancestors was innovation. Do you realize how much technology we've lost since the Great Eruption?"

Of course she did. Her thoughts returned to the message from Samani and of the scores of people strapped to stone slabs. In a trembling voice she responded, "Even if you overthrow the council, you will have to do something about the people across the sea. Surely you won't release them. The technology we do have is reliant upon the oracles. Besides, the prophecies describe total annihilation of our continent."

"Not our continent, Fatwana, our culture. Our way of life."

"That is one interpretation."

"The Society will free all who are enslaved and create a new world that is free of tyranny."

"The people of Andalon deserve freedom, but they're dangerous. How can we help them without destroying the world with their powers? We can't give them the gift of unfettered freedom."

The Dragon's eyes turned dangerous and cool. "They're humans, not cattle. Would you kill a cow for its ability to produce milk?"

"I wouldn't give it weapons with which to destroy our world."

"Our ancestors enslaved the world with idealism. They meant well but lived so comfortably that they forgot the value of adversity. Without the right pinch of salt, mankind would never have developed civilizations. Have you never wondered why the first cities weren't founded on tropical islands?"

"No."

"It was because life there was too easy. When life is too easy you don't care about developing literature or writing. The same goes for a life that's too difficult. If you're constantly worried about food supplies or shelter you never invent wheels or mathematics."

"What are you saying? That our ancestors grew too complacent?"

"Exactly. They were too accustomed to easy lives and lost everything when the caldera erupted. Their world warmed to the point that the oceans flooded their cities and they grew desperate. When the eruption launched their weapons, every other nation responded in kind, killing over eighty percent of the world's population. For a time, they lost the knowledge to rebuild their own technology, and what we have today is patchwork at best."

"I know the history, tell me what it has to do with the people of Andalon?"

"They're the master race and deserve to rule over mankind, Fatwana."

Unable to hide her shock she raised her hand to her mouth. "I've heard that before."

"Yes. You have. Your brother taught that to me. They were engineered before the collapse of civilization and brought to life by a fledgling society, one desperate to replace their satellites and computers. Our ancestors made improvements to the human mind."

"But those experiments failed."

"Quite the opposite. They were highly successful and produced foresight and manipulation over the elements. But many of the powers terrified the Council because they threatened their control over the subjugated citizens. They seeded the three unpopulated continents with their laboratory rats, culling out the undesired traits and farming the rest for use by the covens."

"And enslaving oracles through a promise of transcending to the afterlife."

"That is correct, Fatwana." The Dragon returned a smile to his face, laughing off the seriousness he once held. "Alas, that's what governments do. They make empty promises that convince blind followers to give up their free will in exchange for fairytales like equality and prosperity for all."

He leaned back in his chair and poured from a bottle of wine. Fatwana recognized the numbers seven, five, and four on the label, having seen them before in Chancellor Jakata's office. "What's your ultimate goal?"

"At some time before the Astian people were corralled into communes and complexes, they were convinced to give up their ability to think and defend for themselves. Overthrowing the Council is our only avenue. Then we will forge a new world that blends cultures as well as bloodlines."

Fatwana stared deep into the man's fiery eyes, trying but failing to find his true intent. This man was godlike; so confident and arrogant. "And who is better to lead both the Andalonians and the Astians but you?"

He answered with a wink and a tip of his glass. After a moment he spoke again. "You brought the information we requested?"

"I did." She pulled a storage device from the hidden pouch in her robes and handed it over. "Twelve hundred years of Ka'ash'mael prophecies."

"Twelve hundred?" Cassidy interrupted with shock in her voice. "But Andalon is only a little over eight hundred years old."

Fatwana nodded agreement. "This version of Andalon is."

"I don't understand."

The Dragon answered, "The council has reset Andalon three times and the Southern Continent twice."

"Reset?" The Society agent's confusion grew.

"Revolutions and unrest are common in Andalon and oftentimes appropriate to control population and technological advance." Fatwana could not keep the sadness out of her voice as she spoke. "But occasionally the situation gets out of control when the powers awaken at a quicker pace."

"Like now, due to renewed volcanic activity." The Dragon added.

The lead sister nodded. "Like now. When that occurs the Falconers and Jaguars fall behind in their duties of finding and controlling the latents before they can fully work their emotant powers."

The Dragon added, "When they can no longer work effectively from behind the scenes, the council steps in. They send military to cleanse cities in such a way that resembles a natural disaster."

Fatwana agreed, "And sometimes they completely wipe out populations and reseed the continent."

Cassidy calculated. "The last time was eight hundred years ago?"

"Yes. The Andalonians have never advanced this far or this quickly, and wouldn't have, if the Society hadn't been helping them along for the past fifty years." The Dragon took another long sip of the wine and looked at the glass. "Damn this is a fine vintage."

"How much have you interfered?" The question came from Fatwana.

"Helped," the man corrected, "not interfered. About thirty years ago our agents stirred up the Pescari war. The Council couldn't let the Esterlings lose, so they provided cannons and black powder to the continent. Our sources now tell us that a group of Andalonian revolutionaries have invented rifled firearms."

Horror struck Fatwana as she remembered the industrial activity in the underground city. "You plan to give them advanced weaponry? They'll destroy us all as prophesied!"

"Of course not! I plan to intercept the Astian soldiers sent to reset the continent. I'll take their weaponry for us and secure our own uprising." He took another sip. "As far as the prophecy goes, that's why we needed your records. We need to know just exactly how he will bring the destruction when the time comes.

"Modern weaponry combined with their powers? Isn't that obvious?"

"No. I think that the event will be much more destructive and magnificent than your imagination allows." He leaned in close and added, "And that is precisely why I need your prophecies. So that we can stop him in the act."

Fatwana felt her heart sink and her stomach churn. "You're insane to believe that you can stop the prophecy or even control the fate of the destroyer."

The Dragon chuckled and gestured around the once holy place of worship that surrounded them. "Except for the fact that there is no fate, only free will. Nothing is predetermined, Fatwana, and soon we will walk beside the true gods, those designed by mankind."

Terror gripped the lead sister, suddenly aware that she knew too much of The Society's revolutionary plans. "I must go. I need to return to answer The Council's summons."

The Dragon slowly shook his head. "No, I'm afraid that you won't. I need you to aid your brother in his work and to ensure that he doesn't fail." He took a final swig from his glass. "You have work to do in Andalon."

# Chapter Twenty-Four

It was noon before Flaya returned to the windmill. She was out of breath from running nearly the entire way and startled Taros when she barged through the door. He sat up quickly with his knife drawn. "What is it?"

"There was trouble in Weston last night."

His eyes narrowed with suspicion. "What kind of trouble?" In his mind he imagined the worst kind.

She leaned against the doorway as she spoke between deep breaths. "A riot broke out in the Pescari district. Your uncle led warriors against the soldiers and drove them out."

"I'm sure that he had reason to do so."

"Taros..." She fell to her knees, hands on her stomach.

He ran to her, kneeling down with both hands on her shoulders. "What is it, Flaya? Are you well?"

"Yes, just a cramp from running." She lied. The pain was unbearable and felt more like her heavy womb ripped from within. She had missed her monthly and, although she hadn't seen any morning sickness, her body had already changed. Her nipples were hard and both breasts throbbed with pain from the swelling. *I won't be able to hide the baby for long,* she thought. "Taros, there is more that you need to know about Teot." She felt him pull back with worry. His uncle was his only family.

"What about him?"

"Felicima has blessed him as well. He wields her power just as you."

His face paled, then he breathed out relief. "Then I'm really not a god?"

"No. You're a man, but I believe that you are both chosen by her to deal out justice and punish those who are prideful and threaten her people."

"Who else knows?"

"At first only I, but I'm sure that my grandfather will work it out soon if he hasn't already."

"Daska." Hatred hissed as he spoke the name aloud.

Flaya felt that it was finally time to reveal the truth. "My grandfather opposes you. He speaks of a legend passed down through the time, back when the Falconers still visited our villages and before we settled on the Steppes of Cinder."

"What is the legend?"

"It was prophesied that a man would steal Felicima's power and wield it as his own, eventually destroying his own people. Taros, he thinks that's what you've been doing."

Realization settled in his eyes. "And if he knows that my uncle wields it, he likely sees him as Felicima's savior of our people. He will proclaim him the true shappan?"

"I'm afraid so."

"My uncle will not challenge me with Shapalote. He's loyal to me."

"Daska has been telling him lies, Taros. We don't know how much of them he believes."

"Flaya?" Taros sat back with eyes on the floor.

"Yes, My Love?"

"Are you really?"

"Am I really what?"

"Are you really My Love?" His voice was steady with cruel undertones. "Why have you been coming to me, every night for all of these weeks?" He steadied himself for her reply, remembering the rush of uncontrollable power the last time he asked a similar question. "Flaya, why did you come to me and convince me to lie with you?"

"At first I came at my grandfather's insistence. He has wanted us paired so that he can keep eyes on you."

"So, you never loved me, either?" He flinched at the memory of acrid burning flesh and hair as he poured his anger into Sarai. *I never meant to harm her.*

"I've loved you since before, Taros."

Hope and doubt dueled in Taros' mind. "Before what?"

"Before Cornin shunned your mother after your father fell to him in Shapalote. Do you remember? We were young, but we used to play together."

"No. I don't remember much at all before the day he gutted my father alive. He left him for the vultures and didn't even give him a proper funeral. He left him on that hill for an entire year until the animals and insects had picked him clean. Only then were we allowed to cast his remains into the fumarole. But it was too late for him to rejoin Felicima."

"I remember." She moved to his side and held him. "I loved you even then, Taros, but my grandfather forbade me from visiting you with the shunned, despite that you chose to live among them to be near Lynette."

He lifted his eyes to meet hers. "You speak the truth?"

"Yes. That's why I was so jealous of the Westonese girl. She touched and teased you and I watched her set up your heart to break." Her cheeks darkened when she added, "When he finally told me to find you and to bear your child, I did so gladly, My Love." His eyes turned to her stomach and she nodded. "Yes. Feel." She gently grabbed his hand and placed it low across her womb. "It is yours, Taros."

"You are with child? My child?"

"Yes." They cried together for several minutes. Him with joy and she with fear that the child would look more like the city guard.

# Chapter Twenty-Five

Campton Shol watched the laborers wading the river. The stones would take years to completely clear, but the engineers suggested that flow could be returned within a few months. In the meantime, they would have to dig out and relocate the ships one by one to other ports; a monumental task when they were required immediately. For the first time since his father had tasked him with securing Andalon, Shol realized the complexity of his situation.

"We have word from Weston that will please you, My Lord."

Campton turned as Kestral approached. "It's about time you bring positive tidings. It seems that you and your rookery have done nothing but lose until now." He pointed down at the collapsed bridge and asked, "Children did this?"

"Yes. We only expected one emotant with affinity for water. Once we had him secured, a second powerful spring emotant revealed her presence. She caught us unawares and collapsed the bridge to secure their escape. They then ran eastward into the forest."

Shol shook his head in frustration, biting back words of condemnation. "What word do you bring?""Cassus Eachann reports from Weston. The trap is set for the summer emotant and we shall have him in custody soon."

"The trap is set?" Shol's cheeks danced with anger and he responded with a raised voice, "This news means nothing! So far, we've lost Falconers every time we've attempted to capture or kill a pure emotant. I want results, not optimistic prognostication!"

Kestral nodded then added, "He secured most of the Pescari in a single location within the city and contained the rest in underground mines. He's planning to purge the continent of fire emotants with a swift genocide once the boy is dealt with."

Shol considered the news. "Boys and girls? It seems that our power over this continent is collapsing because of the acts of children. It's bad enough that Braston has control over those you had collected in Diaph. Speaking of Diaph, did your scouts figure out why we've had no word in a week? What is the status of the harbor repairs?"

"The city has been completely razed, My Lord. Northern Raiders attacked during the full moon and left it in ruins."

"Razed?" The administrator could not contain his shock. "How did they defeat our Falconers?"

"We do not know. The marauders burned the husks, so we were not able to recover my brothers and sisters."

"What about the Rookery?"

"Burned as well."

"That will significantly impact my father's quotas." Grave concern crept in, sending Campton's heart racing. "If we cannot turn these losses around very quickly then Chancellor Jakata will surely reset this factory."

"The southern ground is finally green enough for our army to march on Eskera. They departed yesterday at dawn."

"They cannot fail, my old friend. They must capture and kill Robert Esterling."

"We've set a trap for him as well. He and Braston will be destroyed together very soon."

"You'd better be right, Kestral." Lord Shol stood silently, watching the workers for some time before speaking again, "Did you say that the children traveled east when they left?"

"Yes, My Lord."

"Prepare ten thousand troops and a full contingent of Falconers. They're marching toward Estowen's Landing in the morning."

"Estowen's Landing? But that city has long been abandoned."

"I don't believe it remains so."

Rain soaked the ground during the night, and the chill in the air worked its way into Shon's joints. *I'm getting too old for the forest,* he thought over the popping sounds in his knees and the crackle in his hip. He could have remained in Estowen's Landing and awaited Marque's scouting report, but he had grown bored from inaction and decided to meet his friend along the road. He had hoped the morning walk would relax his mind.

He rubbed his shoulder as he made his way down the trail, massaging out stiffness from an old war wound. More than a decade before, he had taken an axe in the chest while defending Brentwood from marauders. Mornings like this reminded his wound that it never properly healed. He reached to his hip and touched the sharp blade of that very axe, thrown by none other than Braen Braston.

When he formally met the man several months before, Wembley felt outrage that his niece had aligned with the demon from the north. But his attitude had changed over time. Braston had charisma, a dangerous trait in a leader, but he had proven that he also led with compassion. Like Shon, he built bonds with the men and women who followed him and genuinely cared about empowering others around him. Their agreement was the reason that his outlaw band sat idle through the spring, instead of harassing Imperial patrols as they did before winter.

The two men had agreed to align their forces toward a common goal. Together they had raided Diaph and conquered Pirate's Cove, a task that had before been viewed as impossible. Since the attacks, his outlaw band had grown into an army of three thousand fighting men, each trained on Sippen Yurik's rifles. Their ability to move silently through the forest and hide in plain sight made each man more dangerous than a hundred Imperial soldiers.

He paused in the roadway, listening to the Black Forest of Diaph and detecting a subtle change in the insect songs. He pulled out his tobacco pouch and placed a plug between his cheek and gums. Speaking into the woods he said, "Good Morning, Marque."

Abruptly twenty men rose from the ferns surrounding him, including his jovial friend. "Aye, a good morning indeed, Boss." Marque strode over and the two grasped forearms.

"What news do you bring?"

"There's a large group of refugees fleeing Diaph. They're moving south toward Middleton instead of making the trip westward to Eston, and that's confounded our scouts."

Shon raised his eyebrow at the mention of the city. "Why are they fleeing Diaph in the first place? We left it mostly intact and they had enough food to survive winter."

"They've left because there's nothing left but ashes and stone, Boss." Marque waited for Wembley's shocked expression. Knowing that he had his full attention he continued, "A few days ago, raiders from Fjorik attacked in force. They looted and pillaged then set every building aflame."

"How big is the group of refugees?"

"Several hundred. Mostly women and children, but a few men of fighting age walk with them."

"We can accommodate them in The Landing. Send word that we have food and warm shelter." Shon shared his tobacco pouch with his friend.

"I already did. I knew you'd want that, so I left a few guides camped along the roadway." Marque paused to load his lip then continued. "How many more emotants have shown up? We didn't see any along the roads toward Eston."

"So far only a few out of Middleton. I don't think our system is working."

"I'd give it more time, Boss. The Falconers will be cracking down as more awakenings occur, and that will scare those in hiding toward us."

"Aye, but we're running out of time. With those on loan from Braston we have trained twenty to fight alongside our troops."

Marque flashed a hand signal to his men who immediately faded back into the underbrush of the forest. Once alone he addressed his leader, "When do we get to fight again, Shon? The men are restless, they just aren't telling you."

"Soon. Braston said to wait and so we wait."

"But these are your men, Boss. They follow you and none of us trust the Northman."

"I understand but I gave my word that we'd wait. With his ships and our army, we're better as a team." He grasped his friend's shoulder and pulled him into a close embrace. "Let the men know that I share their concerns about Braston. But Eusari is one of us, and he has her loyalty. Once we drive out the Esterlings and their Falconers we can reconsider our alliance if need be."

"Aye, Boss. I'll spread the word."

Shon watched Marque disappear into the forest. After he had gone, the former constable spit dark tobacco juice onto the road. *I'm itching for a fight as well, My Friend.*

# Chapter Twenty-Six

Robert Esterling watched from the window of the keep. The sunrise painted the sky deep shades of red and orange that met the blue with a layer of pink. The marshes beneath the eastern glow reflected the magnificent colors and almost reminded him of the burning steppes he had witnessed in Weston. But this glow signified a different kind of threat. An army loomed across the beautiful horizon.

He had spent his entire life agonizing over and training for the trials required to assume the throne, but the past few months proved a tougher endurance test than any the council could impose. His friend and father, Maximus Reeves, constantly reminded him that life is the best teacher. So far, he had passed every test, but not without his share of defeats. After the past few months, he had swallowed more than enough humility and came away each time with more wisdom. He no longer worried over the trials and did not need them to prove that he was fit to rule. He only needed to defeat his brother.

But for a moment the young king yearned for freedom from his obligations. Part of him wanted to get away from the war with his brother, to take Sarai away to the coast for some much-needed rest and relaxation. They hadn't had a moment to themselves since their marriage ceremony, and a honeymoon would lighten both their spirits. But responsibility is the price of adulthood and his debt to the kingdom grew every day.

"Robert." Max's gruff voice interrupted his thoughts and so he put them aside for later.

"I saw riders pressing their steeds hard from the east. I assume they're our scouts. What's the report?"

"Aye. The army's a few days out and it's worse than we feared."

"How many Falconers?" The last time he fought his brother's troops they had underestimated him and sent ten. He had barely won then, but had since grown stronger and more familiar with his powers. Despite his newfound confidence, any more than ten would be worrisome.

"At least twenty by early count. But they're driving ten covered wagons and we have no idea how many more lurk within. I think it's a trap and should expect thirty or forty." Max's face wore a mask of worry that he normally wouldn't show to the world. The past few months had worn on everyone around Robert.

"What do you think we should do? We can't flee, they'd catch us in the open field. We can't leave by boat; we don't have enough to load the troops and we'd never make it past the blockade."

"Lourdes and I shared the same thoughts. If it came to this, we agreed that you need allies."

He of course meant Braston. "No. Absolutely not. We can't trust a pirate." Robert walked to a large table in the center of the room and stared at his charts, hoping to find a way out of the fight or toward victory.

Max put his hand on the boy's shoulder and spoke gently. "Sometimes we have to face that we can neither win nor retreat without help, Son. You're in that spot now. Reach out to Braen. He has ships and, if Horslei is telling the truth, he has weapons that can destroy the blockade and get us out this corner."

"He also has emotants who can help us fight, Max, but at what cost? Mercenaries always cost you more than you're willing to pay. What's his price to win this fight for me?"

"You need to ask him that question, Robert."

A knock at the door caused both men to turn. Captain Titus entered with a grave expression and dire news. Robert put on his regality and stood tall when he asked, "What is it, Titus? More news from the scouts?"

"No, your highness. One of your newly recruited naval officers reported a personal matter that requires your attention."

Max interrupted, "If it doesn't affect the coming fight then it needs to wait. The king can't handle personal conflicts right now."

"General, with respect I wouldn't have brought it to you both if it wasn't relevant."

Robert's interest piqued. "Go on, Titus. What's the grievance?"

"Captain Matthieu Dominique's personal manor was broken into. His ship's logs and ledgers were stolen and his son, well..."

"What about his son?"

"His throat was slit while sitting in a chair. The coroner believes that the wounds were made by cutlasses. Dual wielded cutlasses, sire."

Robert and Max shot each other a look and clearly shared a thought. Max asked, "Dominique was formerly of The Cove's service, wasn't he?" Titus nodded. "And two men from The Cove recently arrived."

Robert nodded, "And both wield dual cutlasses."

Titus added, "There's one more thing. The boy did not struggle. It appears that he was tied up, based on the posture of the body when it was found."

Max raised an eyebrow. "What do you mean, 'appears,' was he tied or not?"

"There were neither ropes nor marks to signify that he was bound by traditional bindings, sir."

Realization hit Robert in the gut. "Air. He was bound by air. Unless another emotant is in the city, it was either me or Marita who bound him. Titus, arrest Horslei and Pogue and bring them before me immediately."

"Aye, sir. And the girl? What are your wishes for her?"

"Take her to Sarai. Don't make her feel afraid in case you trigger her magic. Let Sarai meet with her privately, but keep guards close by just in case." To Max he added, "You still want me to trust Braston?"

Alec Pogue wore chains for the first time in his life. He stared down at the iron bracelets, marveling how many times he had clamped them on other men when he was on the other side of the law. Oddly, they affected him less than he had expected, but he had grown apathetic to many situations since he lost Mattie. His only anxiety at the moment was his desire to find her and the irons further slowed that progress.

"Can we get things moving? I've business to attend to."

Three high ranking military officers stared down. The oldest was completely gray and the hard sort, battle worn and surprisingly fit for his age. "Answer our questions and you can get on with it."

"I claim diplomatic immunity. I operate under a letter of marque signed by the guild and council of The Cove. Any crimes you accuse me of are sanctioned and you have a duty to release me under their authority."

The middle-aged general stared him down with cold eyes as he spoke, "Cold blooded murder isn't protected, Captain Pogue."

"General Reeves, I presume? I assure you that I've committed no such crime." His thoughts immediately shot to Marita. He could still visualize the moment when the blades split the skin and spilled the boy's life. *Surely, they won't prosecute a child.*

"Someone did, and they used your blades." Reeves watched him curiously.

*Watching for a lie, General? I know your methods because I interrogate men for a living.* "If you've proof then you should present it. But King Robert needs an alliance with Braston, and these accusations are impeding that process."

"King Robert is better off making alliances with men of honor."

"If you doubt Braston's honor then you truly don't know him. That man keeps his promises."

The older general spoke. "Max, we're not getting anywhere with him and we don't have to. Horslei already gave up the girl."

Pogue watched the men for signs of a bluff and found none. *Dammit, Amash!* He made up his mind to comply. "She's only a little child. Please keep that in mind."

Reeves grabbed Alec by the tunic and lifted him from the chair, snarling into his face. "You don't get it, do you? Every action that a child makes was taught by an adult they respected and loved. I saw the way she drew those blades across the boy's neck, and I've seen it before. Your style of swordsmanship is a closely guarded secret, but masters of the dual blade call it 'crossing the crimson river,' don't they?"

Alec did not respond. He was correct, just as Horslei had been. Marita had watched him use the technique aboard *Desperation* and even gave him her silly thumbs up. Realization hit and tears flowed for all of the children but especially his own missing daughters. *They're only children but we're using them like pawns.* His heart broke knowing they would forever be affected by the kidnapping.

Reeves tossed him down in a heap and the tears continued to flow. *If only I had searched for Mattie sooner,* he thought as he wept. After the sobs had ended, he looked up at the men staring down. "Yes. She learned the move by watching me. We had no intention of harming the boy and only wanted answers."

"Answers to what?"

Alec began with the disappearance of Mattie and the girls and ended with the death of Adolphus Dominique, choking up when he repeated the confession by Stefan Nevra. The other military men said nothing as he spoke and asked no further questions. After he had finished the men gently helped him from the chair and walked him to a holding cell.

# Chapter Twenty-Seven

Marita sat comfortably across from The Lady. She had earlier introduced herself as Sarai, but that was total nonsense, now that she knew that The Lady was the rightful Queen of Eston. As such she had no first name. Kings did, but queens did not. They were always, "My Lady" or "Your Highness," and "The Lady" sounded better than "The Highness."

The lady had been beautiful once before someone had burned her face and neck. Now the queen was only halfway beautiful. The other half was perfectly scarred in a way that went beyond beauty, and Marita couldn't stop admiring the deep lines and circles of crumpled flesh.

"Marita," The Lady asked gently, "Where did you and my brother go, tonight?"

The question didn't make sense in her head. Queens didn't have commoner brothers because their brothers were princes, and both Alec and Amash were certainly not princes. *Princes come from frogs, silly lady,* she thought and stared up at the woman with a smile. She always smiled nowadays. *Smiling keeps away the bad thoughts.*

"Marita," the lady asked again, "Where did you and Amash go tonight? Did you go to a house and sneak in through a window?"

"I'm not allowed to say, Lady Sarai." She used the name only to please the woman and her fancies. She was, after all, a highness. "We keep secrets because we're pirates!" She leaned in close to the beautiful woman with the spellbinding scars and looked around, then added with a whisper, "We have a code." The corners of the queen's mouth curved into a smile, so she shot the lady a thumbs up. Thumbs up mean that everything is going to be just fine, no matter how bad the situation felt. Her mother had taught her that before she went away.

"Would that code keep you from telling a secret even to a queen?"

"I would only tell you if you were my queen and not someone else's."

The Lady's eyebrows shot up quizzically and she asked, "Do you have another queen, Marita?"

Realizing that she had hurt her feelings, she gave the lady another thumbs up and showed her teeth to make her feel better. Careful to maintain the smile she answered honestly, "I have Captain Eusari. She isn't a queen yet, but she will someday marry Captain Braston and be Queen of The Cove. But not until after the elections." The lady seemed confused again, so Marita gave another thumbs up and smiled as big as she could, squinting her eyes as she did. She hoped that the lady would feel better soon because her cheeks were growing tired.

"Elections?" Sarai mused. "I don't understand."

"Braen and Eusari and Amash are running for a new kind of office against Adamas Creech and Lord Nevra." She spit when she said the traitor's name, just as she had seen some of the other sailors do. The lady watched it land on the carpet. "After they win the people will let them be in charge. It was Captain Braston's idea. He's really nice, and the people like him." The Lady frowned down at the spit and Marita again flashed a reassuring thumbs up. Her hand and cheeks were beginning to cramp from all of the comforting.

"Sweetheart, who killed Captain Dominique's son?"

"I did." That was an easy question to answer since it didn't violate the code. She told the truth and didn't harm anyone else's reputation in the process. She gave another thumbs up just in case the highness doubted her truthfulness. She was a pirate after all.

"Why?" The Lady's face had grown serious and one might have described it as crestfallen.

Marita again leaned in and whispered, "He saw me do things that Alec didn't want him to see."

"So, Captain Pogue asked you to do it?"

"I can't tell you without breaking the code, Your Highness."

"I... I need you to tell me, Marita."

The air currents shimmered as if something had disturbed them. Before her powers had awakened, she would have likened the movement to a gust or a breeze. Now that she could see the currents, she knew that this was different. The girl focused her mind on the ripple that flowed in under the door. Vibrating as it traveled, the current carried the echo of movement by several large men.

The lady faded from her sight as Marita allowed her mind to travel. She had so far been unable to bond with a bird like some of the other Dreamers, but this trick of hers was one that no one else had discovered. She called it "drifting" and gave herself over to the current that bore her spirit through the palace. The woman's words muffled as Marita glided under the door and down the hallway.

She soon found the source of the disturbance. Alec walked among several soldiers but not as a part of their company. He wore shackles that bound his hands to irons around his ankles, forcing him to shuffle instead of stride. Tears rolled down his cheeks as the men led him down the hall, but his hands were bound too low for him to wipe them from his face. She observed his guards opening the door to his apartment and roughly shoving him inside. Unable to balance he fell hard upon the bare floor with a slap. Marita snapped her spirit back to her body with sudden outrage.

Sarai watched as the girl's eyes glazed over and her posture stiffened. Something had changed in Marita, almost as if she had fallen asleep with her eyes open. The queen waved her hand in front of the child's face and shook her leg gently. The girl did not respond. "Marita are you okay?" Blank eyes answered back.

She was about to run for help when the girl suddenly moved. Eyes fluttered and the smile disappeared, replaced by a look of hatred and vengeance. A gust of wind rushed through Sarai's chambers, sweeping her hair across her face and blowing the many ruffles of her dress toward the door. The massive oak boards burst outward, cracking under pressure and splintering wooden shards into the hallway. Marita calmly stood and strode from the room.

Sarai rushed to follow. "What's wrong? Where are you going?"

The girl answered, "I'm going to free Alec."

Sarai stared in shock as the girl kept walking. *How did she know? My job was to keep her distracted while they questioned him.* "Marita! Wait!"

The girl paused and thrust her single thumbs up over her shoulder without turning. She walked to the staircase and up a flight to the next floor. Six guards met her in the hallway, staring questioningly. With a wave of her hand all six flew across the hall with a clatter of armor and grunts. She bound each man with shimmering wisps of air as Sarai watched in horror.

One of the doors opened and Robert stepped into the hallway. He eyed his soldiers with a quizzical expression and calmly asked the girl, "Marita, how did you tie up all six?"

The girl paused. "It was easy." Her head cocked to one side as she looked at the king. "I thought you could do it too?"

Five divisions of power were his extent. The girl was obviously stronger than he. Robert shrugged and lied, "I can. But those knots are very intricate. You are incredibly talented."

Marita thrust him a thumbs up and answered, "Thank you. I'm a pirate and pirates tie good knots." She tried the door that imprisoned Alec but found it securely locked. She knelt and peered into the keyhole. A shimmering stream of air coalesced before her face and slid into the mechanism. Robert glanced toward the guards on the floor, confirming that they were still bound. She succeeded in seven divisions as she picked the lock.

Robert reached out a thread and securely wrapped the girl's hands and feet, binding her. She looked over her shoulder and giggled. Almost as soon as they formed, they fell away in a puff. "Silly man. I told you that I'm good at knots and can untie them just as easily." The girl had effortlessly made eight divisions. The lock clicked and the door swung open on its hinges.

Inside Alec rested on his bed. When the door opened, he sat up with wonder on his face. "Marita, what are you doing, dearie?"

"I'm here to rescue you, silly. Come on, let's get Amash and go. We need to go find Mattie."

Alec held up his shackles. "We need to stay here, dearie. We did a bad thing and I will have to stand trial."

"But I'm stronger than them and you're a better fighter. We can just leave, and they can't stop us." She smiled her weird grin at him and gave him a thumbs up. With her other hand she pointed at the shackles and they clicked, locks picked cleanly.

"The code binds us here, Marita. I didn't want the boy to die. I only wanted information."

The girl frowned. "But I killed him. Why are you arrested and not me?"

"It was my idea to break into the manor to find the evidence. I made you bind him to that chair while I forced him to talk. I'm the adult and you are a child, dearie. I'm responsible for everything that happened." His eyes and voice were soft and soothing as he talked. "Just as a parent is responsible for his children."

Sarai watched as the girl's eyes grew wet. She had never seen the girl upset before, and from the look on Pogue's face neither had he. Marita ran into his arms, sobbing into his chest as he held her like a father, comforting and consoling. After a while the girl pulled away and looked up at the captain.

"Mattie and the girls need you, Captain."

"Right now, my place is with you, child. You need a family around you."

"I have one. The entire Cove is my family, but especially you and Amash."

"We've been treating you as a weapon, dearie, not as a child. I made mistakes and should have taught you things besides seeking revenge and killing without remorse. It was my duty to treat you like one of my own children and not a member of my crew."

"I... I don't have a father, Captain, I never have." She snorted back more tears. "I don't even have my mother anymore after the mean men came."

Alec Pogue pulled the girl into a warm embrace and promised, "You have a mother, dearie, you just haven't met her yet. But you will. Just as soon as we can, you and I will sail southward to find Mattie. Then you'll have a proper family again. Until then you need to listen to the queen and be good to the soldiers. Braen will negotiate our release."

Marita nodded with her head against his chest. In the hallway the men were instantly freed and began clamoring to their feet. Robert held up a hand that stilled their movements as he addressed the prisoner. "I give you my word that she will be treated as a guest until your trial." After a pause he added, "I'll also reach out to Braston."

Sarai took the little girl's hand and gave her a smile and thumbs up that made the girl giggle. She returned the gesture and exited the room with the queen. After they were out of earshot, she asked Marita, "What was it like to be raised by your mother? I lost mine when I was little and was raised instead by my father." She listened intently for several hours as the troubled child opened up with her life story for the first time. It took all of the queen's effort not to lose her composure until after the little girl had fallen asleep in her chambers.

# Chapter Twenty-Eight

Kali knelt and patted the head of the fox. It had followed them all day, but finally approached. Unlike the dogs in Logan, the animal was wild and not as easy to connect with, but she had finally succeeded. With a grin she turned her head toward Johan who looked on with amazement. "See? It's just like you and the fish."

"So, what we did at the bridge was the same?"

"I think so, I feel animals and plants all around me. Sometimes I can bond with them and make them do things."

"It's the same for me but with water." He scrunched his face up in thought. "Except when the Falconers attacked. I've never made the water do that before."

"Maybe it was because you were scared. My powers feel different when I'm angry or upset."

"Yeah, maybe." The pair walked for a while following the path eastward. Unlike the roads closer to Eston, they found the trail more difficult the farther they traveled. Finally, Johan broke the silence. "How did you find out about Estowen's Landing?"

"There was an old man in Logan preaching about The Falconers. He talked about powers like ours and said there are others like us scattered around the Empire."

"Yeah, there was an old woman in Norton doing the same. She said that it wasn't safe for me and called me an 'emotant' before telling me to head east. At first, I thought her daft, touched in the head, even."

Kali nodded. She remembered having thought the same of the preacher in Logan. "But now? After the bridge?"

"I know it's real and I'm glad that you're my friend. I'm happy that I'm not alone."

His words stirred a strange feeling inside Kali. She had been alone for so long that she rarely let it bother her. But when he spoke the word "friend" she realized that she had indeed been missing something in her life. Besides the strays in the Logan alleyways, there was no one else in the world that she could call a true friend. She looked closer at Johan and really noticed him for the first time since they began their voyage.

He was a sweet boy, unlike the wolfpack in Logan. He seemed to sincerely care about keeping Kali safe, even though she was confident that she could do a better job for herself. His blue eyes drew her gaze, something that happened more frequently since the bridge. Something about them made her feel less like being alone. When he spoke, she jumped back into reality.

"What are you looking at me like that for?"

"Oh!" Kali felt a deep blush feel her face. "I don't know." She lied, "You had mud above your eye."

"Right here?" He wiped at his face.

"No. There." She pointed.

He made another attempt, smearing the mud over a bigger area. "Did I get it now?"

She looked at his face, now brown and streaked worse than before. "Yes. Absolutely you got it." She tried to hold back the laughter but when it came, it spilled out like a river that had once been dammed.

"You laugh funny."

Putting a hand to her mouth she abruptly stifled her chuckles. "What do you mean by that?"

"It's cute and I like it." His own cheeks blushed a little when he said the words.

"I see." And more awkwardly she added, "Thank you." They continued in silence after that, with her occasionally looking up at his smeared and dirty face and trying not to laugh out loud.

After a while they came across an area where two roads converged. A large caravan camped at the crossing. The children could tell that it was a hodgepodge collection of misfits. Strangely, there were no horses, mules, or oxen pulling their loads. The luckiest pushed carts while the rest dragged sacks full of whatever they could carry. In the center of their camp was a cookfire where an old woman wearing a black shawl ladled out stew for those gathered.

The inviting smell wafted across the teen's noses and Johan started forward.

"Wait!" Kali warned.

"What's wrong?"

"We don't know these people. How can we be sure that we can trust them?"

"They are obviously not outlaws, if that's what you mean. I see women and children mostly." He urged her forward. "Come on!"

Before she took two steps, an arrow shot out of the woods causing them both to jump. Soon a huntress emerged from the tree line, holding her bow at her side. She casually walked past the pair and retrieved Kali's now dead fox.

Anger filled the girl who challenged the woman. "That was my fox!"

Confusion crossed the newcomer's face as she puzzled the words. "If the animal was your pet, then I'm deeply sorry." The raven-haired hunter gestured to the pitiful group of people ahead. "But these people have walked for days and have further yet to go. This fox will go into the stew and bring them closer to their destination."

"He was my friend and he trusted me."

The woman paused and turned around, boldly asking, "You were bonded with the animal?"

Shocked that the hunter understood, the teen answered truthfully, "Yes, I was, and I felt his pain when he died."

"Then I'm sincerely and deeply sorry. I did not think to question why it followed so closely behind you." She pointed toward the old woman standing over the stew pot. "Come with me. I must introduce you to Pearl."

The stew was more hot water and vegetables than a proper stew, but Pearl added herbs to flavor the pot. Luckily, she brought along salt and herbs that would keep up the caravan's strength and stave off cramping as they journeyed. Madelyn had ventured into the forest with her bow and would hopefully bring back meat. Pearl's companion had many talents, one of which being skilled with the archaic weapon.

She lifted her eyes from the kettle and squinted down the road. Although she was close to eighty years old, her eyesight had mostly held up during her years in Andalon. Pearl was surprised to see that Madelyn was trailed by two teens and carried a fox by her side. *Good. The meat won't be tender, but it will give the people protein as we travel.* When the trio was in earshot she asked, "Who are your friends?"

The girl answered first, "I'm Kali and this muddy mess is Johan." At her words the boy reached up and smeared his already dirty face worse than it had been. The girl laughed at his futile attempt then reached out her hand in greeting, "I assume you're Pearl?"

"I see that my companion has already told you my name." Madelyn shrugged and went to work on skinning the animal, carrying it off and around a wheelbarrow, presumably taking it out of sight of the others. "What else did she tell you?"

"That she was sorry for killing my fox."

"Your fox? You owned the animal?"

Kali shook her head, "No. I was bonded with him at the time she killed him. That's why she said to talk to you."

Excitement filled the heart of the old woman and she nearly dropped the ladle into the stew. With a shaking hand she carefully set it aside, trying to appear relaxed. "It's not often that I meet someone who can bond with animals. What else can you do?"

A defiant undertone entered the girl's posture as she answered, "Let's suffice to say that's all, until I decide we can trust you."

After narrowing her eyes, she demanded, "How do you know about bonding?"

Pearl liked the girl and thought she resembled her own spunky self when she had joined The Society. "It's the reason that I've spent sixty years on this continent, dearie. I've been waiting for you and the others to awaken."

"You aren't from here?"

"No. I am from far away."

The boy named Johan finally broke his silence. "Are you from the Southern Continent?"

"No, young man, I am from..."

Kali cut her off before she could finish. With wide understanding eyes she marveled, "You're from Astia?"

Once again shocked by the girl's words, Pearl inquired, "How do you know of Astia, dearie?"

"The old man in Logan told me about it. He said that the Falconers farm emotants for our powers and kill those with powers they don't want awakening."

"That's very true, Kali." Pearl could not believe her ears. "Where are you two headed, dearie? Where were you traveling before Madelyn killed your fox?"

"Estowen's Landing." Johan said the words before Kali could answer, earning him a threatening look.

"Why Estowen's Landing? The Fjorik raiders depopulated the town over thirty years ago. Now there's nothing except abandoned streets and a crumbling pier."

"That's not what we believe. We were both told that there's a place for us and other emotants. Like a school even." The boy had ignored the girl's protests, obviously quicker to trust strangers than she.

Pearl suddenly felt worried. If Samani were gathering emotants then Estowen's Landing was ideal. She motioned for the teens to sit on a fallen log nearby. "You're welcome to journey with us. We're what's left of Diaph and we're headed to Middleton. I have a sister there who I need to contact."

Johan asked, "Why not go to Eston? Isn't that closer than Middleton?"

"It is, but these people are not safe there. The city is doomed to fall when the rebellion occurs."

Kali broke her recent silence, "How is Middleton safer?"

"It's too far and dangerous for the northern navy to sail that close to The Cove. And right now, the Pirate's Guild also wars with the Fjorik King."

Shouts of alarm interrupted their conversation. Pearl's attention turned to Madelyn who quickly grabbed her bow. Soon five men clad in dark green entered the camp, empty hands raised peacefully. Pearl shouted, "What is the meaning of this?"

One of the men answered, "Peace, Mother." Despite his words, the rifles on their backs sent panic through the old woman, as she quickly realized how deeply Samani had already interfered in the rebellion. Another of the men tossed a bag down near the kettle.

Pointing to the sack the first man continued, "We brought you supplies that we've foraged to aid your journey. We know what happened in Diaph and only want to help you along your way."

"How would you know, unless you were the outlaws who aided Braston in his own raid on our city?" Pearl demanded.

"Aye, we're those outlaws." The man confirmed. "But when we raided, we attacked only the Falconers and the soldiers who fought against us. Your city was destroyed by another whom we are sworn to defeat."

"If that is true, then we owe you thanks for the supplies. Now leave so that we may also continue along our way."

"We actually hope to lead you to Estowen's Landing, Mother. We have resources to put you all on a ship and can take you wherever you'd like. But this forest is dangerous, and many of you won't make the journey down south."

Pearl turned and stared at the children to whom she had been speaking. They were listening to the exchange with wide eyes and whispered something between them about Falconers. Then movement caught her eye near the fire. Although the ladle rested on a stump nearby, the stew slowly stirred inside the pot as if by a ghostly spoon. Her attention snapped to Johan and she immediately understood. Turning back to the outlaw she responded, "I too think it's best that we travel with you to Estowen's Landing. A boat ride would accommodate my old bones nicely."

# Chapter Twenty-Nine

Braen paced the room anxiously, awaiting the election results with growing impatience. Eusari and Sippen waited with him while Gelert slept curled up at his master's feet. Sebastian also napped on a sofa nearby. The boy had been tied to Braen's hip as much as possible.

The team had been using the network more frequently, and, With Marita in Eskera, Eusari had grown accustomed to Caroline and helped her fine tune her craft daily. The girl was a fast learner, although quite obstinate. Eusari liked the girl who currently napped next to Samani in the counting house. She would relay his messages to Sebastian.

Someone had started calling the children "Dreamers" although no one could remember who. It seemed fitting since they passed their messages in a sleep state, so the term stuck. "You won district one, Braen." The boy muttered Samani's words. "Eusari came in second, and Amash third. Creech won fourth and nothing for Nevra. Things are working out as planned."

Braen took a drink to settle his nerves. "That's good news."

Sippen remarked, "Only fuh... four more duh... districts left." Although not in the race, he was as nervous as his lifelong friend.

"District two is in" Sebastian mouthed. "Eusari took first with a sweeping margin followed by Braen and Amash. Creech was again fourth and Nevra had one vote."

All three adults let out a long breath. So far things were going well. The two districts had been the smallest, so they settled in, knowing that it would be some time before the other three reported. Eusari broke the silence, "Any more word from Amash and Alec?"

"Not a thing. Last I heard the prince still won't speak with me. He thinks that it's a trick, and that we are trying to kidnap him, or something worse. The damned kid's paranoid."

"He's an Esterling, Braen. They don't trust anyone, and he thinks you killed his mother."

"We need him on our side. I've been giving it a lot of thought, and we need to help him win his war."

"That's not our fight, Braen. It doesn't matter which of the whelps win, either one will have to accept you in Fjorik after Skander is dead."

"No. I don't think Marcus will ever tell the people the truth about Crestal's death. Our best hope is Robert."

"Cinder's crack, Braen, there's a problem." All eyes shot toward the sleeping boy. "Our switch boxes didn't make it to the rest of the polling sites. Some of Creech's men interfered and the crew had to dispose of them."

Eusari shot Braen a hot stare. "Switch boxes? What did he mean by that?" When he didn't answer she stood and set down her drink. "Dispose of what, Braen?"

He immediately realized that he had let her down. He cringed as he answered, "Fake ballots."

"What?" Her angry eyes reflected both shock and disappointment. Gelert rose from his nap growling low and deep.

"Creech closed the gap in several districts so Samani packed some boxes. He planned to switch them out before counting."

"You promised me that the elections would be honest, that if we won it would be the will of the people."

"I did."

"I trusted you. After everything that you know I've been through, you still lied to me?"

"Samani insisted..."

"Samani only does what you tell him, Braen!" She was so angry that she shouted, "Hell, he worships you and thinks the prophecies foretold your coming, for Cinder's sake!" She stormed out of the room and shouted over her shoulder, "This is on you!" The door slammed behind her and the wolf with a definitive crash that woke Sebastian.

Sippen slowly rose from his chair and set down his glass of wine. "Buh... Braen. I nuh... never thought you'd stoop so luh... low." He shook his head at his friend and the large captain felt his heart break at the disappointed look. "I need air."

Braen's eyes followed his best friend from the room, anxiety strong in his gut. *I screwed this up,* he thought, *I should have talked to them both before I acted.*

From the sofa Sebastian yawned and stretched, "What made them angry, Captain Braston?"

"I did something I shouldn't have, but it's going to be okay. Family forgives." But in his mind, he thought, *except Eusari. She'll hold a grudge for decades.* "Can you sleep? We're waiting for more news from Samani."

"I can try." The boy settled down and soon drifted off. "Two more districts reported. District five picked Creech first, you second, Eusari third, and Amash fourth. No votes for Nevra."

Braen closed his eyes and breathed. Creech had won the market district. Despite his campaigning, the old money had made a statement.

"District four is in. Creech, Braston, Thorinson, and Horslei in that order. Two votes for Nevra."

Braen picked up a quill and parchment and scribbled calculations. That made Creech and Amash tied in third with one district left to report. Thankfully the voters had eliminated Nevra, but Amash had to beat out Adamas. He took another deep breath and thought about Eusari. She may be consoled to know that she was elected fair and square, after all, but he doubted she would. The fact that he even attempted to rig the votes would push her far away. He hoped she would speak with him soon.

The boy on the couch stirred in his sleep, snapping Braen from his private thoughts. He watched Sebastian with concern. Something about the way the boy slept had changed. He seemed restless and less relaxed, almost as if experiencing a nightmare. Braen walked over and placed his hand on the boy's forehead. His skin flushed hot and sweat beaded along his hairline, but he could see that his shivering arms had formed tiny bumps of chicken skin. Something was wrong.

He tried to wake the boy, but failed and the child groaned and shifted positions. As he rolled over Braen saw that his back had drenched with sweat through his tunic. Alarmed, he shook the boy but stopped when he heard him cry out with pain from his deep sleep. He ran to the door and called for help.

Sebastian and Caroline sat across from each other in the dream world. They and the other Dreamers had learned how to construct the world however they wanted. Caroline perched atop an enormous mushroom while fairies flitted around her. Sebastian rode atop a giant luminescent salamander. Strange looking trees and flowers towered over them and birds resembling chickens flew overhead or rested on branches.

"Braen pissed off Eusari. She stormed out of the room."

"She'll forgive him." Caroline hugged her arms around her chest and mocked the adults, "She's in love with him."

"How can you tell?"

"Because I catch them kissing all the time. Also, he sneaks into her room at night and they get naked together."

"Ew! That's gross!"

"No, Silly. Its romantic! They're going to get married and have babies and someday she'll let me babysit."

"All the way naked?"

"Yes. That's what grownups do to make babies."

"Really? That's all?"

"Pretty much. They get naked and roll around in bed and then nine months later a baby pops out of the woman."

"That's grosser than gross. Wait, where does the baby come out?"

"I think the belly button, or from down below. I'm not sure."

Sebastian pondered that for a while, thankful that only women had babies and relieved that he wouldn't have to squeeze one out from "down below." Of course, he remembered an old man in his village who peed out rocks sometimes. He heard him say one time that it was like giving birth. "I think you're right. I think they come from your pee hole."

"Probably." Caroline relayed a message from Samani and went back to playing with the fairies.

Sebastian passed it on and tried to teach the salamander to rear up like a horse. So far, he was largely unsuccessful at anything except standing in one place. Finally giving up he turned his attention back to his friend. A woman stood behind her in a feathered hood and with arms crossed. "Why did you create a Falconer here, Caroline?"

"I didn't, Silly. Why would I do that?"

He pointed behind her and she turned, letting out a bloodcurdling scream at the sight of the specter. Instantly she was gone from the dream world, probably awakened by fear. Sebastian continued to stare at the strange feathered lady. "I know you aren't real. You can go away now."

"How can you be so sure?" Her voice was creepy and without emotion.

"Because everyone knows that Falconers are men."

"I'm not a man, yet I'm a Falconer."

"A made up one in the dream world."

"I'm real. I have the same powers as you and can travel here as well."

"You don't have the same powers. You swallow beads and steal our powers. Braen told me that you make the beads by farming us in your rookeries."

"Why are you not afraid of me, child?"

"Because I'm stronger than you are."

"Are you sure of that?"

"Yes, I am. Marita is the only one stronger than me, and she can divide her power fifteen times without hurting."

"That is impressive. How many times can you divide? What about the others?"

Sebastian suddenly grew suspicious at the woman's questions. "I'm not telling."

"You already told me that the most any of you can wield is fifteen separations of power. That tells me plenty, child."

"I'm done playing here and I think Caroline isn't coming back. Goodbye." Sebastian tried to return to Andalon, but suddenly realized that he had lost his pathway back. Panic gripped him as he tried to focus on his body in The Cove. The specter continued to watch him with eerie calm as he wrangled within his mind. Beneath his legs, the salamander transformed into a crocodile, biting and chomping at the boy on his back. Sebastian reacted quickly and wrapped its powerful jaws with ropes of air. Then he leapt off and ran into the forest.

Above his head the flying chickens turned into piranha fish that bit at his flesh as he ran, chasing him deeper into the dream world. One of them latched onto his arm and tore a chunk of meat from his bicep. The wound pulsed with pain as he ripped the monster free and tossed it aside. Another bit at his leg and ripped a chunk from his calf muscle, causing him to tumble onto the ground. He was soon overtaken by the fish who latched on and munched their way to bone.

All at once they were wrapped in net of air and pulled away in a single movement. Looking up Sebastian recognized Marita standing over him. She flashed him a thumbs up, letting him know that he would be fine. Afraid that he would bleed out on the ground, he scanned his wounds only to find that they had fully healed. He scrambled to his feet and stood next to his friend.

"What are you doing here?"

"I brought a friend to talk to Braen." She pointed over her shoulder and a young man standing behind her.

"That's Robert! You found him!"

"It turns out that he's King Robert, and his full name is Robert Esterling."

"You're Robert Esterling?"

"Yes, I am." He looked around in amazement. "You kids built this place?"

Marita nodded her head. "We're working on it, but it's a lot of work." She turned to Sebastian. "Why were you running?"

He felt his stomach drop when he thought about the strange woman. "There's a Falconer here."

"Here?" Esterling scanned the woods for threats.

Marita frowned. "Why didn't you just wake up, Silly?"

"I... I couldn't. I think she had me blocked somehow."

"She?" Robert seemed confused. "You saw a female Falconer?"

"Yes. That's why I thought she was make-believe at first. I thought one of you other Dreamers put her here as a joke."

"Take us to her." Esterling motioned for him to lead and Sebastian took them back to the clearing. The crocodile had turned back into a salamander and the woman was gone. "She was right there."

"Well, she appears to have left. Can you try to get back to The Cove? I need to speak with Captain Braston." Robert leaned against the mushroom and Marita hopped up on a rainbow- colored rock nearby.

"I can try." Sebastian closed his eyes and reached into his mind. White lights coalesced around him, resembling stars. He focused on the space between the glowing orbs and felt outside of his body with his mind. Soon he found a pathway that led to a familiar spot. He flowed along the ether until a clear image emerged of his feverish body and Braen kneeling beside him. Other people stood around the room while Sippen held his wrist. With a rush he rejoined his physical husk.

The boy's eyes shot open and he gasped a deep breath that caused Braen to jump. "Calm down, Sebastian. You gave us a fright for a moment."

"I need you to come back with me."

Braen turned to Sippen who appeared as concerned as he. "He must still be feverish. There's no way that I can travel with him."

But Sebastian insisted, "I think there is, Captain Braston. But we need to hurry, Marita is there and so is Robert Esterling." Every adult in the room looked at Braen.

# Chapter Thirty

The walk to the mines took the pair longer than they had hoped. Taros insisted that they circle around several times to ensure that they weren't followed, and they rested twice when Flaya felt cramping in her womb. When they finally arrived, they were shocked to find the roadway unwatched and not guarded. The path to the opening wound around a creek, filled but not full after the recent rains. A makeshift wooden bridge led up and over, but not too steep that workers couldn't push carts with ease.

At least fifty mules were corralled nearby. They brayed alarm at the sudden appearance of the Pescari teens, some kicking and snorting in protest. The commotion forced the pair to duck behind a watering trough and wait. Just as Taros feared, a sleeping watchman had been resting nearby.

The Pescari man stumbled and staggered as if he had been drinking dragon water during his watch. He circled the mules, shouting for them to quiet down. When one bit at his arm he reacted, picking up a board. He lifted it high above his head and swung with force. It burned instantly, scorching his hands and falling harmlessly as ash atop the mud.

Taros left his hiding spot and faced the man, now crying out from the pain and fearing Felicima. "You have failed the goddess."

"She didn't see me strike out, Shappan!"

"No." The chieftain agreed, "But I did." The watchman knelt before the teen, begging for mercy. Taros felt the heat rising and screaming for release, but he contained it within. "Take me to the others," he ordered, "so that I may cleanse my people of their sins."

The entrance was unremarkable, merely an opening in the hillside framed by large support beams. Taros paused before them with claustrophobia coursing through his body. *My people were meant to roam above the land, under the full eye of Felicima,* he thought, remembering the first time Sarai Horslei had led him into a stone building. Gentle words from Flaya broke him from his worries.

"We have no other option, My Love."

"I know," he answered with hesitation, "but even this feels wrong. We have been exploited by the leaders of Weston since we arrived. Don't you find it strange that Cassus Eachann found a ward for us in the city so quickly?"

She replied, "I never thought about it."

"None of us did. He had set the perfect trap, a section entirely walled within the larger city with steel gates to lock us in." He ran his hand along the fresh timber at the opening of the mine. "There are no gates here, but this also feels like a prison." To the sobering watchman he asked, "How deep does the mine go?"

"It is not deep, Shappan. The vein is large but close to the surface."

"How large?"

"Some of the crew have suggested that it runs for miles toward the city."

"Where are the workers?"

"Just up here, Shappan." Once inside Taros, allowed the watchman to lead him and Flaya down the passage. After a while the tunnel opened into a cavern. Stone walls had been erected in much the same fashion as the city, with apartments for sleeping and living. Inside, miners slept on cots. "The night crew works below and will swap with the day workers in a few hours." He pointed at another row of doors ahead. "Up there are the kitchens and laundry where the women work."

"Wake them and send a runner to gather the workers. Our brothers and sisters in Weston are in dire need of help."

The man immediately went to work rousing sleeping miners, each annoyed at the early awakening. They slowly emerged, one by one with dirty faces that seemed to make the whites of their eyes glow in the lamplight. Their irritation quickly evaporated at the sight of Taros and the men and women knelt piously before their chieftain. Soon the others emerged with pickaxes and shovels in hand, joining their comrades in genuflection.

Taros cleared his throat and began, "Our brothers and sisters in Weston are imprisoned by the city guard and need help."

One of the men cried out with a tone of defiance in his voice, "Where have you been, Shappan?"

Before he could respond another voice called out, "We thought you had abandoned us!" Soon the cavern was filled with shouts of dissention and righteous anger. Taros listened intently as the men aired their troubles, emboldened by months of fending for themselves below ground.

The question soon grew into angry shouts and Taros raised his hand. Fearing his fiery wrath, the crowd abruptly silenced and cowered before him. His heart broke in that moment. *They have only followed me out of fear*, he thought. *Why else would they follow me from the Steppes of Cinder and across the Forbidden Waste.*

When he spoke, his voice was low and full of honesty, "I did leave you, although I never ventured far. I spent my days praying for Felicima's guidance. This land and its people have a culture that is strange to us, and many of our brothers and sisters have tried to adopt their ways. But assimilation is not the answer. I realize now that the goddess led us here to work alongside the Andalonians, to teach them humility without setting her aside to embrace their sinful ways."

Many of the men shuffled and their faces fell at his words. They surely pondered their own indiscretions. Taros continued, "Cassus Eachann and his other chieftains take advantage of us. They compel us to labor and pay the taxes that increase their wealth while we cling to poverty. He claims that he is our benevolent father, but he is the true chain that imprisons us."

His words struck a chord attuned with the feelings of the crowd, and many of the men drummed their chests to a rhythmic war beat.

"Yes, the time for war is at hand. Beat the drum of war so that we can free our families from the city and drive out the people of Weston." The pounding grew louder until all fists beat breast in the dark mine, thunderously echoing down the shaft.

And then the walls and floor shook violently. Pieces of rubble fell from the ceiling, worked free by the quake. The men leapt to their feet, preparing to run from the mine until cackling laughter froze them in their tracks. Taros strained his eyes toward the entrance and spotted a hooded figure silhouetted against the flickering light from the lanterns above. "Beat your drum of war, abominations!" The laughter was inhuman as it echoed through the cave. "You will not escape this prison and you will all die very soon!"

Taros noticed a second figure seated on the ground and adorned with animal skins. The woman swayed faster as she muttered strange words, then placed her hands to the ground. Another quake, much more powerful than before, shook the teeth in Taros' head as the entire tunnel collapsed between him and freedom.

# Chapter Thirty-One

"This is the dumbest thing I've ever done, Samani." Braen lay atop his bed while his friend pushed a chair next to him for the boy. "Didn't you say that there's a chance that I could die?"

"Only if you transcend to the Ka'ash'mael." He held up a pouch of black oracle beads pilfered from the Diaph rookery and gave them a shake.

Sippen sat at on the other side of the bed, facing the wall with slumped shoulders and wearing an expression of deep concern. "I duh... don't like it, Braen. Suh... Sebastian nearly died, and he knows his way back." His oversized head shook back and forth. "Besides, it could be a trick of the Falconer like the flying puh... piranhas. How do you know it's really Eh... Esterling?"

"I don't. But we sent Marita there to find him and we need to make contact if he's finally ready to parlay." Braen readjusted his massive shoulders on the bed in an attempt to get comfortable. He tried to make the move seem casual so as to hide his intense dread and nervousness. "Are you ready, Sebastian?"

"I think so, Captain Braston." The boy hopped into the chair and sat facing his skipper. "I've slept a lot today though."

Braen liked the boy, especially after his help during the raid on The Cove. Unfortunately, they had many casualties on that day, including the Dreamer Suzette. Sebastian had watched her die on the deck of *Ice Prince* and carried a melancholy ever since. "Then I'm ready also." He popped a bead into his mouth and washed it back with water. "Tell me what I need to do."

Both the man and the boy closed their eyes and Samani guided them through. "Let the darkness smooth out in your mind. The light from the room will slowly disappear and you will see dots form that resemble stars. Watch for a swirling pattern like a whirlpool."

"Okay, I see it."

"Push your mind toward it, slowly."

Something felt wrong to Braen. His stomach twisted. "Samani, I'm feeling weird, like the bead is burning."

"That's normal. Relish that pain, because it will be in your muscles soon and that pain is worse than any you've ever felt."

"I don't think so. This is strange." All of a sudden, his stomach retched and spilled its contents on the ground. The bead landed with a splat on the ground and Braen fell backward onto the bed. The onlookers watched his eyes roll back in his head and his mouth foam as if in a seizure. The voices of the other men echoed in Braen's ears.

Sippen moved to help, but Samani grabbed him and pulled him backward. "This is part of it, Yurik."

"Thuh... then why did he vuh... vomit it up?"

"Because the essence of the bead contradicted the way his body is wired. It's like if you were to put one person's organ inside of another; they would have to match each other perfectly."

"Why would suh... someone put..."

"Your medicine hasn't progressed far enough for that, Sippen. Just trust me that his body rejected the autumn essence."

"Thuh... then how will it work?"

"The reaction will briefly allow him to share properties from both for a few minutes."

Their muffled voices finally tapered off and the bearded captain's eyesight grew completely dark, falling into the stars that Sebastian had described. A voice in his head called out to him, "*Braen, follow the vortex.*"

"The entire thing is a vortex and I can't stop spinning, Sebastian."

"*Don't talk to me with words, use your mind. We're linked now, but I don't know for how long. Let go of your husk.*"

The sensation sickened the large man as he slipped into the abyss and he tasted more bile in the back of his throat. "*I don't think that I can, Sebastian.*"

"*You must. If you don't release now you may be lost forever. Follow the vortex and let go from your body. Just like taking a breath and letting it out.*"

Braen could hear the boy's voice much clearer in his mind the more that he spoke, suddenly understanding what he meant. His muscles were tensed from the oracle bead, and he had been more focused on the physical sensation than the mental connection. Giving in to the swirling pattern, he felt his body slacken and then let go, suddenly releasing the pain that coursed through his extremities.

He could see Sebastian flying beside him as they tumbled through the velvety darkness. Faces appeared in his mind, orbiting the man and the child as they fell. "*Stay focused on the vortex and ignore the images, Captain. They're a distraction made by your brain.*"

The boy's words sounded unusual from one so young as they rumbled in Braen's head, but he stared straight ahead and did as he was told. "*Who are they?*"

"*Distractions, Braston.*"

One of the images briefly passed directly in front and he recognized Hester. She wore dark clothing and a woolen hood that partially hid her troubled blue eyes. She walked as if in pain and Braen cried out for her as she boarded a longboat. "*Captain! Focus!*" The sharpness in the boy's voice drew his attention back to the abyss ahead. "*We're almost there!*"

A light at the center of the vortex glowed brighter as it rushed toward the pair. Soon, Braen could make out a spinning sphere of blue and green with swirling white clouds. He marveled at the awesome sight, unable to look away. *I wonder if our world looks the same.* All at once a brilliant flash of light erased all images from his mind and he opened his eyes.

They stood in a green meadow next to a river capped white with rapids splashing against rocks. The blue sky above carried fluffy white clouds floating on a quiet breeze. The same draft tickled the tops of the blades of grass and they waved up at him. *But it's spring*, he thought, *where are the flowers?* He thought about the colorful tulips that grew in Fjorik, popping out of the soil as their bulbs are warmed by spring. He nearly jumped out of fear when hundreds rose out of the ground all around him.

"Nice! I thought we were missing something."

Realization passed over Braston. "This is the world the Dreamers built?"

"Yes. It's quite beautiful, isn't it?"

"Stunningly so." And he meant it. Beauty surrounded him on every side.

"Braen!" The voice of a young girl called out from behind, and he turned to see Marita sitting at a small white table with four chairs. Beside her sat a young man with dark hair and sad eyes. He was skinny, not malnourished, but certainly lacking in brawn as he sipped from a tiny set of cups and dishes. "This is King Esterling! Come join us for tea!" Braen smiled back at her silly grin. She gave him a thumbs up while sipping from her own porcelain mug.

"The pleasure is mine, Robert." Braen stretched his massive hand out to the boy who eyed it suspiciously.

"You don't address me as 'king' or 'your highness' when we meet, Braston? Do you imply equality?"

"Damned right I do, but I imply it with the deepest of respect as a kindred king whose brother also sits upon his throne." He stood there with hand outstretched until Robert finally stood to return the greeting.

"Seems we do share a similar seating arrangement with our respective families."

"Sit down, boys. Drink your tea." Marita beamed as she spoke.

After everyone had taken their seats Robert cleared his throat while Braen frowned at his cup, then changed it into a wine glass filled with his favorite Esterling vintage.

The boy began to speak with a slight shake to his voice. "I'll start by setting some ground rules for the meeting."

Braen nearly choked on the wine and laughed as he interrupted. "Drop the formal parlay bullshit, Robert. No offense, but we don't have the time. You need a navy and I have one. You need more ground troops and sophisticated weaponry, and I have them as well." He gestured at the children sitting beside him. "As you can see, I also have a team of emotants trained to use their powers in both combat and support roles." Marita shot him a thumbs up and he winked back at her. "You need us to win back your kingdom, and I need you to legitimize my own claim in Fjorik. Do we have a deal or not?"

Robert sat down his cup and pointed at Braen's wine glass. "Do you have any more of that you'd like to share? There seems to be a shortage of good wine in the kingdom of late." With a wave of the bearded man's hand, the teacup transformed into a golden goblet. The tea inside turned burgundy with striking aromas of toasted oak. The young man took a sip and smiled. "So that's where all the 754 went."

"It's a pleasing vintage, to be sure."

The boy king agreed. "To be quite sure." He took a deep breath and let it out. "You're correct. I need your help, but I've no reason to believe that you won't try to steal the empire away from my family after you get your kingdom."

Braen nodded. "True. You only have the assurance of my word as a Braston."

"As a Braston? We'll need stronger ore than that if we're to forge an alliance."

"Spit out what you need, Robert. And don't give me any of that 'bend the knee' bullshit. The world has been saturated with enough of that crap to choke a dragon. Just tell me what you want."

"Horslei and Pogue filled me in regarding the 'advanced weaponry' that you mentioned. I want my entire army outfitted and trained in rifles and pistols."

"That's it?"

"And I want my blacksmiths to have full access to your weaponsmith facilities. I want them to learn the entire process from start to finish."

"Agreed." Braston reached out his hand.

Robert narrowed his eyes with distrust. "Just like that? I'd figured that would have been your deal breaker."

Braen sighed. "I told you already, we don't have time to negotiate and we both need each other's help."

"But my army outnumbers yours and would have a considerable advantage after I have control of my own weapon development."

"Cinder's Crack! Don't you get it, Esterling? The world around us has changed. You and I know that more than most since we've awakened."

Robert digested his words with a thoughtful expression. "Then we have a deal."

"Great. Let's shake and be done."

"We have other pressing matters as well." He sat up straighter and took a long swig of wine. "Two things. One, my brother's army is only a couple of days march away."

"That's not a problem, sieges take time to set up, and I can get my fleet there in a matter of days."

"That will prove helpful," the young prince agreed.

"I assume you want a full evacuation?"

"Aye. That I do. Can you accommodate three thousand men?"

"Have them ready," Braston commanded. "What was the other matter?"

"This matter regards your emissaries." The young king looked at Marita whose eyes fell to the tea set. She dropped her smile as well as her gaze.

"What about my 'emissaries?' I trust they have been treated well?"

"It appears that they had a side mission in Eskera and broke into the personal estate of one of my newly recruited naval officers."

Braen let out another chuckle. "You mean Captain Dominique." Marita turned her head and spit on the ground at the mention of his name. When she noticed both men watching her, she smiled and gave a thumbs up.

"A simple pilfering of personal logs escalated to the death of his son. The facts are public knowledge, and all three must stand before me in trial."

"All three? I don't understand." Braen turned his eyes to Marita with realization. "Marita, you...?"

She bobbed her tiny head. "Yes, I killed him, Captain Braston."

"Turn them over to me."

"I'm afraid that I can't."

"Then you'll turn over Dominique and I'll oversee his trial for the transgressions against Pogue. He's wanted for kidnapping and engaging in the illegal trading of slaves."

"I can do that."

"Just get my team out with your men and onto my ship. We can discuss this resolution once you're onboard."

"Then it's a deal, Braston?"

"Yes. It's a deal, Esterling." The two men grasped hands and shook as equals before standing to take their leave. They both turned when Sebastian began to laugh maniacally.

"Sebastian?" Braen knelt beside the boy and placed his hand on his shoulder. "Are you okay, son?"

"You are both idiots and deserve your waiting deaths." The boy began to laugh, and his body heaved in time with the cackling. "You're all children playing with powers that you don't deserve to wield. It's just too bad that we can't keep you in stasis within our rookeries. I would have enjoyed consuming your essence." Sebastian's laughter intensified as he spoke until convulsions overpowered his ability to speak. Braen and Robert stepped forward and eased his seizing body to the ground.

"What's happening, Marita?" Braen shot her a worried glance.

"I don't know!" Tears filled her eyes as she thrust two thumbs upward.

"We need you to figure it out, dearie." The captain pressed. He watched as she sent a sliver of glistening air toward Sebastian, feeling the boy's body and mind. Her eyes shot immediately to the forest and she slowly raised a finger, pointing to the tree line where a horde of Falconers emerged into the daylight.

Braen and Robert stood and moved beside Marita. At their feet, Sebastian's seizure ended but his skin began to ripple as if a million spiders crawled beneath it. The girl answered, "She had control of him, but I cut her off."

"She?" Robert seemed confused.

One of the Falconers approached the trio standing over the boy. From the way her robes clung to her frame, they could tell right away that she was a woman.

Marita stepped forward and raised her fist at the specter. "Go away! You can't harm us, here!"

"I don't have to, My Dear. I'll kill you soon enough in person."

Braen scooped up Sebastian's limp body and turned to Marita. "Can you help us get home." She nodded and touched her palms to their foreheads.

Braen's eyes shot open with alarm and looked around the room. Samani and Sippen were there and Sebastian slept quietly in the chair. "Wake him up!"

"What happened, Braen?" Samani looked puzzled.

"Sippen, get the ships ready. We're leaving for Eskera."

The pier buzzed with activity as men readied the fleet to sail. Eusari stood with Braen, listening to him and Sebastian retell their experience. She was happy that they were both well, but she also seethed with anger that Braen had casually taken such a risk with both him and the boy's lives. "Sebastian, go on and board *Malfeasance.* I need to talk to Captain Braston."

"Yes, Captain." He looked pitiful but had sworn that he would be fine on the voyage. He was not physically hurt, only terrified after the Falconer had taken control of his body when he was stuck in the dream world.

"Eusari, I..." She cut him off.

"I haven't forgiven you yet."

The corners of his lips curled up and his gorgeous eyes glistened with his charming mischief. "You said, 'yet.' So, you are saying that you will."

"Don't get your hopes up." She looked around to ensure that no one was listening. Despite his and Samani's attempt to rig the election, the outcome turned out honest in the end. However, Creech had beaten out Amash and would serve as the third head of the triumvirate. As such, he tried to block this mission to aid the Esterling boy and would have been successful had it not been for her vote and approval by the emergency war council. "We have a lot to talk about, but I'm not ready. To be honest, I don't even want to sail in the same fleet as you today."

"I understand." He appeared terribly sorry for his actions, and it was so hard to remain angry. But she dug in her heels and kept him distanced. He continued, "After we take out the blockade, why don't you bring back any captured ships and prisoners that we can press into service?" He turned his eyes to the water to avoid hers. "That way you won't have to be near me, and you can have time to think things out."

Eusari wanted to scream inside but kept her demeaner calm. *Damn him. Doesn't he get it? I don't want time to think things over, I want him to love and comfort me. I want him to wallow in his torment and grovel at my feet!* Instead of speaking her thoughts aloud, she casually stated, "That suits me just fine, Captain Braston." *Stupid girl,* she screamed in her head, *He'll have to figure things out during the voyage!*

She pushed past him with her shoulder, careful not to touch him with any part of her hand except her glove. She boarded *She Wolf* without glancing back a single time.

# Chapter Thirty-Two

*Malfeasance* loved the open seas. Four masts heaved against the strain of the full canvas stretched above, capturing the wind and making it hers to control. The sleek curves of her hull sliced through the Southern Ocean as she led the race to Eskera, the rising sun reflected from her armored skirt and lighting up the water below her draft. At her highest point, a banner announced the admiral at her helm with the tentacles of the Kraken crushing ships against the black colors of the Pirate's Guild.

It had been years since Braen had put a newly built ship through its paces, shaking down the lashings and learning her limits. The last time had been aboard *Ice Prince,* he and Sippen had stood beside his father, challenging the newly commissioned ship and putting her through exercises. Like that day many years ago, Yurik smiled with pride while the crew marveled at his engineering prowess.

Braston placed a hand on his friend's shoulder and voiced his approval. "She's your greatest marvel, my friend. We're going to have to slack sails to let the others catch up."

"I tuh... told you she wuh... was fast." The little man's smile filled his face and his eyes glistened behind the spectacles.

Braen looked over his shoulder at twenty-nine vessels racing behind his flagship. The ships of the line trailed out, ready to relay his orders and take down the enemy blockade. Although he had commanded fleets before, he had never controlled so much firepower. Each vessel possessed the new rifled cannons and Sippen had even added explosive rounds to increase the impact of the volleys.

Sippen pointed over the side at the shadowy shapes following the wake of *Malfeasance.* "Thuh... they're still thuh... there."

"Yes. I sensed them the moment we left the harbor and they seem intent on following us to Eskera." The bearded captain looked thoughtful. "It's funny, but every other time they connected with me, I experienced intense emotions like hopelessness. This time they latched on immediately and I feel more in control than before."

"Buh... because you are ruh... resolute in your mission, Braen." Sippen pushed his spectacles back atop his nose. "You know that this is thuh... the right thing to do." He gestured at the trailing fleet. "They follow you like wuh... we do."

The words from his friend meant much to Braen and helped heal some of their recent division over the election. He only wished Eusari would be as forgiving. She hadn't spoken to him in a week, except to go over battle plans for this attack. He longed to speak with her and to get her alone so that he could explain his rationale. Mostly he wanted to apologize, but she had avoided him at every chance. He looked back at the black ship halfway behind the line. Soon she would peel off with her own fleet to attack the enemy from the flank.

Gunnery Sergeant Krill ambled up on his wooden leg, a comical sight with his black eyepatch and beaming smile. He had painted an odd-looking eyeball on the patch, making him appear more ridiculous. "Lookout reports sails on the horizon, Cap'n. It be time to split off from the rest."

Braen nodded. "Signal the others." He watched as Krill turned to the signalman. The spindly man grabbed a series of flags and ran them up the yardarm. Braen did not recognize the hand, presumably new to the crew. *So much has changed,* the captain mulled, *there was a time when I knew everyone on my crew by name.* He made a mental note to meet the young man after their mission.

Soon the other ships responded, and the order was relayed to the entire fleet within minutes. Braen could almost feel the tension in every sailor as they squared away their sails. *She Wolf* departed with the others, curving away to hit the western ships, and his heart sank as he watched his lover leave. His eyes lingered on the dark canvas heaving against the wind, his heart yearning for the captain who steered a different course.

Crewmen on the deck readied for battle, tying down loose objects that could potentially fly around and cause more damage from the enemy. Krill and Sippen oversaw the preparations, checking the knots and rigging while ensuring that the powder was dry and at the ready. Instead of a somber mood laden with anxiety, the men aboard *Malfeasance* appeared ready for the fight and excited to try out the new weaponry. The only anxious man on board was Braen.

Thoughts about the rendezvous with Robert raced through his mind, wondering if the boy would keep his end of the bargain. His father had once warned him of the Esterling family, emphasizing that their deals always benefitted themselves more than their allies.

A quiet voice broke him from his brooding, and he looked down at Sebastian, gaunter than he had been before the episode with the Falconers, eyes older than they should be against that youthful face. He was lucky to live, and the boy knew it. "Captain Braston, there are Falconers on one of those two ships."

Braen gestured at the sails. "Those two?"

The boy nodded, "I think the one on the right, but I'm not sure."

"I need you to be certain. Can you reach out without detection?"

Although his face paled from fear he nodded again and answered with a shaky voice, "I'll try."

"Good boy. I'll get you closer and you can tell me when you know for sure." He pulled out his spy lens and peered at the signal masts of both vessels. They would see him soon and he wanted them to alert their comrades. Red and blue flags raced up the yardarms and the galleons turned against the wind. As Sebastian predicted, their sails remained full of the Falconer's aid. "Krill, they see us and are moving to join the line. Load all guns!"

Sebastian exclaimed, "The one on the right, Captain!"

Braen focused the lens on the starboard vessel and soon a single hawk rose into the air. It made a beeline to warn the main fleet and the bearded northerner smiled. "Good job, Sebastian. Keep calling them out as we go. They'll probably be wondering how we have wind as well, so hang back. Don't get too close just yet."

"Aye, Captain." The sails fluttered briefly as the boy allowed the others to gain a slight lead.

They followed the outline of the vessels for an hour before lookouts identified more sails. The main fleet consisted of forty galleons, the full strength of the Soston fleet. These cruised toward the nearest then allowed them to move into the lead of the convoy. "They've committed, gentlemen! We've got a battle on our hands!" The crew let out a war whoop that lifted his heart. "Signal the others to move forty degrees to port. We need natural wind to pull this off." With a grin he called out, "Ready the starboard!"

Braen's line drifted away and his opponents gave fierce pursuit. They held both the wind from the north as well as the aid from the Falconers. The enemy captains would have confidence in their attack, with Braen's fleet vulnerable and fully exposed on their withering starboard flank. He would have to heave to port into the northern wind to have an angle of defense, but the enemy ships of the line would fire repeatedly as they moved past in a trailing single file. They would mercilessly pound his fleet until his revolution lay beneath the Southern Sea.

But with the Dreamers on board, the direction he led the Imperial fleet would open up two surprise attacks. They would expect the first as he turned to port, with starboard cannons at the ready. But a second hard starboard turn would surprise the foe and make rapid use of his portside guns as well. With proper timing, he would fire off two broadsides as quickly as they reloaded their first. His faster loading would also ready him for the next vessel, firing two more shots each as his fleet snaked between their line against the wind.

He called out angles to Krill who was bent over a slate with Sippen. "Fire when you have them, Mr. Krill!"

"Aye Cap'n! Second round will be explosives on your order!"

"Make it so!"

The enemy line moved into position and fired their first shots toward *Malfeasance.* Imperial cannons roared to life, breaking the tranquility of the spring day on pleasant seas. Most of the guns hit their mark, striking the vessel below the waterline, but mostly bouncing off the armored hull. Sippen's rifled weapons responded immediately, shooting faster and truer than their foe's. Wood splintered into the sea as Braen shouted for the second attack.

"Sebastian, give me wind to snake starboard! Get me in between those ships!" The sails turned to the northeast and filled with an unnatural wind that quickly blew them north and east of the enemy. Braen glanced over his shoulder to confirm that his trailing fleet had followed his lead. They were also ready on the portside. "Where's the Falconer, Sebastian?"

"Second ship, Captain Braston!"

"Krill! Fire both broadsides at both ships!"

"Aye Cap'n! You heard the man, you bilge rats! Prepare to reload your guns like your wenches want another tumble!" He glanced at Sippen who nodded. "Fire away, you rapscallions of the Southern Sea! Fire!"

Deafening shots rang out as both starboard and portside guns exploded. Each hit their mark. In response, the second vessel turned toward them with aid from the Falconer, breaking the line and moving into range for a last-second starboard volley. Krill screamed over the ringing in Braen's ears, "Hurry, you swabs! We can't let them get a shot off. Crab legs tonight if you get the rounds off first!" Each gunner signaled one by one and then Sippen nodded again. "Fire, you cold hearted turd chasers!"

Sippen's guns fired and projectiles screamed through the air with trailing whistles. The challenger exploded into a series of fireballs as each made impact, several igniting the powder stores. Braen's crew cheered as they loaded the next attack. But a second ship accelerated around the debris of the first, turning so that it would fire off a shot before *Malfeasance* could ready. The bearded captain shouted, "Brace for impact!"

As he shouted, he reached out instinctually and felt the beasts below the surface. *You've helped me before when I was in danger, please take that one out first!* When he opened his eyes, he saw that the dark shapes raced toward the target. His heart beat fast as they sped toward the ship and adrenaline surged in his chest as he replaced the fear with rage.

Braen Braston became a fearsome sight atop the forecastle of *Malfeasance.* His face no longer appeared calm and friendly, but twisted as if possessed. His beastlike roar caused every man on deck to pause in their loading and to stare at the animal leading their attack. As if answering his call, the tentacles from one of the Krakens wrapped around the hull of the enemy vessel, crushing it into splinters.

"Where's the next Falconer, Sebastian?" His voice roared demonically as he screamed the question, causing the boy to jump slightly and the sails to luff. "Hurry, Boy!"

Sebastian sputtered out, "Thuh... The fifth ship, Captain Braston!"

The crew watched in wonder as the second dark shape hurtled toward the ship, rendering splinters in the same manner as the first. "Next target! Now!" Blood poured from Braen's nostrils, staining his yellow beard orange. Veins throbbed in his contorted face and every muscle in his body flexed as he raged.

"Nine!" The crying boy shouted and then added, "Twelve, fifteen, eighteen, and twenty-two!" One by one the Krakens ripped apart the vessels containing Falconers, and one by one the sails of the other ships fell limp as they tried to turn into a position to fire.

As they passed the line of ships, Braen screamed at Krill, "For Cinder's sake keep them firing, Mr. Krill! Take the others down!"

Krill shook himself from his dumbfounded amazement and relayed the command, "Fire!" The ships trailing behind contributed their own ordinance and the remaining enemy vessels shook as masts fell and men hurtled into the ocean.

Sebastian kept yelling over the explosions, "Twenty-eight, thirty-two, thirty-seven, and forty!"

Soon, all of the ships containing Falconers had been destroyed and the water, once clear and blue, had become a frothy pool of floating wood and canvas. Braen fell to the deck in exhaustion and Sippen hurried over. "Do you see Eusari?" He asked his lifelong friend who shook his head.

"More sails, Captain!" Krill pointed westward as forty more ships raced into position. These would have the natural wind no matter if they held Falconers or not.

Braen rose slowly to his feet, steadying himself between Sippen and a sobbing Sebastian. "Turn us north and get us out of their range!" Suddenly the sails of *Malfeasance* fell completely limp. All eyes turned to the little boy clinging to the captain with tears flowing down.

"I... I can't do it anymore. I'm so afraid!"

Braen bent down and glared at the boy. He was a gruesome sight with his bloody beard and equally scarlet eyes. "Don't quit on me now, Son! We need you!"

"She's dead, Braen!"

"Who? Who's dead?"

"Suzette!" Sebastian fell to his knees and sobbed at an image burned forever in his mind.

"Of course, she's dead! She died months ago!" He remembered the death of the defiant little girl who had stowed away during their attack on The Cove. He and the boy had watched her impalement by a three-foot-long splinter, a shard from *Ice Prince's* broken mast.

"I can't... I can't do it, Captain Braston."

"You'll find a way, Sebastian. You will find a way, or we will die." The other ships raced by *Malfeasance,* leaving their admiral dead in the water as they attempted to curl around the enemy fleet for a better vantage.

"Captain, we have company!" Krill pointed toward five galleons breaking off and steaming fast toward the Cove's flagship.

Braen reached out to feel for the Krakens but they had left his side, fleeing his control the moment his rage had subsided. In the distance, a black ship led fourteen others into position behind the main force. The newcomers fired into them, providing the cover needed for the rest of The Cove's ships who opened full broadsides. The battle on the horizon raged as Braston and his crew stared at Sebastian.

The captain knelt before the boy and gently grabbed his shoulders. "Son hear me. They are stealing our wind and if you can't get it back, we'll be like Suzette. Do you understand that?" The Dreamer nodded. "Then I need you to catch us up to the others."

Sebastian regained his footing and walked to the rail. There he committed the contents of his stomach into the sea before turning to face the crew. His eyes rolled back into his head and he fainted onto the deck.

Braen scrambled into action, shouting orders and taking the helm in his hands. Adrenaline surged as he gripped the wood of the giant wheel, reaching out to the water lapping against the bulkhead. The entire ship groaned as he turned the rudder to starboard, catching the current that he created around *Malfeasance.* The ship turned very slowly, too large to adapt quickly to the change in heading.

Braen felt panic rising but focused on the water, trying to aim the ship into a position of attack. *I can't die here,* he thought, *I've got too much to finish.* On the horizon he saw *She Wolf* and the others exchanging fire with the few remaining ships. *At least Eusari will succeed after I'm gone.*

The five ships raced toward him in a line that would allow them five broadsides to his one. There was no way that he could take down even a single vessel. *I love her. I never thought I'd love another besides Hester, but I do. If only she would have forgiven me so that I could tell her to her face before dying.*

Braen returned from his melancholy just long enough to notice that the sea around him had calmed considerably. When the battle had begun, the waves were cresting between three to five feet, but now the ocean was smooth as glass around the ship. He reached a second time, feeling for the water a thousand yards out. He felt the warmth of the spring sun in the upper layer and began to draw upon that portion, heating the ocean above the cooler waters of the abyss.

He thought about Marcus Esterling and how easily his rogue general had cut down the boy's mother. Anger brought his mind back to Artema Horn and how he had tricked Eusari into delivering Braen to Skander. She handed him to the very man who had stolen both her virtue and childhood in a single horrendous act. *He is full of confusion not evil, and I could never hate my brother.* But somehow, in that moment, Braen envisioned how he had harmed Eusari and found a way.

The crew of Malfeasance stood frozen on deck, staring out at the storm brewing overhead. They snapped to attention when their captain roared at the sky. His guttural voice vibrated in their chests when he shouted, "Batten down everything that's loose! Tie yourselves off and get that boy below decks!"

One of the boatswain mates grabbed Sebastian and scurried below while Krill ordered about the crew and pointed at the incoming vessels. "The Cap'n aims to blow the men down, you blimey bastards!" He grabbed a line and lashed his body to a gunport. "Grab your hempen halter and tie off or you'll feed the fishes!"

The bearded captain let out another howl that ended with a thunderclap. The darkened skies swirled and swelled as rain punished the sea. Just as the enemy ships reached the edge of the storm, the winds raged out Braen's fury and spun tightly around the pirate vessel, forming an eyewall hundreds of yards across. The northerner took control of every molecule of water from the sea to the clouds of the storm, battering the enemy with a violent savagery that tore them apart.

One of them, a four masted galleon, managed to reach the calm waters of the eye and issued their challenge. They came around swiftly and fired a deafening broadside that ripped into *Malfeasance*, testing her armor. Thankfully the masts stood tall and the hull defiantly remained intact. The marvel of engineering fared much better than the crew, many of whom cried out with agonizing screams as shrapnel ripped at flesh.

Braen looked around the decks. Most crewmen had tied off at his order, but several lay scattered among the splintered planking. Once again, anger darkened his heart as he watched blood wash over the newly stained boards, permanently scarring his flagship and marking her a true warrior. One man in particular caught his eye. Krill lay moaning among the guns with his painted eyepatch staring at the heavens. His mangled and bloody hands were still caught in the rigging, and an ear appeared to have been sheared off. Rage erupted from Braston's chest at the sight of his friend, once again injured in his service. His face contorted as he bellowed at the water, screaming for it to obey.

With port guns still loading, the enemy vessel tried to come about, but the fierce northern warrior had given in to his anger, as berserk as the rampaging warriors of his homeland. Instead the enemy galleon spun counterclockwise with the water churning beneath and pushing hard against her hull. Using the ocean as his weapon, Braen turned the attacker's guns toward the sky, causing the Imperial crew to roll and slide until the heavy cannons crushed them against their starboard rail.

Both ships filled the eye of the storm with wails of misery and pain, but the devil aboard *Malfeasance* could not hear the cries. He was one with the water and could only hear the creaking sound of the vessel as he slowly rolled her completely over, leaving her keel to dry in the sun. One by one sailors and soldiers pierced the foamy surface, gasping for life. A gentle hand touched Braen's arm but he could not feel it for his rage. "It's over, Bruh... Braen," Sippen stuttered, "luh... let's fuh... fish them out."

Ignoring his friend, the Kraken King leaned against the railing and screamed at the terrified men in the water, "The ocean belongs to me!" After a glance at Krill trying to untangle himself from the lines, he added as froth spewed from his mouth, "There shall be no quarter!"

One of the men abruptly disappeared beneath the waves. The swimmers frantically turned and tried to climb the overturned vessel, but the barnacles were razors that shredded their calloused hands and put more blood into the water. Another man shot downward as if pulled, and the sailors further from the ship began to clamor over those against the hull.

Braen laughed at the sight and bellowed a final, sickening curse, "There's no escape, and the penalty of bringing harm against my crew is death!" The sharks leapt from the water with their massive white teeth bared, snatching their prey from the surface as they sunned before quickly diving below to feast. The water around the overturned galleon turned pink as red mixed with the white foam of their frenzy. Every man aboard *Malfeasance* stared in silence while their captain licked his lips at the sight. Only Sippen wept.

Having finished the battle that Braen had mostly won, Eusari steered *She Wolf* through a sea of debris. Most of the ships they had faced had been decimated, although Sippen's team of engineers would no doubt rebuild a formidable fleet from the usable wreckage. She had already dispatched a salvage team to gather the most seaworthy, and these would follow her and Braston's engineer back to The Cove.

Though it dissipated quickly, she noted a faint cloud of blood in the water around the enemy ships encircling *Malfeasance.* The flagship softly rocked in the strangely still ocean, drifting like a ghost in the desultory current without correction or heading. The chilling quiet was the only remnant of the battle that raged inside the storm that Braen no doubt conjured during the fight. Thinking about the storm raging inside the man sent shudders through her spine.

She had been watching the northerner carefully since they had met, and she now realized that the younger Braston was actually two men. Most of the time, he was the quiet and endearing Braen, eager to please and to calm the world around him. This man was charming and loving of everyone while constantly forgiving and ready to move on with amiability, even if with his brother who has hurt him and others the most.

The other man more closely resembled that very brother, full of anger and rage. In a moment he would turn dark and become the devil who had killed her father. When the demon took him, Braen would lose sight of the world around him and focus instead on the brutality of his destruction. He was impossible to stop when he went berserk, seemingly able to tear the world apart with his bare hands and teeth if it stood in his way.

As she pulled alongside, Eusari laid eyes on a gruesome sight and knew instantly that the Devil of Fjorik had returned. The deck boards of the shiny new vessel had already darkened from the blood of the battle. Everyone topside wore bandages that, despite their fresh application, were in much need of change. Even Krill's hands and head were tightly bound. He sat on a coil of rope with a needle and thread, frowning down at a project he was intent to finish. It was probably another absurdity by the man she considered to be of questionable sanity.

She spied Sippen standing over Braen. He held out a rag, but the captain refused to take it. The reason the engineer offered it was clear, his friend's beard and chest were saturated with blood that could have possibly been his own. She called out to the little man, causing both to look up, "Sippen!"

"Yuh... Eusari!"

"Let's get going. I want to get these ships towed back immediately." She glanced down at her blood-stained lover, a horrible sight to be seen. *Lover. But is he really? What are we, he and I?*

"Eusari." Braen's voice was still low and gravely, no doubt hoarse from screaming like an animal. "Can we talk?"

"Not now." She looked around, "This isn't the time or place." Her eyes rested on his bloody beard she added, "Nor are you the correct Braen."

She turned on her heel and led Sippen to *She Wolf.*

# Chapter Thirty-Three

Robert stared at the army amassed outside his walls. In all his life, he had never seen such a tremendous force poised for an attack in one place. This was more along the lines of the army that Maximus and Merrimac had led against Krist Braston and the Pescari before his birth. Blazing bright campfires dotted the landscape in perfect rows, stretching vastly into the horizon.

General Reeves stood next to Robert, sharing in the awe of the moment. "And thus, begins the siege, My Liege."

"I've never seen one. How long do we have until they attack?"

"Months. Maybe even a year. Our army is small, and this city is wealthy. With rationing we can hold out at least through the summer."

"We don't have to, Max." Robert turned to face his mentor who he now knew as his true father. Staring into his eyes felt almost as if he looked into a mirror of the future. "I contacted Braston and he's on his way to pull us out."

"That was wise, Robert. Why did you change your mind?"

"Something troubling that Marita said to me. If Pirate's Cove has both a fleet and an army, much less a contingent of emotants, then we'll need to forge an alliance with them."

"With power like, that he may not stop with Fjorik. Doesn't that ambition still worry you?"

"Yes, it does, and that means that I'll have to betray him first. But in the meantime, he provides an opportunity to fight Marcus now, instead of waiting for him to slowly kill me."

A gruff voice from behind caused both men to turn around. "Your brother isn't going to kill you slowly, and he most certainly isn't planning a siege." Mac pointed to the army outside the walls. "Look again, closer."

Robert did. He strained his eyes at the glow of the fires and scanned the rows. "They aren't pitching tents."

Max added, "And their artillery is behind the auxiliary lines."

Lourdes grunted approval at their observations. "They'll attack us soon. Thank the gods you got word to Braston. I was coming up here to tell you that he's arrived. He has twenty-five ships mooring in the harbor as we speak."

Robert pointed at the army. *The woman Falconer must have told them our plans. They will attack tonight before we can evacuate.* "I think it will be tonight?"

The old Major General shook his head in agreement. "I expect them to attack as soon as they can punch a hole in the wall. It will take hours of bombardment to knock down these walls. They're twenty feet thick. No, they can't do that in one night."

"Get the citizens to safety and the soldiers to the dock. I want to pull everyone out before sunrise."

Max responded, "I'll get word to Titus to make it happen." He offered his son a crisp salute and then ran down the stairway to spread the alarm.

"Max!" His mentor paused. "Get Sarai aboard Braston's ship."

"And the prisoners?"

Robert nodded. "Bring them in chains. I pledged to give them over but they're still my captives."

Reeves frowned deeply. "That may spark a contest between you."

"No. I made a deal. Take Captain Dominique into chains as well, in the name of The Cove."

Max gave another salute and hurried down the stairs, calling officers to him and dispatching them with the orders. Robert watched his father, wondering how the man had changed so easily from his mentor to his most loyal general.

"He loves you deeply." General Lourde's voice changed in the night, sounding less battle hardened and more grandfatherly.

“That’s something I’ve known my entire life.” His eyes met a kindly stare from the older man. “Why did you help me kill the Falconers during the battle, Mac?”

Lourdes looked at the young king with curiosity. “Four months ago, I would have doubted that powers such as yours existed outside of the Falconers.”

“And now?”

“I don’t know what to think.” Max sighed. “I’m an old man still playing soldier and getting involved in affairs that I’ve really got no business aiding. But I’m a weapon of sorts, one that you polish, oil, then set in an armory until it’s time to use it.”“And then?”

“And then I kill rather effectively. I’m good at one thing, Robert. I’m skilled at choking out the enemy and killing them on an open battlefield.” The greyed general let out a long sigh. “But even that’s changed. With powers like yours free in the world I’m a relic of the past. I can’t create strategy for your coming war. All I can do is help spot trends to help you stay out of traps.”

“I think you’re wrong, General. You’ve served both my fathers over the years, and you’ve always stayed on top of changing times.” Robert looked thoughtful. “Didn’t you perfect the use of artillery against the Pescari?”

“I did. But I’m an old dog playing new tricks when it comes to magic.” Movement attracted their eyes back to the wagons. Mac pointed. “What do you think’s in those, Your Highness?”

“I think that we’ll find out tonight, but I am assuming it’s full of Falconers ready to trap me.”

“Are you sure?”

“Yes.” The boy nodded, remembering the horde in the dream world. “I think they’re hiding more feathered freaks.”

“Can they lash you from here?”

“Only if they know my precise location. Usually a binding requires line of sight. I think I’m okay from this distance on such a large wall.”

“Want to test that theory?”

“Actually, I do.”

"Shake the tree, son. See what falls."

Robert closed his eyes and focused the air surrounding him. He drew it into a gale that he sent down the wall and across the line of soldiers, knocking over entire squads. The canvas atop the wagons ripped from the buckboards and lifted into the sky as the Falconers threw up shields in defense.

"Who in the god's names are they?"

Robert opened his eyes and stared down at the humans and the animals in the wagons. The giant cats were ferociously strong and sleek, able to run down a soldier laden with armor. The people were nearly naked, clad only with animal skins that matched the beasts laying peacefully among them. The hoods on their heads were identical to the faces of their cats. One by one they crawled from the wagons and moved into position beside the Falconers. Robert counted five of each to every wagon.

The fifty cats sat on their haunches and the fifty people sat on the ground with legs crossed, dark skin glowing eerily in the fire-light. They began to sway and dance with their arms in the air as if choreographed. They hummed as they undulated, adding to the curiosity of their ministrations. In unison, they placed their hands on the ground and the ground began to shake to their rhythm.

Robert turned to the old general with a look of concern. "I think we should run. Get everyone off the walls."

"Go!" Merrimac Lourdes shouted at the boy king, pushing him toward the stairs.

As Robert sprinted away, he looked over his shoulder to see the old man waving his arms at the archers. They stared back with confusion. The shaking intensified beneath the wall and the king stumbled several times before he was safely away from the crumbling structure. Looking up, he watched in horror as the stones disappeared beneath Merrimac Lourdes, causing him to lose his footing. Arms flailed as the general fell from the height along with several dozen bowmen, heavy granite falling like rain atop their lifeless bodies on the ground.

Horns sounded from the direction of the attacking army, shaking Robert from his moment of frozen horror. Cannons roared outside and soon pounded against the walls, severely weakened by the quake. Shards of rock exploded inward as the artillery beat against the crumbling stone. A large section collapsed in a cascade of debris which kicked up a dust cloud that climbed fifty feet into the air. He sprinted toward the docks.

Just as promised, he found twenty-five ships berthed in the harbor. One of the vessels stood out among the rest, glowing in the torchlight that reflected metal plating. A black flag with the image of a giant squid flew atop the main mast and Robert sprinted toward it. He could see that Maximus was already organizing the loading of troops onto the boats and fear fueled his sprint to his father.

The shaking had ceased, but the troops below seemed not to understand the imminent danger that closed in on the city. Max looked up from a conversation with Captain Titus. "What is it, Robert?"

Wheezing and out of breath, the oldest Esterling brother stopped to weave air into his lungs. They burned from the effort, but he didn't have time to control his breathing on his own. "The wall has fallen!" He panted with his hands on his knees. "Lourdes is dead, and they've breached the perimeter. Get them aboard!"

Max shouted at the soldiers boarding Braston's ship, "Make way!" They moved to the side and he half pushed, and half dragged, Robert aboard. He then shouted to the soldiers to double time the loading. They ran aboard the ships with as many duffels and satchels as they could carry.

Braen casually strode toward Robert, reaching out his hand with a wink. "King Esterling, I presume?"

"No time to talk, Braston. My city wall has fallen, and twenty thousand troops are funneling into the city."

Something in the man's casual demeanor changed, and he dropped his hand. He turned to a one-eyed man with a bandaged head and hands. "Krill! Signal the other ships! Break out the guns and prepare to repel boarders!"

Robert's head spun as the crewmen jumped into action. They hauled up long wooden boxes and flipped open latches to reveal contraptions with metal tubes and wooden stocks. On every ship the men manned the rails, kneeling with the instruments pointed in the direction of the wall. His own men continued to board the vessels, ushered below decks as quickly as they loaded until every man was off the pier.

The Northern captain shouted above the cacophony of panic from the regular army. "Steady your aim, boys!" The first line of soldiers rounded the row of buildings that led to the pier. With swords drawn they sprinted down the wharf. "Fire!"

Robert jumped at the explosions. Every crewman aboard every vessel fired into the advancing army, dropping them one by one as they ran. As soon as one man fired and reloaded, a man behind him would stand and fire. As he reloaded the man in front was ready and thus the cycle continued. Eventually the vanguard lay dead on the pier and the second wave faltered, hanging back to analyze what transpired.

A moment of panic gripped Robert. He ran to Max and shouted over the explosions, "Where is Sarai?"

"I haven't seen her, but I sent Titus to fetch her and the prisoners!"

"Braston! Can you hold them off a little longer?"

The bearded pirate narrowed his eyes. "What's wrong, Esterling?"

For a brief moment, Robert saw a darkness pass through the man that raised an alarm in his mind. "We're waiting for several more from the palace, and I need to ensure they get through."

"And my friends?"

"Among them."

"Then I'll go with you." Turning to the one-eyed man, he shouted, "Krill! I'm going ashore. Cover us until I get back. If I'm not back before the troops are loaded, get the fleet out of here!"

Max stepped in front of Robert and put a hand up. "Absolutely not! I can't allow you to do this, Robert!"

"Max. I'll be fine. I can do more out there than you or anyone else. Now move aside and get the men aboard."

After a moment, Reeves stepped aside without argument. "Be careful, My Liege."

"Always." A screech overhead announced the arrival of Arne and the pirates jumped backward as the giant eagle landed gently on Robert's shoulder. He spoke to his feathered friend, "Go find her!" With another squawk, the great bird rose into the air and took off in the direction of the keep. Robert ran after him and Braston followed.

Braen marveled at the confidence in the boy. They raced through the streets, avoided invaders, and ducked through alleyways that would have otherwise confused the bearded captain. He caught glimpses of the massive eagle flying overhead and kept reminding himself that the Esterling prince could see through its eyes. *Handy trick, that.* When Robert stopped running, Braen nearly bowled him over.

"What's wrong?" He asked with concern for his friends.

"They're just ahead, half a block."

Braen drew his cutlass and axe. "Then press forward, Boy! Why hesitate?"

The young man wheeled with eyes ablaze. "That's the first and last time you'll call me 'boy,' Braston."

"This isn't the time to argue over titles, Esterling." Braen grew restless, eager to race into battle to save the others.

"From now on, you'll address me as King Esterling, King Robert, or Your Majesty. Realize your place if you want me to refer to you as King Braston."

"Again, this isn't the time!" Pointing down the street he added, "We're running out of precious seconds and the Falconers will find them before we do."

Something in the boy's face changed, causing Braen worry. "What is it?" He asked, "What are you so afraid of?"

Robert turned in the direction of their friends. "Something much worse than Falconers. I've dealt with those, but I don't know how to fight these."

The northerner felt his back straighten with alarm. "Start talking and tell me everything we're up against."

"Tonight, there were others with the Falconers, men and women dressed in animal skins and accompanied by large jungle cats." There're too many of them ahead, and they have Captain Titus and the others pinned down."

"I'm not worried about cats." Braen pushed by the boy and started walking down the street.

"The earthquake earlier was their doing," Robert called after, freezing the large man in his tracks.

"Earthquake, you say?" Braen felt his hopes sink. "And they have animal companions?"

"Yes."

"Shit. They're just like Eusari then."

"You've seen them before?""I've seen something like them, and they're more powerful than we on dry land." He asked, "How many did you say are ahead of us?"

"I see fifteen of the beasts, but I assume there are Falconers as well."

"Then we need to come up with a plan."

# Chapter Thirty-Four

Captain Titus hurried into the keep. General Reeves had stressed urgency, and so he sprinted toward the royal apartments. The quake had slowed him a little, but he had recovered with renewed vigor when he realized that it had not been a natural phenomenon. He pounded on the Queen's door until she answered. Concern weighed her scarred face.

"What was that shaking, Titus?"

"I'm not certain, Your Highness, but I think the walls are falling. Robert wants you to hurry and meet him aboard Braston's ship."

"Braston's here?" She scrunched her nose in a grimace. She had never cared for fighting men and considered them just above pirates. "They made a deal?"

"Apparently so, Ma'am. I have to gather the prisoners." He quickly glanced down the hall, worried that they were running out of time. "Please hurry and meet me downstairs." She nodded and began scooping clothing into a bag. "No time, Your Highness! We don't have time to grab valuables."

Sarai paused and looked at the items she was packing. None of them were necessary for their escape, least of which was the silver mirror in her hand. She stared at the scars distorting her image and threw the gawdy item on the bed with disgust. "Even so, I do need to pack a few things. You go and I'll meet you downstairs."

He raced to the staircase and down a flight. The guards in front of the two rooms snapped to attention as he approached. "Gather all three and bring them outside. The girl too. Hurry! We have to get to the docks."

One of the soldiers looked at the door behind him. "Are you sure that's wise?"

"Open the damned door and let her out." Titus pushed open the other door and the two men inside rose instantly to their feet.

The older man, Pogue, spoke first. "What's going on? We felt the quake."

"We believe that they're attacking tonight." Sounds of artillery resounded, confirming his words as one of the guards stepped around Titus with shackles.

The other man, Horslei, pointed. "What are those for? Where are you taking us?"

"Braston is here to extricate us from the city, but you're still the King's prisoners until your trial." Titus felt urgency as the cannonade briefly paused. "We're running out of time. Put these on and let's go."

Pogue shook his head. "If they're breaching the walls then we'll go peacefully but without chains. Bring our swords."

"Absolutely not!"

A woman's voice spoke from the doorway. "Amash, if armed, do you pledge to turn your weapons over when we get to the boats?"

Horslei first exchanged a look with Pogue but answered truthfully to his sister. "If we get aboard *Malfeasance* alive, we'll figure it out then." He pointed at the soldiers gathered in the room. "But each of us is worth ten of them in a fight, so it's in your best interest. Besides," he pointed at Marita, smiling and standing behind Sarai, "we all know she's the biggest badass in the group."

Titus heard shouts from the streets below. "We don't have time for this. I won't shackle you, but I won't give you swords."

The small squad led the queen downstairs where they met up with two more soldiers and Captain Dominique. The pirate captain growled at his captors, rattling his chains in anger. When he saw Pogue and Horslei his face contorted with rage. "What's this? I'm bound like an animal while these murderers walk free?"

Titus shoved him forward as he passed. "Move." To the small contingent he ordered, "Get us to the ships as quick as possible." And then he added, "The queen is your priority if things go wrong."

They emerged into a warzone. The enemy flowed into the city but were slowed as they funneled through three fallen sections of the wall. *That's good*, he thought, *the bottleneck will slow their advance.* From the direction of the docks, Titus heard small explosions and shouts. Luckily for his squad the soldiers ahead seemed intent on aiding in that battle and weren't fanning out to storm the rest of the city. "We'll have to go around the buildings on the right to avoid the soldiers. Hurry!"

They sprinted down the street with Dominique staggering and tripping once over the chains. His guards hauled him up immediately and half dragged him as they ran. "Take these damn things off and let me run!"

"Quiet, Fool!" Pogue hissed under his breath, "You'll bring them down on us!"

"Too late." Horslei pointed at the sky, "Their spies already spotted us."

Titus squinted high into the clouds, thankful for the light of the fires illuminating the bellies of two large hawks circling above. "I think we're okay. There's only two of them."

"Only two?" Dominique faltered and again fell to the ground. With a moan he tried to right himself, but he again tumbled, striking his head on bricks. "These chains will get us all killed if you don't release me," he wheezed softly, holding his hand to his bloodied forehead. "I want out of here as bad as you, and my only option is with Braston." He held his outstretched hands for Pogue, defiant and refusing to budge any further.

"Oh, for Cinder's sake let him loose, Alec!" Horslei pointed up at the sky and the looming raptors. "Marita, can you do something about those?"

The little girl smiled and quickly thrust him a fist with an upward thumb. *She is so odd and touched in the head,* Titus lamented as he went to work on the pirate captain's shackles. With the turn of a key they dropped to the ground with a metallic thud.

"And now my feet," the slaver ordered, and the captain knelt to comply.

A screech from above turned his attention toward the birds, just in time to witness one turn midflight and attack the other. "That was her?" He asked Amash with amazement in his voice. "I didn't know that was possible."

"She does a lot of things we don't expect." The answer came from Pogue who placed a fatherly hand on the girl's shoulder, giving her a squeeze of approval. With his other hand he pointed at the waterfront. "Let's move."

Before anyone could take a step, six sleek cats sauntered into the street ahead of them. A low growl from behind revealed that nine more had circled their flanks. The animals were enormous, and each rivaled a northern sabre cat with their massive jaws. Captain Titus quickly ordered his soldiers, "Cover Queen Sarai!"

"For Cinder's sake, someone give us our blasted swords!" One of the soldiers complied and Pogue, Horslei, and Creech joined the fighters as they formed a circle around the woman and the girl.

The beasts abruptly leapt as a unit and Titus swung his blade, catching one of the great cats in the shoulder, deflecting its bite. His own muscles screamed from the impact, having struck a solid beast. Movement caught his eye, and he watched in awe as two sword masters went to work. Amash Horslei and Alec Pogue wielded their dual blades like artists painting canvas, with deliberate strokes that colored the world around them.

The two men danced amid a flourish of steel as they spun and sliced through flesh, felling beast after beast. Pogue ducked under the jaws of one and immediately sidestepped an attack from a second. Titus watched as instinct alerted the man to a third attack from behind. Kneeling to the ground, he spun onto the opposite foot and drove his blade upward and into the animal's heart.

Horslei fought with the same graceful technique. His fluid evasiveness rivaled the agility of the cats, dancing and weaving while biting their hides with steel. At one point the man whirled and faced two attackers from opposite directions. They flew through the air with teeth bared and Amash knelt, making a smaller target as the beasts converged. At the last moment, he crossed blades and drove both points home, disappearing beneath the massive cats with the tips of his blades protruding from their backs.

In seconds, the two men had fought off the initial attack, driving back eight of the jaguars and felling seven. Titus and his squad continued to protect the queen and the young girl beside her. "Form up," he shouted, "prepare for a second assault!" Before the men could move, a gust of wind pinned the team up against the wall. Unable to move, he and the others were like insects in a collector's frame. The captain felt ivy branches twisting around his arms and legs, locking him in place as he tried to speak over the sustained wind. "Marita!" He choked out the words, "Do something, dearie!"

Marita felt the tiny tendrils curl tightly against her arms and legs as her clouded mind cleared. The sudden arrival of the giant cats had terrified her, and, in her panic, she had forgotten to protect her friends and Lady Sarai. Other than Gelert, she had never seen such a massive animal. *I could have protected them,* was her final thought before a sudden gust of wind pressed her and her friends tighter against the wall. The pressure took her breath away, causing her to panic and momentarily lose sight of the threads woven by the Falconers. Black and brilliant specks swam in her vision as each breath drew less air than before.

She tried to reach out to feel her restraints, but they were of a different substance. Although she could feel something coursing through the veins of the branches, the sensation was different than when the girl touched the air. Her thoughts turned to her mother, standing like an apparition before her. *Why can't I feel the vines, Mama?*

"Because they are of a different affinity than you possess, sweet daughter." Her mother was as beautiful as the day she died, long auburn hair brushing her shoulders and framing her smiling face.

*What is affinity, Mother? I don't know that word.*

"It means that you are sensitive to the air and the vines are of the soil, bound in carbon and the leftovers of decay."

Marita understood her mother's words. Over the past few months she had learned to master the swirling gasses and molecules that surrounded the world and reached into heaven. It made sense that the ground would have similar molecules that other emotants, like Eusari, could touch. *Help me understand, Mama.* She pleaded with deep sadness in her heart. *Why are these evil people trying to hurt us?*

"Because I sent them to find you, Marita. I was worried that they would teach you how to hate and sow chaos."

*That doesn't make sense, Mama. They are a family to me, and I love them. I'm looking after them and teaching them to smile like you showed me.* Tears fell down her tender cheeks as they talked. *I even give them the sign of hope that you taught me!* Marita managed to stick her tiny thumb up into the air and smiled broadly for her mother.

"Marita!" Someone screamed beside her. "Marita, don't listen to her!" The voice of Alec Pogue drew her closer to reality.

"But it's Mama, Alec."

"No, dearie! Your mother is dead!"

His words confused Marita because, although she knew that her mother was passed on, he should see that Mama stood before them, wiping the tears from her crying face. She smiled at the tender touch of her fingers against her cheeks.

"Look closer at her face, Sweet Dear!"

"But she's here, Alec." She protested. "She's here to take care of me."

"She's a Falconer, dearie! Open your eyes and see!"

Marita's eyes focus against the spots swimming before them, resting on a vile specter. Instead of flowing auburn hair, she stared at a bald head without even an eyelash. This woman's eyes were round and not hazel as she remembered. Two blood red orbs stared up at her, piercing the night with intensity. Something about the specter's features were familiar to the child, as if she had seen them before.

The girl reached out and found the Falconer's mind. They only touched for a brief second, but it was enough for Marita to know that she had been deceived. Her voice changed in that moment and she once again felt anger rise within. "Your sister thinks you're dead, and your brother would like to know that it's been you trying to hurt the Dreamers."

The Falconer frowned at the words, then her eyes grew wide with realization. She tried to back away from Marita as the girl wrestled away the winds pinning the squad to the wall. With a heave, they suddenly changed direction and hit the specter in the chest with full force. She flew backward in the air, slamming against a building hard enough to shake dust from the masonry. As she lay motionless on the ground, a bound Marita gave her a smile and an upward pointed thumb.

# Chapter Thirty-Five

Eusari remained silent the entire voyage to The Cove. The battle had ended quicker than she expected, given the improved weaponry and use of emotants. Braen had been right about their military application and she was losing the fight to keep the children out of combat. *He's been right about a lot of things,* she pondered, *am I wrong to chastise him for the elections?* Peter Longshanks approached her on the starboard rail.

He gestured toward the fleet of broken vessels in tow behind her fleet. "Sippen said that we may have to scuttle one of the frigates if we take any longer. It's taking on more water than we feared." Eusari nodded. She had worried about a few of them but having the engineer on board helped, even if he appeared deeply troubled. His eagerness to join her on the return voyage had surprised even her, as he rarely left Braen alone to fight and usually preferred to stay at his side.

Her voice was coarse from lack of use when she answered, clearing her throat as she started to speak, "Tell him to wait until we know for sure. We captured twenty-seven ships, and, although one may seem expendable, we'll need many more when we go up against the Eston and Norton fleets." She turned away from the water and faced her friend. His eyes met hers with the kindness of a father waiting to speak with a troubled child. "Just spit it out, Peter. I know what you've been waiting to ask."

"When are you planning on forgiving him, Eusari?"

"I already have, I think."

"You think?"

"I'm not used to this. I never expected to trust anyone again, and I'm still learning how."

"He loves you. We all know it and so do you. You can't expect a man to keep every promise. What's important is that he keep the big ones."

"Which are?"

"How well he takes care of your heart and your body." Her wise friend leaned with both forearms on the rail and stared out. "I was married once. Did I ever tell you that?"

"No." She waited questioningly for the story. "What happened?"

"I was a lot younger then. Please know that, especially when I describe how I treated Racinda."

With her interest peaked, she nodded agreement, not wanting to interrupt.

"I was a mate aboard a transport barge in Eskera at the time. I spent a lot of time upriver in towns like Logan and Weston. Unfortunately, the captain committed to a contract out of Norton to help move the capital to the new city of Eston. That kept us quite busy as merchants flocked to lease the prime spots atop the Span."

"I remember that time. It was right after I was... after I was sold into service on board *She Wolf.* The first time I sailed under the bridges, I marveled at the engineering. They seemed to brush the sky above me."

"Aye, dearie. Many a citizen was caught up in the excitement of the city. Not only was it impressive, but it would finally stop the northern aggressors from reaching the inland cities and farmlands."

"How long were you stationed there?"

"A year, but a day was too long, if you ask me. We made hundreds of trips across the lake before we were informed that we would extend for another year. I wrote to my wife, asking her to move to the new city, but she didn't want to leave her family in Eskera. We fought through written words if you'd believe that."

"Racinda stayed behind."

"Yes. Gave me an ultimatum to come back then or never. But I was under contract, see? I couldn't break it without them branding me as an outlaw. I was locked in for another year."

"We argued for quite a few months via letters, and I finally grew so resentful that I let a lass turn my head in Eston. She was a beauty and willing to share my bed when we were in port."

"Peter, you cheated on your wife?" She never expected such an admission from her friend. Oddly, she wasn't angry with him and appreciated his candor."Aye. I loved Racinda very much, but I was lonely and hurt." Eusari could see tears of contrition forming in his eyes as he spoke. "One day, she surprised me by stepping off a boat with a wee one at her side. I'd never known that she had born a child, but I suddenly understood why she wouldn't leave her parents. He had been sickly, and she hadn't told me about him out of fear he wouldn't survive infancy."

"She came to you after he was well enough to travel?"

"She did. She had finally decided to give the new city a chance." Peter turned his face away, letting the wind dry his eyes. "She knocked on the door and met my lover at my apartment while I was working the docks."

"Peter..."

"I broke her heart. I came home about an hour later and met both women sitting at my kitchen table with the wee lad playing on the floor beside them."

"What did they do?"

"They both kicked me out and I moved onto the barge until after she and the lad could book passage back south. I wrote to her every day for two years, but she never answered, and I assume she never forgave me."

"I wouldn't have either. I'm sorry, but I understand her stubbornness."

"Aye. That's why I'm telling you. Captain Braston failed to keep a promise, but he never broke your heart. I hope that when he returns to The Cove in a few days that you've made up your mind on the matter."

"Why is it that you always seem to know the right words to say to me, Peter Longshanks?"

The First Mate bent down and scratched her wolf behind the ears. "For the same reason that Gelert never growls when I approach. Because you know in your heart that I'm not a threat and that I'll always defend you, My Captain." The wolf let out a sharp bark of agreement and the man rose up, placing his weight onto his peg leg before ambling off. Eusari stared at his back, wising silently that her father had lived long enough to give similar guidance.

"What do you think, Gelert? Do I forgive the man I love?" The beast growled but then settled down with a whine and a whimper. "Yeah. I agree. It's probably best if I give him more leeway when it comes to my heart."

Pirate's Cove was a welcome sight for all of the crewmen who accompanied *She Wolf* and the crippled Esterling fleet. They lined up the prisoners who volunteered service to the Pirate's Guild, rather than drown in the Southern Sea. Each man would be reassigned to a vessel according to their skillset and would assist the coming fight. With so many captured ships, the docks were a spectacle that brought a chuckle from Samani Kernigan.

"Well, Sippen, it appears that you have a lot of work to do."

"As if I di... didn't have enough." The engineer's broad smile revealed his excitement for more projects to oversee. His team of skilled artisans had also grown in mere months, and they cranked out ships and weapons faster than he had believed possible. "Whuh... where's Eusari?" It was difficult to spot one person in the multitude on the pier, even one dressed in black leather and followed by a wolf.

"I haven't seen her since you both arrived."

"Wuh... we need to fuh... find her fast."

Samani glanced at the Northern longboat tied off to a smaller pier. The captain of *She Wolf* rarely missed details and would have questions. He had hurried down from the keep as soon as they approached and hoped to prepare her. Sippen had turned ashen at the news of the arrival and was filled with more anxiety than usual.

A voice from behind made both men jump. "Why is a Fjorik boat in the harbor?"

"Good gods, Eusari!" Samani grabbed his chest and took a moment to breathe after the scare. "You're as bad as your wolf! Don't do that!"

"I'm going to ask one more time." Her green eyes were tinted with red, a sign of her anger. "There'd better be a good explanation for one of Skander's ships tied off in our harbor!"

"She arrived yesterday."

"Who arrived yesterday?"

Sippen answered before Samani could find the words. "Luh... Lady Huh... Hester."

A look of horror paled Eusari's face and she turned, emptying her stomach over the side. Both men stared expectantly, waiting for her to finish. "I'm sorry, guys. I've been ill these past few mornings." Samani could see that her face was flushed. "Why is the wife of Skander Braston in The Cove?"

"She suh... said that she's here to see Bruh... Braen. Wuh... Won't talk to anyone else."

Eusari drew one of her blades from inside her leather tunic. "She'll talk to me." Neither man dared to stop her as she spun on her heel and made for the palace above. They trailed behind, huffing breathlessly behind her, trying to keep up as she climbed the steep streets. Gelert's hair bristled along his back, worrying both men as they chased her through the town.

"She'll kuh... kill her, Suh... Samani!" Sippen's eyes were wide with worry.

"I damn well know that!" Kernigan kept his own eyes locked on the devil who'd replaced the normally calm Eusari. "I just hope that she doesn't kill anyone else in her rampage!"

"Shuh... She's wuh... worrying me."

"I can hear you both." She shot a steely glare over her shoulder. "I have more self-control than you give me credit for." Samani and Sippen exchanged another glance. At the sight of their worry she rolled her eyes and let out a sigh of disgust.

The trio arrived at the tall portcullis of the keep at the same time, the men having hurried to catch up. The guards watched with amazement at the drawn blade in the hand of one of their newly elected officials. One of them moved forward to remind her that blades must be sheathed in the palace. A growl from either Gelert or Eusari stopped him in his tracks. "Wise choice," the other soldier whispered. Samani and Sippen nodded at the men as they jogged past, red faced and panting.

Once inside and out of earshot, Samani pleaded, "Eusari, at least listen to the woman's story first." He let out a high-pitched whelp when the leather clad captain whirled around and pointed the blade at his throat.

"And why in the name of Cinder would I do that?" Strands of hair fell into her face and she blew them out of her eyesight without blinking. "This woman helped kill a king and sent Braen into exile. She's also the reason he can't completely give his heart over to me!" Kernigan had never been this close to the tip of her blade and the feeling unnerved him as she continued. "As long as that woman lives, I'm Braen's second choice. I'll kill her alongside her husband or separately, until all of his ghosts are put away for good!"

"It would be a shame to kill me before thanking me." A woman's voice drifted pleasantly from one of the rooms off the hallway. Eusari spun and, with blade still against Samani's throat, drew another with her free hand and pointed the tip at the woman's heart. Both Kernigan and Yurik held their breath and prayed to Cinder that she didn't hurl it at the queen.

"Thank you for what, exactly?" The words left Eusari's mouth with a snarl. Gelert moved closer to the woman with teeth bared. It was impossible for onlookers to know which wolf poised more danger.

"For getting Braen out of Fjorik. If it wasn't for my warning, he would've died on the gallows."

"Lies." The knife in Eusari's left hand flipped in the air and she caught the tip, bending her arm as if to throw.

"I'm afraid not." Without taking her eyes off the blade, Hester addressed Sippen. "Tell her what happened that day and how you got Braen away."

Eusari kept one eye on the beautiful northern woman but cocked her head toward the engineer. "Tell me fast so I can kill her slowly."

"She's tuh... telling the truth." Sippen's eyes were wide with fear and it was difficult for him to speak. "She suh... sent muh... me uh... a note. Suh... said thuh... that Skah... Skander wuh... would kuh... kill him." Tears formed in the little man's eyes as he recounted the events. "I stuh... stole *Ice Prince* and tuh... took him away."

"Why would you do such a thing if you were scheming with his brother?"

"I never schemed, Dear. I love Braen with all my soul. I got him safely from the kingdom and then did what I had to... endured what I had to for my own survival." Something changed in the queen's countenance and her beauty was briefly lost in a private hatred of her own. "I despise Skander more than you can ever imagine."

Eusari drew her arm back and sent the knife flying end over end. As soon as it stuck in the wooden door, she drew another from her tunic and readied it to throw as well. Hester didn't flinch when the knife flew at her face, but a trickle of blood from her ear ran down her cheek. "Don't presume that you understand my hatred for your husband. Speak like we're friends again and the next blade is in your throat."

Hester's spoke with cool calmness. "I'm sure that he's done nothing to you that he hasn't done to me." She touched the blood from her wounded ear. "I see that you like blades and bloodletting as much as Skander."

The tip of Eusari's knife wavered briefly in the air but she recovered and reared back to throw. Rage had consumed her, and she prepared to murder the heart's desire of Braen Braston. Hester turned her back and pulled the strings of her dress with a single motion, letting it fall to the floor in a heap. The only sounds in the hallway were three gasps and the metallic thud of a knife falling to the floor.

# Chapter Thirty-Six

Braen waited impatiently beside Robert, worried that they were taking too much time. The prince flew as his bird high overhead, peering at the scene below. They had crept as close as they dared, careful not to make any noise or attract attention. He shifted his weight nervously, anxious to charge in.

"There are three on the rooftops and three more on the ground." He had been searching the area for traps or surprises, but so far found none. The small group of soldiers escorting Sarai attracted the entire attention of the Falconers. "Wait. Now that's odd." He paused for a moment longer than Braen could hold his patience and the bearded man grabbed his axe from his belt. "Marita seems to be speaking with one of them."

"What about the strange looking ones in animal skins? How many of them do you see?"

"I counted fifteen cats, but I only see five of the humans."

"Then we need to avoid anything living like roots or branches. We should also watch out for anything that could topple over on us."

"I agree. Are you ready to deploy the fog?"

"I am. Let me find a water source." Braen reached out with his senses until he found the sewer pipes several feet below the street. He nodded to Robert who inverted the warm and cool air, ready to trap the water vapor. Within minutes several streets around them were completely obscured from both ground level and bird's eye view.

"Get ready to do your thing, Braston." Something in the boy changed as he spoke, gaining more confidence and authority.

"Okay, I found the source beneath the vines." Braen could feel the roots protruding into the cistern below and hoped that their plan would work. The sewer flowing into the cistern resembled a maze, with branches flowing into a single major artery just a few streets over. The spot beneath his friends was one of the larger catacombs but was unfortunately upstream from the bountiful main vein. He divided his mind as he focused on the water, pushing against the source above and holding tight to the flow downstream and willing it not to leave his grasp.

He could no longer feel the roots as strongly as before, but they held enough moisture to attempt Robert's plan. His body burned as he attempted a third split in his mind, focusing on wicking the water from the roots. At first, the dripping beads of water barely splashed against the dry stone of the sewer, but one by one the droplets fell like rain. Soon a monsoon washed through, adding to the ever-growing lake he held downstream. He nodded to the Esterling King to begin. Focused on the task, he barely heard the screech from above as the giant eagle dove into the fog.

Marita watched with curiosity as the fog materialized in the street. Quickly, she recognized the changes in the air around them and smiled at Braen's cleverness. *This is how we got into The Cove,* she remembered. *That means he and Robert are nearby.* She tugged at the vines holding her to the wall and frowned at their strength. She would have to wait for whatever they had planned.

Careful not to alert the Falconers, she reached out to the king with her mind, *Robert, where are you?*

*I'm close.* The response was brief. *You and the others will be able to break free soon. Arne will give the signal. Then I want you to keep the six Falconers busy while I find those controlling the cats.*

In an excited voice, she spoke to her friends, "When I give the word, I want everyone to break loose and charge the kitties. I'll take care of the six Falconers."

Everyone looked confused as they stared down at the pacing jaguars and specters. The two still on their feet were helping up the female. Sarai spoke, "Marita, there are only three. Are you feeling okay?"

"I'm fine, Lady Queen. When Robert comes, we need to act quickly, so that I can find the other monsters."

"Robert is coming?" Sarai's voice betrayed concern for the safety of her love. She had hoped that he was already aboard the ships.

They were interrupted by a loud screech as an eagle rushed by in the dense fog. His appearance was quickly answered by screams from the Falconers as he connected and ripped at flesh. Marita focused her senses above and found six birds diving to help their masters. She removed the air from beneath their wings and they plummeted like sacks of flour tossed from a window. As they landed, sounds like wet towels slapping on stone made everyone grimace.

The twisted branches around imprisoned arms withered and shrank, becoming brittle. Marita was the first to rip free of the wall, shouting for the others to follow. As each fell to the ground beside her, she sent three lassos of air onto rooftops, grabbing ahold of the other three Falconers and pulling them stunned from their roosts. The sounds of their landings were far more gruesome than their birds and closely resembled breaking branches.

The soldiers and former prisoners grabbed their weapons from where they lay and charged the great cats. Three managed to escape into the fog, but most of the squad trapped the others, butchering them with ferocious strikes until wisps of air formed a net that fell down upon the fighters. Unable to escape, the soldiers quickly became prey for the great cats who had returned for an easy kill. Leaping atop the pile, the beasts went to work clawing and biting at the bound men.

Marita watched Amash and Alec attack the beasts, fighting off one and killing two. Unfortunately, Captain Titus seemed to have been recaptured in the net with the others, and blood poured onto the sidewalk as he and his men wailed. Looking around, she noticed that Captain Dominique was nowhere to be seen. The girl screamed into the night, "Lift the fog, Robert!" She shouted again, "Quickly!"

The fog dissipated rapidly, and she spotted the cowardly slaver running the opposite way from the docks. She cast a net of her own with blinding speed, caught his feet, and toppled him to the ground with force. Amash and Alec raced away to retrieve him, while Marita stared down the remaining Falconers. The three on the ground had broken free of Arne's attack and faced her directly, awe in their eyes and impressed by her power. She smiled at them and gave a thumbs up.

Their first attack came swift and without warning. Wisps of air shot out around her, not as shackles but finer. The threads spun fast, closely resembling a cocoon as they flew. She sidestepped their attack with foresight, trails of events yet to come blurring toward where she had stood. *Clever,* she thought.

"You made a mistake tonight." She said with a smile, dancing and spinning around like she was at a fair. "You see, I've never been able to work magic inside a living person." Addressing the woman, she added, "But now I know that you're already dead." She first attacked the two men, reaching into their lungs and stealing their breath. While they drowned on dry land, Marita bound Ashima Nakala.

Robert Esterling stepped onto the street, dumbfounded by what Marita had accomplished in mere seconds. *She's so powerful,* he marveled. He looked up and down the street, straining his eyes for a glimpse of the humanoid Jaguars. Arne screeched above and immediately shared his sight, peering into bushes outside of a money changing house. He conjured a wind so powerful that the bushes lay flat and revealed five half-naked monsters sitting cross-legged and in a trance.

Braen shouted through clenched teeth, obviously struggling to hold the water. "They're conjuring another quake, Robert!"

The king nodded and threw a web of air around them, hoping to interrupt. But they kept swaying. Movement to his left caught his eye and he responded, "Not a quake, Braen!" He pointed to the five dead Falconers. "Look!" As the Jaguars swayed to their own music, the birdlike men raised up from the ground onto their feet. The three who had fallen snapped their broken legs into place, then walked toward the young girl standing over the bound woman. "Marita! Watch out!"

She briefly flashed the king a smile and thumbs up before wheeling around and sending a powerful lash. All five creatures again fell to the ground and she ripped the air from their lungs. Robert watched as it flowed out of their noses and mouths and as she used it to bind their hands behind their backs. And then the ground rumbled.

"There must be more!" Braen shouted.

Arne screeched and circled a high wall beside a tailor shop. "There!" Robert replied. Before anyone could respond, the tremor grew to a roaring quake that fell every building in the city square. His first thought was of Sarai, and he threw a shield of air around her and Titus's men. They were no longer bound, but he could tell that many had died, and most were bleeding. The stone of the building rained down and fell in piles around them.

"Marita, take Sarai and run!" Robert bellowed, "Get her to the ships!" She grabbed the Queen's hand, dragging her down the street and away from the specters. Amash and Alec returned with their quarry and he ordered them to follow and protect his wife.

Pausing, Marita yelled for them to also carry the bound female Falconer. "She's important! Grab her and bring her along!" Confused, but obliging, Horslei scooped her into his arms and ran to the ships,

Robert watched the sky for Arne, who responded with another screech. "There!" Once again, a blast of air revealed five more Jaguars seated and swaying to their eerie music.

"Do something about them, Esterling!" Braston screamed into the night.

"I can't. I can't take on all fifteen!" As soon as he spoke, the street fell out from under Braen. Robert watched in horror as the bearded captain fell into the cistern, followed by Titus and his injured soldiers.

The stone at the floor of the cistern met his body with a crushing thud. All at once every part of his body ached and Braston lay stunned, unable to breathe. *You're okay,* he told himself, *find out if anything's broken.* He flexed his hands and feet, then rolled over and tried to stand. To his left Titus and his soldiers lay bloodied and still on the stone. The captain's face had been sliced to shreds and a giant nail from a jaguar's claw protruded from his left eye.

He whispered a prayer to the gods for the fallen men and regained his footing, thankful that he hadn't met their same fate. The entire street above was gone, replaced with the nighttime sky. The steep walls were smoothed from decades of flowing water, preventing him from climbing out. He was trapped.

Robert's face appeared overhead. "Are you alive, Braston?"

"Barely so, but yes, Esterling." He flexed his hand, sore from the fall. "Get out! Go save yourself before they awaken those Falconers again."

` "I need to get you out first!"

"Don't be a hero on my account. Just promise that you'll acquit my friends and give Dominique his due."

The boy looked up, suddenly showing fear on his face. "It's too late, Braen. They're already up and the Jaguars are walking toward me." The fearful look grew into horror and he added, "Everything is coming alive now! The trees are even walking toward me, Braston! I'm trapped."

"Hang in there! I'm trying to get out!"

"Cinder's Crack, you won't believe this." His voice broke as he yelled down to Braen.

"What now?"

"Every stray animal in the city is moving toward me. Hurry, I don't think I can get away."

"Step back from the edge and be ready to run as soon as I release the water!"

"But you'll kill yourself in the process!"

"If I do, I do." After a pause he added, "If I do, then tell Eusari that I love her and that I'm sorry."

"I have a better idea, Braston." As soon as he spoke Robert jumped into the cistern, rolling as he landed and running to his side. A bubble of air formed around them as he said, "Let go of the water and let's get out of here."

The deluge of water rushed into the cistern, washing the men, living and dead, out to sea.

Sarai followed Marita to the docks where Maximus Reeves waited aboard a glittering copper-sided ship. The others were already leaving the harbor, and this lone vessel remained at the pier. She collapsed as soon as she was onboard and watched the crewmen drag the Falconer and the slaver across the brow. Out of breath she tried to talk. "Robert's still back there with Titus and Braston." Max drew his blade and began to run down to the dock.

"Wait!" Marita called to the general. "Robert just told me that we need to go without him. That he and Braen will catch up."

A bandaged Krill ambled over. "Where are they, dearie?"

"They're floating down the sewer to open water. Robert's showing me what he sees through Arne and will help me find them."

"No!" Sarai screamed, "Send soldiers back for him!"

Krill ignored the Queen's orders. "All due respect bein' givin', but aside from Marita, we don't know or trust any of you." He tottered on his wooden leg toward the girl. "Do you swear on me lost eye that you know they be safe?" She nodded, then smiled and gave a thumbs up. "Good enough for this scallywag. Let's shove off!"

It took an hour for them to find the duo, bobbing in the ocean in their air bubble raft. Once they hauled them in, Sarai ran to her husband.

"They're aboard, Mr. Krill!" Max's voice boomed and Robert stood to survey the situation.

Turning to Braston he ordered, "Get us out of here!"

# Part III
# Arising Powers

*Life of misery,*
*Death not binding,*

– *The Oracle of Astian, 754$^{th}$ year of order*

# Chapter Thirty-Seven

Skander tightly clenched his jaw, rising anger seething within. Hester had fled. She had left him and traveled south toward Braen. He felt searing humiliation and could already hear the world laughing at the pathetic king in Fjorik. Rumors would surely spread; mostly of his inability to control his queen or keep her in his bed. The only thought that soothed much of his fury was the sound her elixir had made as it had shattered against the bedchamber wall. *The bitch will welp my pup!* Of that he was sure.

He had brought his fleet north to make brief preparations for their next attack. Unlike Diaph, Middleton would fight back, and he planned to hone his new weapons before the battle. Pushing thoughts about Hester aside, he focused on his looming challenges. The foremost regarded the Imperial fleet. Most of Middleton's warships were on the Southern Ocean participating in the Eskera blockade. He could easily handle any resistance to his armada, especially with control over his powers growing.

His second concern was the sheer size of the bay. Middleton sprawled across many finger-like inlets reaching deep into the land. Although access to water suited his powers, several batteries would stand ready to pick off his ships if he ventured too deep. That job would depend on foot soldiers as his army moves door to door, fanning out and looting all they could carry. Each team would be accompanied by members of his newest elite squad, crushing anything that stood in their path.

That had been the most important reason for returning to Fjorik. He wanted to outfit his newest weapons in such a way as to invoke terror within his enemies. Skander had designed a special uniform and adorned them in pure white furs with hoods crafted out of the head of the northern sabre cat. He stood before an eerie assemblage of nearly one hundred men, women, and children. The ages of his children mattered not, and even the elderly stood in full dress before their father and lord. Each eagerly awaited his words.

Skander's army formed rows around the Sabre Cats, watching with trepidation. They stood at parade rest in columns facing the new weapons, and also awaiting his address. He briefly glanced at the meager force of berserkers that had once been his elite fighters. They were useless now, except for nostalgia of an earlier time. *So much has changed, but so much more is yet to come.* Unable to contain his excitement, he let out a chuckle as he stepped forward.

"My children!" He threw up his arms as he spoke, indicating the Saber Cats, "Terrible things were done to you, despicable acts that can never be erased or forgiven." He watched their eyes as he spoke, large as they soaked every word and eagerly seeking his approval and love. "You were given away by your families or taken by force to that place. Remember always, that horrible laboratory from which I rescued each of you personally." He smiled benevolently when he said, "I, alone, love you enough to gift you both a family and a purpose."

Wails of an infant abruptly erupted in his mind, threatening to interrupt his speech. They cascaded louder but he concentrated hard, trying to ignore them as he spoke. Then his father's voice also boomed in his head, temporarily drowning out the cries. *How can you be their family when you've destroyed your own, Skander? Do you even know how to love?* He pressed his hand to his temple, slightly easing the pain, and continued his address.

"You were born as gods instead of people and thus your families rejected you. They gave you to the Falconers to have and lord over. They gave you away without concern of your well-being. They kept you alive to dream but never to walk the earth. But I freed you so that we can create a new world, together, as gods!" He pointed to the sky.

Storm clouds brewed, but no rain fell from the black swirling mass above. Lightning licked the sky in the glowing form of a sabre cat and the crowd recoiled in fear. “Don’t be afraid, my children, for I would never harm you without cause.” He pointed to a familiar figure amongst them. “Brion, step forward so that the others may know you.” The man with a child’s mind walked toward Skander, trembling with fear. “Tell them what you did to me when you awoke.”

With chattering teeth, the man-child answered, “I used air to throw you across the room, Father.”

“Henceforth, my children, no one will strike me or my soldiers without facing my wrath. You are gods but lesser than I. You rule over air, whereby your father rules over life giving water.” He pointed at Brion, “Witness the penalty for disobedience!” A single bolt of lightning cracked down from the heavens, striking him in the chest. The man fell limp, heart having immediately ceased beating.

*You enjoyed that, didn’t you? That poor boy did nothing but act out instinctively.* His father’s voice again boomed loudly in his mind, this time forcing his eyes closed.

Despite the pain, he continued, “The city to which we sail contains a prison very much like the one that enslaved you. When we arrive, do not be afraid of the people who will fight to keep your brothers and sisters from joining us in freedom.” He smiled against the wails and the booming insults in his head, “Their penalty for defying the gods will be death, and we shall execute them all.”

The soldiers popped to attention and sent out thunderous applause as they rhythmically pounded swords against shields. Cheers rang out as they praised their king, calling him the true northern god. Skander waved back, smiled, and basked in the love that he had always craved but never received.

*All I ever wanted was for you to recognize my greatness, father, but you always loved Braen more.* His smile abruptly dropped into a scowl when Krist Braston answered, *And I always will for as long as he lives.*

The king whirled on his heel and left the cheering crowd behind. He shouted a command that brought his first mate running to his side, "Artur!"

"Yes, My Liege?"

"Ready the boats for the voyage but set one aside for the berserkers." A sneer curled his lips, showing yellow teeth, "I have a special mission for them, one that will bring in some extra coin."

"Where are you sending them, sire?"

"Farther south than Fjorik has dared to sail."

Mattie walked with the master of the house, not beside him, but a step behind as suited to her position as steward of the manor. She nodded along as he listed off his requirements for the dinner party. The banquet would be huge, she imagined, even larger than the extravagant feasts hosted by Artema Horn.

"And over there is where I expect to find the peacocks," he said.

*Yes,* she thought, *more extravagant, indeed.* "Have there been any more confirmations? I want to ensure that we don't run out of food."

"You had best not," he cautioned, "but we will stress the pantry for sure. Here," He pulled a wad of letters from his pocket and shoved them toward her, "I believe that brings the count up to one hundred and fifty-two lords."

"That's a lot of lords," she remarked, "does the title even have meaning down here?"

"Of course it does!" A sly smile crossed his face, "Although, only a handful of them really matter."

"I'm beginning to understand that." Mattie nodded her head thoughtfully as she flipped through the letters, reading the names and mulling over the various titles.

"Take this Viscount, for instance." Charro reached out a dark slender finger and pointed out a name at the top of one. "Scalia purchased his title a mere fifteen years ago." He frowned, "In fact,

I recall that he purchased it from our dear friend, Nevra, when he moved his operations to The Cove."

"So Nevra was a Viscount?" Mattie hated even speaking the name aloud, but she was honestly interested in the workings of wealth on the continent.

"At one time he was, in title, yes."

"So titles are purchased?"

"Along with the land and holdings."

She pondered aloud, "So, if he sold his title, then he isn't a lord at all?"

"Oh yes, he is very much a lord. In fact, his holdings rival only my own in Cargia."

"But, you said that he sold the title to Viscount Scalia."

"I see that you are confused. But that is expected since you hail from Andalon where titles are acquired through birthright and have nothing to do with holdings." He cleared his throat and continued, "Through shrewd purchases, Nevra rose to the level of Duke, like me. He sold only the portion of his holding that included the estate and manor house."

Shock filled her face. "So, he sold only the estate and that was large enough to make the buyer a Viscount?"

Lord Valencia nodded like a proud schoolteacher. "My dear Mrs. Pogue," he explained, "Stefan Nevra still owns a very profitable estate in Cargia."

"Define profitable."

"His empire is the center of all trade for the entire continent. He receives taxes on the docks, the warehouses, inspection of goods and the transportation of talent."

Mattie felt her stomach drop and she swayed with vertigo. "That monster controls the economy of the entire southern continent?"

"Not entirely. I still control a sizable portion. But yes, between myself and Stefan we steer the economy of our continent." He waved his hand dismissively, his eyes suddenly betraying some regret over holding the conversation. Mattie realized that it was improper to discuss these money matters with his steward. "Now, that will be all, Mrs. Pogue. Make sure that everything is in order and ready for the feast."

"Yes, My Lord." She bowed and was about to leave when he cleared his throat.

"And I want you to purchase attire for your daughters that is suitable for the occasion. With any luck we can find them work as ladies in waiting for some daughters of the other lords."

She paused and cocked her head with suspicion. "You want to sell off my daughters, Lord Valencia?"

"Not at all." He smiled softly like a caring father reassuring his child, "I want to ensure that they can rise in station, much as you have, Mrs. Pogue. As the daughters of my steward, they deserve the opportunity to become more than scullery maids." Another thought crossed his mind and he added, "Who knows, maybe one of the lords will take a liking to one of them and promote her to consort."

Mattie stifled a gasp, but smiled disarmingly. "I will pass that hope on to the girls."

"Also..." His face puckered and voice broke off as he considered something sour.

"Yes, My Lord?"

"Make sure that, on the night of the dinner party, you and your daughters stay inside the manor house. Do not wander far from the main hall."

"Why is that, My Lord?"

"Just ensure that you remain close. I have taken a liking to you, Mrs. Pogue, and want to keep you safe."

*Keep me prisoner, you mean?* She bowed slightly and then headed back to check on the kitchen staff. There was still so much to prepare, she thought, *Stop taking so long and rescue us, Alec!*

# Chapter Thirty-Eight

Shon Wembley watched the refugees with growing disappointment. He had hoped the scouting reports were wrong, but his eyes confirmed they were mostly women, children, and elderly.

Marque shared his concern. "They're going to be a burden until we can ship them south."

"Aye. That they will."

"At least the woman holding a bow looks like she can actually use it." With a smile he added, "If she can hit a target the lot isn't a total loss."

"Be honest. You're interested in her for other reasons." Shon offered his friend an approving nod, "Although, I'll admit that she's nice to look at."

"I'd rather stare at a pretty girl than your ugly mug." Marque pointed at a cart pulled by a teenage boy and a girl. "That old woman has got to be eighty or ninety summers, at least!"

The woman with the bow exchanged words with a scout then spoke to the teens. She pointed at Shon and they began walking toward him. The ancient woman riding in the cart stared him down as they neared. "Marque. You talk to them, I'm not in the mood to deal with beggars.

"It was your idea to invite them."

"Aye, but at the time I'd hoped they'd be useful." He turned to make his exit when the old woman called out, "Mr. Wembley!"

*Shit,* he thought, *damned scouts told her my name.* He put on a fake smile and faced the group expectantly. "What can I do for you, Mother?"

"Why are you gathering emotants?" The question wiped the smile from his face and replaced it with a look of shock. "Close your mouth! You look like a buffoon," she ordered.

"How did you know that we're gathering emotants?" His eyes darted to the teenagers and back to the old woman hopefully.

"These youngsters each received a missive and were told to come to this place. What I want to know is where is Samani Kernigan?" She made a show of looking around then added, "Because when I find him, I'm going to drag him out by his ear."

Shon finally found his voice and responded, "He isn't here, Mother. He's currently in The Cove planning our next move against the crown."

"So, he isn't just aiding revolutionaries, he's leading them?" To the woman with the bow she added, "He's violated every code by which we've lived our entire lives." Her companion nodded her agreement. "How many emotants have you recruited and what are you using them for?"

"That's sensitive information, Mother. I don't even know your name."

"Tell Samani that Pearl has arrived. This beautiful woman your friend is ogling is named Madelyn and the children are Johan and Kali." She stepped down from the cart with a hand from the boy. "Show me your emotants."

Next to Shon, Marque laughed hysterically, causing Wembley to turn. "What's wrong with you?"

"You said that you wanted them to be useful. I'd say you can retire and let her run the entire show. You've finally met your match, Boss!"

Shon punched his friend in the arm then gestured to the newcomers. "This way, Mother. I'll show you everything."

Kali and the others followed the man named Shon to a group of buildings on the northern edge of town. She immediately noticed eight teens standing in a clearing between the buildings. The oldest gave an order and a whirlwind spun through the field. He gave another and the vortex split into eight separate funnels. Kali squeezed Johan's hand and whispered, "Air!"

Wembley overheard and responded, "Yes, so far that's all we've found. What's your specialty?"

"You're assuming we're emotants."

Shon winked back and pointed at thumb at Pearl. "She already said that you were, dearie."

Kali rolled her eyes and responded, "I'm able to do things with plants and the ground."

Abruptly a black bear ambled out of the grove of trees on their left.

Marque lifted his bow, but Shon stepped in front. "Lower it and watch," he said.

The animal approached and then reared up on its hind legs. Shon started forward and placed his hand on its paw. "Beautiful animal, Kali. Have you bonded with her long?"

"Oh, I'm not bonded with her. I'm bonded with that fox over there." Wembley's eyes grew wide in shock as the bear roared into his face. He stumbled backward and fell, scooting away in terror as Marque again lifted his bow. Kali's childish laughter froze both men in their tracks and they watched the giant beast nuzzle against the girl's chest. "That was too easy! You guys are funny!" After she had laughed at their expense, her face turned thoughtful. "How did you know I could bond with her?"

"My niece shares the same powers and is bound to a wolf. Can you also make the ground quake?"

"I haven't tried that, but I can do this." She pointed at the grove of trees and the party turned. Three tall pines ripped their roots from the dirt and began dancing around in the meadow, spinning with elegant pirouettes. After a few moments they bowed to the onlookers and returned to their beds.

Pearl, who had quietly watched the exchange, let out a low whistle and remarked, "Now that's impressive."

By now the other teenagers had noticed the newcomers. They hurried over and Shon made introductions, pausing at Johan. "What's your power?"

"Water. I can't really show you right now." He gestured around the meadow. "I've nothing to draw from."

"Actually, you can do quite a bit. Can you sense the creek flowing in the east?"

Johan closed his eyes and concentrated. When he finally opened them, a plume of water shot westward, spraying the buildings like a fountain in a market square.

"Great work! We've got some other ideas for you as well. Braen Braston has worked out quite a few combinations that you can try with the other emotants." He motioned to a taller girl in the group. "Beth, why don't you show them the barracks get them settled in?" With a grin he added, "You should introduce them to Akili." The girl smiled broadly at his suggestion and shuffled the others toward a long building. After they had left, Shon addressed the old woman. "How do you know Samani Kernigan?"

The lines of wisdom on the old woman's face deepened as she considered old memories. "I mentored him and brought him to Andalon more than twenty years ago."

"So, it's true, then?" He turned his eyes to the children playing tag in the field. "He really is from the other continent?"

"He's told you truthfully."

"Why?" Wembley had struggled internally with this question since meeting the man. "Why is he here and what's his goal?"

"He and I are part of The Humanitarian Freedom Society. I recruited him over thirty years ago out of the Winter Oracle. I brought him and another young recruit to Andalon, where we've worked our mission."

"What exactly is your mission, Mother?"

"We were to blend in and observe your people for signs of a fulfilled prophecy." Worry crept into the old woman's eyes. "But from the sound of things, he's no longer observing and has progressed to interference."

"You've been expecting the emotants to emerge for more than twenty years? Why observe if you've no intention of exploiting their powers? At least Samani is aiding our cause for the greater good of Andalon."

She rounded on the former constable, suddenly less feeble and more intimidating than before. "Our prophecies foretell the coming of a destroyer who will destroy the world."

"Ours or yours?"

"Mostly ours, but there are many of us who believe that his destruction will affect all the continents." She sighed and slumped down, again looking tired and old. "Both of my protégé's were young and overly passionate about their role in Andalon. We later disagreed on key doctrines."

"Like what?"

"They had a different view of The Destroyer's role."

"And what was their belief?"

Rustling of leaves caused them both to turn as two women emerged from the woods. The older of the two stared intently at Pearl who responded with a gasp. "Fatwana Nakala?"

"Continue your story, Perlana. Just what exactly is my brother's belief regarding The Destroyer?"

# Chapter Thirty-Nine

Captain Frederique Titus had died, of that he was sure. Vivid memories remained of the jaguar ripping at his flesh and drenching him in blood, both his own and that of his men. He also remembered the ground falling away beneath him and hitting the water below. But he had blacked out when stones and debris rained down. At one point in the sewer drain he had come to, gagging on filthy water and counting himself lucky that he had not inhaled and flooded his lungs. But he vaguely remembered feeling the unmistakable burn within his chest as if he had.

He coughed and sputtered on the beach, spewing rancid water on the sand. Every time his body convulsed to push out the fluid, his temples crushed his brain like a vice. Flashes of light behind his eyes reminded the military officer that he was again living, even if he had wished otherwise. He finally fell in a heap and allowed his body to slip again from consciousness.

When he eventually decided to rejoin the awakened world, Titus found two men casting shadows over his body. "Looks like a Captain from what's left of his uniform, Sarge."

The second man asked, "Are you sure about that? There's not much left of it or him."

"Positive, Sarge," the first man responded, "that makes two officers in two days."

"Who?" Titus tried to stand but his legs weren't ready. He collapsed in the sand face first.

"Don't try to walk, Caps. We've sent some privates for a litter. We'll get you back to camp." The man called Sarge knelt down beside him and asked him the question he feared, "But first, we need to know what side of the war you're on."

Caution urged him to silence, to only state his name and rank as he was trained. "I am Frederique Titus, Captain in the true Esterling army."

The enlisted men shared a laugh before Sarge asked, "Which Esterling army, Mate? Right now, that makes all the difference in the world."

Titus suddenly realized that he no longer cared if he lived or died by their hand, especially since he was confident that he had already passed. He responded with assertion, "The true king, His Royal Highness Robert Esterling." He again passed out, this time from the effort of speaking the words.

When he awoke the third time, he found himself laid out upon a cot within a tidy military tent. Several soldiers passed by the opening, but no guards appeared to linger outside. *They must not believe me to be much of a threat in my current state*, he reasoned. Pain radiated from his right eye. He felt along his face with cautious fingers, gingerly touching the bandages around his head. Someone had placed extra packing around that eye, so he assumed the trauma had been significant.

His stomach growled as he moved into a sitting position, and he suddenly realized how hungry a dead man could feel. Looking around he spied a bowl of stew left out on the ground next to him. He gave in to the appetite and devoured the contents without tasting. It went in and stayed down easily.

Belly full, the captain rose from the cot and stretched his sore and aching muscles. They were especially painful where the large cat had bit his shoulder. He pressed on the wound, palpitating and checking for infection. Finding it surprisingly clean and healing well, he tried his luck by stepping outside. Several men sat around a campfire, cooking a stew and laughing about former exploits. *All soldiers are the same*, he reasoned, *and these men have obviously been together for many seasons.*

One of them, appearing older and more battle-worn than the rest, gestured at Titus as he approached. "Get in order, the officer's awake."

Another of the men laughed but pointed at the bowl. "Hand that to me, sir, and I'll give you seconds."

"Thank you, that would be nice." Looking around the camp, Titus counted tents, estimating that the force was easily over two thousand men. He felt confusion rush in. "I see no banners, for whom do you march?"

The man he now recognized as Sarge responded with a chuckle, "For us, mostly. And also, for the future of Andalon."

"Deserters?" Titus had no tolerance for men who left their posts, considering them little more than highwaymen.

"You can say that, sir. But we like the term defectors. It better suits our consciences."

A glimmer of hope rose in the officer's chest, "So, you ride for King Robert?"

"Not yet, but we hope that he'll accept us. Now that we have you and the general with us, the Major thinks we'll stand a better chance."

"General?" Shock mixed with hope as he asked, "Which general?" He had no idea if his commanding officer had survived, but he prayed that the sergeant would speak the name.

Before the soldier could respond, a gruff voice called out from behind, "Captain Titus!"

He turned slowly, disappointed that Merrimac Lourdes was in the camp instead of Reeves. He once again hoped that his mentor hadn't perished in the attack. "General Lourdes!" He proffered a sharp salute, despite the pain that wracked his shoulder.

"Join us!" He gestured toward a young officer in a crisp uniform standing beside him. "We have some planning to do. When Robert returns, we're going to end this war once and for all."

Merrimac Lourdes quickly briefed Captain Titus. "So, they marched back to Soston and left only a small cadre behind for city defense."

"How many is small?"

"Roughly fifteen hundred."

"We've two thousand and could easily handle a force that size. But how many emotants stayed behind?"

"That's the thing," the old general explained, "it appears they left none." He pointed at a spot on the map. "Major Smythe here scouted them at this location. They were camped along the road and were clearly on their way back to Soston."

"I can't say they didn't leave any Jaguars behind, but it's hard to tell when they ride in those covered wagons. I know for sure that they left with nineteen Falconers."

"The original count was twenty."

The major looked up, hopeful. "Maybe the king killed one of them?"

Something about the conversation jogged the captain's memory and he searched the events of the battle for the missing information. He vaguely recalled a female Falconer, but couldn't remember her fate. "It's possible."

Mac continued, "I'm assuming they left one or two surprises in Eskera. They wouldn't want to hand it back over to Robert after all the trouble they went through taking it." Both junior officers nodded their agreement. "But let's say that the city forces are all conventional. That would open up the possibility that we can be inside the walls when Robert returns."

Titus stiffened at the general's optimism. The man usually tore apart every contingency of a plan before acting. He felt that he should urge caution, "The collapsed sections of the wall were localized. I'm sure they'll have it well fortified."

The smile on Lourdes' face was distinctly out of character when he answered, "But we won't besiege the city."

"Then how do you propose we take it?"

"Through the back door that you discovered."

Confusion overwhelmed the captain. Perhaps the head injury was affecting his memory, but everything felt strange and out of place since awakening on the beach. "I discovered no such entrance, General."

"Quite the contrary, Frederique. You've provided us a way in."

Major Smythe cleared his throat. "My men found you on this section of the beach." He pointed to a spot on the map nearly two miles west of the city. "Given what we know about the current and from your story about falling into the sewer, my scouts found a hidden entrance here."

"Unprotected?"

"Somehow the bars had been pulled away from the tunnel, ripped off with the strength of a Kraken, if you want to speculate."

"Braston?"

Lourdes nodded. "That's what we think. It's probable that he and King Robert escaped through the same tunnel that spit you into the ocean. Given his affinity to water, it's likely one of his sea creatures helped them pry the bars."

"Surely the army's posted guards at the entrance."The major shook his head, "Not as far as we can tell. They seem pretty confident that Robert's attack will come from the harbor and have committed the bulk of their occupying force there."

*Odd,* Titus worried, *that these men have so much confidence. They are set on a single plan without contingencies.* General Reeves had taught his protégé better, but the captain had always assumed that Max had learned his caution from Lourdes. "When will we begin the attack?"

"Our men will slip into the city in groups of five until we have a force large enough to surprise the sentries on the wall. Then, they'll open the gates and let us in as well." The general and major shared a smile, "The entire operation should be over by midnight tonight!"

# Chapter Forty

*Malfeasance* arrived shortly before sunrise and Braen marveled at the number of ships in the harbor. Dying light tugged at the riggings all around him, desperate to illuminate the rolled canvas tied on the many yardarms. Most of the ships were ghosts, their crews having already disembarked days before. Those who aided the egress from Eskera would soon join them in the brothels and taverns of The Cove. Braen Braston had pulled off the impossible, and, in only a matter of months, compiled an armada that rivaled that of the Esterling Empire.

The new arrivals led by Braston were the only activity in the harbor, starkly contrasting the bustling city alive atop the hill. He watched as Robert's soldiers stared wide eyed at the pier and breathed the fresh air carrying tropical scents and robust sounds of joy and comradery, starkly contrasting the Estonian cities that reeked of oppression. These visitors, committed to war on foot and steed, had never dreamed that such a magnificent city like The Cove existed. The place of legend and intrigue loomed around them, changing their perspective on their own lives and freedom.

A child's voice broke Braen away from musings and he turned his attention to the boy beside him. "Where's *She Wolf*?"

The bearded captain scanned the ships a second time. As the boy had pointed out the distinct black ship was not among the others. "I don't know, Sebastian. She should have arrived and had no reason to leave. Perhaps you could reach out to Caroline?"

The boy's eyes turned sad and studied the decking. "I don't want to go back there, Captain Braston."

Remembering the lady Falconer chained in his hold he nodded, "I don't blame you, Son, but you've got to conquer that and move on. Fear will destroy your ship if you try to head around it. Treat it like a storm and sail directly into the wave, keeping it under your bow until confidence assures that you're safely over. If you allow fears to sail at your side, you invite a capsize instead of putting them astern."

The boy nodded meekly. "I'll try again tonight."

"Good lad. Now, help Krill with that rigging. His hands aren't what they used to be." The Gunnery Sergeant inclined his head at mention of his name, then briefly held out two fists toward his skipper. Each had a gap where the middle finger had been ripped away during battle and Braen imagined the ghostly digits fully extended into the air. "What's wrong, Gunny? Did you lose your ability to communicate properly?"

"I cannot hear you, Captain," the grinning man responded, reaching for an item hanging from a necklace. Holding it outstretched he advised, "you must speak into me good ear!"

Braen responded with a grin of his own then turned a frown toward the empty berth on the pier. In his mind, he yearned for the dark outline of *She Wolf* and the company from her leather clad captain. *I messed things up so badly,* he thought, *she was the best thing to ever happen to me and I ran her off.*

"Braston." A curt military voice barked his name as if it were a command.

"What can I do for you, General Reeves?"

"King Robert is anxious to disembark so that we can meet as a council. How much longer until we can."

Braen pointed a patient finger at the brow, lowering into place under the watchful eye of Krill. "Any time you please, General. But I'd let them tie it off first. Armor doesn't float very well." His crassness surprised even himself, but the interruption of his private thoughts had provoked irritation.

"Buh... Braen!" A stammering voice shouted up from the wharf and the northern captain felt his melancholy lift at the sight of Sippen's approach.

Suddenly wanting to leave the vessel as badly as the infantryman, he grabbed a dangling line and climbed onto the rail. With a look over his shoulder he shouted to his one-eyed friend. "You have *Malfeasance*, Krill!" Before swinging over the side he added toward the general, "I'll meet you all at the palace. I'm going to stretch my sea legs." He landed softly on the pier and let go of the rope

"That was druh... dramatic," his engineer said through a wide smile, "shuh... showing off for the general?"

"Not at all. I was merely in a hurry to see my best friend." Braen allowed worry to cross his face, suddenly vulnerable in front of his only confidant. "Where is she, Sippen? When did she leave and where did she go?"

"She luh... left last night."

"Why? What did she say? Last I spoke with her she'd promised we'd work things out between us."

"It wuh... wasn't yuh... you, Braen." Yurik stepped aside and pointed down the pier. Samani Kernigan approached with a vision at his side.

Hester's bright yellow hair graced her shoulders and she wore a regal gown of Fjorik style. The dress had been dyed purple, the color of a queen. On her back was a brilliant white cloak with fur lined edges resting gracefully against her pale skin. Even before Braen could lock onto the sapphires that smiled back, he caught her scent of northern lilac. His legs wobbled as he struggled to breathe.

Captain Adamas Creech had been quiet since the armada had broken the Eskeran Blockade, pondering the changes in the world directly around him. He suddenly felt naïve at the ambition he had once held after the disappearance of Artema Horn. He now humbly reflected that his desire to rule was a passing fancy. *Braston was*

*right that the world has changed. Men no longer rule over the land, not when gods wield true power.*

He no longer held quarrel with the northern captain and understood that his previous resistance was tied to his aversion for everything Fjorik. He viewed their tactics as barbaric and lacking strategic genius. They took what they wanted regardless of the effect on the people they robbed. That was why he had resented Braston's interference in The Cove, and why he had worked so hard to undermine the man who had nearly destroyed the city.

Despite his feelings against Fjorik, he could no longer deny Braston's military prowess. The man was a leader as demonstrated during the battle. *He's a tactician with undeniable instincts.* Adamas watched him seated at the head of the table. Only weeks ago, he would have made a point of challenging the man by sitting in the chair first.

The boy king cleared his throat, breaking Creech from his thoughts. "I want to start by thanking you for pulling my army out of Eskera."

"This isn't your meeting." The words came from Braston's mouth with a coolness that froze the room.

"Excuse me?" Robert Esterling couldn't hide his shock at the sudden turn in the northerner. Even Creech was taken aback. Looking around, he noticed that everyone at the table had stiffened.

"I said that this isn't your meeting to lead. You are in The Cove, and therefore have no power here." The boy's ever-present bodyguard and mentor began to speak, but Braston cut him off abruptly. "It isn't your meeting either, General Reeves. I'd appreciate if you'd wait your turn." Both Estonians clamped their mouths shut at the insult but remained quiet. "We're missing a key member of the triumvirate. Captain Creech, unless your vote agrees with mine, we will be unable to decide on the evidence regarding Captain Dominique." He gestured to the ships log on the table. "We'd be forced to await the return of Captain Thorinson."

Adamas briefly tapped his finger on the table then looked the northerner in the eye. "I'm ready to find the man guilty of slaving."

All eyes shot to him with surprise. "I recommend that a sentence of death be carried out with his body displayed on a gibbet."

Braston raised an eyebrow then proceeded. "Thank you, Captain Creech. I second both the vote and the recommended sentence. It appears that there'll be no need to await the return of Captain Thorinson."

Samani Kernigan cleared his throat and asked, "What about the fate of Nevra? Since you are both suddenly in agreement of something, dare we press our luck for a vote on his crime?" After he posed the question, all eyes immediately returned to Adamas.

"Although I can't stand the bastard, I don't see any clear evidence that he participated in the crime."

"You were present during his confession, were you not?" Braston spoke the words like a knife slicing through the air and bleeding the air from the room.

"Aye. I was. But he's a braggart and a blowhard, a child who was grasping at his throne. I can't make my vote until we have testimony from someone involved in the planning of the crime. Since Dominique is quiet and his son is dead, we need to find Pogue's wife and children."

Braston nodded private thanks and Adamas returned the gesture. "Then it's agreed that Amash Horslei and Alec Pogue will make haste to the southern continent and retrieve Mattie and the girls."

Esterling interrupted, "Absolutely not! Those men are wanted for conspiracy against a sailor in my navy!"

Braston responded, "The last I looked, Your Highness, you were king of a dream and dreams don't float imaginary ships."

Robert Esterling stood in anger, but his wife placed a calming hand on his arm, softly urging him to his seat. *He also has quality of leadership, but he's still a child after all*, Creech thought.

Braston wasn't finished and continued, "Mr. Creech, do you agree that we should pass a formal request to King Robert Esterling stating that we will officially recognize his sovereignty under stipulations set forth by The Cove?"

"You suggest that we make demands of our own?" Adamas couldn't help but chuckle at the bold move by the northerner.

"Aye! The first of those being renegotiated terms with the taxes we pay to the crown."

Braston added, "Exactly, along with payment for services rendered during his war. We are, after all, providing services that place us in violation of terms with his brother.

"I think we could iron those out. Shall we also demand the immediate pardon of prisoners?"

"Aye. Specifically, Captain Pogue and Amash Horslei."

Robert looked at his wife who wisely nodded. He collected his composure and asked the pirates in a calm voice, "And what of Marita?"

Braen clapped his hand down on the table with enthusiasm. "I'm glad that you asked! She is a minor and therefore culpability must be passed to her parents."

"Except that she is an orphan."

"Was."

Esterling sat up in his chair curiously. "What do you mean was?"

"An hour ago, Captain Pogue presented me with a petition of adoption, placing full guardianship of the girl under him and Mattie. Captain Creech, do you approve of the placement?" He handed Adamas the document who looked it over briefly.

"It seems to be in order."

"Good, then the pardon is extended to her as well."

Just like that, the Esterling King had been defeated at the table. Creech watched his cheeks redden while the pirates removed the wind from his political sails. Instantly, Adamas felt genuine sympathy for the boy. When the young man finally answered, he somehow found dignity in his bearing. "Present me with the new terms and I will agree. But I will have some of my own as well."

Braston nodded and waved his hand dismissively. "Of course. We'd expect nothing less. I'm assuming that a renewed attack on your brother's forces are among those?"

"Yes. I've been told that a force of defectors has left Marcus' service, and I need help to find the bulk of that force. Then I'd like to mount an attack first on Eskera and then up the Misting River to retake Weston."

"If you retake Weston then I demand that you place Horslei in power." Braen's words were spoken without taking his eyes off the young queen, patiently awaiting her expression. She calmly gripped her husband's forearm in response.

"I can agree to that."

"Good. Captain Creech, would you like to accompany King Esterling up the river and help him reconquer the cities?"

"Aye. That would be an easy task if I had a contingent of Dreamers to aid in the effort.

"I agree."

Esterling eyed Braston suspiciously, "Where are you going if not with us?"

"I believe that Captain Thorinson is seeking personal vengeance against my brother."

"Where is he?"

"His wife thinks he's headed south to Middleton. I plan to meet up with Eusari and attack his fleet. I will take twenty ships, that should be all that I need with our improved firepower."

Kernigan opened the door and a beautiful woman glided with confidence into the room taking a seat next to Braston. She moved her chair closer and Adamas stifled a smile when Braen scooted his awkwardly away. He watched the exchange between Braen and the northern queen with budding curiosity. *There is certainly a history between Braston and his brother's wife,* he mused, *and affairs such as these are easily exploited.* Several times she placed her hand on the bearded man's arm, and each time he pulled away. *But his eyes are conflicted.* Creech could tell that his political rival harbored feelings for the regal woman.

The next hour was spent listening to the woman describe the mind of Skander Braston. Everyone in the room lacked surprise at his mental anguish, but were shocked when she described the pleasure with which he committed his crimes and perversions. After she had finished, she again touched the northerner's arm as she rose to leave the room. The touch visibly unsettled the large man and Braen lowered his eyes with fleeting confidence.

After Hester had left, the military men discussed strategy and organized their resources for the invasion. Braston finally excused himself to retire. The conflicted look remained. *That man is far more complex than the northern brute I had assumed.*

A clearing of a throat pulled his thoughts back to the room and Adamas turned to meet a palace page. "Captain, a message has come for you."

He held out his hand and received a dirty missive, haphazardly folded and sealed with a simple dot of candle wax. "What's this?" He turned it over in his hands, noting the lack of a seal. "Did you dig this out of the trash?"

"No, sir. One of the brig sergeants handed it to me. Said that it was highly important and that I should rush. I would have brought it sooner, but I had to wait outside until your meeting ended, Captain."

Creech waived the boy off with an annoyed shooing gesture then broke the wax, curiosity winning his attention. *Lord Stefan Nevra respectfully requests your presence in his stateroom. Please attend as soon as possible.* Adamas shoved the note into his pocket with a chuckle before scanning the others. No one had paid any mind to the arrival of the errand boy. With a final draw from his mug, he excused himself and headed for the dungeons.

The brig was musky and damp, not unlike a storeroom of a seasoned vessel. Creech liked the smell, but hated walking into the prison to meet with Nevra. *Horslei and Braston should have allowed Pogue to run the rat through,* he thought, *that would have saved us the trouble of further dealings with the pox ridden bastard.* He well remembered the day when the former king had revoked his letter of marque, forcing him to go into hiding in the city. Of course, on that day had also launched his own uprising. Although it had failed with Braston's arrival, he still enjoyed the backing of many key supporters in The Cove.

When he reached the first station, he observed several men sitting around a table playing cards. A brawny soldier stood and opened the gate, allowing him to enter the guardroom. "Good day, Captain Creech. Please remove your sword. You may hang your belt on that hook."

"Are you worried that I'll speed up his execution?"

"No sir, we cannot allow the prisoner to gain access to weapons. Do you have any sharp objects in your clothing?"

"Just this." Adamas drew a dagger from a hidden pocket in his tunic and placed it on the table. He frowned deeply when he noticed the other men eyeing it greedily. "What happened to you?" He asked a man wearing a bloodied bandage on his neck.

"Oh this?" The guard pointed at this neck. "It's nothing. I nicked it on the practice field."

Creech allowed the men to lead him to the cellblock. Something felt out of place, and his raised hackles urged caution. The men seemed bored with their duties, but that wasn't what caused his discomfort. He felt flanked as they made their way to the cell. "Does it take all three of you to escort me?"

"He's a high-profile prisoner, Captain. We take every necessary precaution." The soldier paused to open the door with a large brass key.

Adamas gasped when he saw the sight behind the door. The page boy sent to deliver the message lay bound on the ground, gagged and unable to move. Nevra knelt over him, a short metal shiv placed over the boy's heart. A red-eyed rat sat calmly perched on Stefan's shoulder, staring down at the messenger.

"It's not long, but it will serve the purpose on one so small." The prisoner shook his head mournfully. "It seems somehow wrong to kill the messenger." With a single motion the sharp metal spike drove deep into the child's heart.

Creech leaped forward but the guards abruptly grabbed him from both sides, pressing him down on the ground. One of them stepped forward and produced a long dagger. "Use his own, My Lord."

The lunatic standing over the boy giggled with glee as he carefully accepted the blade. He eyed the captain with strange lust as he undid the buttons on his jacket, placing the tip of the point just below his breastbone. "I should have killed you before instead of entrusting that task to Pogue. At least now you will have no choice but to finally serve me."

Adamas felt the cold steel enter his chest and the room fell dark.

# Chapter Forty-One

Hester fought back her frustration. She had hoped that Braen would be excited to see her, but he was too melancholy over his leather-clad nymph, Eusari. Worse, he refused to speak with her alone and had pointedly been avoiding her. She felt her belly, *thank god it won't show for another month.* She was running out of time and would have to try a different approach.

Her first stop was to find Delilah. The older woman was in the kitchens, mixing a tea for Samani Kernigan who sat back in a chair with feet on the table. They abruptly stopped talking when she entered. *So, they share secrets as well?* "What are you two planning?"

"Nothing, dearie. Samani and I go way back." Delilah looked down at her concoction, making a quick end to that line of questions.

"I was looking for that drink you had prepared for me."

"You'll have to see Gretchen for that."

Hester let out an impatient sigh and then stormed from the room. Halfway down the hall she stopped, then crept back to listen at the door. She was quickly rewarded with more than she had hoped when she heard Kernigan ask, "So, everything is going as planned back home?"

"Yes. The Dragon has stepped up bombings against the Astian Council, and those blowhards are afraid to leave their compounds. His agents are in every factory and commune, stirring dissent and promising redistribution of wealth."

"Then, it's almost time for him to return so that we can begin the second phase."

Delilah agreed, "Yes. It won't be long before we can get the destroyer in place." Hester watched as the woman drifted toward the man, wrapping her arms around his shoulders with an embrace.

"Soon, we'll be able to launch the revolution and return home to a victory." Kernigan placed his hand atop hers in a surprisingly intimate display of familiarity.

The northern witch responded with a soft kiss on his ear. "Do you truly believe that he's the prophesied one? You're confident in this?"

"I do. He matches the description perfectly from the few Ka'ash'mael visions that have seen him."

Delilah stood and began reciting a strange sort of poetry. "Come, witness their salvation! Rise the Kraken from the depths, dealing destruction and slaughter. Watch him destroy our legacy."

"On land the monster roars and walks, death surrounds in light and shadow. Destroy the seed before it roots. Emotions of water but born of land, lord of beast and friend of man. All forces of nature have awakened, chaos sown without distinction. No longer controlled by boundaries, siblings consume each other."

Hester watched as Delilah returned to a pot of boiling water, ladling tea into a cup before saying, "Don't forget the rest." She handed her lover a cup.

"How could I?" He blew on the hot liquid then sipped before continuing, "Pain and suffering early known, raised a king without a crown. Life of misery, death not binding."

"And you're positive it's him?" Hester heard the old woman scoot a chair to sit with Samani.

He replied, "We've spent our life's work seeking him out. I'm certain it's him."

There was more, but Hester moved away down the hall. She quickly found Gretchen in her room writing in a journal. The girl raised her head when the queen approached. "It's on the nightstand. Give it to him in strong wine for maximum effect."

"It had better work."

"He'll be asleep, but aware enough for you to convince him." The girl finished talking and looked back down at her writing. Hester took that as a dismissal and departed.

She tried once more to find Braen. After several minutes of searching, she finally cornered him in a hallway. She forced him to make eye contact. "Why are you avoiding me?"

He peeled his eyes from hers and glanced impatiently down the hallway. "I'm not."

"Yes, you are." She placed her hand on his arm and stretched her neck to get in front of his gaze "You're acted like you've never loved me."

"I did, for a time."

"What's different, Braen?"

"Well, for one you're married to my brother."

"No longer. I've left him." She smiled in a disarming way, hoping to put him at ease. "At least admit that the feelings are there."

"Of course they're there, Hester! Not a day went by for two years that I didn't think about the life we should have had! Not a night passed that I didn't mourn your memory or dream of your perfume!"

"Then love me now, Braen."

"I can't. My heart belongs to Eusari and I won't be unfaithful. She deserves loyalty for the first time in her life, and I aim to keep my promises."

She was irritated by his chivalry, but feigned understanding. "Then I won't pursue you any longer, Braen." She dropped her eyes to the ground and walked away with her most convincing crestfallen air. Although she didn't turn around to check, she was certain that he watched her leave before entering his war room.

While he made plans with the boy king and the other pirates, she slipped out of the palace and made her way to the docks. Men scurried, setting about preparations to get underway. They were so busy loading crates and tying lines that no one noticed her slip aboard *Malfeasance.* From there it was easy to find his stateroom. She tried the door and it opened without complaint. Once inside, she set up the room and found a wardrobe in which to hide. Then Hester waited.

"So, it's decided then?" Braen asked the question while looking directly at Robert.

"Yes. Captain Creech and I will take thirty ships and a contingent of Dreamers to Eskera." He tapped his quill on the parchment as he ticked off each item. "We'll move north to Weston, retaking the city by force and await you and Eusari. Then we'll move on Loganshire and later Eston. Meanwhile, your forces at Estowen's Landing will attack the Logan river and harass convoys in the area."

Samani Kernigan rushed into the room, slamming the door loudly and getting the attention of everyone in the room. "We just received a message from Estowen's Landing!"

Braen watched the man with expectation then asked, "And?"

"Their northern fleet is grounded!"

"How's that possible?" Robert sat up stiffly in his seat.

"Yes," Braen asked, "how?"

"Apparently, two emotants escaped several Falconers by dropping the western bridge across the River Logan! That re-routed the current around the city, and their entire fleet is stuck in the mud!"

Braston turned his attention back to Robert. "That changes things. You should reconnoiter with Shon Wembley in Estowen's Landing and attack Eston straight away!"

The boy looked thoughtful. His general leaned forward and whispered into his ear. The king nodded, then addressed the others. "We can't act on intelligence that we haven't confirmed for ourselves."

Braen glared at the young king with irritation, then asked in a calm voice, "Are you both complete idiots?"

General Reeves stood in defiance. "What are you implying, Braston?"

"I'm not implying anything. I'm plainly stating that you raised this boy as an overly cautious tactician." Braen kept his voice low and calm as he spoke, "And if you don't take this opportunity, then the war is prolonged and Robert risks letting his kingdom slip farther out of his hands."

Robert Esterling found his regal bearing when he answered, "It's about trust. You are the son of Krist Braston and the brother of Skander. My experience with you so far is that our alliance is tenuous. You never act unless it lends you the advantage."

"I am not my family."

"No, but you would benefit from feeding me false information and then surrounding me with an army loyal only to you. I will rule the empire, Braston, not you. Your ambitions are buried too shallow and were easily exposed."

Everyone in the room stared at Braen, awaiting his response. He sat quiet for a time, then raised his glass, turning the wine against the light. He inspected its hue for several seconds, admiring the composition. When he finally spoke, he did so deliberately. "Everyone I've met since fleeing Fjorik has tried to push ambition on me, but I've rejected each and every opportunity." He downed the contents of the glass then added, "Now you accuse me of being over ambitious." Reaching across the table he plucked a bottle and refilled his drink. "No one has ever, in all that time, asked me what I truly want for myself."

Robert took a moment to refill his own glass then asked, "What do you want, Braen Braston, Son of Krist?"

"I want my father back from the dead, for one. Then I want my brother cured of the madness that afflicts his mind. I want my mother, who died in his childbirth, to have survived and raised Skander as she reared me."

"I can't provide either of those, what do you want for yourself?"

Braen's serious eyes locked on Robert's with intensity and answered, "Not a gods damned thing." He gestured around, "I didn't want The Cove, but duty obliged that I take it and make it better. I don't want Fjorik. The north holds too much of my melancholy and would remind me daily of what's been ripped away." He tipped the glass all the way back and drank the rest of his wine before adding, "And I certainly don't want your precious empire. When this is over, grant me a large plot of land in Loganshire on which Eusari and I can retire. Hell, maybe we'll raise children and vineyards."

"I think I finally believe you, Braston." Robert again refilled his glass and added, "But we're not ready to attack Norton. I'll return to Eskera to find the deserters and then move on Weston."

"By Cinder's Crack, Esterling!" Braen pounded his fist on the table, spilling drinks and causing everyone to jump in sudden fear. More calmly he said, "Take what you need and whoever will join you." He scanned the other shocked faces. "What about each of you? Who's coming with me? Who's going with him and who's helping Shon?"

Adamas Creech cleared his throat and addressed the boy king. "I'm sorry, but I agree with Braston. I'll assist him in Middleton against Skander."

Robert nodded. "I understand."

Amash Horslei answered next, "Alec and I spoke. He and Marita are going to free Mattie and the girls, and I need to get to Weston." To Robert he said, "I'll still assist, if you can get me inside my city." The young king responded with a nod.

Braen addressed Horslei, "I've had a gift sent down to *Desperation*, one that would be useful for Alec when the time comes. Ensure he gets it and also the gold to ransom back Mattie. Tell him to remember our earlier conversations and to retire with his family. I'd remind him myself, but I'm getting underway at first light."

Samani turned toward Braen and cautioned, "Don't underestimate your brother when you find him."

"You'll not come with me to see this end?"

"No, Friend. I have to meet with contacts who are arriving in Estowen's Landing. Delilah and I will travel together. You and I can meet up, later, after this is all finished."

Braen stood and adjourned the meeting. "Then it's settled." Without another word, he strode from the room, letting the door slam. Once in the hallway, he remembered Hester. *Shit*, he thought, *I don't want to sleep in the same palace as her.* He decided the best chance for rest would be on board *Malfeasance* and made his way to the docks.

While he walked, he thought about Eusari. *I've got to find her. She left because she believes that I love Hester more.* That was the problem with loving two women, and he had realized that he would always have feelings for both.

The activity on the pier had died down considerably, but many of his crewmen were making preparations to get underway. He spotted Krill. "Quiet night, Friend?"

"Aye. We all be hungry to fight Skander and avenge your father, Cap'n."

Braen placed his hand on the gunnery sergeant's shoulder and looked him in the eye, pointedly avoiding the painted patch on his other. "What will you do after all this is done and I retire, Cedric?"

"How kin you even ask such a question, Cap'n?" A frown crossed the gunner's face, "And why're you using my given name?"

"Because this is finally a time to be serious. This is it, and I'm done. As soon as we deal with my brother I'm settling down. Robert Esterling can finish the fight."

Cedric Krull abruptly dropped his smile and spoke deliberately, "Braen, you know that I will always be at your side. You can always count on both Sippen and I, till the end and beyond." A tear formed in the sailor's eye as he spoke, "Besides, you'll need me on that farm of yours to keep the farmhands in line."

"Just don't call them 'turd chasers,' that means something else to landlubbers."

Suddenly jovial, Krill smiled and responded, "Aye. That it do!" Braen laughed as his friend winked his eye.

He was still smiling when he entered his stateroom. Someone had set out a snack and a bottle of 754. *Thoughtful Sippen*, he thought as he pulled the cork. He breathed the aroma deeply, taking in the rich bouquet. He poured some, then swirled the liquid in his glass, watching the legs drip down the back. Before he sipped, he again breathed in the luscious accents, honoring the masterpiece that would someday be gone from the world. *What a shame that will be when the world is robbed of one of its greatest treasures.*

He alternated sipping from the glass and preparing for bed. He carefully placed his boots near the foot of his rack, a tradition of seafarers always ready for battle. Then he deliberately removed his clothing, folding each item separately and placing it on a nearby chair. When he was finished, he realized how tired he really was. Braen yawned deeply as slumber quickly overtook him. Within minutes the bearded captain slept.

Sleep comes to us in different forms. It evades some and overly consumes others. In a perfect form, the act restores and refreshes our bodies so that we can function daily in a stressful world. But there are some who dread this function of body to such a degree that it provides no benefit save the eventual awakening from terror. I am speaking of dreams.

Braen was no stranger to them, and one particular nightmare burdened his sleep far too long. It plagued his nights and antagonized his mornings. He both yearned for it and lived with anxiety that it would arrive. The man enjoyed no respite, since there was no escaping when it arrived. The dream always began with the scent of lilac.

Braen walked hand in hand with Hester, taking in the soft aroma of her perfume. He had given her the scent, having found a small case aboard a sloop bound for Middleton. She wore it on that special day, specifically for him, and both lovers hoped that they would soon take their relationship to a higher level. That is, unless shyness won out over their young nerves.

They made their way down to their favorite picnic spot. The tulips would be in bloom, and he had promised her a surprise. “Keep your eyes closed, but don’t trip on any rocks.”

She laughed with excitement, "I'm trying to! Stop making me laugh!" She didn't keep them closed, however, and sneaked adoring peeks at him with his patchy beard. It was nothing more than tufts of blonde fur. She tugged one of these.

"Ouch! That hurts!" They both laughed.

"When do I get to see my surprise?" She asked, staring into his blazing blue eyes.

He would never forget how she looked in that moment with sun reflecting off her yellow hair, so long that it reached the middle of her back. He touched the fine strands, marveling at the softness that rivaled only her skin. "You can see it now." He gestured over her shoulder and smiled as she turned to look.

During the end of the past spring, he had dug up hundreds of yellow tulip bulbs from another meadow. He had kept them frozen through winter and replanted them here among the field of red blossoms. She gasped when she read the message, "I love you, Hester!"

Tears of joy filled her eyes as she realized how intricately he had planned and worked on the gift. "I love you, too, Braen!" She wrapped her arms around him, and they kissed so passionately that they fell to the ground. They laughed and giggled as they rolled in the field, until Hester climbed astride his hips. Although suddenly shy, he allowed his body to react to the pressure of hers. Feeling him, she responded by slowly unbuttoning her blouse, smiling at the shocked expression on his face.

Braen lay on the soft grass, eyes closed with a gentle spring wind brushing against his face. He breathed in deeply, smiling widely as the breeze brought soft lilac to his nose. He held that breath in, praying to the gods that he would never forget both this moment and her scent.

Her body pressed harder against his, her firm breasts exposed against his bare chest as they slipped from her half-unbuttoned blouse. His arms held her warm body and his mouth searched for hers, her soft supple lips dancing and teasing his own. His body pulsed with blood as he felt her hips press into his, rubbing slightly with pressure. After they had pulled away, she whispered, "I wish that you were not leaving me, Braen."

"I have to go, Hester. Father is taking us raiding in Loganshire at a place called Brentway. He said that we're to become men."

Smiling, she reached her hand down and grabbed ahold of his pulsing manhood. "You're more than man enough now, Braen."

He laughed and kissed her again, rolling her over on her back as he did. She nodded and shyly smiled her consent. He fumbled at the buttons of his breeches, hurrying to finish the task before they changed their minds. The two made love in the meadow amidst the tulips, creating a memory they would carry their entire lives. After they had finished, they napped in a lover's embrace, steamy bodies cooled by the spring wind and the scent of lilac.

# Chapter Forty-Two

Eusari had lain in her stateroom and cried the entire voyage to Middleton. Peter Longshanks had tried several times to check on her, mostly to ensure she was eating. She never once opened the door to speak with him. She had asked not to be disturbed on the voyage, but was thankful that he loved her enough to check. She had Gelert, and that was the only friend she wanted during her misery.

The wolf lay beside her on the bed, facing the door. Her face was buried in his fur, wet from her tears. "I shouldn't have left, but I couldn't bear to see his reaction when he arrived." Gelert let out a soft whine of understanding. "What have I done?"

She raised her head at a knock as Peter's voice called through the wood. "We're arriving in the bay, Captain. You've got about thirty minutes, is all."

"Thank you, Peter." There was a time in her life when she would never have spoken those words. Life had groomed her hard demeanor and only depended on herself for too long. Meeting and falling in love with Braen had taught her so much more regarding herself and about life. To Gelert she whispered, "He taught me how to love and be thankful. I want so badly to trust him right now, but I'm so afraid that he'll choose her over me." *I'm so stupid,* she thought, *I knew he'd eventually hurt me, and I never should have let him in.*

Her thoughts turned to that fateful night on *She Wolf* when she had violated and beat Braen unconscious. *I was so wicked before, until he taught me how to love.* "How can he be so full of forgiveness to everyone? Even if he chooses her, I know that I should forgive him and move on, but I can't. Not with all the changes in our lives." The wolf whined again and nudged her belly with his muzzle. "I don't know what to do."

Another knock on the door informed Eusari that they needed her topside. She dried her eyes and pulled a cloak over her shoulders. The hood completely covered her face. When she emerged, she walked up on Peter and Devil Jacque in a heated argument. "What's the trouble, boys?"

Longshanks tried to make light of the conversation. "Nothing, Captain. We're merely disagreeing about our role."

"What about your role? You'll all stay aboard while I infiltrate and work the city until he arrives."

Jacque interrupted, "Captain, with all respect, you've trained us to fight and that's what we want to do. Many of us wish we were getting some action and plunder."

Eusari pulled a knife from her sleeve and toyed with it, cleaning her nails. In a low rumble she purred, "It seems that you've been questioning a lot lately, Jacque. Can I count on you or not?"

He stepped back, eyes on the knife, and answered, "Of course you can, Mum. I only ask that you allow me to accompany you in town. You've trained us well, and you'll need a partner if something goes wrong."

"I have Gelert."

"With all due respect, Mum, you need a partner who blends in slightly better with the city folk."

Eusari mulled his words carefully and found wisdom. "It's true that movement through the city would be easier in a disguise rather than shadow. You may come."

"Thank you, Captain."

"Then it's settled." She slipped the knife back into its hiding spot and got down to business. She pointed around at the scenery. "Middleton is situated on a series of inlets and bays. The primary entrance is heavily guarded. Once we slip in, we will have to hide *She Wolf* in a spot that can egress without difficulty, as well as avoid Skander's attention when he arrives."

Peter frowned. "That's a tall order, Mum. Where do you suggest?"

She pulled out a chart and pointed at a tiny cove nearby the financial district. "I think we should situate here."

He nodded his approval. "Because when Skander makes his attack he'll pick a spot close to the plunder?"

"Exactly. He'll also want to remain near the entrance of the bay in case something goes wrong." She paused, remembering the night in Estowen's Landing when Marcus' men killed Sa'Mond. At the time, she had believed her world destroyed, only later to learn that it had grown vast around her. "Hear me now when I tell you that Skander Braston is a coward. He attacks the weak and flees at first hint of trouble."

"But Middleton isn't weak, Captain. Middleton would be difficult to take, even with King Robert's and Shon's combined forces and the Kraken's sea power."

"I know, and that's what troubles me." She gave Gelert a scratch behind his ears to calm herself more than him, then added, "I don't think he's here to conquer. He's here to raid and send a message to Braen." She again fell silent, ending the conversation and turning her back on the two men.

The city sprawled before Eusari, so large and spread out. *He's here for something specific. Whatever could he need or want?* Her eyes scanned the buildings for a clue but finally gave up and went below to change her attire. If she were to walk the city streets she would need to fit into the crowd.

A few hours later, she walked the city with Devil Jacque at her side. They were dressed like a merchant and his wife, out for an evening stroll. They made small talk as they meandered through the streets, Eusari often complaining about the ruffle of the skirt. "I can't move silently with this crap on. I sound like crushed wrapping paper when I move."

"Aye, and this jacket restricts my arms. I should have worn a vest."

She looked up at her crewman. "Jacque, what's really going on? You've been so bitter and openly showing disdain for my decisions. Are you unhappy on my crew?"

"No, Mum. It's not that, at all."

"Then what? Tell me."

The tall pirate, not near as articulate as Peter Longshanks, grew quiet as he searched for the words. "I'm craving the action. It's literally the only outlet I have."

"What else troubles you?"

"I can't tell you, that, Mum."

"Please stop calling me 'Mum.' When we're alone you may use my name."

"Eusari." She watched him closely when he spoke the word aloud. He resembled a child tasting new candy, eager to try it, but wary of the taste. "I've got a bit of a crush on you, always have. Before I was afraid to approach because of Sa'Mond, he'd have taken my jewels and fed them to a shark if I'd tried."

"And now?"

"Braston's a difficult man to best in any contest, much less a duel over a lady's affections."

Eusari felt a laugh slip out at the thought, then quickly grew grim at the thought of Braen alone with Hester. "Well, it wouldn't have worked anyway. You're on my crew and I don't fraternize with my cohort."

"Then I'll leave your crew and switch to another vessel, Mum."

"No need for drastic measures, Jacque." She decided to let him down easy. "We're friends and that's the extent of our relationship."

"Even if Braston were out of the picture?"

She nodded, "Even then. I'm not looking for a harbor to drop my anchor in permanently." They walked along and quickly reached the financial district. Eusari pointed at a large building with several soldiers milling about. "There's the bank and city vault."

"It's impenetrable."

"Aye. He'd need cannons to get inside." She looked around, "Where do you think the armory is? That's where he's likely to hit as well."

"I remember the map showing it closer to the shore battery."

"Then let's head that way." As they walked, she thought about their own raid on Diaph months before. One of their chief targets was the armory and looted it quickly. The only surprise of that night had been the Rookery and the people within. She remembered the glowing tubes in the ceiling and the naked bodies laid out on stone slabs. The tubing running in and out of every orifice made her sick, even to this day. She hated slavery in every form and fashion, but the act of farming people for powers was most despicable.

"What did Shon's dispatch say about Skander's raid on Diaph?""What do you mean?"

"I remember reading that the city had been burned after Skander found the armory empty."

"Aye, that's what I recall. That seemed like a waste of time, to me. Why would anyone take the time to raze an entire city that's already been plundered?"

"Usually to cover something up." She focused on that detail. *What would Skander have found in Diaph that he would want to cover his tracks?* She mentally checked the jail and armory off the list. The batteries were also useless to him. She stopped in her tracks when they rounded a corner, suddenly standing before a simple stone building that looked odd against the rest of the city architecture. The structure lacked adornment and two Falconers stood in the doorway speaking with a constable. Eusari felt her dinner rise into her throat. "Jacque, he would have also found the Rookery."

She abruptly pulled her crewman into an alleyway. Devil Jacque's eyes were wide with questions and asked, "What? What is it that you're afraid of?"

"We need to get back to *She Wolf* straight away. If he found the Rookery, then he found the emotants inside!" She gestured toward the building across the street with fear in her eyes. "He's not here to raid, he's here to gather more!"

All of a sudden, horns sounded throughout the city, announcing invaders in the harbor. Skander Braston had arrived.

Middleton loomed in the distance but Skander focused on the knife in his hand. He held the tip against the hard wood of the rail and carefully scored a deep line. Not satisfied with the groove, he tried a different angle, cutting across the first. He frowned at his work and sighed, but a glance at the city ahead slightly comforted his mood. Flesh was much more satisfying to carve.

Artur's voice broke his concentration, "Sails!"

Skander turned to the gathering behind him. Each was eager to hear their father speak. "Behold the city that conspired against you, my children." The Sabre Cats swayed collectively, humming with eyes closed and focused on the air over Middleton. The sails on the incoming vessels fell limp, impotent and lifeless as the warships drifted without a current. The stolen wind gathered into a visible vortex above the harbor, swirling and raging.

The skies above darkened instantly, turning the whirlwind black. An electrical storm raged within the massive spiral, barely able to contain the current. Everyone within miles felt hair stand up on end as city dwellers stepped outside to investigate the phenomenon. Then the northern king added his own theatrics. The people of the city stared and called out in alarm, unable to turn away their collective gaze.

All at once, the Braston sigil burned brightly. Skander had warned his crew, who averted their eyes unlike the unfortunate citizens watching in awe. The retinas of those looking on were burned instantly, the image permanently fused in their vision. Cries of pain clashed against the sound of the storm, a churning roar that rattled shutters and shattered glass. Above it, all could clearly hear the wails of an infant.

When the vortex split into a hundred tornados the crews of his armada gasped in awe. The electrically charged demons fanned out into the city, lighting rooftops afire and inciting panic in the streets. Everywhere the blind fumbled in darkness as they found themselves unable to flee. Many collapsed in heaps as loved ones raced from their homes, desperately trying to bring them inside. Then Skander released his army.

# Chapter Forty-Three

The streets of Weston had been wrapped in eerie calm all evening, but storms often followed tranquility. Percy Roan hurried through the empty streets with eyes darting back and forth. He was early for his meeting, but rushed to outrun a growing anxiety. Since the riot, he rarely went out at night, a new habit adopted by most of the people of Weston. Heightened paranoia created images of buckskin-clad warriors leaping from shadows, and even the most rational of city-dwellers questioned their safety.

When he reached the palace, he breathed a sigh of relief and gathered his nerves before making the journey up several flights of stairs. He found Eachann atop the highest tower, standing next to a roaring fireplace and watching the city below. His focused attention fully rested on the Pescari district. The refugees had been isolated for more than a week, but stood as defiant as before. Surely, they would soon acquiesce to the governor's demands.

Percy watched the lawmaker with growing concern. Politicians often changed platforms, but this sudden switch in policy confused the accountant. The decision to go after the Pescari weapons made sense, but the way he went about it seemed provoking. It almost appeared that the man, prized for his humanitarianism, planned the uprising. *There must be intervention by another party*, he mused, *a wealthy and more powerful investor.*

"Spit it out, Percy." The politician turned to his friend with expectant eyes.

"You knew this would happen?"

"A Pescari uprising? I thought it a possibility."

"That's why you picked the lower district," Roan mused, "you were able to trap them at the first sign of trouble." He scratched his chin for a bit then asked, "You intentionally provoked them by taking their weapons?"

"The Esterling boy and Horslei were right about these savages, Percy. You saw the damage that boy wrought on Weston the night they arrived." He pointed at the sector below. "And now at least one more of them has the same power."

"Where's the boy named Taros? How do you know he won't return to free his people, Cassus?"

"Right now?" The city leader smiled proudly, "He's trapped hundreds of feet below ground, completely separated from open flame and slowly running out of air to breathe. He's trapped."

"It sounds to me like you want them all to die. Each and every one. Him by suffocation and them by starvation."

"If they do, the blame won't be mine. The people of Weston will believe that I tried everything in my power to make this cohabitation work, but the nature of the Pescari ruined it."

"And you're once again the savior of Weston who has united both the war hawks and the humanitarians." Percy felt bile rise from his belly but forced it down. Stealing from the wealthy rested fine on his conscience, but these people were helpless. After he had collected himself, he got down to more business-like questions. "Why did we invest so much in the infrastructure if this was an elaborate scheme for genocide?" Without waiting for an answer, he added, "And why didn't you tell me your plan?"

"Because you wouldn't have understood. There are forces at play that make us look like fleas on a dog, Percy." The governor grew quiet, chewing on his own words for a while before adding, "The best we can do is take pride in the contracts we've issued, and trust that after the Falconers cleanse the city we can rebuild."

"You made a deal with the Falconers?"

Eachann's stoic expression reacted at the mention of the specters, but quickly recovered. "After the Pescari are gone we'll restore the sector to its original glory. Perhaps it'll become the center of high society?"

Roan digested his friend's words, sickened that their entire constituency had eagerly lapped up his lies. He tried to reason excuses for his friend's behavior. *We really are powerless to the Falconers*, he thought, *how could he have refused them?* He almost told that to Cassus, to let him know that he understood, but Eachann enjoyed the misery below.

Percy considered his options. If he left now, he had enough wealth to build a plantation on the southern continent. If he stayed north, he could curry favor with whichever of the Esterling brothers won out. He may even find a way to grasp political power in one of the other cities. *Soston sounds nice,* he thought, *but so does Middleton.*

A messenger burst into the room, panting and out of breath. "Your Lordship!"

"What is it?" Eachann replied, lighting a southern cigar with a coal from the fireplace.

"The Pescari are attacking a section of wall."

The governor stood quietly, drawing shallow puffs. His face glowed an eerie red against the twilight. "It's time. Let's go rid the city of pests, Percy."

Teot howled with rage as several warriors fell at his side. Their initial attack had been swift, testing the wall above the Elder's Lodge. They had tried to use stealth and set homemade ladders against the stone, ready to sneak their way toward the Northern gate. They climbed only halfway before archers, cleverly hidden atop the walls, popped up and picked his scouts off one by one.

He had tried a technique that he learned from Taros, to burn the weapons in the air, but each hit their mark and dropped the entire first wave. He walked to a warrior and plucked an arrow, turning it over in his hands. The metal tube was unlike anything he had ever seen, shiny and silvery in appearance. Curious, he ordered another squad up the ladders and watched closely.

This time, when the archers revealed themselves, he noticed the strange devices in their hands. Instead of holding the bow vertical this contraption was held flat and horizontal to the ground. Also made of metal, the bow made a ringing sound after firing the bolt. Once again, his men plummeted to their deaths with pieces of steel protruding from their bodies. He tried and failed to burn the weapons, and futility replaced his anger. He ordered his men back into the lodge so that they could prepare his other plan.

Taros rested with his back against stone. Though the tunnel was pitch black he could still imagine Flaya's features, lying beside him with her head resting in his lap. He marveled at her beauty. *Why did I take so long to notice her?* He felt her breast rise and fall as she slumbered, unconsciously breathing in what little air remained in their tomb. Most of the miners slept as well, many having quietly accepted their fate in hopes that they could die without pain.

But sleep evaded Taros and he prayed to Felicima for the first time in months. *I know that I am far from your sight and no longer feel your power course through my body. Please grant me one final gift with which to avenge your people. Grant me the strength to escape and free them from captivity.* He closed his eyes for a moment, squeezing back silent tears. He slowly opened them to Flaya's voice.

"I love you," she said.

"And I love you." His hand reached for her silky hair, stroking it carefully. "You should sleep while I find a way out of here."

"I've slept enough." She snuggled deeper into his lap with a smile. "I want to die knowing that you held me when I breathed my last." After a while she touched the ground and added. "At least the rocks are warm. I expected it to be colder beneath the surface because we are so far from Felicima."

Taros nodded, having wondered the same. "I'm surprised she can reach us this far."

"Felicima can do everything, Taros. You know that. She is everywhere." She sat up beside him, feeling for his hand and locking her fingers into his. "Daska says that our world came from her fire when she breathed out. What was once molten hardened into the stone around us, and her flame burns eternal beneath the surface. That's why we're not cold."

The shappan also placed his hand on the ground, feeling the warmth. *Like the caldera and the fumaroles*, he puzzled. "I've seen molten rock spew from the ground. I saw it when I cast the bones of my father into the Caldera."

"What was it like?"

"Flame lived everywhere, it flickered into the air and melted the ground around it. Rock flowed like rivers of fire before it cooled." Thoughts of that day flooded back into his mind as trapped images were set free. He remembered praying to Felicima for strength on that day. Strength so that he could challenge Cornin and avenge his father. Tears rolled down his face at the memory. He had cried then as well, except those tears had fallen into the fiery river and sizzled when they made contact. "How large do you think the caldera is, Flaya? Beneath the surface, that is?"

"Daska says that Felicima's river flows everywhere beneath the stone."

An idea leapt into his mind and his eyes abruptly shot open. He stood up from the ground, releasing her hand. "Find a torch and light it, My Love."

"The miners said that would waste the air, Taros."

"Do it. I need to draw from the fire, and I need to be able to see the walls." He heard the sound of striking flint as sparks flew in the dark. Soon the cavern was illuminated, and he recognized a sleeping miner nearby. He roughly woke the man with his foot, commanding him, "Get up. Lead me deeper into the mine and show me where you dig the coal."

The laborer frowned at the open flame, then turned to lead the way. After a few minutes, they came to a place where the walls changed. Instead of pink granite, the walls were marbled with soft black coal. Taros reached and felt the dark substance with his hand. It was cooler than the rock around it. "I wonder if there are rivers of this?"

"The vein stretches everywhere, Shappan."

"Does it reach the city?"

"Aye, we were told that we are digging toward Weston."

Taros turned toward his lover and placed his hand on her shoulder. "What I am about to attempt is difficult, Flaya. I'm not sure how many of us will die in the process."

"Do it," she whispered, "so that we have a chance to die like Pescari."

He nodded and faced the seam of coal running through the wall. He placed both hands against the stone and concentrated on finding Felicima. At first, he felt nothing more than the gentle warmth from before. Deeper and deeper he reached past the rock, searching for his goddess buried beneath the world. Regret over his earlier doubts brought forth memories of his many blasphemies as he felt for her power.

He finally understood that he was not a god. He was an agent of Felicima and nothing more without her glory. *She will be there*, he thought, *slumbering deep in the Caldera.* He remembered her fiery bed in which he had tossed his father's bones and formed the image firmly in his mind. The torch puffed out and the tunnel darkened instantly, but Taros could see the fire deep within the rock. He pulled this toward him and channeled the flame into his body.

He heard Flaya and the miner gasp from behind, but he paid them no heed. More and more of the heat was drawn until two molten pools formed in the rock beneath his hands. "Run." The words came out as a whisper, but Flaya and the laborer fled as fast as they could. *Felicima guide my hand,* he begged, groaning into the darkness against the pain. The air was quickly consumed around him as he directed magma into the river of coal.

At first it burned slowly, but the young chieftain funneled more heat until the entire vein burst into a raging inferno. The fire exploded past him into the shaft, threatening his people resting near the entrance. But Taros resisted the heat, catching and turning the flames. With great effort he pushed them deeper into the soft black substance, turning it shades of red, orange, and yellow. Somewhere deep in the rock ahead, another blast from trapped gases shook the tunnel and Taros saw the world through the eyes of Felicima.

# Chapter Forty-Four

Alec Pogue stared in awe at the cliffs overlooking Cargia. The last time he had business in the harbor, he had done the same, filled with wonder and speculating what treasures lay atop the steep bluff. He never had the opportunity to solve that mystery, as the city officials had ordered his ship to leave as soon as cargo had been exchanged. Foreigners were rarely allowed past the docks.

Marita's voice snapped his attention to the matter at hand. "The harbor master is asking for our bill of lading."

Alec reached into his pocket and drew out a parchment, yellowed by the oil used to waterproof the expensive document. He handed it over to the tall man, whose dark skin contrasted his white beard. The top of his bald head beaded with sweat against the afternoon's humidity.

"What is this," the official asked, "some kind of joke?"

"Not at all," the captain replied. "He asked for a security detail to ensure delivery and I must accompany the cask safely to the manor."

"Absolutely not!" The man's hands trembled with worry as he spoke, betraying his insecurity. "Law strictly forbids the entrance of foreigners into the city."

"Except," Alec instructed, "during rare deliveries of luxury items."

"But a cask of this importance requires the attention of the local magistrate."

"I think that Lord Charro Valencia outranks the magistrate, don't you?"

"I can't allow it," the harbor master protested, "not without..." He leaned in close, "Not without certain assurances."

"A bribe?" Pogue let out a chuckle and placed a satchel of golden coins in the outstretched palm. "Here are your assurances. Now, how do I get up to the manor house?"

"Follow the main road through the city until you reach the square. Turn left and continue out the eastern gate. The road curves up the cliffside and leads only to Valencia's estate."

Alec placed another satchel in his palm and ordered, "Have a hitch and wagon ready on the pier with five additional horses at the ready."

"I am not a valet, Captain!" The dark man blanched with disgust at his treatment as a domestic. Alec opened another purse and counted out six imperial talents, placing them directly into a pocket on the man's waistcoat. The man nodded, "They will be ready within the hour, Captain Pogue."

Alec smiled as the greedy man scampered across the brow to order about some idle slackers. "Gold is a funny thing, Marita." The girl had rarely left his side on the voyage, glued to every conversation and watching him lead the crewmen through the driving of the ship.

"How so?"

He looked down at the sweet little girl with tender pride, the same given to a daughter by a father. "It can open doors."

"What if the price is too high?"

"Then it buys the whole damned thing."

She nodded agreement then shot him a smile and a thumbs up. Of course, he understood her mind much more deeply by now, and knew that she didn't have a clue what he had just meant.

"Get your things, dearie," he told her. "We're going to get Mattie and the girls."

The road to Valencia Manor curved up the steep bluff, making it a longer trip than expected. They had ridden more than an hour, backsides already sore from the rigid seat atop their wagon. The higher Alec and Marita climbed the smaller they felt. The vantage was perfect for gazing at the scenery, but the young girl focused mostly on the city below. All the people resembled ants, scurrying here and there as they lived their busy lives.

She asked a looming question that had been burning in her mind. "Why do they look so small?"

"I guess it's just perspective. Everything looks smaller when you're looking down," he answered.

She slowly nodded, her trademark smile notably absent. "Just like people," she mused.

"Yes. That's why they look smaller."

"No." Marita corrected. "Just like people when they're in charge. Like King Robert and all the others. The people below them look smaller, like insects, and they forget that they are really people." She bit the inside of her cheek as she pondered something deeper. "That's why nobody is getting along," she insisted. "They can't see things from everyone else's point of view."

Alec stared at his adopted daughter with surprise. "Yes. That's exactly the problem," he replied as he recovered from his shock. "That's why Robert and Braen are having a difficult time getting along. That's also why I want to take you, Mattie, and my other girls away from all the politics." He glanced upward at the looming manor house as he mentioned his family, suddenly realizing how large it really was. Earlier it had seemed normal size from the road. *Braen and Mattie are right,* he thought, *and,* as *soon as the girls are safe, I will retire. We'll start a nice farm somewhere.*

"Make way!" Shouting from behind broke his concentration and he pulled the wagon to the side of the road. Another carriage, just as elaborate as the last, ambled up the road at breakneck speed. The driver shouted as he whipped the horses, "Move out of the road for the lord!"

"How many fucking lords do they have down here?"

"Don't use profanity, Marita."

"I'm a pirate. Pirate's cuss," she responded stubbornly.

He didn't press. Her words had echoed his own thoughts. It was the fifth to pass them and a procession of wagons could be seen further down the road. They had picked a good time to visit the manor; with all of these visitors he and Mattie could easily blend into the crowd.

"Alec." Marita tugged at his sleeve and he turned toward her.

"Yes, dearie?"

"Why is Braen's old ship here?"What do you mean?"

"Look out there." She pointed off into the distance at the haze atop the blue ocean. "Don't you see it?"

Pogue strained his eyes, unable to see anything in the distance. "No. I don't. But it can't be *Ice Prince,* he wrecked her in The Cove."

"I remember, Silly. I was there with Eusari." A gust of wind suddenly blew down from the cliffside, sweeping over the road and toward the sea. He didn't know how she did it, but he knew that she was riding the breeze to get a better look. "I was wrong," she finally admitted. "She isn't *Ice Prince.* She just looks like her."

Alec froze in place. "Fjorik longboat?" He shook his head. "They don't venture this far south."

"Well nobody told them that and there's one rounding the bluff."

"What do the crew look like? Pirates or northerners?"

"Definitely north men. Their beards are wild and not combed like Braen's." After a pause she added, "Ew!"

He pressed, "What is it?"

"Their teeth are really sharp. They look like they filed them down to look like wolves."

*Berserkers.* thought Alec. *Why are berserkers in Cargia?*

Mattie fussed over the kitchen staff, ensuring perfection no matter the task. The soup needed salt, the smokers were too hot, and no one had adjusted the dampers. The stuffed eggs weren't stuffing themselves and so she put Lexi on that task. So much rode on this banquet that the steward worried she would faint away from the stress.

Alexa looked up from the half-peeled potato in her hands. "Try and relax, Mother."

"Try and relax?" Mattie whirled on her youngest daughter. "Every lord in the southern continent is arriving at our door as we speak. You want me to relax?"

"Alexa's right," Lexi agreed, "you're all worked up over nothing. It's only a big party."

"Only a big party?" Mattie stared at her girls, marveling at their unified defiance. She walked to the window, threw open the shutters and pointed at the rows of elegant tents pitched in the yard. "Outside there are nearly one hundred lords competing with one another. Each of those tents cost a vast fortune and are filled to the brim with whatever luxuries would make the others envious. These people aren't here to party, they're here to show off their wealth and reinforce their political relevance."

She returned to her girls, both of whom eyed the ground with humility. "If our lord doesn't make the biggest display of wealth, then he loses importance in the eyes of the others. Our job is to put on that show, down to the tiniest detail." She pointed at a bubbled crepe, "Like that." She picked it up and flipped the pancake over in her hands, scrutinizing the obvious misshapen form. "This will not do." In a single motion she flung it like a frisbee toward the waiting trash container. "Now get to work."

Alexa finished skinning the last potato. She was stiff from hunching over the tub, so she stretched and yawned.

Her mother eyed her suspiciously, no doubt wondering if she would try and duck out of more work. "No time for yawning, dearie."

"I'm sorry, Mum. I just need to walk around and do something active."

"Well then, you can run these out to the men smoking the meat." She gestured at a box of boar haunches and ribs. "Can you lift it?"

She knew that she could, but hefted it cautiously just in case. It lifted easily enough. "Anything else I can take?" She was thankful for her mother. Since they had been taken from The Cove, she had grown closer to the woman, bonding in ways that most teenage daughters don't with their parents. But that wasn't to say that she and Liza weren't starting to crave their independence. Especially the older sister who was already of marrying age.

"Take these herbs and spices. Please and thank you, dearie."

She smiled back at her mother, feeling deeply sorry for her earlier defiance. Of course the event was a big deal. She had no right to suggest otherwise. "I'll hurry back," she promised.

"Please do. There's so much more that needs done." Her mother looked up from her chopping and added, "And Alexa!"

"Yes, Mum?"

"Stay near the manor house. Valencia said that we aren't to wander from the grounds of the main property while his guests are camped."

"Of course!"

The teen had no plans to wander near the camps. She had seen glimpses of the other lords through the kitchen window and wanted nothing to do with their flamboyance. She also saw the hard men who had accompanied them, hired mercenaries who would love a piece of a vulnerable young woman. She would be careful not to wander far.

She found the smokers fully manned and bellowing sweet smoke. She handed the crate to the lead chef and turned to leave when a figure caught her eye. Charro Valencia was clad in a garment as colorful as the peacocks currently meandering the front lawn. He walked with his hands in the sleeves of his robe, eyes forward as he made his way toward a dense grove of orange trees.

Two guardsmen, Jon and Petr, followed closely behind. They carried a large chest between them, swinging it as they walked. Alexa couldn't help but notice the jingle of coins inside as they passed. She glanced briefly at the kitchen window and then back at the lord, suddenly forgetting her desire to stay close to the manor. Curiosity had already won over her feet and they carried her up the walk toward the orchard.

When she reached the trees, she found a place to hide out of sight. She ducked behind a bush and waited, watching as the lord stood unmoving in a clearing. His guards were less patient. They shifted their weight anxiously, eyes scanning for movement. Soon, two more men approached from the south. Alexa let out a startled gasp and clamped her hands over her mouth.

She had never seen a Fjorik raider until she had met Braen Braston. Her father had often brought him into their home to teach the girls about the land in northern Andalon. They had both been frightened at first, terrified that he would be true to the depictions in stories and paintings. They had expected a terrible visage clad in furs and with filed teeth that gnawed lustfully for their teenage flesh. Instead, he had been cultivated, educated, and refined. He was handsome instead of ugly, and he had quickly charmed the entire family.

The men speaking with Valencia were not Braen Braston. They were hideous barbarians with unwashed bodies and matted manes of hair. Their beards were soaked and stained by their last meal, undoubtedly raw by the bloody tint. They resembled animals more than they did men. Charro seemed not to notice their appearance or, more simply, did not care. He ignored one as it drew out an axe, gnawing on the handle like a dog would a bone.

"You get the other chest after the deed is done," the lord promised. He gestured around the clearing. "My men will leave it in this very spot."

"Just make sure that you do," one of the beasts replied, "or your palace won't be safe." As quickly as they had arrived, they had gone, disappearing into the woods while laughing at their private joke.

Alexa closed her eyes, wishing that she had paid heed to her mother. *Why couldn't you have stayed close to the manor,* she thought. *They could've killed you!* Once she was certain that Lord Valencia had left as well, she rolled over and opened her eyes. A man far viler than the berserkers loomed over her body with an evil grin, licking its lips and salivating as he tasted her fear. The man's animal skin hood made it appear as if he were the manifestation of a jungle cat.

"Lord Valencia!" The nearly naked figure called out and the lord of the manor returned. "It seems that you were not careful and have been overheard."

Charro shot Alexa a look of pity, no doubt the last she would receive in this world. To the beastlike man he said, "She's only a girl."

"Nevertheless she must be dealt with." The creature leaned in so close that Alexa could smell the oil on his skin.

"She is nothing I cannot handle. I assure you."

"If we are to continue with our arrangement, then you will leave her for me to deal with." The hideous man reached down and stroked her skin with a mud caked finger, causing her to flinch. She whimpered as he caressed her lightly, humming softly.

"Our agreement will not change. The attack will thin out any resistance and solidify my rule over the entire continent. That is what your handlers demanded, is it not?"

"Yes..." The specter mused, humming louder as he continued to stroke Alexa's face. He reached down with both hands and firmly clamped her cheeks.

"No," she pleaded, "please don't." The girl tried to pull away, but his grip was strong and his music enchanting. Soon she could hear his voice echo in her mind.

*Don't resist, child. I will not harm you. Give in to me and you will soon forget everything you have seen and heard.*

When she finally stopped her struggle, she knew his words were truth.

Mattie watched as Alexa casually strolled through the kitchen door. The girl had been loafing somewhere, gone a full hour. "Well," she said with a hint of sarcasm, "look who finally decided to join us."

"I'm sorry, Mother. I dropped off the meat and came straight back."

"We'll talk about this later. Right now there's too much to prepare. Go wash up and dress in your serving attire. Then you can join your sister in the banquet hall."

"What about the stuffed eggs? Surely they're not ready?" The girl turned to the table where her sister had been working. When she had departed for her errand, the table was empty. Now several hundred eggs sat beautifully on their serving plates, garnished and ready to serve. "Oh," she remarked, "Liza did that faster than I could have."

Mattie harrumphed then chased her daughter from the kitchen. "Go get ready!"

# Chapter Forty-Five

A solitary ship traveled northward toward Estowen's Landing. Samani stood on the lee deck, keeping dry as he watched ocean spray wash over the topsiders. A boy of about ten summers kept wind in the sails, oblivious to the foam and mist. He looked silly in his rain slicker, hands in the air like he was conducting an orchestra of air. Kernigan barely knew the young emotant.

Braen had called him Jasper and promised that he could take Samani and his cargo safely north without incident. He was one of the younger children, so far kept out of the fighting and more dangerous missions. At first, the crew had seemed concerned, leery of trusting such a small child with their lives, but they quickly warmed up to the hard worker who seemed to love his job.

A woman's voice broke the silence. "Would you've ever believed that we'd be walking openly among so many emotants?"

Kernigan turned and greeted Delilah as she slid in beside him. "Honestly, no." He gestured toward the child, "But isn't this what we'd hoped for when Pearl brought us across the ocean?"

"It is. But imagine what it will be like when they can walk among the entire world." The two watched as Gretchen brought a small bundle to Jasper. The boy ripped it open and quickly consumed the meal within. "She's got your stubbornness, Sam."

"I noticed that. Does she share my gift with the bead?"

The two watched as the girl walked slowly across the deck toward a hatch that led below. "She does, but unfortunately, we've nearly exhausted our supply. What we brought across the water lasted longer than expected, but thirty years is a long time and we'll run out soon."

"Don't worry, we gathered plenty during the raid on Diaph and I can restock your supply." He gestured toward the child channeling the wind. "Hopefully we won't need the beads much longer." They stood silently for a moment before he asked, "Did it work? Has Gretchen produced any other Ka'ash'mael visions?"

"Only the one regarding the brother." Delilah looked expectantly at her former lover "Are you sure that we have the right Braston, Sam?"

"I'm positive. Besides, Braen has Eusari and the others. There are plenty of factors that will contribute to the process."

"Pearl will tan our hides when she realizes what we've done."

He shook his head. "We haven't done anything. And, despite what she may claim, we certainly haven't influenced the prophecies, Delilah. All we've done is identify key players and point them toward their destinies."

"I don't think she'll see it like that."

"She's eighty years old, what's she going to do? As long as Braen and Eusari are together at the right time, it'll go as prophesied. He's running to her as we speak, and the three will be together when it happens." He paused for a moment then added, "Then Pearl will have to step back while we coax the second phase." Samani turned, suddenly feeling chilled by the ocean spray. "Speaking of the second phase, let's go below decks and speak with what's left of my sister."

Pearl paced the kitchen waiting for Madelyn and the children to return. She had tried to prevent them from leaving with Shon Wembley, but they had insisted. His scouts had reported a column of soldiers marching toward Estowen's Landing and he quickly set up an ambush along the road. Despite her protests, the young Kali argued that she and Johan had a duty. "The soldiers followed us from Eston, so we have to help," she had insisted. Pearl finally relented and sent Madelyn along to keep the children safe.

A voice interrupted her thoughts, "Why did you take my brother, Perlana?"

The old woman looked up with tired eyes, exhaustion hanging beneath them. "I didn't take him, Fatwana. He begged me to bring him across the sea."

"I'm sure that's how you remember it, but I see it differently. You played upon his passion for knowledge and promised him answers."

Pearl nodded at the truth in the lead sister's version of events. "That doesn't mean that he wasn't persistent."

The younger woman handed the elder a mug of cider then relaxed in a chair beside her. The two women sat like that, sipping the hot liquid and staring at the door expectantly. It was Fatwana who finally broke the silence. "The prophecies are dangerous, Perlana."

"It's Pearl now, Dear. I haven't gone by my given name in thirty years."

"I don't care what you call yourself, don't evade the subject. You're playing with fire."

The old woman took a long sip from the mug, then held it in her lap with crooked fingers, the warmth feeling good against her frail legs. "We came here to observe, but your brother may have meddled too much in Andalonian affairs."

"Even a little is too much." The lead sister took another sip then asked, "How bad is it?"

"I won't know until I get my arthritic fingers around his throat." Fatwana raised an eyebrow and Pearl continued, "His assignment was to watch The Cove.""The Cove? What Cove?"

"Pirate's Cove. The locals call it simply, 'The Cove.' He somehow rose in the ranks to serve in the Inner Sanctum of the Pirate King. At first, I was supportive because he was in a position to expand our network. He had spies in every portside city on the continent. If it touched water Samani knew its gossip and news."

"He always was industrious."

"Industrious? Your brother is a damnable genius. His network grew so strong that he cut me out of his chain of command. After only a few years I even worked for him as part of his network."

"Perlana... Pearl, we had a Ka'ash'mael prophecy that revealed a powerful winter emotant."

"I know. I believe that it read, 'All forces of nature have awakened, chaos sown without distinction. No longer controlled by boundaries, siblings consume each other.' Don't look so shocked. We have agents in both the council as well as every oracle. Not a prophecy is recorded that we don't see."

"I didn't realize..."

"That the Society has such a far reach?"

"Exactly." The old woman placed her gnarled fingers on the slender hand of Fatwana. "My Dear, you must accept that the Chancellor and the Council are corrupt. They exploit these people and hide it from the Astians."

"The beads."

Pearl raised an eyebrow. "You know their origin?"

The lead sister nodded, tears welling in her eyes. "Samani found a way to contact me through a Ka'ash'mael. I don't know how he did it, but one of the brothers in my oracle saw the inside of a Rookery through his eyes." She buried her face in her hands. "It's awful! We are consuming their essence!"

"That's true, Dear, and that's the true mission of The Society. We must free these people without letting The Destroyer wreck our culture."

"That isn't what The Dragon would lead you to believe."

"The who?"

"The Dragon. The leader of The Society?" Pearl stared back dumfounded so Fatwana described him. "Red hair, alluring smile, completely beautiful and ageless. He was a little smug and overconfident for my taste, but he was a very convincing man."

"Fatwana, The Dragon isn't our leader!"

"Well you could have fooled me! He described a plan to topple Chancellor Jakata and the entire Council."

"Topple? Jakata? My Dear..."

Horns in the distance alerted the women, and Fatwana rushed outside without waiting for Pearl to finish. The old woman, also distracted, shuffled outside to witness the commotion. Cheers in the distance suggested a victory, but her worry would continue until she confirmed that all three of her wards lived. She wrung her hands until the ache in her joints grew unbearable, then she paced. She wished that her eyesight were as strong as in her youth.

The shouts of triumph grew closer and she finally spotted the children. Soldiers had hoisted them on their shoulders and paraded toward the outlaw town with rifles pointed toward the sky. Kali and Johan were forefront ahead of the others. A smiling Shon Wembley led the procession. Madelyn followed closely behind wearing a grin of her own. Pearl finally let out a long-held breath and sat down to await the news.

Madelyn wasted no time in giving her report. She collapsed into the chair next to her mentor and gave an in-depth account of the battle. She began with the positioning of snipers in the forest and wrapped up with the final retreat of the survivors. Usually one abhorrent to violence, the old woman felt herself intrigued by the details.

Even Fatwana listened intently. "He used ravens to blind The Falconers?" That part had surprised her.

"He did. He said that they'd used the tactic before, but it was much more effective with the help of The Dreamers."

"So, the Falconers were useless in the fight?"

"They were. They picked them off easily, and then Kali opened a crack to swallow the few who survived the initial attack. Johan rerouted a creek and flooded the crevice to drown them."

Pearl felt her heart sink at the thought. "They're too young and innocent for such exposure to killing." Madelyn nodded that she agreed, a sudden sadness on her face as well. "How many soldiers were there?"

"Shon said that there were at least ten thousand, but Marque estimated twice that number." Her eyes took on a sparkle at the thought of the forester as she talked. "It was difficult to tell on such a narrow road."

Pearl calculated. "That's a quarter of the Northern Army."

"That's what Marque said." She blushed a little when she mentioned him again. "Shon wants to press westward and attack Eston. With their ships grounded and many of their Falconers gone, he thinks the war will be over within a month."

Despite the good news, something about the details worried the old woman deeply. "Where are the bodies of the Falconers now?"

"We left them in the hole." Shock and panic consumed Pearl and she tried to stand but then slipped back into the chair. Madelyn jumped to her feet to assist. "What is it?"

"He has to go back! You can't leave behind the body of a Falconer or they find a way to come back!"

Madelyn sprinted off to find Marque and gather a squad of scouts. Then they raced away to burn the bodies. When they returned a few hours later, Pearl learned that her worries were justified. The bodies of the Falconers were gone and so was the multitude of soldiers. They didn't have to wait long to learn where they had gone. The attack came with nightfall and disrupted their celebrations.

# Chapter Forty-Six

The entire voyage from The Cove to Eskera was filled with strategy and planning. Maximus Reeves wanted to establish a perimeter around the harbor, weakening the city defenses over time with steady bombardment. The superior firepower of the pirate vessels was impressive, and he was eager to make use of it while minimizing the losses of Robert's limited ground troops. The only drawback to such strategy was the potential for heavy civilian casualties.

King Esterling had suggested adding a frontal assault, ferrying his army and cadre of emotants to a safer section of beach further east. After a short march they could easily take advantage of the missing section of wall where the northern gate had formerly stood. He felt that their new weapons would easily cover an attack as they sent in squads. The only lingering concern was over how many Falconers and Jaguars remained to assist the occupying force. Without spies inside the city the invading army was blind.

Eskera looked exactly the way they'd left it, except for the lack of smoke and flame. Robert marveled at the sight, realizing why sailors were addicted to their trade despite the hardship of living on the sea.

"It's beautiful, isn't it?" Sarai's question caused him to turn.

"It truly is," he responded.

"I worry about the people of the city and fear for their treatment."

"Hopefully we can retake it soon, without punishing them further." Robert turned his attention back to the expansive harbor, noting that the absence of ships cast an eerie warning. "I wonder how many troops are within."

"Look there!" She pointed toward a small boat rowing toward the fleet. The tiny craft had pushed away from the pier and flew a flag of parlay from a makeshift mast.

"Maximus!"

"Yes, My Liege?" The general hurried over to the rail where Robert and Sarai watched the vessel.

"Someone wants to talk. Why would they parlay after driving us from the city?"

"It could be a trap. Maybe they have Falconers aboard?"

Movement atop the city walls caught the trio's attention. A large banner unfurled from a prominent section of wall, clearly displaying the Esterling sigil. Robert smiled when he saw the eagle gripping a red rose, a detail disturbingly absent from the new standard flown by his brother.

General Reeves shared the same thought as Robert. "I'll row out to meet with them."

Titus hated the sea. Truth be told, he commissioned in the army to avoid working for his father, a wealthy importer from Middleton. Had he remained, his father would have forced him to captain a vessel that did little more than ferry sugar and tobacco from the southern continent. He had refused and the tossing of the rowboat confirmed that his choice had been wise. With the enlisted men watching closely, he held down his breakfast, but not without great effort. Sarge gave him a knowing wink, but did a good job of focusing the others on the oars.

He ran a flag of truce up the makeshift mast as they approached the larger ships. The looming hulls were markedly different than he had ever seen. These were a hybrid resembling both Fjorik longboats and the heavier beasts assembled in Middleton drydocks. *Braen Braston has changed this world,* he thought. Not long after Robert's sigil unfurled atop the walls, Titus spotted sailors lowering a gig over the side of the lead frigate. A few minutes later, he was tied alongside and sitting face to face with Maximus Reeves.

"Well now, if this isn't a surprise!" The commanding officer grasped forearms with his aide-de-camp and brought him close in an embrace of respect and camaraderie, tipping the boat as he did. After they had pulled back, he pointed at the captain's eyepatch. "I see that while we've been rubbing elbows with pirates you've decided to look the part."

Titus gingerly touched the adornment on his face. "Yes, it seems that I narrowly survived an attack by a jaguar."

Max nodded. "Robert told us about that. He said that the last he saw you, he thought you dead in the cistern."

Titus felt his pocket at his side, fingering the animal claw within. Sarge had given it to him as a trophy after surviving the attack from the beast. He had claimed that they had plucked it from his now useless eye. *Funny,* he thought, *that I don't even remember the surgery.*

Reeves gestured toward the city. "Don't tell me you took the city on your own?"

Titus smiled warmly at his friend and answered, "Honestly, I didn't do much at all. This was all General Lourdes' work."

The smile disappeared abruptly from Reeve's face and a quizzical expression took over. "But Robert said that Mac died when the wall collapsed." Hope filled the old soldier's eyes. "Are you telling me that he survived?"

"Apparently so," Titus responded, "but I don't reckon I know what could actually kill that man. He's proven indestructible up until now."

"You've got that right! Who are these soldiers?" Max indicated the enlisted rowers.

"Loyalists to Robert, sir." The men behind him beamed proudly at the description. "They found me nearly dead, lying on the beach. They took me in, fed me, and took me to Lourdes. I want to petition for full pardon of each of the deserters..."

Sarge interrupted, "Defectors, Captain."

Titus smiled. "I mean defectors. They and their Major got us inside the walls, and we were able to take the city in a single night."

"So, the city is truly ours?"

"Aye, General, with two-thousand loyalists and defectors eagerly awaiting his arrival. He finally has enough to fight this war, sir."

Robert Esterling disembarked amid fanfare and cheers from both soldiers and civilians. Although he had departed Eskera in the dark of night and under heavy enemy fire, his return would be recorded in history as miraculous. He had dressed for the occasion in a brilliant white uniform that seemingly caught the sun, reflecting off polished golden buttons and aiguillettes. Atop his head he wore a glorious crown with bright red rubies in the shape of his mother's rose.

He silently thanked Braen Braston for insisting that he allow Sarai to commission the uniform with jewels and precious metals donated by The Cove. A "loan" the pirate had called it.

His queen walked with confidence at his side, a stunning sight in a regal gown of crimson splendor that accentuated the rose in his crown. The vibrant color could be seen from every rampart along the harbor, and the tiara upon her head sparkled like stars on a perfectly moonless night. They were flanked on both sides by bannermen waving the Esterling crest and the crowd cheered at the display. Their shouts echoed off the heavens for the young king who had quickly recovered both the city and their hearts.

A makeshift stage had been erected on the wharf and every eye was on the ceremony. Merrimac Lourdes and Maximus Reeves awaited their monarch with wide smiles, proudly watching as their young protégé celebrated his second victory.

"Nice work, Mac." Reeves spoke the words to his former mentor over the wild applause.

"It was really nothing," the much older officer replied. "It's the least that I could do for the true heir of Charles Esterling!"

Maximus froze at the words, doubt creeping in and making him wonder. "Say that again, Mac? I couldn't hear you over the crowd." Despite his sudden concern, he smiled disarmingly.

"Hmm?" Lourdes' eyebrows lifted questioningly then quickly recovered. "Oh yes, of course only we know the truth about Charles." In a whisper he added, "I said it like that for the ears." He gestured around. "As far as this crowd should know that is the solitary truth."

Reeves nodded his agreement, worries settled as he turned to watch Robert. The king had reached the platform and he and his bride made their way up the steps. "I often wonder if Lady Crestal knew before they were wed."

Lourdes did not take his eyes from the young king. He asked, "Knew what?"

"That Charles was sterile," Max explained.

"I'm sure it was discussed beforehand, or else she wouldn't have lain with Matteas Brohn. At least one of his boys made a strong leader."

A shockwave of fear passed through the younger general. He was about to press his old mentor, but Robert had arrived. Both men genuflected to their sovereign, hands across their breast in a sign of fealty.

"Arise!" The young king ordered, "Let's speak upon this glorious occasion."

Both men recovered and stood with heads bowed in respect. "King Robert," Merrimac began, "I give you the city and people of Eskera, liberated in your name as you commanded."

"You deserve a triumph, General, but while time is scant, I offer you instead a boon!" Robert moved in closer to the battle-hardened warrior, placing his hands on his shoulders in a public display of favor. "Speak what you will ask of your king!"

Maximus watched the exchange with a mixture of fear and caution, alarms surging through his mind. *Did the fall affect his memory?* He quickly recapped the older man's behavior. *The attack on the city was rash,* he thought, *and certainly would have advised against the risk or urged caution instead.* But that wasn't enough to distrust his friend, now standing inches away from the king. *Robert was certain that he had died in that fall!*

Max felt his stomach lurch as he remembered Braen and Robert's report of the Jaguars. Each had retold how the specters reanimated dead Falconers. His instincts screamed warning. If Merrimac Lourdes was an agent of the enemy then he had the perfect opportunity to strike. He suddenly stood too close for Reeve's liking.

He quickly moved to separate the two. "Your Highness," he asked, "perhaps the general would ask for clemency for the men who aided in the seizing of the city?" He broke script as he spoke, pushing past his old mentor and stepping between the two men. The words barely escaped his mouth before cold steel enter his ribcage. His vision swam while the onlookers scrambled to defend their monarch. Slowly he slid to his knees, eyes on Robert who watched with horror and with feet frozen by shock. Maximus Reeves whispered out his final breath, "Run!" Darkness replaced the image of his son.

Robert watched as blood spewed from his father's side, staining his white uniform as he collapsed onto the stage. Behind Max stood General Lourdes, face twisted in hatred as he tried to free a dagger caught between his protégé's ribs.

"Run!" Max spit blood as he spoke his final words, spraying the king's jacket with pink froth.

Dumbfounded, Robert stepped away from the danger, confused and suddenly frightened. Lourdes finally freed the blade, wrenching it out with the cracking of bone and a hiss of escaping air. The blood that gushed from the wound came from the general's heart, punctured by the long blade. His father was dead.

Mac cursed loudly and stepped forward with the speed of a younger man. A shot rang loudly from Robert's left, dropping the decorated warrior.

Amash Horslei frantically reloaded his smoking pistol while chaos ensued all around. He shouted at the king, "Get to the ship, Boy!"

Meanwhile the defectors had drawn blades and clashed with the king's soldiers. Gunfire echoed on the pier, drowning out the loud clash of steel upon steel.

Someone shouted, "To the king!" Guards quickly surrounded Robert, leaving Sarai to stand defenseless.

He pointed at this wife and called back to Horslei, "Protect the Queen!"

One of the defectors stood over a slain soldier, holding the man's rifle in his hands. He whirled around, looking for the king. Finding him surrounded, he quickly aimed the barrel at Sarai. Everything moved in slow motion then, as Robert tried to shove aside his human shields. A shot rang out, loud and terrifying as the projectile hurled through the air. It moved fast, despite that time had slowed for the king. He reached out instinctively, sending a blast of air to meet the object before it struck his love.

Too late to fully change the trajectory, his wife fell to the ground. He was trapped, unable to move from behind his guards. Robert watched with horror as Lourdes regained his feet and rushed toward Sarai. The older man laughed maniacally as he raised the blade above his head, oblivious to the loss of blood from his belly. He brought the point of the blade down with force, intending to pierce her heart.

Another shot rang out from Amash's pistol, and the general fell atop Sarai. Robert shoved one of the guards aside and lashed Mac's body with air, ripping him from atop his queen. He stared intently for signs of life, willing her chest to rise. She was too far away to tell, and so he fought against the soldiers now dragging him toward the ship and safety.

Strange sounds hummed from atop the wall, and the king strained his eyes to watch the citizens move aside. There, he watched twenty Jaguars swaying and singing from where they knelt atop the palisade. Turning again toward the wharf, he watched as every fallen soldier rose, including the body of Maximus Reeves.

Robert Esterling watched in horror as the dead rose to attack his men a second time. The scene resembled a nightmare, just as it did on the night that he and Braen Braston had battled side by side. *What has died is never meant to walk again*, he thought. Watching as his father cut down two of his own soldiers he added, *especially when evil has replaced the goodness that once dwelled within.* This day would end as the last, he feared, with the Jaguars forcing him to flee. Looking around he took inventory of the battle.

His cadre of emotants were forming up near the ships. Some tried to help the soldiers, but it was difficult to intervene when both sides fought so closely together. Nearby, Amash had gathered up his sister and was calling for Robert to follow. "Get behind the line! We need to organize them the way Sippen taught you!"

*Rank and file*, the little man had called the tactic. The first line would fire, then back into the line to reload. Then the second line would fire and so on. There was method to the new weapons, and they would only be effective when used correctly. He nodded to Amash and sent a blast of air toward the Jaguars, momentarily breaking their rhythm and concentration. That bought some time, but, just as he attacked, horns sounded in the city.

Arne, sensing trouble through his master, launched from the flagship and soared skyward. Then Robert finally assessed the situation. *It can't be,* he thought, realizing that Marcus' army had arrived. *They must've been lurking nearby.* And then he realized the worst, *they've been hiding outside the city and have Falconers!* Several large raptors attacked the eagle as it flew, harassing the bird and trying to blind the king on the wharf.

Robert hated Falconers. But he had fought against the hooded specters before and had some luck. They were easy enough to defeat with the element of surprise, but that was not the case here. Worse, they had again joined forces with the Jaguars, and that meant they would kill with improved cunning and efficiency.

A sword swung through the air, barely missing his neck as he dodged, and the scene around him again slowed. Maximus Reeves recovered from the miss and swung a second time, this time aiming for Robert's hamstring. The young man's chest suddenly felt tight and he began to wheeze. *Not again*, he thought, *he knows my weaknesses and will recognize my breathing sickness.* Reanimated father or not, the monster swinging the sword meant to kill the king.

Wisps of air shot out and grabbed the general's wrist while another lashed his feet. Robert pulled them tight, tripping him up and causing him to swing wide. But then the interference came. Tendrils of air shot out from an alleyway nearby. Robert threw up a shield that narrowly blocked the attack, then split his mind a third time and caught the sinews that had flown toward him. He coiled these around and around until they formed a thick rope as wide as a mooring line. He swung it up and over the wall, catching each Jaguar in the chest and sending them sailing toward the hard streets below.

Amash nodded his approval and the two rushed to join the others in the rearguard. Robert yelled to rally his men. "Form up! Fall back and reform!" The loyal troops raced after their sovereign, falling in as he passed and forming tight rows as they reached the piers.

Amash looked around, still holding his sister. "I don't like this. We're trapped and they can cut this boardwalk to pieces when they reach the batteries!"

Robert looked up, taking notice of the defectors who were nearing those very positions. Thankfully most of the citizens had fled and were off to hide in their homes. The king turned to the nearest ship and shouted to a crewman, "Signal the others! Aim your cannons at each of the gun mounts and fire at will!" What happened next was a cacophony of explosions ripping through the harbor defenses and spraying rubble, slowing the advance of the reinforcing troops.

His eyes darted to Sarai in her brother's arms. Her chest moved, although he could tell that it was labored. Two deckhands carrying a stretcher raced across the brow, crossing over and recovering their queen from the pier. They hurried her to the waiting ship's surgeon. *Aboard what?* Robert let the thought distract him momentarily. *This ship doesn't even have a name and I'm using it as my flagship!* A broadside from the nameless vessel roared overhead, striking the nearest harbor defense just as a group of defectors reached it.

A brief moment of clarity followed and King Esterling shouted commands at his men. They were finally in position, the front line fighting with bayonets against the pressing mob. "Second rank, ready and take aim! Fire!" The explosion sent the opposition flying backward. Turning to the ship he called to the captain, "Get some sharpshooters on the rails! Take down anything that looks like a Jaguar!" By now the first rank was ready and he ordered them also to fire.

The soldiers slowly backed the attackers down the pier. With artillery flying overhead to soften the enemy flanks and snipers keeping the Jaguars busy, Robert was able to get a foothold on the wharf, just in time for a harbor cannon to take out the pier they had been standing on previously. The ships rocked but continued their cannonade. *Sarai will be safe onboard,* he told himself. The cadre of emotants around him quickly found their footing in the battle. In short time, they had captured fifteen of the Falconers, tying them down and lashing them to anything they could find.

Robert looked around for the Jaguars, but could no longer find any. When the dead ceased rising to fight, he finally realized that they had fled the battlefield. He called the ceasefire. One by one he and his cadre of emotants dispatched the Falconers, tendrils of air acting as nooses along the city wall. Only when they stopped kicking, did he know that it was safe to visit Sarai.

To Amash he ordered, "Do what you need to do, but I want the dead burned, even our own."

Once aboard the ship Robert made straight for sickbay and found his wife. She rested comfortably but was very much alert. He asked the surgeon, "Can't you give her anything for the pain?"

"No, Your Majesty. I'm afraid that I cannot."

"Why not?" He asked, quickly losing patience.

"Because," answered Sarai, "it would be dangerous to your heir."

# Chapter Forty-Seven

Percy Roan watched intently as archers circled the Pescari District. The warriors had tried several times to test the new weapons, but were repelled each time by the crossbows. From this vantage he felt safe and away from imminent danger, but he worried for the city. Usually a man without principles, he strangely felt compassion for those trapped. They could not possibly defend against superior force and new technology.

*Even if the Pescari are killed,* he thought, *this humanitarian crisis will remain a black mark on the people of Weston for generations.* He turned his attention to Eachann standing with his new feathered friends. Occasionally the governor would point, and they would converse about tactics or argue over the best angle for the final attack. And then the moment the accountant feared most came to pass.

Pescari warriors began darting about, tossing torches into piles of debris that Roan had not noticed before. Huge bonfires roared against the darkness, lighting the night with a hellish flickering. A solitary figure emerged into the open. Careful to remain out of range of the new weapons, he stood defiantly in the center of the district. One by one the fires would extinguish, then a fireball would explode atop the walls and send crossbowmen scrambling for safety. As each fire was consumed, scouts would dart out and ensure it was relit. Soon, the flames launched over the walls into the market district, igniting rooftops and threatening the entire city.

Percy watched as the Falconers took charge of the battle, moving into position and weaving the air around them. A spinning vortex formed above Weston, drawing the flames from burning buildings and sucking them into the sky. He watched with awe as they swirled the fire and carefully placed it directly into the center of the Pescari District. The man below tried desperately to steal back the flames, but it was too late his own weapon had been turned against his people.

The cyclone split into several firenadoes that attacked homes and lodges, instantly sending people running into the night. The awful screams clawed at Roan's ears, threatening to haunt him forever.

"Well Percy, that ought to finish them off, don't you think?" Eachann's words broke the accountant from his trance.

"That's horrible, Cassus."

"Don't blame me. He's killing his own people. The Falconers are merely protecting the rest of the city."

Percy felt that he could no longer bear to watch the carnage. He turned his back, but couldn't tune out the screams. Each one became a woman or child running from their homes and consumed in fire. He stood like that, with his back turned, staring eastward into the night and hoping no one noticed his tears.

In the distance, a soft glow reflected in the moisture on his face. He gasped, unable to believe his eyes.

"What is it?" Eachann heard the sudden expression and turned.

With an outstretched finger Roan asked his friend, "Isn't that the direction of the mine?"

Cassus strained his eyes against the night and cursed. "By Cinder's Crack you're right!"

Jagged red lines of flame reached outward from the site like rivers grasping for the sea. They grew rapidly, making their way toward the city. Off in the distance an explosion revealed that the flames had found a buried deposit of gas, sending a fireball high into the sky. The sudden interruption caused the Falconers to turn away from their ensemble of terror, facing the new threat without expression.

Eachann's voice shook, suddenly realizing that the tide had turned. "That's impossible! He had no access to that kind of flame!"

Percy had seen a coal seam fire once in his childhood. That fire had raged for weeks before spring rains doused it enough to damper the heat. But this was a different kind of flame, as if the Caldera of Cinder had suddenly moved eastward and aimed its eruption directly at Weston. As it approached the city, he could see that the ground had cracked and was splitting wider. All around, gasses bellowed hell into the sky. But the true threat raced alongside the flaming fissures. Riding atop horses and armed with Pescari weapons were the miners following their young leader. Taros advanced on Weston.

Even from horseback, Taros found it easy to control the inferno, pushing it along the seam toward the city. Whenever he had channeled flames in the past, he had been blinded by rage and possessed limited authority. But now, having bonded with the fires of Cinder, he felt completely dominant and bent the blaze to his will. Up ahead, he sensed several more pockets of flammable gases and guided the fire toward along the branching veins.

As he neared the city, he noticed several glowing vortices ravaging the Pescari District. He reached out and easily plucked the heat from these, holding it in for later use. Up ahead a line of soldiers formed atop the city wall, waiting to fend off his warriors. A wide grin formed on the shappan's face as he realized that they perched above one of the chambers of explosive vapor. The report of the blast was deafening as both the stone and their bodies ripped apart before him.

He surrounded the city with a blazing ring and quickly sought out ways to weaken the foundation of the walls. He focused on those imprisoning his people and went to work, stretching out with his mind. As he did, he raised an image of Felicima high into the sky so that his people would know the source of both his power and their liberation. The vibration of the crumbling stone shook the countryside as the walls disappeared into the glowing chasm below.

Taros and his entourage reached the entrance easily enough. Once inside Weston, he ordered the miners to fan out and attack the soldiers within. He dismounted and climbed the stairs to the nearest parapet, burning alive any sentry who dared to challenge. Eventually he found the source of the cyclones that had harmed his people. Twenty hooded specters flanked Cassus Eachann atop the city wall. They stared defiantly.

He addressed the leader of the city and ignored the others. "Sarai trusted you and believed you would treat my people well."

"I did not start this fight, Taros." Cassus gestured at the burning Pescari district, "This came from your own people, and our arrangement has changed."

"Sarai once told me that you serve your people and would do so for my own." The young chieftain fanned outstretched fingers toward the Falconers. "But you serve yourself and these false gods."

Eachann roared with laughter. "False gods? Don't you see yourself as one, Boy?"

The burning image of Felicima settled above Taros' head, pushing the city leader and the Falconers back to avoid the heat. "There are no gods, Andalonian, only the goddess Felicima and we are her children." Fire exploded from the fingers of the shappan. But as soon as he attacked, the flames instantly disappeared, snuffed out as the Falconers removed the air around him. Even the image of Felicima extinguished along with every fire in the city.

Eachann laughed as wisps of air shot out, lashing Taros' hands and feet. They bound him tightly in place. A sphere formed around the chieftain trapping him within. Suddenly helpless, the boy's thoughts returned to the winter day in the courtyard below the palace. He had lashed out with fury after Sarai had rejected his love, burning her with his unintended outburst. Prince Robert had bound him with similar magic, nearly suffocating him within that bubble of air.

Taros should have been terrified, but he had learned much during his self-imposed exile. His months spent in the watermill had been with purpose. It was a place to grow stronger and learn more about himself without interference by anger or other sources that fueled his flame. He knew that he had many virtues yet to learn.

Foremost was mercy, previously unknown to the shappan but exhibited by Robert Esterling. He lived to fight the Falconers by that man's choice alone. But mercy had no place during this night above Weston. Wrath was also a virtue when delivered appropriately.

He could not defeat the shield of air from within, that had been his mistake when fighting Robert. He had tapped and used up his own supply, choking his internal fire and almost snuffing out his lifeforce in the process. This time Taros remained calm, another lesson learned in his fight over Sarai's charred body, and he breathed deliberately as in the mine. He closed his eyes and focused on the air outside the bubble, plentiful and infinitely abundant, as he sought Felicima.

Below he spied his uncle. The man stared with a face full of embarrassment, humility, and fear. Teot's eyes darted from his nephew to the feathered entourage who held the shappan prisoner, searching for a way to free him. The boy's hands quickly danced, returning the man's attention back to him. They danced again, forming figures and spelling out the silent language of the scouts. *I am not in danger, lead the people from the city, quickly, so that I may destroy those who blaspheme against our goddess.* Teot nodded and quickly signaled the others.

Not surprisingly, the Falconers and Eachann remained focused on Taros, ignoring the flood of people racing over the crumpled outer wall. Taros had been their real quarry, but the agent of Felicima was finally ready to strike back. His opponents had cut him off from all sources within the city, but had forgotten one vast presence beneath their feet. Underground the goddess burned through the coal seam, building up heat with such intensity that she would no longer be contained.

He drew that fire up into the granite upon which the city had been built, melting and swirling it into a pool of magma. Pressure built beneath the foundation of the entire city, with ground rumbling slowly at first, then growing into a deafening roar. All over Weston bricks fell from buildings, raining onto the streets below. Soon, not only the Pescari fled, but thousands of citizens trampled women and children to escape the terror.

The pressure inside the shappan was great, and, when Taros could no longer hold it, he addressed Eachann and the Falconers one final time. "When you die, you will meet my goddess. I pray that you are welcomed by her. For the sake of mercy, I pray that she fully consumes your soul so that you may finally know and fear her true power." The eruption was deafening as molten rock spewed into the night sky and the new caldera swallowed every stone of the city.

Taros watched as the Falconers and the city leader slid into the molten rock below, not diverting his eyes until the shield of air finally evaporated. Looking down, he realized that the swirling red and yellow pool reached up to his waist. With a frown he ripped his smoking buckskins from his torso. He dipped his fingers, unburned as they were, into the magma. He was blessed.

He waded toward the collection of his people waiting on the distant shore. When he finally emerged, he found Flaya approaching with a blanket which she lovingly wrapped around his naked body. He abruptly shivered from an unknown cold despite the heat all around.

"Taros," she said, "your name means brave and you are the truest named warrior of the Pescari."

"My Shappan!" A deep voice called from the wretched ranks of the Pescari, once again reduced to refugees without a home. "I beg your forgiveness, Shappan!"

Taros turned slowly, exhausted from the battle, just in time to see Teot press through the ranks. When he reached his nephew, he knelt on all fours.

"What have you done that requires forgiveness, Uncle?" Tears fell from the older man's eyes onto Taros' bare feet, steaming and disappearing as they contacted his skin. "Rise and look at me, Uncle, I am confused."

"I stole the power of Felicima, Taros! I used it as my own, acting as her agent in your stead."

"Uncle, no one can steal the power from our goddess. If you wield it, then you truly are her agent, just as I. Your shappan is not angry. On the contrary, I am happy that you have been blessed with her power."

"But there is more." Teot refused to look at his nephew as he drew a Pescari sword from his side and offered it up. "I beg you to remove my head from my shoulders and leave my bones to rot so that I may never face Felicima's judgement!"

"I don't understand, Uncle."

Daska stepped forward, clearing his throat. When Taros' eyes met his, he explained, "Your uncle offered a challenge in your absence. He demanded Shapalote if you did not return willingly, and he professed his defiance against you."

Taros looked lovingly upon his uncle, resting a hand on his shoulder. Kneeling down he forced the older man to look directly into his eyes. "You are my only blood, Uncle. If you uttered these words, then you are forgiven."

Teot stared up in shock. "But forgiveness goes against the goddess!"

"I once believed that as well, but I have since learned differently. Besides, you were influenced by another traitor who convinced you to accept his will. You will be held blameless."

All eyes turned to the elder standing behind Teot. Daska's eyes grew wide in fear, suddenly aware of his fate. "No! You cannot! You are an abomination! You were prophesied as a destroyer of cities!" The old man gestured toward the cooling black circle of magma that had once been Weston. Fumbling in his satchel, he retrieved an old and faded parchment, holding it up so that all could see the drawing of a boy destroying a city with fire. "Behold," he shouted, "look upon the face of your destroyer!" The crowd gasped at the similarities to their leader.

Taros motioned for his uncle to rise. "If you shall redeem yourself, it will be through the death of this traitor, Teot."

Upon hearing the words, the warrior stood and approached the old man, still professing blasphemies against his nephew. He grabbed the man from behind, easily lifting him over his head. The elder thrashed and flailed, the parchment falling to the grass as he did, but Teot ignored his objections. He walked toward the fiery red center of the caldera and tossed in the enemy of Felicima. Taros nodded his approval.

No one noticed when Flaya bent down and retrieved the parchment, quickly stuffing it into her dress. They were focused too intently on the path of the river next to the caldera. As the magma cooled, the water slowly seeped in and began filling the crater. By morning the city of Weston was unrecognizable and replaced by a lake instead.

# Chapter Forty-Eight

Alec stared at the sky, willing the sun to finally set. Time ran differently this far south, with longer days and barely any notice of winter. His best guess was that nightfall was only an hour or so away, but the orb clung to the place where it hung, refusing to sink lower. He shifted his weight on the hard bench and let out a sigh of impatience.

"They're checking every wagon," Marita pointed out.

"Yes." He focused his attention on the gate, a delicate wrought iron beauty interwoven with aromatic orchids. Two sentries checked vehicles while six more manned ornamental parapets that were clearly more for show than function. Shouting up ahead filled him with anxiety as a merchant was turned away, sent back down the long road to the city. Marita laughed at the curses he screamed at the guards.

"What's a son of a flatulent tavern turner?"

"Never mind that, forget you ever heard him say it." He eased the horses forward and settled in behind a cart of entertainers. The driver ahead handed over credentials and waited.

"That isn't fair. If you're my father now, then you have to teach me about the world."

"I don't have to teach you everything. Some things you will have to figure out on your own."

Marita feigned hurt, then muttered under her breath. "Don't be such a tavern turner."

"I'm not a woman, so I can't be a tavern turner."

"Oh!" A look of triumphant understanding lighting her face. "It's a prostitute!"

"How in Cinder's crack did you figure..."

A shouted order from the guard cut off his words, "Next!" The man waved the cart through and reached out a waiting hand. "What business do you have at the manor?"

"I'm delivering a gift from His Excellency Braen Braston."

"Never heard of him! Turn around and leave."

"Braen Braston is the newly elected member of the triumvirate in Pirate's Cove. Your lord would like very much to receive this gift."

"Elected member of the what?"

The other guard moved to the rear of the wagon and climbed aboard. He shuffled his way toward the cask with a small hatchet.

"Don't touch that."

His command caused the first guard to growl, "What're you hiding, northerner?"

Alec calmly handed over the bill of lading and waited. Soon the man's hand trembled. "Surely not!"

"Yes. I advise you to allow us entrance straight away. The heat has not been good to the load."

Regaining his composure, he shouted at the man on the wagon, "Get off, Bruce!"

"Why?"

"I'm waving them through!" He handed the piece of paper to Alec and added, "Besides, an old man and a young girl are no threat." Pogue ignored the insult and spurred the horses forward. They were inside the gates. He drove the wagon directly to the main building of the manor, but was turned away. They directed him to the servant's entrance near the pantry.

This door was also guarded, but not by mercenaries. The portly woman who met him was a nightmare. She lorded over him with arrogance, despite her lowly status in the household.

"I told you to come back tomorrow," she barked. "Lord Valencia will not be disturbed until after the banquet!"

"I'm sorry, Miss..."

"Pritchett!"

"Miss Pritchett. Can you at least notify the steward that I am here? I am here on especially important business that cannot wait until tomorrow."

"She won't be seeing you, either."

"Then will you please tell her that Captain Alec Pogue has arrived with a gift and message from Pirate's Cove." The reddish faced woman blanched at his name.

She quickly regained her composure and screamed, "Come back tomorrow!" The door slammed so firmly in his face that the frame shook.

"She knows who I am," he growled. "Mattie's in there, for sure!"

"What now," Marita asked?

"I suppose we move the cart to a safe place and start searching for another way in."

The man had said that his name was Captain Pogue from The Cove. Penelope Pritchett leaned against the door, barring it with her body.

Mrs. Pogue rounded the corner to the pantry, alarmed by the slamming of the door. As much as Penelope hated the woman, she had no choice but to talk to her.

"Who was at the door?" The steward asked, "Was there another delivery?"

"No. Just some riffraff," Pritchett explained. "I told them to come back tomorrow."

"I'm sure that whatever business they had can wait. Thank you, Miss Pritchett."

As quickly as she had arrived, Mattie Pogue had left. Penelope waited to a count of ten, then scurried down the opposite hallway. Three more turns brought her to the great hall. The tables were set in the fashion chosen by the new steward. Of course, the layout was hideous and unsuitable for such a grand event, but there was no time to gawk at the woman's botchery.

She spied two house guards, trusted men to Miss Pritchett. These men were not hired mercenaries like the others, these had been in the lord's employment for a decade. She walked directly to the older man, Petr, and addressed him. "There is a man causing alarm outside."

"Then go alert the sentries. We've been tasked with inside security," he replied.

"I overheard him say that he was here to kill Lord Valencia."

"Oh you did?" Petr laughed her off. He was trusted by her, but not her favorite.

"What exactly did he say, Miss Pritchett?" Jon was a patient man, much more polite than his partner.

"He has a little girl in his wagon, and I heard him tell her that if we didn't let him in the house, then he would find a way in. He also said that he is on a mission from Pirate's Cove and plans to assassinate Charro."

Petr let out a laugh. "That was nice of him to say all of that in front of you, wasn't it?"

"This is serious!" She stepped forward, staring down into his eyes. In a low voice she added, "Do you want the lord to know that you've been coming around my quarters drunk? He might want to know that you like to offer coin for a tumble with the lady servants."

"You wouldn't."

"Yes. I would. Do you want to check this man's story out or not?"

"Aye." Peter reluctantly turned and followed as she stormed toward the main entrance. Jon followed, loosening the clasp that held his sword.

The house security asked again, "May we help you?"

Alec glanced at the woman from the pantry. She stood behind the guards beaming with smug satisfaction as if she had already beaten him. "I need to see the lord of the manor."

"That isn't likely to happen ever. Tell us why you are here."

"That's our business," Marita shouted up at him defiantly, then turned to Alec and smiled, sticking her thumb into the air.

"You mean pirate business?" The older of the two men laughed.

The girl answered, "As a matter of fact, yes. And you'd best let us inside to see the lord if you know what's good for you."

"Marita," Alec cautioned, "I can handle this." To the guards he insisted. "This can all be cleared up as soon as I speak with Lord Valencia. I bring a gift from Braen Braston, leader of Pirate's Cove."

"The prince of Fjorik? Now we know you're lying. Lord Stefan Nevra leads The Cove, last we heard."

"He doesn't any longer. Please, may I have five minutes of Valencia's time? We've come a long way."

"No," the older man replied, "you'll be coming with us for further questioning. Of course, we're really busy tonight, so we'll get around to our questions in a few days if you're lucky."

"I don't have time for this." Alec placed his hand on the pommel of one of his swords. Miss Pritchett screamed, "He's drawing down!"

Both guards drew their own and Alec froze in place. "Easy now! There's no need for anyone to get hurt!" He raised his hands with palms out to show that he did not want a fight.

"That sounds like a threat. You'll be lucky if we don't just run you through and save the questioning."

Shouting from the visitor tents caused everyone to pause. Then northern horns of war blasted loudly from the tent city.

"The longboat," Alec exclaimed.

The woman blanched, "What are you talking about? What longboat?" Then she had a thought. "Did Braston send you to distract us while his men attack the manor?"

"No!" Alec shook his head in frustration. "When we were coming up the road, we saw a longboat rounding the bend. If they're attacking, then it's Skander Braston, not Braen." The shouting intensified and quickly turned into screams of pain. Soon steel rang against steel on the other side of the manor. "We have to aid them!"

"Petr," the younger guard said nervously, "It's started early. We need to get into position!"

The older guard advanced, "You won't be aiding anything!" He lunged forward with his sword swung high and arcing downward.

Alec reacted on instinct, drawing his blade from his left hip and raising it with a high parry. The man pressed forward, moving in too close for the sword master to draw his second blade. Pogue pleaded, "Stop!" But the second sentry rushed forward with his own sword, swinging it low and slicing through a tendon. The captain groaned as he crumpled to his knees, with one sword drawn and the other still at his side.

A rush of wind blew from the south, blasting the attackers backward. The fat woman toppled over as well. With skirts over her head, she fell into a heap of petticoats. "No," Alec tried to scream to Marita, but she was already moving toward the men. With a single motion, she drew the sword from Pogue's belt, holding her hand out for his primary. He shook his head defiantly, "Don't do it, Marita! You don't have to."

"Nobody fucks with my family," was her reply as she lashed his sword with tendrils of air. It ripped from Alec's hand and flew into hers as she moved between her adoptive father and the attackers.

Marita set her feet and balanced into a stance she called 'shit in your britches.' She had learned it by watching Alec and Amash. She did not know the correct term and coined the name because they looked to her like they were dumping in their pants. They had never noticed the close attention she had paid to their many hours of practice. They also failed to realize that the girl had picked up a few skills on her own.

Both of Alec's attackers scrambled to their feet and held their swords at the ready, unsure whether they should charge the young girl. She never gave them a chance to make up their minds. She glided like the wind as she moved beneath their blades, transitioning to ‘left-handed windmill slice,’ a move that allowed her to attack with her right hand before finishing the older guard with another slash from her left. The move was quick, and the man lay dead before an incredibly surprised Captain Pogue.

Now settled into ‘circle your arms like a ballerina,’ she paused long enough for the second man to turn and face her. She parried with a left-handed ‘punch the sword’ and stabbed his abdomen with her right in a move she called ‘belly blow.’ The man stared at her smiling face with disbelief.

Alec’s voice met her ears, breaking her attention from her dance. “Finish him, dearie. That wound will kill him, but not quickly enough.” He glanced toward the fighting near the tents, a battle raged between berserkers and the mercenaries hired by the lords. “We’ve got to find Mattie and the girls.”

Marita nodded, then drew her sword from the guard’s gut, scrunching her nose at the mixture of blood and shit pushed out by his ruptured intestines. The man dropped his sword and grabbed his belly, trying desperately to push his insides back in. He slid to his knees and Marita crossed her swords. She knew the actual name of her next move, ‘crossing the crimson river.’ Unlike the last time she used it, she knew that once you crossed the river you could never return. She crossed him over, nonetheless.

“Help me up, Marita.” Pogue’s voice wavered, betraying the pain in the back of his leg. He was wounded, but not as seriously as she had previously feared. “I think I can stand.”

“But can you fight?”

“Yes. Where did you learn those moves, dearie?”

“By watching you and Amash, Silly!” A thought crossed her mind and she frowned, suddenly worried. “Are you upset with me again?”

“Actually, this time I’m quite thankful.” Marita offered up his swords and he took them, pointing one at the plump woman on the ground. She still lay on her back, eyes wide after watching Marita kill the two guards. Alec placed the blade to her throat and growled, “Where is my wife?”

"She's in the grand hall, no doubt serving the lords."

"Take us there," he barked.

The woman clamored to her feet and led them toward a secret entrance into the manor house. "Here's the door, please let me go, sir."

"No, you will stay with us and take me to Mattie. I don't trust you not to bring more guards." She pressed on a set of bricks, causing a section of the wall to break away and swing inside. "When I came by earlier, you knew exactly whose husband I am. How do you know my name."

"No, sir!" She pleaded "I was scared and wanted to warn Mrs. Pogue in case you were lying."

Marita pushed by the sniveling woman and entered the passageway first. "She's lying, Alec."

"I know she is, dearie."

"Can we kill her?" The woman let out a miserable whimper at the suggestion.

"Alas. No, we should not. We may need her."

"Pity." Marita moved slowly through the passage, leading the way and feeling around in the dark. "Where does this passage lead?"

"To the pantry."

"We'll just see about that," the girl responded. A gust of wind blew past the trio, despite the closed door behind them. Marita travelled with her mind along the breeze, scouting ahead. As she rounded a corner, she encountered a door that easily pushed open with the gust. All that lay ahead were stacks of dry goods along tall shelves, each meticulously arranged and organized. Satisfied, she snapped her mind back into her body. "That was the truth. It's the pantry and it looks safe."

"Good," Alec responded. "We are so close now I can't even bear it."

"Captain Pogue?" Marita bit her lip, worried how to say the next bit. She was trying so hard to be a good daughter to him and what she was about to say had been bothering her.

"Yes?"

"I'm sorry you heard me say the 'f' word, before I killed those men."

"It's okay, dearie," he replied, "sometimes it's an appropriate word to use. I would say that was good timing." He placed a gentle hand on her shoulder, giving her a light squeeze.

"Oh, I'm not sorry I said it, I'm sorry that you heard me say it." Even though it was dark, she shot him a thumbs up and a smile of reassurance. *Everything is perfect right now*, she thought. *I can't wait to meet Mattie!*

# Chapter Forty-Nine

Braen awoke to the creaking of timbers and the sound of water lapping the hull. He could tell by the spacing in the waves that they kept a fast pace. *That's odd,* he mused, *surely the crew would not have shoved off without waking me.* He opened his eyes and rolled over, eager to slip on his boots and head topside to investigate.

Hester lay on her side, facing him and smiling. "Well, good morning." She placed her hand on his chest and he sat up in shock.

Shock was replaced by anger when he realized the state of their undress. His eyes shot to the empty chair beside the bed. "Where are my clothes?"

She gestured to the crumpled heap on the floor. "You threw them off in your passion, or don't you remember?" A look of worry crossed her face and she added, "Were you so drunk last night that you don't even remember making love to me?" She pointed at the empty bottle of 754 on the table.

"That's impossible," Braen protested, "I only drank one glass before falling asleep! I recorked that bottle!"

"No, you drank so much at your meeting that you apparently don't even remember sending word for me to join you!" She looked put out and stood from the bed. When she turned her back Braen laid eyes on his brother's handiwork. His heart broke and his anger softened into concern for Hester.

"He did that to you?"

"Yes. And that's not all I've endured."

"I'll kill him." The captain's cheeks began to dance as he ground his teeth in rage. "I'll gut him and leave him to the sharks for this."

A quiet knock at the door turned his attention. A meek voice from the other side begged, "Buh... Braen, can you cuh... calm down? The suh... seas are getting ruh... rough."

"I'm sorry, Sippen!" The bearded captain gathered up his clothing and began dressing.

Hester sat naked on the chair beside him, staring with a wanton smile. "It's been a long time since we've been alone."

He pleaded, "Can you please put on some clothing?"

She looked down at her body and raised her hands in a shrug. "What does it matter? It seems that I remember what we both look like, since I can recollect last night."

"Did we?"

"Did we what? Do what we did as horny teenagers?" Her cheeks curled into a devious smile. "Did we have sex, Braen? Is that what you want to know?"

"Well, did we?"

"Yes, we did." After a pause she added, "And it was amazing."

Braen grunted his displeasure and fought to pull on his boots, fumbling in his hurry and dropping one to the deck. "I need to go."

"I wish things had been different, Braen. I wish that you had been crowned and we had married as planned."

"My father always said to 'wish in one hand and shit in the other, just to see which one fills up quicker.' I finally understand what he meant."

She wrinkled up her nose. "How crass."

"How wise." He finally pulled on the last boot and made for the door. "You made your choice on the day you went to Skander. You broke my heart in a million pieces and I've spent my life trying to get over you."

"But have you?"

His thoughts immediately turned to Eusari. *Poor Eusari. I can't tell her of this, or she will never forgive me. Demon's nipples, what have I done?* "Undeniably, yes. I finally have, and I am in love with another." He swung the door open and strode out, letting it swing on its hinges.

Suddenly aware of her nakedness, Hester ran to shut it. But just before she did, a one-legged man with an eyepatch walked by and whistled, "Looking good, Hester!"

"Piss off, Cedric!" She screamed as she slammed it tight.

"I already did, Hester!" Came the muffled reply from the other side.

Braen arrived topside to find that they had pushed far during the night. Sippen manned the helm, having recently relieved Krill to lay below. "I'm duh... disappointed in you, Bruh... Braen."

"I'm disappointed in myself. Believe me when I tell you that I don't remember any of it. It's strange, like I was drugged or something." Silence passed between the two friends as *Malfeasance* raced along. "How far have we travelled? I don't suppose we could come about and drop Hester back in The Cove?"

"Nuh... not a chance. We're arriving in a cuh... couple of hours."

Braen pondered the situation ahead. If his brother is already in Middleton, then he would have two battles to fight. One with him and then one with Eusari. *She will be furious when she sees Hester aboard.* "Has Sebastian reached Caroline, yet?"

"Nuh... no. The last we huh... heard is that Eusari wuh... won't talk to you."

"We need to find her. Tell the boy to try and track *She Wolf* from the air." He frowned at dark clouds on the horizon. "Isn't that the direction of Middleton?"

Sippen nodded, "I thuh... think it's smuh... smoke."

"Then it's already begun. Order the men to battle stations and let's be ready for anything."

Eusari felt the chill of the storm before she saw it above the harbor. Thankfully neither she nor Jacque had been looking directly at the flash, so they were spared blindness. Even still, as she blinked against the sudden brightness, the image of the Braston sigil graced her eyelids. *He's a monster and must be stopped!* The air around them suddenly felt alive and her hair stood on end. With quick thinking, she grabbed her crewman and pulled him to safety. They tumbled into the muck of the street just as the ground where they were standing exploded with lightning.

The two scrambled to their feet and ran, dodging debris and people scampering for safety. An old woman ambled out in front of them and Jacque collided with a crack of her bones. The two toppled to the ground with a thud and various groans. The woman, worse for the incident, lay sprawled on the ground, staring at the sky with eyes forever scarred by the Braston sigil.

"I'm blind," the woman kept repeating to no one, "all I can see is the cat! Gods take me now! I'm blind!"

Eusari grabbed Jacque's arm and pulled him to his feet, muttering, "Be more careful!"

"I'm sorry! I didn't see her!" After a brief pause, he added with a smile, "I guess she didn't see it coming either."

"Not the time!" With an eyeroll she groaned, "All you men are as bad as Krill!"

"Aye, I know that we arrrr..."

Eusari ignored him as she wheeled around a corner, nearly crashing into a squad of soldiers. In the middle of the unit stood an ancient man dressed in the white furs of a sabre cat. The man pointed one finger and the pirates flew into a wall, crashing hard against the bricks. The soldiers rushed forward with swords drawn, eager to finish them off. Instinctively Eusari reached out with her mind.

Nearby she felt several shrubberies. These came to life and thrashed and flailed at the Norsemen, luring them to turn and fight them off. The strangely dressed emotant giggled with merriment as he watched the soldiers fight against the bushes, sounding more like a child than a man of many years. Eusari took advantage of the distraction to reach out further for something to bond.

She found a tree that was neither too small nor too large. With a grin she brought it to life. The oak stepped out from its bed, lumbering toward the northern invaders who were too busy chopping at bushes to notice. She compelled her new weapon forward, swinging a massive branch toward the elderly man's head and cracking his skull from behind. With the emotant down, the tree lumbered toward the others, grabbing ahold and squeezing them breathless.

Scrambling to her feet, Eusari shouted over the roar above, "Hurry! We've got to get to the Rookery!" They rounded the bend and surveyed the scene in the harbor. Skander's ships had landed and his entire army disembarked. Movement at the harbor entrance caused her heart to flutter when she recognized a shimmering flagship with four billowing masts leading twenty frigates. "It's *Malfeasance*," she shouted, "Braen came!" In an instant she forgave any and all transgressions, whether real or perceived. *Even if you screwed her, I forgive you*, she thought, *thank you for coming after me!*

Braen eased *Malfeasance* into the harbor, eyes fixed the mayhem ahead. The entire city burned, and more than fifty lightning infused tornados flung bolts indiscriminately. "What the hell is this?"

"Looks like Middleton, Cap'n!"

"Thanks, Krill." The Gunnery Sergeant proffered a salute and went about his duties preparing the guns. Braen stared back at the carnage with sympathy for the people dying in the streets. "Sippen! Signal the others to load explosive rounds. Take out every one of his ships!"

The little man complied and soon the longboats in the harbor were reduced to splinters.

Braston lifted his spyglass and surveyed the pier. A lone figure stood defiantly shaking his fist, his backdrop a fiery hell storm. "There he is. Drop anchor."

"No, Braen."

The bearded captain bristled at the defiance. In thirty-five years, he had never heard Sippen refuse his order. "You want to take him on alone to keep us out of harm. But this time I won't let you." The engineer stepped forward. "Don't you get it? Every time you try and do things yourself, you push your friends a little further away. By trying to save them suffering, you intensify your own."

Braen stared back in shock. "You didn't stutter."

"Buh... Because my words were spuh... spoken with confidence."

In that moment he saw his friend differently. The friend he had always viewed as thoughtful and loyal wasn't. He was more than that. "Why haven't you stood up to me before?"

"Buh... Because you wuh... weren't ready. Yuh... you've been buh... busy teaching luh... leadership to all of us, that you fuh... forgot to listen to yuh.. yourself." The little man pointed at Skander on the pier. "Yuh... you can't do it by yourself. You need us."

"What are you implying, Sippen?"

"That you luh... look around at the buh... bigger picture." The little man gestured toward the city.

Braen eyed it closely, this time searching out the source of the fires. A storm raged overhead, and tornados swirled through the streets. All around people ran from their homes and into hysteria. "He's an emotant?"

Yurik nodded.

With spyglass to his eye, Braen focused on a squad of northerners clashing with city guardsmen in the streets. "Demon's nipples. He has an army of air emotes."

Sippen took the glass and watched quietly for a moment. "Suh... Sebastian!"

The boy answered right away, "Yes Mr. Yurik?"

"Make a shuh... shield of air around that bucket."

"That one?" The boy pointed aft.

"Yuh... yes. Duh... Don't let anything through." The boy nodded and a shimmering field surrounded the container. Sippen pulled his hand cannon from his belt, aimed, and fired. The pail flew across the deck. "Thu... That was your strongest?" The boy nodded and the engineer pointed at the pier. "Puh.. Put us ashore, Bruh... Braen."

The bearded captain marveled at his friend's wisdom then ordered the crew, "You heard the man! Break out rifles and pistols and prepare to storm the beach!" To his friend he added, "But I fight Skander alone."

# Chapter Fifty

Kali and Beth were exhausted but in good spirits, resting idly in the center of town. Akili, it turns out, was an amazing sight. A snowy owl, she was pure white with streaks and speckles of black along her wings and back. She had taken to Kali, and the three had quickly become good friends.

During the battle, Beth had been extraordinary, at least in the eyes of the teen who had never met an air emotant. The tall teenager defied all of the former street urchin's expectations. She had tied up one of the Falconers while holding off three Jaguars. Of course, she had raved all evening about Kali's contribution and how she killed the feathered specters by swallowing them with the ground.

The younger girl thought of a trick and brought out a mouse from under a nearby woodpile. As soon as Akili caught the movement, she shot into the air, circling twice before diving down to snatch up her dinner. Kali released the rodent at the last moment, feeling a little bad for the critter but happy to feed her new friend.

The rider from the forest nearly trampled the bird as he raced in, heedless of whoever or whatever stood in his way. The next rider was Madelyn, tall and graceful in the saddle as she raced past, yelling for the girls to follow. They shot each other a knowing look, then clamored after. They reached the house just in time to hear the news. The bodies of the Falconers and soldiers were gone, taken from the battlefield in a matter of a few short hours.

*Who could have been close enough to remove them,* Kali thought, *surely our scouts would have seen the wagons?* She started to whisper the question aloud to her new friend, but was interrupted by shouts from the edge of town.

Madelyn had dismounted and pulled a rifle from a sling attached to her saddle. She shouted, "You girls with me!"

Shon's revolutionaries were already forming into squads, ducking behind buildings and shooting at shadowy figures on the forest edge. Soon several thousand enemy soldiers burst from the woods, running toward Estowen's Landing. Kali was confused, these men had blood on their uniforms, so much that it had to have been their own. She tried to create a crevice between them and the town, but she could not. Fear gripped her like it never had before. She yelled to Madelyn, "My power's not working!"

Gunfire boomed from the west and Madelyn shouted back at the girl, "Forget that," she yelled, "get control of those!" With a finger she pointed to another section of the woods, one with massive spruce trees reaching at least thirty feet into the air. She watched in horror as forty of the stockiest ripped their roots from the ground and lumbered toward the frightened people fighting for their lives. Chaos and confusion ruled as the enemy raced in from every direction.

"Do something!" Madelyn screamed into the night, again indicating the giant trees.

"I... I can't! There's too many!" Kali felt suddenly weak and worthless in the fight.

Beth placed a calming hand on the girl's shoulder, whispering four words before racing away to offer what little aid she could. Akili flew overhead, screeching into the night as the tall girl whipped up a violent whirlwind, swirling wildly and causing the trees to bend forward against the vortex. Abruptly, a pack of large cats raced past the trees, leaping and biting at the girl. They were large like northern saber cats, but smokey black in appearance instead of white. In no time at all they were upon the teen. She lay on the ground, screaming in pain as they tried to rip her apart.

Madelyn called over the noise, eyes wide and fearful, "What did she say to you?"

Kali choked back tears at the horror in front of her eyes. "She said, "I believe in you." She began with the jaguars. Recognizing that someone controlled them, she reached deep into their minds, feeling for a connection and tracing it to the forest. She focused on slicing the threads neatly, then replaced them with bonds of her own. The roaring animals stepped casually aside, and Kali rushed to her friend, bleeding badly from her wounds.

"The trees!" Madelyn screamed, pointing at the animated monsters making their way toward them. "Leave her and focus on the trees!"

But Kali couldn't pry her eyes away from the dying teen. Staring down she flinched at the sounds of battle. Rifles exploded nearby and men and women screamed, causing tears to form on her cheeks. She placed a hand on Beth's forehead, feeling for a spark of life. A white blur caught her attention as Akili swooped down and landed next to his bonded. He hooted in panic, pecking at the girl's hand and trying to wake her up.

"I'm sorry, little guy. I know you loved her." Kali tried to soothe him with her words, but he was too panicked.

Rough hands grabbed Kali and tugged her away, screaming in her ear, "Stop the trees or we will die!" Madelyn pointed as one of the trees began smashing the nearby house with its branches, pounding and crushing the walls. As the roof collapsed, Madelyn shrieked, "Hurry! Pearl is in there!"

The trees were harder to wrestle from whoever had bonded them, but Kali was able to take control of the closest. She sent it toward the others with flailing limbs and kicking roots. The sight would have been funny if the town was not losing the battle, but she choreographed kicks and punches as the great spruce took down each of the others in turn. Thoughts back on Beth, she returned to her friend's side, finding her lifeless.

Johan's voice snapped her attention, "How can I help?"

Through tears she responded, "We need rain. Lots of it!" He knelt and held her hands, focused on the clouds forming overhead. As it began to fall, Kali closed her eyes and felt for the vines climbing around the city and on the walls of its buildings. Roots absorbed the water and the stems stretched out like ropes down every street. Soon, thousands of men struggled against their entanglements. She had slowed their advance, but only momentarily.

Kali opened her eyes and whispered to Johan, "Can you make lightning?"

"I... I've never tried," he responded.

"Aim for the trees," she ordered.

Samani sat silently across from Ashima, taking in her features. She barely resembled his baby sister. Although the eyes were the same, these orbs stared blankly ahead, devoid of emotion or any spark they once held. Only a few strands of hair were left on her head and even these were slowly planning their escape from her scalp. Her skin was ashen white, not pink and rosy as when she had once blushed with laughter.

Delilah asked, "I don't understand. How is she a Falconer?"

"That's the great secret of the oracles. Like Andalon is a farm for emotant essence, our former homes were farms for these abominations." He reached out a timid hand and touched his sister's cold face. "Oracles are chosen because of their natural sensitivity to the bead. Not everyone can travel through the Da'ash'mael and fewer can reach the Ka. Only the strongest will prophesy, and those who 'transcend' are worth more to the Astian Council dead than alive."

"So there really is no afterlife?"

He gestured toward Ashima. "I don't think so, unless this is it. I'd like to hope so but seeing this walking husk reinforces my doubts."

"How do they bring them back? And why as Falconers?"

"Not just Falconers. The Jaguars are created in the same fashion, only from the autumn oracle."

"Why not the other two?"

"Water and fire are more difficult to control. I believe that it's possible to bring them back, but why would the Council create forces of pure destruction like water and fire?" He shook his head. "No, they're as arrogant as the gods of ancient mythology. They would know better than to create titans because they fear the same power struggle."

Delilah marveled at the specter chained before Kernigan, "She's so lifelike, it's hard to tell that she's actually the walking dead."

"She was my sister," he said with a pang of disgust, "I can tell."

"We'll have to destroy her."

"I know. But for now her connection to the bead is expired, so she's cut off from the collective. She's strongly under their control, however, and will never give us intelligence or anything else that could be useful."

"Could we wrestle away control?"

"I've thought about that option as well. It is very much possible and there is a way, but Eusari will never do it. She's too self-motivated and fickle regarding the war that they're fighting. No, she'll never lend practical aid to ours." He stood, turning his back on the depressing reminder that his sister had perished. "When the time comes, I'll do it. I owe Ashima that much at least."

He and Delilah left the room, turning the key in the lock as they departed. Knowing that they were nearing Estowen's landing, they headed topside for some fresh coastal air. The breeze had warmed since the last time he had sailed these waters, but the chill was enough to ache his bones. He scanned the northwest, looking for signs of the hidden city, but found none. They had concealed it so well.

By the time they had pulled into the harbor he paused. Thunder echoed from the forest, met by distant shouts. *No,* he grabbed the railing to steady himself, *it can't be.* He strained his eyes, peering into the night.

"Samani!"

"I hear it." He threw open the hatch and called below, "Gretchen!" The girl sprinted topside. After she had joined him on the rail, he thrust an Astian bead into her hand, ordering, "I need my wits about me, take this and tell me what's going on!"

The girl nodded and tossed it back, swallowing it dry. Soon she described a warzone with unbelievable details. The dead walked and trees marched on Estowen's Landing. Then lightning exploded from a cloudless sky.

Kali knelt over Beth while Johan gave her cover. She placed a hand over her friend's eyes, feeling for lifeforce and willing her to wake up. She released more of the vines, not so much that Shon Wembley's army would be overrun, but enough that she could reach deeper into her friend. She felt her there just out of reach. Akili must have sensed her purpose and landed on the girl's shoulder. He stared down at his bonded mate, cooing and grunting his displeasure.

"Let go of her," Kali whispered to the owl. "Break your bond so that I may find her." He must have understood, because he spread his wings and let out an angry cry before rising into the sky. He flew high, up and away. As soon as he was airborne, the girl felt movement within. There was a spark of life. She reached deeper and found Beth, struggling to remain within her body but partially restored by the gift from her bird. Kali did the only thing she could think of and poured herself into her friend.

Beth's eyes snapped open and she sat up. Kali cried out with joy, "You're alive!" But the older girl stared blankly at her friend, as if waiting for something. "Beth, do you know me?""Yes. My name is Beth."

An explosion ripped into the nearest of the trees, spraying charred splinters. The battle had grown closer. Kali reached into the vines, connecting with the entire network from the edge of town to the forest. She squeezed, choking and tearing at every soldier she held in her grasp. She could see through the leaves now suddenly feeling omniscient. On a small bluff overlooking the village, she spied several scantily clad men and women adorned in animal skins and kneeling on the ground. Their humming and swaying made her nauseous.

"Johan," she said as she pointed to the clearing, "aim your lightning at that ridge."

Pearl breathed her last with Fatwana by her side. The lead oracle had always resented the woman, blaming her for stealing away her brother and corrupting him with lies and government conspiracies. Yet, as the frail woman lay trapped beneath the rubble, she had earned pity from the eldest Nakala sibling. She had thrown away any chance for transcending to the afterlife.

After the battle outside had subsided, she and Cassidy strolled outside to watch the Andalonians pick up the pieces. The devastation was sickening, with hundreds of bodies dangling from vines and nearly every building uninhabitable. Their magic was truly an abomination, and she no longer wondered why the council had worked so hard to keep it a secret and so far away from civilization.

Several of the emotant children had gathered around a young woman, once tall and graceful, but now staring off into space as if she had gone mad inside.

"She was dead," one of the boys said. "But Kali brought her back."

Fatwana clasped her hands to her mouth, filled with sudden revulsion. She turned to her partner, but Cassidy seemed unfazed by the comment. *By the oracles, I think she's even smiling a little.* She was about to verbally rebuke the young woman when she suddenly froze, shocked by the sight of a man and a woman making their way through town. Although it had been many years, she recognized her brother immediately.

He did not see her, nor did he seem surprised by the carnage. He strode directly to the children and addressed several of the oldest as if they were closely acquainted. They laughed at his jokes and beamed with pride as he slapped them on their backs triumphantly. They loved him, almost as one would admire a father or a teacher.

He bent down and spoke with the strange girl, the one they claimed was reanimated. Then he took her hand and helped her to her feet. With kind words he told Kali, "I can help you teach her to be like herself again, but first I need you to meet someone I care about very deeply." Kali and the tall girl followed him toward town and Fatwana heard him say, "I'm hoping you can help her just as you helped Beth."

Fatwana was too shocked and disgusted to follow.

# Chapter Fifty-One

Mattie sighed a breath of relief as the guests arrived in the main hall. Dinner preparations had gone smoothly, and the place settings were stunning. Each centerpiece contained a dazzling display of orchids grown in Charro's own nursery. The decorations enchanted each guest as they entered, and she watched as several paused to gawk at the giant ice sculptures. Each peacock was twenty feet tall and had been carved from a single block of ice.

Lord Valencia arrived not long after the last guest had been seated. His arrival was celebrated with fanfare and met with great applause by his guests. The gown he had chosen for the occasion was adorned in plumage and purple feathers that would make even the peacocks jealous. The man was beautiful in all his splendor, captivating the room as he moved to a small stage in front of the sculptures.

"My fellow nobility." He paused after speaking, allowing the applause to die down and the people to settle. "I want to welcome you to my home." He had to wait another moment to allow for a second eruption of applause. After a few moments he continued, "Tomorrow we will discuss many aspects of economy, politics, and security of our united continent. But let's save those topics for tomorrow, because tonight we feast!"

Mattie marveled at the way the man captivated the entire room. She would have believed him a god had she not been working so closely with him. He made his way to the main table where his steward stood with a serving jug. She noted how his robes waved on the breeze as he strolled with unrivaled confidence.

She held out a glass which he nodded and took with a smile. As he sipped, he whispered, "An excellent job well done, Mrs. Pogue."

Although praise from the man was rare, it was not entirely a foreign concept. Nonetheless, she was caught off guard by the compliment. She stammered, "Thank you, My Lord."

"I shall grant you and your daughters the evening off. You may retire to your chambers."

"Thank you, Lord Valencia, that's very kind, but I think we should remain here and treat your guests."

Charro's features suddenly dropped, revealing his darker side, "That wasn't a request, Mrs. Pogue." Frowning at his wine glass he added, "Is this Estonian? What vintage is this?"

"It is, My Lord. I believe it is a 752."

"It will have to do. What a pity there isn't a bottle of 754 left in the north. I would sell half my lands for a case. That way I could sip contentedly as I sit upon my balcony and watch the northern continent burn." Discussing the wine had restored his usual cheery demeanor.

"I will dig around in the cellar and try to find a bottle."

"Don't bother, if there was a drop of 754 on this property, I would know it. Now, about your girls. I'm serious about you taking the evening off. These parties usually turn rowdy and somewhat..." He paused to find the word then added, "provocative. I would hate for any of my guests to assume that you or your daughters are on the menu."

"Thank you, My Lord." Mattie suddenly felt very foolish for challenging her employer. As good as he had been to her, she should have realized that he was just being overly protective. "I'll gather Liza and Alexa at once and retire."

He suddenly looked around the room, his eyes betraying a hidden concern. In a shaky voice he asked, "Have you seen Jon and Petr?"

"They left with Miss Pritchett about thirty minutes ago. I'm sure they'll return soon."

He felt at his chest, pulling out a necklace with a large key attached. He began to fidget, rubbing the key and turning it over in his hands. *Odd,* Mattie thought, *I've never seen him so nervous.* She followed his darting eyes, first to the main entrance to the hall and then to a large hearth nearby. She wondered, *what has him suddenly so afraid?* And then the doors burst open and chaos rushed in.

The tents outside were ablaze, backlighting mercenaries rushing about with swords drawn and drenched with blood. Every head in the great hall had turned, just in time to witness a man falling to his knees with an axe buried deep in his back. His face landed hard on the floor and the nobles gasped with fear.

Mattie spun around to address Charro, but he had already moved away. He had the key out, desperately trying and failing to place it into a hidden slot by the mantle. His hands shook so badly that he dropped it twice, stooping down to pick it up each time. He resembled a deranged peacock as his colorful robes flapped behind him. A scream drew her eyes back to the entry.

Liza was frozen in place, staring out at five large men storming the room. Each was clad in northern furs with wild beards and faces covered in blood. They roared menacingly, sending the party goers into a panic as they turned over tables. The nobles scrambled away in terror as everyone fled the berserkers. Everyone except Liza.

Mattie shouted for her daughter, "Liza!" But the girl couldn't hear her mother's cries. Her feet were frozen in place.

Another cry came from the servant's door, "Mother!"

Mattie tore her eyes from her eldest and watched as Alexa entered the hall carrying a large platter of stuffed eggs. Three of the raiders continued their dash toward Liza, while two made a charge toward her sister. She would have to choose only one to aid.

As a mother she had only ever felt this helpless once, and memories of that morning in The Cove haunted her daily. She was unable to prevent strong hands from forcing her and the girls into a wagon to be sold like livestock. But her greatest failure had been when the men had arrived. She should have fought them off, screamed for the girls to flee as their father had taught them. But she had cowed.

She had offered up hers and Alec's life savings and then penned the very note that had prevented him from searching.

At the kidnapper's prompting she had written, *Alec, I am tired of living in The Cove. This kind of life is not what I had wanted for our daughters and I've taken them away. You are married to your career and I refuse to be second behind that kind of mistress. Don't try to find us. Mattie.* As a mother she would once again prove worthless, unable to protect her sweet babies. She was about to watch them lose their maidenhood and probably even their lives.

Her body moved before she even realized that she could. Her hand reached down, drawing a sharp blade from Lord Valencia's place setting. Her feet stepped forward one after the other until she felt herself running toward Alexa. She was the closest. Her arm raised the blade, ready to plunge it into the soft neck of the first berserker she could reach. Her eyes darted, first at her youngest and then at Liza. The men were upon her flailing body, ripping at her dress and fighting over which would take the spoils first.

Someone caught Mattie Pogue from behind and a voice pleaded, "No! There's no saving them! Come with me and I will keep you safe."

Glancing back toward Liza, she could see that the bodice had been ripped free from her chest and the corset cut clean through. Her sweet daughter's white breasts were exposed to the animals who drooled and bit at her skin. *Fight them,* she pleaded in her mind, *fight them off!* The knife came down with vengeance, stabbing into the flesh of the man behind her and digging deep into his thigh. Suddenly free, she rushed toward Alexa's assailants with the knife raised above her head.

Liza's screams intensified, turning into moans that a mother should never hear from her daughter. There was nothing she could do for her, but the knife came down, just as one of the men had forced Alexa onto the table and ripped the laces at her back. The blade found the soft part of his neck. She pulled the knife free. The raider's right hand gripped his throat, slipping off the gush of crimson that foamed with his final breaths.

The second man, unfazed by the sudden death of his partner, raised his axe and swung wildly. The heavy piece of steel hummed as it fell, racing forward to steal Mattie's life. She stumbled backward, slipping on the wet floor and toppling into the table behind her. The weapon missed slightly, cutting deep into the solid oak next to her head. He grunted as he wrenched it free, raising it high and screaming as it came back down. Mattie knew that she had once again failed as a mother.

Marita heard the screams echoing down the hall. They were close and a battle raged on the other side of a heavy door. She pressed forward, eager to drive off the northern raiders. Captain Pogue placed a hand on her shoulder, urging caution.

"They're only men," she argued. "They aren't Falconers or even those nasty Jaguar things," she protested."

"Still, I don't want to lose you." The scream of a young woman rang out, wrenching the girl's heart. *Too similar,* she thought, *it isn't her, but I can save this one.*

She jerked away and sprinted into the great hall. Alec tried his best to keep up, but his injured leg slowed his pace. She burst through the servant's entrance just in time to watch a woman stab a steak knife into the neck of a raider. His partner swung his axe, burying it into the table beside her beautiful face. As he pulled it free, Marita wrapped a noose of air around his throat and swung the other end around a rafter above. She didn't have time to finish the job, only to keep him out of reach of the woman. He swung his axe wildly above his head, unable to cut the invisible cord.

Amid the panic she could see noblemen and women trying to flee the hall, running in circles and tripping over or trampling each other in their haste. Crazed berserkers continued to rush in, eager to claim their spoils and bathe in blood. She and Alec would stop them, but first she had to find that certain young woman.

Near the entrance, three men pushed and shoved as they fought over a particularly pretty girl roughly the same age as her mother had been. One of the brutes had his weight atop her, trying to pry her legs as she fought back. She had done a good job of it so far, but was losing strength of both body and will. In a futile attempt, she bit the man's arm, causing him to roar with laughter.

And then Marita no longer saw the young woman. The cries and moans now belonged to her own young and beautiful mother, Floret. When these same men had come to Atarax, Marita had been powerless. She had lay under the bed, unable to pry her eyes from her mother's, as the men worked their evil, taking turns until they had exhausted her spirit. Her mother had kept their attention well, keeping their heads turned and their minds on her to protect her little girl.

Marita had cried at the sight, but her tears had been silent, rolling down her face and pooling on the floor as she clamped her hands over her mouth. Just before her mother had given up the fight, she had raised her head for the last time, locking eyes with Marita with a final smile as if to say, "It's going to be fine." Then, with one last gesture of reassurance, Floret used all of her strength to raise a single thumb into the air so that her daughter would know that she had died strong in the end. It had been her dying act.

The girl on the table in the great hall was losing strength. Marita wiped a tear and charged headlong toward the three brutes. She pushed with all of her might and a blast of wind sent them flying backward against the stone wall. She drew the swords she had won from the manor house guards, and glided with her shoes a foot above the floor, surfing along with both swords outstretched. The wind carried her toward them at a deafening speed, so quickly that two of the men barely had time to lift their heads from the brick. She lopped them off in a single coordinated strike.

The third man had witnessed the flying girl and a puddle of piss formed between his feet. He dropped his axe, folded his hands, and prayed to his gods to save him from the demon hovering before him.

Marita felt the air envelop her entire body as she loomed with hair blowing gently in the breeze. *I should have tied it back,* was her single thought before she sent him down the river to join his friends.

Steel clashing against steel rang out, suddenly returning her back to the moment. Behind her Alec was fighting against four berserkers. He was slowed by his injury, but flowed with the grace of the breeze. He felled two of the men just as three more rushed to aid their comrades. Marita lowered herself slowly to the ground and then rushed to aid him.

Charro Valencia lay on the ground, holding his wounded leg. He had received cuts and scratches in his life, but privilege had protected him from serious injuries such as this. He swooned at the sight of his own blood. *Father was wrong,* he laughed with just a hint of hysteria, *there's nothing blue inside of us to make us noble.* He looked around at the room, littered with noblemen and women and painted crimson with their death. *Inside we only have the red of commoners. What really sets us apart?*

He had been too busy focusing on his own wound that he had failed to see the girl enter. But the gust of wind had shaken him from his trance, and he marveled as she flew atop an invisible breeze. *How old is this girl? Twelve summers? Thirteen?* After she had dispatched the three berserkers, she turned to face a man in his early forties.

Charro knew right away that the man was Captain Alec Pogue, the husband of Mattie and father to her two girls. *They favor him,* he noticed. He had finally come for his family, a man of action and violence, but passionately filled with tender love. Despite that he was in his early forties, the swordsman fought like a young man, fast and agile. He deserved his wife and family.

It only took about ten minutes for him and the little girl to kill every marauder who entered the hall. When they had finished, the man scooped his wife into his arms, hugging her tight as if he'd never let go of her again. Liza and Alexa, upon seeing their father, rushed over and joined in the family embrace. The other girl, the ferociously special girl, stared at the exchange with longing and timidity. It was clear to Charro that she wished to join in.

Finally, Mattie stepped back and smiled sweetly, fully aware that this little child had saved her life as well as those of her daughters. "dearie," she asked, "what is your name?"

"My name is Marita, Mrs. Pogue."

Mattie smiled a mother's love toward the girl, walking toward her as gently as one would creep up on a rabbit. "Where are your parents, Marita?"

"Right here. You are all that I have now. You and Captain Pogue have adopted me."

Mrs. Pogue turned to her husband, "Is this true, Alec?"

He nodded, "Yes, Dear. I am bonded to her like a father, and I hope that you will love her as much as I do."

Mattie held out her arms in an offered embrace and Marita rushed in. "I owe you my life and my love, sweet Marita. Thank you."

The girl pulled back and smiled up at her new mother. Then she raised a single thumb into the air toward Alec before wrapping Mattie into another hug.

# Chapter Fifty-Two

Skander stared as his longboats exploded into kindling. He locked eyes on the lead vessel attacking his armada. The magnificent creation boldly reflected the roaring flames of the city. His mouth watered as he coveted his brother's enhanced firepower, laughing maniacally as cannons fired in rapid succession. *What's his will be mine*, he tittered. He raised his hands into the air and welcomed the attack.

Artur approached, pointing at the flagship. "They're making for the beach, sire."

"Let them come. Signal the others and form a shield wall along that street. We'll stop their advance." He strained his eyes, focused on a form in the water. "Give me your spyglass, Artur!" His first mate complied, handing over the copper instrument. While his crew disembarked and rowed to the shoreline, Braen casually strolled across the water toward Skander. "It's true," he marveled, "he shares my powers. My brother's a fool and believes we can duel this out in single combat."

He returned the eyeglass to a dumbfounded Artur, then stared down at the water lapping the pier. He willed the surface to take on a solid state and a ten-foot circle of firm ice formed before his eyes. With a smile he walked toward his brother, the pathway keeping stride beneath him. The two men met in the middle.

"Brother," Braen began, "It doesn't have to end this way."

"How is that?" Skander let out a chuckle. "With you dead?"

"No, Brother. With us killing each other." He gestured around. "We're surrounded by water and can pound at each other until sunset.

All we'll accomplish is the total destruction of the city." He pointed at the burning buildings. "And you've already ensured that fate."

Skander knelt and placed his hand in the water. He felt the molecules form into a frozen spear which he drew out and held like a javelin. "So, it will be hand to hand combat then?" He hurled the ice formation, watching his brother flinch out of the way. As the target moved, he flung his axe with his left hand. Braen grunted as the blade stuck in his back and Skander rushed in with knife and sword drawn.

Eusari watched from the pier as the two brothers fought in the harbor. Skander had the early advantage and lunged at his wounded brother. Braen deflected the advance and swung his axe hard enough to send the other man crashing backward on the ice, hitting hard enough to knock out his breath. She watched in horror as he reached and pulled his brother's axe from his shoulder blades.

By then, Skander had recovered his feet and the two became a wild flurry of steel, brutally swinging at the other with devilish desire to hack them into pieces. She had seen her lover rage like this before, and the berserker blood howled inside him as he backed his younger brother toward the edge of the ice. When the smaller man ducked, Braen nearly tumbled off the platform, momentum overtaking his rage.

"Kill him!" The scream came from *Malfeasance* and Eusari stared in shock at the blonde woman atop the deck. She was clad in white furs and wrapped in Braen's battle banner. "Kill him and retake your throne beside me, My Love!"

All hope that Braen had rejected the northern queen's advances sailed away in that moment, filling the leather-clad woman with sadness and loss. She watched as Hester held the banner over her head and let the wind wave the image of the Kraken for all to see.

The sudden appearance of his wife in support of Braen sent the usurper into a rage. He ran toward his brother's ship with blades shimmering from the lighting above. When Braen tried to follow, a great white shark leaped from the water, jaws snapping as it crashed onto the ice. The platform cleaved in half and the older Braston fell, nearly slipping off the edge.

Ahead the two armies stood ready, but neither side advanced. Their eyes were locked on the two princes, battling the outcome in the bay. Eusari watched as two figures moved atop the ship berthed closest to *Malfeasance*. One of the newcomers pointed toward Braen while the other swung across the water, landing behind Hester and ducking behind some crates.

By then the northern king had reached the ship. The captain of *She Wolf* gasped as his icy platform slowly raised from the water, positioning himself to step aboard. Her eyes turned toward Braen who was no longer running toward the ship. Instead a dark shape had formed beneath him and a creature emerged. He stepped onto the Kraken, riding its back as it glided toward his ship and his brother.

Eusari saw the sniper take aim and she raced along the shore toward *Malfeasance*. Two shots rang out. Skander turned at the first and fell at the second.

Braen felt the bullet tear through his skin and burrow deep into his chest. He could barely breathe, his lung punctured straight through. Gasping, he felt the beast fall away beneath him, dropping him in a heap on the deck. The connection between him and Kraken weakened as the monster fled back to its home in the briny depths, abandoning its master. He rolled over and stared at the body of his brother also sprawled out on the deck. The bullet had taken the northern usurper through the right eye, killing him immediately.

He crawled toward Skander, reaching for his hand and slipping on the bloody deck. *I love you brother*, he thought without concern for the snipers still in hiding, *no one understood your sickness, but I.* Braen tried to speak but sputtered blood and froth into his beard as he fell across his brother's chest, holding him in a loving embrace. Tears raced down his cheeks as he mourned the last of his family. With a bloody finger he closed the open eye.

A shadow let him know that a figure had emerged. Looking up he could see Adamas Creech with two pistols drawn, both pointed at his heart. He managed to cough out a single word before the pirate pulled both triggers. "Why?"

Blackness was the response.

Two more shots could be heard as Eusari and Devil Jacque scrambled up the cargo netting to board *Malfeasance.* Behind them, chaos ensued as the white robed figures in Skander's army wailed in agony. A glance over her shoulder revealed that the northern raiders were charging Braen's smaller force, ignoring those dropping to coordinated gunfire. Sippen and Krill stood among the defenders, desperately trying to hold the firing line and resist the advancing horde.

When she topped the rail, she laid eyes on a gruesome sight. Both Skander and Braen lay on the deck with a pool of blood forming around them. Hester's white furs were crimson as she lay across the older brother's chest, shaking his lifeless form and begging him to arise. Adamas Creech stood behind her reloading one pistol with another pointed at her head. A flash of steel flew through the air as one of Eusari's knives hit home, piercing his throat. She quickly followed with two more, each taking him in the chest and dropping him to his knees. Both pistols fell with thuds on the wooden decking.

A shot rang out from behind, narrowly missing her. She whirled, drew her pistol, and fired, striking a deckhand in the chest. He dropped the rifle that had downed Braen. "Grab him and get him over the side, Jacque! Drag him to *She Wolf!*" Her own ship wasn't far, and she had no hope to sail *Malfeasance* with only a two-man crew and a spoiled northern queen. She grabbed Hester by the armpits and pulled her from Braen. "Get over the side and follow us to my ship." The blonde woman nodded and followed Jacque and Eusari as they lowered the bearded captain with ropes.

Sippen saw them struggling to move Braen's heavy body and rushed over. The sight of his longtime friend stopped him in his tracks and tears welled up, choking off any further questions. He asked, "Who?"

"Creech," was the reply. Eusari surveyed the scene. The Dreamers held a shield around the defenders, but were losing the fight. The white robed zealots were coming to their senses one by one after the death of Skander and were testing the shield for weaknesses. "We're outnumbered and don't have much time. We've got to get him aboard *She Wolf*!"

Krill ambled over quickly, despite his wooden leg. "Gods above, I'll kill whoever did this." His jovial demeanor gone, he clenched his teeth and grimaced to hold back tears.

"I already took care of it, Krill. Help get him aboard *She Wolf*, while I hold them back." She pointed at the frontline, quickly crumbling against the flooding horde of axes and shields. Heaps of dead crewmen piled on the sand as Krill led the survivors in a panicked retreat toward the black ship.

She knelt then, dress flowing around her in the sand of the beach. One by one she pulled her silken gloves from her hands, staring down at the multitude of scars. Each cut represented a transgression against her innocence and a loss of childhood. She focused on these, marveling at the power contained within.

When they had stormed Pirate's Cove in the Fall, she had channeled her pain to aid the battle. Then, she had allowed confidence to flow through her scars as she regained control over her destiny, something she had long believed impossible. On that day she grieved the loss of her father Franque and her mother Anne, both tragically ripped from her world. She also grieved Sa'Mond, her truest friend before meeting Braen. Fighting back tears, she pressed her hand to the beach and felt the gritty cool sand against her skin.

She poured love into her cuts, love for her family and friends, but most of all for Braen. He had taught her not to bottle her feelings and that it was acceptable to express them. Anger and love were normal emotions, as were laughter and yearning. He taught her to strike a balance within her heart, and to express them all without fear. Fear of forgetting the hurt.

She had spent far too many years clinging to a multitude of pains. If she grieved, then she would move on and forget her parents. If she forgave those who harmed her, then she would grant them victory over her body and mind. If she loved, then she would open herself up to new hurts. But Braen did not give her pain, he granted her life.

Forgiveness and love poured through her hands and into the sand, swirling the beach under the feet of the invaders and causing them to sink. Down they slid into the ground as the zealots behind them broke into a panic. When they finally realized the source of the power, it was too late, and the army had slipped beneath the surface.

A powerful blast of air sent Eusari toppling backward, just as a black wolf raced before her eyes. She sensed from Gelert a command to run toward their ship and she did, as quickly as she could. She left in such a hurry that she left behind two silken gloves discarded on the beach. He drew the attention off of her just long enough to escape, then paced alongside as they made their way to freedom.

Once aboard, she gave the order to get underway. "Shove off!" Turning to the children she shouted, "Sebastian! Caroline! Give us the wind!" She collapsed on the deck next to the lifeless body of Braen.

"Which heading, Captain?" Peter Longshanks knelt beside her. "Do we return to The Cove or Estowen's Landing?"

"Our strength accompanies Robert Esterling to Eskera. Take us there right away."

Despite the many people standing around, she allowed herself to shed tears over Braen. Hester did the same nearby, and the two women shared a moment of solidarity for the man they both loved.

Eusari leaned in close and touched one scarred hand to his forehead. She placed the other on his chest, feeling the wounds.

Although he was dead, she wondered if it would be possible to bring him back. *Are you in there, Braen?* She thought, reaching out with her mind and seeking a glimmer of life in his. *And if you did return, would you be the same?* Deep in his brain she felt a shimmer of electricity, barely a lifeforce but enough that she believed she could draw him back. She focused harder and began to pour her own into him.

But as the light grew, she realized the truth. If he returned, he would do so with too much of her lifeforce and not enough of his. He would walk among them, not as Braen but as an extension of her. He would no longer be the man she loved. That man had died. Instead she would control both his mind and body, and no one deserved a life of slavery. *That would be no kind of relationship*, she cautioned her heart.

Speaking with her mind to the spark within she said, *I love you, Braen. I will raise our child to learn compassion and forgiveness.* She pulled away and allowed what was left of Braen Braston to slip away into darkness. When she finally stood, she placed her beautifully scarred hands on her belly and felt the child move. *At least I'm no longer alone.*

After the sounds of battle had finally subsided, Lord Stefan Nevra emerged from hiding. He calmly left Adamas Creech's stateroom and made his way topside, mulling over mixed feelings regarding the outcome. Both Braston brothers were killed, and for that he was pleased. But Eusari had dragged away the stronger of the two, interfering greatly with his plans. He blinked his eyes against the glimmering fires throughout the city, soaking in their warmth and forming a new strategy.

When he found the three bodies, he knelt first beside Creech and ripped open his shirt. The new wounds were extensive, with one in the neck and two in the chest. A circular scar rested directly over the heart. Stefan had inflicted that wound in the jail. It had been perfectly placed. He silently chastised Eusari's sloppiness. He placed his hand on Adamas and poured lifeforce until his eyes opened and mouth gasped for air. Nevra leaned in closely and whispered, "Next time stay alive."

He moved to the deckhand behind the crates, leaning in and inspecting the bullet wound in the heart. *Much cleaner work*, he thought, then went to work on him as well. "Go dig up the others," he told the man as he rose, gesturing toward the beach.

"Aye, My Lord." The man turned slightly and Nevra caught a glimpse of the scar on his neck. Frowning at his earlier work, he reminded himself that he had limited options at the time. It was the best he could muster using the sharpened spoon found in his prison mattress.

Stefan then turned his attention to Skander Braston. One eye was missing, replaced by a large bullet wound. He reached his fingers into the gap and felt around for the piece of lead, retrieved it, and tossed it aside on the deck. Pleased that enough of the brain was still intact, he placed one hand over the eye socket and the other against his cheek.

He leaned in close and placed his mouth against the lips of the fallen northern king, kissing him deeply. He then poured more of himself than he had given to any of the others, ensuring control over this powerful emotant. *You will be special, My Darling. You will serve me well.*

The single eye of the Kraken instantly shot open, and a wicked smile curled on his face. "The voices are gone, Father. I can finally think clearly."

Chapter Fifty-Three

Chancellor Jakata leaned intently toward his computer, poring over dispatches. Several more explosions had rocked the capital, and protesters now openly marched in the streets. Food distributions had been interrupted by one of the blasts, and angry residents of the Industrial Sector threatened to riot. In all his twenty-years over Astia, he had never suspected that he would have to turn out troops against his own subjects.

Guarin cleared his throat in the doorway, but the chancellor was too frustrated to give him a glance. "Your Excellency. Fatwana Nakala has completely disappeared, and we have no idea where she's gone. We think she's defected to The Society."

"What did you find by searching her logs?"

"She has indeed been hiding prophecies, and we think she delivered one directly to the terrorists."

Jakata closed his eyes, the soft sound of an orchestra no longer soothing his mood. "Music stop." When he finally opened them, he asked calmly, "Did you question the initiates and reconstruct the missing verses?"

"We did," came the reply from his assistant, "and it isn't good." Gaurin stepped forward and handed the aged politician a simple slip of paper, the message written in the shaky hand of a trembling oracle.

The chancellor read the words carefully, fear consuming his body as he realized the missing part of the puzzle. "Tell Campton that his time is up."

"Your Excellency?"

"Dispatch our special forces to Andalon. We've no choice but to reset the experiment and start anew. Now leave me in peace!"

"Right away, Your Excellency."

A few moments later, Jakata heard a throat clear in the doorway. "Damn it, Guarin, I want to be left in peace."

"Too busy for me, Father? Even after all these years?"

The chancellor snapped his eyes to the door, finding a tall man with fiery red hair. He was regal in stature, bearing himself more like a king than a total shit of a son. "Oh, it's you."

"Yes," the newcomer replied, "it's me." He strolled casually into the room, admiring the Andalonian artifacts on display. He paused at the wine collection, drawing the cork from a partially empty bottle and sniffing long. "This vintage is nearly gone, you know."

"Quite the shame, I fancy that one."

"Most people do, Father."

"What are you doing in Astia? Why did you abandon your post? Can't you see that the continent is falling apart? Yet here you are, pouring the last of my fine wine."

The redheaded man lifted the cup to his nose, sniffing and taking in the bouquet before taking a long sip. With piercing green eyes he stared into his father's soul and asked, "Have you ordered the kill switch?"

"Yes, no thanks to you."

"Then Campton failed?"

"Not yet, but that ending appears inevitable. I'm pulling the plug before he gets himself killed over there."

"Was he always your favorite, Father?"

"No, Artema." The Chancellor handed over his own glass. *No sense letting him drink it all,* he thought. "You were until you abandoned the mission and started playing pirate."

Artema Horn returned to the bottle and tipped the contents into the glass, swirling it to allow air into the aroma. "I wasn't just playing, you know. I learned a lot about politics and scheming while I was away." He handed the wine to his father.

Jakata laughed, "I bet you did." He tossed back the glass, not wanting to savor anything at the moment. "Why did you choose now to return?"

"Because you are weak, Father. The Council has lost faith in you and the Society is sowing chaos."

"What are you implying?"

"That as soon as you are dead, I will petition the Council for succession. With Campton away there will be no opposition."

"Well you'll have to wait a long time, because I'm not going anywhere."

Artema sat down in his father's overstuffed chair with a plop. "Once I'm cozy and comfy in your seat, I can unravel everything our family has worked for. I'll dissolve the Council and restructure everything the way I desire."

"You wouldn't dare!" Jakata took two steps and stopped, holding his head against a sudden dizzy spell. "This world is our legacy! Our ancestor laid the foundation for our family and I'm sworn to protect it!"

"To the death, Father?"

Jakata did not answer the question. He fell to the floor, body wracked with convulsions as he tried to focus eyes on his son.

"The potency of the beads is stronger in someone lacking the ability to use their benefit. It can even act as a poison." Artema leaned close to his father's ear, whispering softly, "You just swallowed the equivalent of all four types of beads at once, Father. The Council will believe that you swallowed them in a vain attempt to further spy upon your little world."

He gestured at the artifacts that cluttered the room. "It's common knowledge that you're obsessed with Andalon. It will make sense that this was a desperate attempt to play god." He rose and placed four beads in a bowl next to the wine; one black, one white, one red, and one blue. Then the Dragon quietly strolled from his father's quarters, ready to begin the next phase of his revolution.

Marcus Esterling paced in his rooms, a virtual prison cell now that he was no more than a puppet played by Lord Shol. He stared out the window for a while, then chose a book and took a seat. He turned it over in his hands. It was hefty, no doubt full of dry ramblings of old men long dead. He read the words on the spine, *Common Law and Trial.* It did not sound appealing. He opened the pages, read two paragraphs, then hurled the tome into the gardens below.

He paused to take in the fragrance of some roses one of the domestics had placed on the hearth. His mother would have found them beautiful in their glass vase. There was just a hint of water in the vessel, and someone had filled it with vibrant glass in the form of polished beads. They were beautiful and every color of the rainbow. He grabbed the flowers by the stem, drew them out, and tossed them on the floor. Then he reached in and pulled out several handfuls of the baubles, placing them into his pocket with a smile.

The king by name only walked to the door, opened it a crack, took a deep breath, then stepped out into the hall. Two of those disgusting Falconers stood waiting, as if they had foreseen his desire for a stroll. *What am I thinking? Of course they knew that I would. They always know my next move.* The young man decided to lead them on an adventure.

He turned left, walked down the main corridor, then made three rights and a left. Every time that he rounded a turn he sped up until they appeared behind. Then he would casually act as if he had been taking his time. They matched his speed each time. When he approached the stairs leading to the watch tower he sprinted, pumping his arms and pushing himself to exhaustion. *Let them foresee this,* he plotted.

As he had hoped, the feathered men sprinted after, running with less effort of body, but definitely hampered by their flowing robes. His plan, as he had hoped in his mind, hinged on their ability to see. Marcus had a theory that their keen vision and gift of foresight was tied directly to their birds. This staircase had no windows and barely even the occasional arrow slit.

As he neared the top, he reached his hand into his pocket and grabbed a handful of beads. Three more steps and he let go, letting them bounce all at once down the narrow staircase. He did this several times until his pocket was flat. Then he spun around, rested on his haunches, and waited.

The specters slipped and slid as their feet met the marbles, stumbling forward and tangling in their gowns. The first Falconer completely lost his footing and the other toppled over him, his bodyweight causing both to slip down the steep staircase. Down they fell, several flights while Marcus laughed hysterically at their demise. After a while, he no longer heard the thudding of their bodies on stone, and so he carefully made his way down.

About halfway down, he noticed something odd. So far, the marbles had reflected the light of the murder holes, glistening and giving away their treachery. But as he rounded a bend, he found three dull stones laying among the shimmering glass. They were black and unassuming, perfectly round and smooth. He snatched them up quickly and slid them into his pocket as he continued his descent. On the way he found several more, scooping them up as well. His only interest in the objects was that they obviously had been dropped by the Falconers.

Marcus passed the two specters three fourths of the way down, laying in a heap, but very much alive. They gingerly tried to right themselves, hampered by broken bones but determined. Both had lost their hoods in the tumble and stared at him with steely eyes that seemed to bulge from their bald heads. He twiddled his fingers at them as he passed, laughing and taunting. Done with his fun for the night, he returned to his rooms.

The light outside had dimmed considerably, but he was nowhere near ready for bed. He took the time to hide the beads in his mattress, all but one, which he passed over each knuckle like magician would roll a coin. For a while he simply stared at the object, marveling at the perfectly smooth texture. And then a thought took over and he decided to test another theory. *Could this be the source of their power?* He popped it into his mouth and swallowed it down with a glass of really shitty wine, the best in the palace.

At first nothing happened, then he felt his body shudder and convulse. Then he was no longer constrained by his shell, with full consciousness floating out into the night. There, far below he could see the textbook he had tossed. It had caught upon a trellis with pages open, fluttering in the breeze. It was this wind that he latched onto, surfing far and away from Eston.

Southward he flew, over mountains and thick forests. Eventually the leafy trees gave way to swaying pines that bowed before him.

Then he saw the white sand of a coastline and circled, watching for movement on the sea. One dark vessel drew his eye as it sailed into the setting sun. A shrouded body lay on a funeral plank, ready to commit to the deep. All hands stood topside, mourning the loss of a beloved sailor. Marcus recognized the ship and moved closer to watch.

Perched upon a yardarm, he realized that he did not see with his own eyes, but of a large hawk. Thus the crew paid him no heed as he watched the proceedings. The bitch that captained *She Wolf* said some words over the body, and then another woman did the same. Both obviously cared deeply for the man and each held their bellies as they talked. Marcus deeply believed that they were both with child.

He watched the crewmembers. A tiny man with a large head and spectacles stared stoically forward, intent eyes focused on the sea and forcibly not looking at the body. A one-eyed man with a long beard and wooden peg leg paced the deck, muttering to himself. A large wolf, black as the night curled in a corner, whimpering and howling out misery that words could never express. Not even for a human.

Eusari stepped forward, bent over, and pulled back the shroud. She gently kissed the bearded man on his lips, whispered some private message, and then tilted the plank and committed his body over the side. Marcus flapped his wings and shot into the sky, laughing and cawing out his joy that Braen Braston was dead. He circled the vessel three times, shouting his promises of revenge and shitting on everyone he could. Then he shot off to the west to learn the fate of his brother.

He found him in Eskera, white uniform marred by crimson and crying over the body of Maximus Reeves. Nearby, lay the remains of Merrimac Lourdes, the traitor and former loyalist to Crestal Esterling's husband. Marcus took the opportunity to take a shit on him, too, as he lay with eyes open to the heavens. He missed and hit Captain Frederique Titus instead. The man didn't flinch. He remained steadfast and comforted Robert, feeding him false hope for the war ahead.

Turning north he sped toward Weston, confused and amazed that the city was gone. In its place stood a glistening lake, red and orange while reflecting the glow of the setting sun. Circling once more he found a line of Pescari wretches. They walked slowly behind a boy and a girl riding atop a steed as black as the night. They headed south, toward Robert in Eskera. Not far behind the procession followed what was left of the people of Weston. They carried both their past and their future in their wagons, but they carried their present on their faces.

Marcus turned north along the Misting River, following it toward Norton and then home to Eston. Things were about to change in his empire. Of course, he would first have to regain control from Campton Shol and the Falconers. He was tired of playing the boy puppet and decided to finally show the world a king.

Eusari lifted the shroud and bent down, gently kissing her lover on the lips. "I love you," she told him. "I love you forever and will always miss you." She touched his face with her hand, no longer gloved. "I couldn't bring you back," she whispered, "you wouldn't have been you if I had. I would give anything to have your arms around me, to finally feel safe. To feel loved." She wiped a single tear and continued, "I trust you, Braen. I trust you and I finally understand why you were placed in my life. Thanks to you, I will be the mother that I had lost. Thank you, Braen."

She pulled back and lifted the funeral plank, cleverly designed by Sippen to commit the body over the side. Braen splashed into the briny Southern Sea and slid beneath the surface, tiny bubbles marking his final resting place.

"Kraken!"

Sippen, who had been watching the water to avoid looking upon his beloved friend, cried out and pointed to the south. Three large creatures passed under the ship and the largest swallowed the shrouded body in a single gulp. As quickly as they had arrived, they had disappeared into the frigid depths. Krill let out a mournful cry and then scooped Eusari up in an embrace, squeezing her tight and sobbing uncontrollably into her shoulder. The man loved by his friends and despised by all others had broken his most important of promises. Braen Braston had abandoned them all.

# Epilogue

Mattie and Alec walked hand in hand, strolling the grounds with Lord Charro Valencia. The trio had business to attend to, especially regarding the terms of indenture. Since it was a beautiful night, they all agreed that this business should occur out of doors. But mostly no one wanted to be reminded of the hell that had occurred in the Great Hall.

The children rested in the manor, eager to get to know their sister. Marita had been a large topic of this discussion, with Alec explaining about emotants and Robert's war in the north. He included the taking of The Cove and the recent elections before wrapping things up with a tale of their escape from Eskera. Charro listened intently without interrupting even once.

After he had finished, Mattie asked the first question, "Are you going back to fight for The Cove?"

"No. I'm finished with that life and all debts are paid." He added, "Braston sent me with gold, Mattie. Gold to free you and the girls and to start a new life. He said to consider it our pension."

Valencia finally broke his silence. "What would you pay for their freedom, Captain Pogue?"

Alec bristled at the question and answered defiantly, "Everything."

"Well, it won't come to that, fortunately." He stopped walking and the husband and wife turned to face him. "I've decided that debt is paid. Mattie, I release you and your children from your indenture."

Mattie let go of her husband's hand and wrapped her arms around the lord's neck, hugging him tightly. When she let go, she kissed him firmly on the cheek and then turned to embrace Alec.

Charro laughed while the couple rejoiced. "Where will you go now? You must find a place to settle."

Alec answered, "We've always talked about Loganshire. I've heard Brentway is nice. But Braen also gifted us some grape seeds in case we ever decide to plant a vineyard. I tried to refuse, but he ensured me that these were of the highest pedigree. To grow wine grapes we would need to settle in Soston."

"Not necessarily," Charro suggested, "grapes grow extremely well in Cargia as long as you are on the leeward side of the bluffs."

"Lord Valencia," Mattie proposed. "You enjoy wine. Didn't you once say that you would sell off half your lands for a case of 754? Well, how much gold to purchase a leeward parcel?"

He laughed, "I may have said that, but rest assured that no amount of any vintage would convince me to relinquish my own titled lands." He thought seriously, then added, "However, things have changed in regard to the local nobility after tonight. There are several small baronies that have opened up if you have enough gold. How much did you bring?"

Alec didn't hold any numbers back, "I have three hundred thousand talents."

Mattie blanched at the number. "Braen Braston sent you with that much gold?"

"He did. He said that I was to recover you and the girls at any cost."

Lord Valencia smiled. "You could purchase the title of Marquis for that sum, but I wouldn't want to take all of your capital. You would need to retain enough for planting costs and purchase of labor, of course."

Alec grinned back. "What kind of title could we purchase if I paid two hundred thousand and threw in an entire cask of 754?"

Charro laughed at the obvious joke. "Why, for that you could become a full Viscount. But do you know what? If you actually had one, I would give you a discount and grant you the title of Lesser Duke."

Duke Pogue responded, "Summon the notary and draw up the paperwork then. Because I have one full cask of Estonian 754 on my wagon."

## Cast of Characters

(Alphabetically)

ANDALON

The Cove

BRAEN BRASTON: Winter emotant. Pirate Captain of *Ice Prince* and *Malfeasance.* Eldest son of Krist Braston and exiled heir to Fjorik.

ADAMAS CREECH: Pirate Captain of *Vigilance.* Political opposition to both Braen Braston and Stefan Nevra.

ADOLPHUS DOMINIQUE: Pirate Captain of *Aggressor.* A slaver known for kidnapping families and selling them on the southern continent.

MATTHIEU DOMINIQUE: Son of Adolphus Dominique.

GELERT: A wolf. Emotionally bonded and connected to Eusari Thorinson.

ARTEMA HORN: Pirate Captain of *Wench's Daughter.* Former pirate king of The Cove. Whereabouts unknown.

AMASH HORSLEI: Son of Abraham Horslei and brother to Sarai. Left Weston University to live a pirating life to spite his father. Classically trained swordsman.

DEVIL JACQUE: Quartermaster of *She Wolf.*

KRILL: One-eyed Gunnery Sergeant of *Ice Prince* and *Malfeasance.* Childhood friend fiercely loyal to Braen Braston. Uncanny ability to estimate range.

PETER LONGSHANKS: First Mate of *She Wolf.* Personal confidant and friend to Eusari Thorinson.

LORD STEFAN NEVRA: Former Duke of the Southern Continent and pirate king. Imprisoned for the crime of slavery.

ALEC POGUE: Pirate Captain of *Desperation* and Captain of the Guard for The Cove.

ALEXA POGUE: Fifteen-year-old daughter of Alec Pogue.

LIZA POGUE: Seventeen-year-old daughter of Alec Pogue

MATTIE POGUE: Wife of Alec Pogue.

SA'MOND: Deceased. Former First Mate of *She Wolf* and best friend of Eusari Thorinson. Eunuched by unknown means in the southern continent.

EUSARI THORINSON: Autumn emotant. Captain of *She Wolf.* Originally from Loganshire, was kidnapped and sold to pirates at thirteen years old. Won her freedom through mutiny. Lover of Braen Braston. Bonded with Gelert the wolf.

TURAT: Deceased agent of Stefan Nevra. Slaver and conspirator of Adolphus Dominique.

SIPPEN YURIK: Engineer and Weaponsmith of *Ice Prince and Malfeasance.* Best friend of Braen Braston. Stutters when anxious.

Dreamers

BETH: Autumn emotant with affinity for air. Bonded with Akili.

CAROLINE: Autumn emotant with affinity for air. Favorite of Eusari Thorinson

JASPER: Autumn emotant with affinity for air.

JOHAN: Winter emotant with affinity for water. Friend of Kali.

KALI: Spring emotant with affinity for earth. Friend of Johan.

MARITA: Autumn emotant with affinity for air.

SEBASTIAN: Autumn emotant with affinity for air. Traumatized by the death of his friend, the Dreamer Suzette.

Esterling Empire

ARNE: An eagle. Emotionally bonded to Robert Esterling.

LORD CAMPTON SHOL: Sensitive to Autumn Oracle beads. Astian agent and overseer of Andalon. Chancellor to the Eston Empire and secret head of the Falconers.

MATTEAS BROHN: Captain General of the Eston Army. Mentor and secret father to Marcus Esterling.

CHARLES ESTERLING: Deceased. Former king of Eston. Unified the kingdoms under the Esterling Empire and drove the Pescari across the Misting River.

CRESTAL ESTERLING: Deceased. Former Queen Regent of Eston.

ROBERT ESTERLING: Autumn emotant. Eldest son of Crestal Esterling. Fathered by General Maximus Reeves. Assumed the title of King of Eston in opposition to his brother.

MARCUS ESTERLING: Second son of Crestal Esterling. Fathered by Captain General Matteas Brohn. Recognized by the council as King of Eston.

KESTREL: Lead Falconer. Childhood friend of Campton Shol.

MACMILLAN LOURDES: Retired General of the Eston Army and Governor of Eskera. Renowned for defeating and driving the Pescari across the Misting River alongside Charles Esterling. Mentor of Maximus Reeves.

MAXIMUS REEVES: Eston General. Former protégé and aide-de-camp to General Macmillan Lourdes. Secret father to Robert Esterling.

FREDERIQUE TITUS: Aide-de-camp to General Maximus Reeves.

Fjorik

ARTUR: First Mate under Skander Braston.

KRIST BRASTON: Deceased. Formerly king of Fjorik and father of Braen and Skander.

SKANDER BRASTON: King of Fjorik. Second son to Krist Braston and husband of Hester.

HESTER: Queen of Fjorik and wife of Skander Braston. Former lover of Braen Braston.

Outlaws of the Diaph Forest

MARQUE: Right hand man to Shon Wembley.

SHON WEMBLEY: Former Loganshire constable. Leader of the Outlaw band living in the Diaph Forest.

Pescari

CORNIN: Deceased. Former Shappan after killing the father of Taros in the right of Shapalote.

DASKA: Elder of the Pescari. Fears Taros from ancient prophesies.

FELICIMA: Goddess of the Pescari. Rises in the east and settles each night west of the Caldera of Cinder.

FLAYA: Granddaughter of Daska.

LYNETTE: Deceased. Mother of Taros.

TAROS: Summer emotant. Shappan leader of the unified Pescari clans.

TEOT: Uncle of Taros.

Southern Continent

PENELOPE PRITCHETT: Former Manor Stewart to Lord Charro Valencia.

CHARRO VALENCIA: Duke of Cargia.

Weston

CASSUS EACHANN: Leader of the Humanitarian Party. Governor of Weston.

ABRAM HORSLEI: Deceased. Father of Amash and Sarai. Former governor of Weston.

SARAI HORSLEI: Wife of Robert Esterling. Assumed the unrecognized title of Queen of Eston.

PERCY ROAN: Accountant. Clerk and notary to Cassus Eachann.

## ASTIA

Astian Council

CHANCELLOR JAKATA: Elected and ruling chancellor over the Astian Council.

Humanitarian Freedom Society

CASSIDY: Society agent in Astia.

DELILAH: Society agent in Fjorik.

THE DRAGON: Society agent in Astia.

GRETCHEN: Society agent in Fjorik.

PERLANA (PEARL): Society agent in Diaph.

SAMANI KERNIGAN (Formerly Samani Nakala): Society agent in The Cove. Was a member of Artema Horn's Inner Sanctum. Advisor to Braen Braston.

Winter Oracle

ASHIMA NAKALA: Deceased. A member of the Winter Oracle who perished revealing a prophecy that powers awakened in Andalon. Younger sister of Samani Kernigan.

FATWANA NAKALA: Lead sister of the Winter Oracle. Elder sister of Samani Kernigan.

Made in the USA
Coppell, TX
09 August 2020